The critics on Michael Connelly

'An excellent thriller that puts Connelly firmly in the frame as one of the stars of American crime writing' *Sunday Times*

'No one writes a better modern thriller than Connelly. Guaranteed to keep you riveted until the very last page' *Time Out*

'Part police procedural, part Big Boys' Adventure book . . . one of those books you read with your knuckles – just hanging on until it's over' *New York Times*

'The best writer of tough detective fiction at the moment is Michael Connelly . . . For those who like a bit of contrariness and astringency in their heroes, Bosch has to come head of the list' *Irish Times*

'Joins the top rank of a new generation of crime writers' *Los Angeles Times*

'Most impressive . . . rich in detail, strong on character, with a fascinating plot that functions on several emotional levels . . . Connelly has, with great skill, given us a detective who inhabits a world filled only with torment, fear and danger' *People Magazine*

'A classic in the genre' *Sunday Times*

'Impressive . . . convincing ambience, a mass of procedural detail, authentic dialogue, a speeding plot and a flawed hero' *The Times*

'A cracker . . . it fairly coruscates with all that goes to make a good crime thriller' *Irish Times*

'His methods of killing and eluding detection are infernally ingenious, adding an intellectual charge to the visceral kick of the hunt' *New York Times*

'One of the most authentic pieces of crime writing I've ever read. It is an extraordinary story, one that engages the reader on the first page and never lets go' James Lee Burke

'Sharp and scary ... as gripping as it is disturbing' *Company*

'In-depth knowledge informs every turn of a wonderfully Byzantine plot ... If you are an aspiring crime writer, buy this bravura display of technique' *Sunday Times*

'Intensely clever, entirely credible ... thrilling, suspenseful and securely anchored in procedure and purpose. Not a false note; deeply satisfying stuff' *Literary Review*

A former police reporter for the *Los Angeles Times*, Michael Connelly is the author of six acclaimed Harry Bosch novels including *The Black Echo*, which was the winner of the Edgar Award. Michael Connelly lives in Los Angeles.

MICHAEL CONNELLY

ANGELS FLIGHT

ORION

An Orion Paperback
First published in Great Britain by Orion in 1999
This paperback edition published in 1999 by
Orion Books Ltd,
Orion House, 5 Upper St Martin's Lane
London WC2H 9EA

Published by arrangement with
Little, Brown and Company Inc., New York, NY, USA

A CIP catalogue record for this book
is available from the British Library.

ISBN 0 75282 694 8

The characters and events in this book are fictitious.
Any similarity to real persons, living or dead, is entirely
coincidental and not intended by the author.

Typeset by Deltatype Ltd, Birkenhead, Merseyside
Printed and bound in Great Britain by
Clays Ltd, St Ives plc

This is for
McCaleb Jane Connelly

I

The word sounded alien in his mouth, as if spoken by someone else. There was an urgency in his own voice that Bosch didn't recognize. The simple hello he had whispered into the telephone was full of hope, almost desperation. But the voice that came back to him was not the one he needed to hear.

'Detective Bosch?'

For a moment Bosch felt foolish. He wondered if the caller had recognized the faltering of his voice.

'This is Lieutenant Michael Tulin. Is this Bosch?'

The name meant nothing to Bosch and his momentary concern about how he sounded was ripped away as an awful dread entered his mind.

'This is Bosch. What is it? What's wrong?'

'Hold please for Deputy Chief Irving.'

'What is—'

The caller clicked off and there was only silence. Bosch now remembered who Tulin was – Irving's adjutant. Bosch stood still and waited. He looked around the kitchen; only the dim oven light was on. With one hand he held the phone hard against his ear, the other he instinctively brought up to his stomach, where fear and dread were twisting together. He looked at the glowing numbers on the stove clock. It was almost two, five minutes past the last time he had looked at it. This isn't right, he thought as he waited. They don't do this by phone. They come to your door. They tell you this face-to-face.

Finally, Irving picked up on the other end of the line.

'Detective Bosch?'

'Where is she? What happened?'

Another moment of excruciating silence went by as Bosch waited. His eyes were closed now.

'Excuse me?'

'Just tell me, what happened to her? I mean … is she alive?'

'Detective, I'm not sure what it is you are talking about. I'm calling because I need to muster your team as soon as possible. I need you for a special assignment.'

Bosch opened his eyes. He looked through the kitchen window into the dark canyon below his house. His eyes followed the slope of the hill down toward the freeway and then up again to the slash of Hollywood lights he could see through the cut of the Cahuenga Pass. He wondered if each light meant someone awake and waiting for someone who wasn't going to come. Bosch saw his own reflection in the window. He looked weary. He could make out the deep circles etched beneath his eyes, even in the dark glass.

'I have an assignment, Detective,' Irving repeated impatiently. 'Are you able to work or are you—'

'I can work. I just was mixed up there for a moment.'

'Well, I'm sorry if I woke you. But you should be used to it.'

'Yes. It's no problem.'

Bosch didn't tell him that he hadn't been awakened by the call. That he had been roaming around in his dark house waiting.

'Then get it going, Detective. We'll have coffee down here at the scene.'

'What scene?'

'We'll talk about it when you get here. I don't want to delay this any further. Call your team. Have them come to Grand Street between Third and Fourth. The top of Angels Flight. Do you know where I'm talking about?'

'Bunker Hill? I don't—'

2

'It will be explained when you get here. Seek me out when you are here. If I am at the bottom come down to me before you speak with anyone.'

'What about Lieutenant Billets? She should—'

'She will be informed about what is happening. We're wasting time. This is not a request. It is a command. Get your people together and get down here. Am I making myself clear to you?'

'You're clear.'

'Then I will be expecting you.'

Irving hung up without waiting for a reply. Bosch stood with the phone still at his ear for a few moments, wondering what was going on. Angels Flight was the short inclined railroad that carried people up Bunker Hill in downtown – far outside the boundaries of the Hollywood Division homicide table. If Irving had a body down there at Angels Flight the investigation would fall under the jurisdiction of Central Division. If Central detectives couldn't handle it because of case-load or personnel problems, or if the case was deemed too important or media sensitive for them, then it would be bumped to the bulls, the Robbery-Homicide Division. The fact that a deputy chief of police was involved in the case before dawn on a Saturday suggested the latter possibility. The fact that he was calling Bosch and his team in instead of the RHD bulls was the puzzle. Whatever it was that Irving had working at Angels Flight didn't make sense.

Bosch glanced once more down into the dark canyon, pulled the phone away from his ear and clicked it off. He wished he had a cigarette but he had made it this far through the night without one. He wouldn't break now.

He turned his back and leaned on the counter. He looked down at the phone in his hand, turned it back on and hit the speed dial button that would connect him with Kizmin Rider's apartment. He would call Jerry Edgar after he talked to her. Bosch felt a sense of relief come over him that he was reluctant to acknowledge.

He might not yet know what awaited him at Angels Flight, but it would certainly take his thoughts away from Eleanor Wish.

Rider's alert voice answered after two rings.

'Kiz, it's Harry,' he said. 'We've got work.'

2

Bosch agreed to meet his two partners at the Holly-wood Division station to pick up cars before they headed downtown to Angels Flight. On the way down the hill to the station he had punched in KFWB on his Jeep's radio and picked up a breaking news report on a homicide investigation under way at the site of the historical inclined railroad. The newsman on the scene reported that two bodies had been found inside one of the train cars and that several members of the Robbery-Homicide squad were on the scene. But that was the extent of the reporter's information, as he also noted that the police had placed an unusually wide cordon of yellow tape around the crime scene, prohibiting him from getting a closer look. At the station Bosch communicated this thin bit of information to Edgar and Rider while they signed three slickbacks out of the motor pool.

'So it looks like we're gonna be playing sloppy seconds to RHD,' Edgar concluded, showing his annoyance at being rousted from sleep to spend probably the whole weekend doing gofer work for the RHD bulls. 'Our guts, their glory. And we aren't even on call this weekend. Why didn't Irving call out Rice's got-damned team if he needed a Hollywood team?'

Edgar had a point. Team One – Bosch, Edgar and Rider – wasn't even up on call rotation this weekend. If Irving had followed proper call-out procedure he would have called Terry Rice, who headed up Team Three, which was currently on top of the rotation. But Bosch had already figured that Irving wasn't following any procedures, not if the deputy chief had called him directly before checking with his supervisor, Lieutenant Grace Billets.

'Well, Jerry,' Bosch said, more than used to his partner's whining, 'you'll get the chance to ask the deputy chief personally in a little while.'

'Yeah, right, I do that and I'll find my ass down in Harbor the next ten years. Fuck that.'

'Hey, Harbor Division's an easy gig,' Rider said, just to rag Edgar a bit. She knew Edgar lived in the Valley and that a transfer to Harbor Division would mean a miserable ninety-minute commute each way – the pure definition of freeway therapy, the brass's method of unofficially punishing malcontents and problem cops. 'They only pull six, seven homicides a year down there.'

'That's nice but count me the fuck out.'

'Okay, okay,' Bosch said. 'Let's just get going and we'll worry about all of that stuff later. Don't get lost.'

Bosch took Hollywood Boulevard to the 101 and coasted down the freeway in minimal traffic to downtown. Halfway there he checked the mirror and saw his partners cruising in the lanes behind him. Even in the dark and with other traffic he could pick them out. He hated the new detective cars. They were painted black and white and looked exactly like patrol cruisers with the exception that they did not carry emergency lights across the roof. It had been the former chief's idea to replace unmarked detective cars with the so-called slickbacks. The whole thing had been a scam perpetrated to fulfill his promises to put more cops on the street. By changing unmarked cars into clearly marked cars, he was giving the public the erroneous impression that there were more cops patrolling the streets. He also counted the detectives using slickbacks when he addressed community groups and proudly reported that he had increased the number of cops on the street by hundreds.

Meantime, detectives trying to do their jobs drove around like targets. More than once Bosch and his team had sought to serve an arrest warrant or had attempted to come into a neighborhood quietly in the course of an investigation only to have their presence signaled by their own cars. It was stupid and dangerous but it was the chief's edict and it was carried out throughout the department's divisional detective bureaus, even after the chief was not asked back for a second five-year term. Bosch, like many of the department's detectives, hoped the new chief would soon order the detective cars back to normal. Meanwhile, he no longer drove the car assigned to him home from work. It had been a nice detective supervisor's perk having a take-home car but he didn't want the marked car sitting in front of his house. Not in L.A. You never knew what menace that could bring to your door.

They got to Grand Street by two forty-five. As Bosch pulled to a stop he saw an unusually large number of police-related vehicles parked along the curb at California Plaza. He noted the crime scene and coroner's vans, several patrol cars and several more detective sedans – not the slickbacks, but the unmarked cars still used by the RHD bulls. While he waited for Rider and Edgar to pull up he opened his briefcase, took out the cellular phone and called his home. After five rings the machine picked up the call and he heard his own voice telling him to leave a message. He was about to click off but decided to leave a message.

'Eleanor, it's me. I've got a call out … but page me or call me on the cell phone when you get in so I know you're okay … Um, okay, that's it. Bye – oh, it's about two forty-five right now. Saturday morning. Bye.'

Edgar and Rider had walked up to his door. He put the phone away and got out with his briefcase. Edgar, the tallest, held up the yellow crime scene tape and they crossed under, gave their names and badge numbers to

7

a uniform officer with the crime scene attendance list, and then walked across California Plaza.

The plaza was the centerpiece of Bunker Hill, a stone courtyard formed by the conjoining of two marble office towers, a high-rise apartment building and the Museum of Modern Art. There was a huge fountain and reflecting pool at its center, though the pumps and lights were off at this hour, leaving the water still and black.

Past the fountain was the beaux arts revival-styled station and wheelhouse at the top of Angels Flight. It was next to this small structure that most of the investigators and patrol officers milled about as if waiting for something. Bosch looked for the gleaming shaven skull that belonged to Deputy Chief Irvin Irving but didn't see it. He and his partners stepped into the crowd and moved toward the lone rail car sitting at the top of the tracks. Along the way he recognized many faces of Robbery-Homicide detectives. They were men he had worked with years earlier when he had been part of the elite squad. A few of them nodded to him or called him by name. Bosch saw Francis Sheehan, his former partner, standing off by himself smoking a cigarette. Bosch broke from his partners and stepped over.

'Frankie,' he said. 'What's going on?'

'Harry, what are you doing here?'

'Got called out. Irving called us out.'

'Shit. Sorry, partner, I wouldn't wish this one on my enemy.'

'Why, what's going—'

'You better talk to the man first. He's putting the big blanket on this one.'

Bosch hesitated. Sheehan looked worn down but Bosch hadn't seen him in months. He had no idea what had put the dark circles under his hound dog eyes or when they had been cut into his face. For a moment

8

Bosch remembered the reflection of his own face that he had seen earlier.

'You okay, Francis?'

'Never better.'

'Okay, I'll talk to you.'

Bosch rejoined Edgar and Rider, who were standing near the rail car. Edgar nodded slightly to Bosch's left.

'Hey, Harry, you see that?' he said in a low voice. 'That's Sustain Chastain and that bunch over there. What are those pricks doin' here?'

Bosch turned and saw the grouping of men from Internal Affairs.

'Got no idea,' he said.

Chastain and Bosch locked eyes for a moment but Bosch didn't hold it. It wasn't worth the waste of energy to get worked up over just seeing the IAD man. Instead, he focused on trying to put the whole scene together. His curiosity level was at maximum. The number of RHD bulls hanging around, the IAD shines, a deputy chief on the scene – he had to find out what was going on.

With Edgar and Rider behind him in single file, Bosch worked his way to the rail car. Portable lights had been set up inside and the car was lit up like somebody's living room. Inside, two crime scene techs were at work. This told Bosch that he was quite late arriving at the scene. The crime scene techs didn't move in until after the coroner's techs had completed their initial procedures – declaring victims dead, photographing the bodies *in situ*, searching them for wounds, weapons and identification.

Bosch stepped to the rear of the car and looked through the open door. The technicians were at work around two bodies. A woman was sprawled on one of the stepped seats about midway through the car. She was wearing gray leggings and a white thigh-length T-shirt. A large flower of blood had blossomed on her chest where she had been hit dead center with a single bullet. Her head was snapped back against the sill of the window behind her seat. She had dark hair and features, her lineage obviously stretching somewhere south of the border. On the seat next to her body was a plastic bag filled with many items Bosch couldn't see. A folded newspaper protruded from the top of it.

On the steps near the rear door to the car was the facedown body of a black man wearing a dark gray suit. From his viewpoint Bosch could not see the man's face and only one wound was visible – a through-and-through gunshot wound at the center of the victim's right hand. Bosch knew it was what would later be called a defensive wound in the autopsy report. The man had held his hand up in a futile attempt to ward off gunfire. Bosch had seen it often enough over the years and it always made him think about the desperate actions people take at the end. Putting a hand up to stop a bullet was one of the most desperate.

Though the techs were stepping in and out of his line of sight, Bosch could look straight down through the inclined train car and down the track to Hill Street about three hundred feet below. A duplicate train car was down there at the bottom of the hill and Bosch could see more detectives milling about by the turn-stiles and the closed doors of the Grand Central Market across the street.

Bosch had ridden the inclined railroad as a kid and had studied how it worked. He still remembered. The two matching cars were counterbalanced. When one went up the side-by-side tracks the other went down, and vice versa. They passed each other at the midpoint. He remembered riding on Angels Flight long before Bunker Hill had been reborn as a slick business center of glass and marble towers, classy condominiums and apartments, museums, and fountains referred to as water gardens. Back then the hill had been a place of once-grand Victorian homes turned into tired-looking rooming houses. Harry and his mother had taken Angels Flight up the hill to look for a place to live.

'Finally, Detective Bosch.'

Bosch turned around. Deputy Chief Irving stood in the open door of the little station house.

'All of you,' he said, signaling Bosch and his team inside.

They entered a cramped room dominated by the large old cable wheels that once moved the train cars up and down the incline. Bosch remembered reading that when Angels Flight was rehabilitated a few years earlier after a quarter century of disuse, the cables and wheels had been replaced with an electric system monitored by computer.

On one side of the wheel display was just enough room for a small lunch table with two folding chairs. On the other side was the computer for operating the trains, a stool for the operator and a stack of cardboard boxes, the top one open and showing stacks of pamphlets on the history of Angels Flight.

Standing against the far wall, in the shadow behind the old iron wheels, his arms folded and his craggy, sun-reddened face looking down at the floor, was a man Bosch recognized. Bosch had once worked for Captain John Garwood, commander of the Robbery-Homicide Division. He knew by the look on his face that he was very put out about something. Garwood didn't look up at them and the three detectives said nothing.

Irving went to a telephone on the lunch table and picked up the loose handset. As he began talking he motioned to Bosch to close the door.

'Excuse me, sir,' Irving said. 'It was the team from Hollywood. They are all here and we are ready to proceed.'

He listened for a few moments, said good-bye and hung up the phone. The reverence in his voice and his use of the word *sir* told Bosch that Irving had been talking to the chief of police. It was one more curiosity about the case.

'All right, then,' Irving said, turning around and facing the three detectives. 'I am sorry to roust you people, especially out of rotation. However, I have spoken with Lieutenant Billets and as of now you have been cut free of the Hollywood rotation until we get this handled.'

'What exactly is *this* that we are handling?' Bosch asked.

'A delicate situation. The homicides of two citizens.'

Bosch wished he would get to the point.

'Chief, I see enough RHD people around here to investigate the Bobby Kennedy case all over again,' he said, glancing at Garwood. 'And that's not to mention the IAD shines hovering around the edges. What exactly are we doing here? What do you want?'

'Simple,' Irving said. 'I am turning the investigation over to you. It is your case now, Detective Bosch. The Robbery-Homicide detectives will be withdrawing as soon as you people are brought up to speed. As you can see, you are coming in late. That's unfortunate but I think you will be able to overcome it. I know what you can do.'

Bosch stared at him blankly for a long moment, then glanced at Garwood again. The captain had not moved and continued to stare at the floor. Bosch asked the only question that could bring understanding to this strange situation.

'That man and woman on the train car, who are they?'

Irving nodded.

'*Were* is probably the more correct word. *Were*. The woman's name was Catalina Perez. Who exactly she was and what she was doing on Angels Flight we do not know yet. It probably does not matter. It appears that she was just in the wrong place at the wrong time. But that will be for you to officially determine. Anyway, the man in there, he is different. That was Howard Elias.'

'The lawyer?'

Irving nodded. Bosch heard Edgar draw in a breath and hold it.

'This is for real?'

'Unfortunately.'

Bosch looked past Irving and through the ticket window. He could see into the train car. The techs were still at work, getting ready to shut off the lights so they could laser the inside of the car to look for fingerprints. His eyes fell to the hand with the bullet wound through it. Howard Elias. Bosch thought about all the suspects there would be, many of them standing around outside at that very moment, watching.

'Shit,' Edgar said. 'Don't suppose we could take a pass on this one, could we, Chief?'

'Watch your language, Detective,' Irving snapped, the muscles of his jaw bulging as he grew angry. 'That is not acceptable here.'

'Look, Chief, all I'm sayin' is if you're looking for somebody to play department Uncle Tom, it ain't going to be—'

'That has nothing to do with this,' Irving said, cutting him off. 'Whether you like it or not, you have been assigned to this case. I expect each of you to do it professionally and thoroughly. Most of all, I expect results, as does the chief of police. Other matters mean nothing. Absolutely nothing.'

After a brief silence, during which Irving's eyes went from Edgar to Rider and then to Bosch, the deputy chief continued.

'In this department there is only one race,' he said. 'Not black or white. Just the blue race.'

3

Howard Elias's notoriety as a civil rights attorney did not come to him because of the clients he served – they could best be described as ne'er-do-wells if not outright criminals. What had made Elias's face and name so well known to the masses of Los Angeles was his use of the media, his skill at probing the inflamed nerve of racism in the city, and the fact that his law practice was built entirely around one particular expertise: suing the Los Angeles Police Department.

For nearly two decades he had made a more than comfortable living filing lawsuit after lawsuit in federal court on behalf of citizens who had collided in some way with the police department. Elias sued patrol officers, detectives, the chief of police, the institution itself. When he filed, he used the shotgun approach, naming as defendants anyone remotely connected with the incident at the heart of the matter. After a fleeing burglary suspect was chewed up by a police dog, Elias had sued on the injured man's behalf, naming the dog, its handler and the line of supervision from the handler up to the chief of police. For good measure, he had sued the handler's academy instructors and the dog's breeder as well.

In his late-night television 'infomercials' and frequent 'impromptu' but cleverly orchestrated press conferences on the steps of the U.S. District Courthouse, Elias always cast himself as a watchdog, a lone voice crying out against the abuses of a fascist and racist paramilitary organization known as the LAPD. To his critics – and they ran from the rank and file of the LAPD to the offices of the city and district attorneys – Elias was a racist himself, a loose cannon who helped widen the fractures in an already divided city. To these detractors he was the scum of the legal system, a courtroom magician who could reach into the deck at any place and still pull out the race card.

Most often Elias's clients were black or brown. His skills as a public speaker and his selective use of facts while employing those skills often turned his clients into community heroes, emblematic victims of a police department out of control. Many in the city's south neighborhoods credited Elias with single-handedly keeping the LAPD from behaving as an occupying army. Howard Elias was one of the few people in the city who could be absolutely hated and fervently celebrated in different quarters at the same time.

Few who revered Elias understood that his entire practice was built around one simple piece of the law. He filed lawsuits only in federal court and under provisions of the U.S. civil rights codes that allowed him to bill the city of Los Angeles for his fees in any case in which he was victorious in court.

The Rodney King beating, the Christopher Commission report excoriating the department in the wake of the King trial and subsequent civil unrest, and the racially divisive O. J. Simpson case created a shadow that stretched over every case Elias filed. And so it was not particularly difficult for the lawyer to win cases against the department, convincing juries to award at least token damages to plaintiffs. Those juries never realized that such verdicts opened the door for Elias to bill the city and its taxpayers, themselves included, hundreds of thousands of dollars in fees.

In the dog bite lawsuit, which became Elias's signature case, the jury found that the rights of the plaintiff had been violated. But since that plaintiff was a burglar with a long track record of prior arrests and convictions, the jury awarded him only one dollar in damages. Their intent was clear, to send a message to the police department rather than to make a criminal wealthy. But that didn't matter to Elias. A win was a win. Under the federal guidelines he then submitted a bill to the city for $340,000 in legal fees. The city screamed and audited it, but still ended up paying more than half. In effect, the jury – and the many before and since – believed they were delivering a rebuke to the LAPD, but they were also paying for Elias's half-hour late-night infomercials on Channel 9, his Porsche and his Italian courtroom suits, his opulent home up in Baldwin Hills.

Elias, of course, was not alone. There were dozens of attorneys in the city who specialized in police and civil rights cases and mined the same federal provision allowing them to extract fees far in excess of the damages awarded their clients. Not all were cynical and motivated by money. Lawsuits by Elias and others had brought about positive change in the department. Even their enemies – the cops – could not begrudge them that. Civil rights cases brought about the end of the department-approved use of the choke hold while subduing suspects – after an inordinately high number of minority deaths. Lawsuits had also improved conditions and protections in local jails. Other cases opened and streamlined means for citizens to file complaints against abusive police officers.

But Elias stood head and shoulders above them all. He had media charm and the speaking skills of an actor. He also seemed to lack any criteria when it came to choosing his clients. He represented drug dealers who claimed to have been abused by their interrogators, burglars who stole from the poor but objected to being beaten by the police who chased them down, robbers who shot their victims but then cried foul when they in turn were shot by police. Elias's favorite line – used as a tagline on his commercials and whenever cameras were pointed at his face – was to say that abuse of power was abuse of power, regardless of whether the victim was a criminal. He was always quick to look into the camera and declare that if such abuse were tolerated when it was aimed at the guilty, it wouldn't be long before the innocent were targeted.

Elias was a sole practitioner. In the last decade he had sued the department more than a hundred times and won jury verdicts in more than half of the cases. His was a name that could freeze a cop's brain when he heard it. In the department, you knew that if Elias sued you, it would not be a small case that would be cleaned up and swept away. Elias didn't settle cases out of court – nothing in the civil rights codes gave an incentive to settle cases. No, you would be dragged through a public spectacle if Elias aimed a lawsuit at you. There would be press releases, press conferences, newspaper head-lines, television stories. You'd be lucky to come out of it in one piece, let alone with your badge.

Angel to some, devil to others, Howard Elias was now dead, shot to death on the Angels Flight railroad. Bosch knew as he looked through the small room's window and watched the orange glow of the laser beam move about the darkened train car that he was in the calm before the storm. In just two days what might have been Elias's biggest case was due to begin. The lawsuit against the LAPD that had become known in the media as the 'Black Warrior' case was set for jury selection in U.S. District Court on Monday morning. The coinci-dence – or, as a wide swath of the public would undoubtedly believe, the lack of coincidence – between Elias's murder and the start of the trial would make the investigation of the attorney's death an easy seven on the media's Richter scale. Minority groups would howl with rage and rightful suspicion. The whites in the West Side would whisper about their fears of another riot. And the eyes of the nation would be on Los Angeles and its police department once more. Bosch at that moment agreed with Edgar, though for different reasons than his black partner's. He wished they could take a pass on this one.

'Chief,' he said, turning his focus back to Irving, 'when it gets out who … I mean, when the media find out it was Elias, we're going to—'

'That is not your concern,' Irving said. 'Your concern is the investigation. The chief and I will deal with the media. Not a word comes from anyone on the investigation. Not a word.'

'Forget the media,' Rider said. 'What about South Central? People are going to—'

'That will be handled,' Irving said, interrupting. 'The department will institute the public disorder readiness plan beginning with the next watch. All personnel shift to twelve and twelves until we see how the city reacts. Nobody who saw nineteen ninety-two wants to see that again. But again, that is not your concern. You have one concern here.'

'You didn't let me finish,' Rider said. 'I wasn't going to say they would riot. I actually have faith in the people there. I don't think there will be trouble. What I was going to say was that they will be angry about this and suspicious. If you think you can ignore that or contain it by putting more cops on the—'

'Detective Rider,' Irving said, interrupting again, 'that is not your concern. The *investigation* is your concern.'

Bosch saw that Irving's interruptions and words, telling a black woman not to be concerned about her own community, had incensed Rider. It was on her face and Bosch had seen the look before. He decided to speak before she said something out of line.

'We're going to need more people. With just the three of us, we'll be running down alibis full-time for weeks, maybe a month. Case like this, we need to move fast, not only because of the case but because of the people. We're going to need more than just three of us.'

'That, too, has been taken care of,' Irving said. 'You

will have all the help you need. But it won't come from Robbery-Homicide. It's a conflict of interest because of the Michael Harris matter.'

Before speaking, Bosch noted how Irving refused to call it the Black Warrior case, instead using the plaintiff's name.

'Why us?'

'What?'

'I understand why RHD is out. But where are the Central Division teams? We're off our beat and out of rotation here. Why us?'

Irving exhaled audibly.

'The entire Central Division homicide squad is in academy training this week and next. Sensitivity training and then the FBI workshop on new crime scene techniques. Robbery-Homicide was covering their calls. They took this one. Once it was determined who that was with the bullets in his head, I was contacted and in subsequent discussions with the chief of police it was determined that we would reach out to you. You are a good team. One of our best. You have cleared your last four, including that hard-boiled eggs job – yes, I was briefed on it. Plus, the main thing is, none of you were ever sued by Elias.'

He pointed with his thumb over his shoulder in the direction of the crime scene in the train car. As he did this he glanced at Garwood but the captain was still looking down at the floor.

'No conflict of interest,' Irving said. 'Correct?'

The three detectives nodded. Bosch had been sued often enough in his twenty-five years with the department, but somehow he had always avoided tangling with Elias. Still, he didn't believe Irving's explanation was complete. He knew that Edgar had already alluded to a reason for their choice, probably a reason more important than the fact that none of them had been sued by Elias. Bosch's two partners were black. That might come in handy for Irving at some point. Bosch knew Irving's desire that the department have only one face and one race – blue – would go out the window when he needed a black face for the cameras.

'I don't want my people paraded in front of the media, Chief,' Bosch said. 'If we're on the case, we're on the case to work it, not for a show.'

Irving stared at him with angry eyes.

'What did you call me?'

Bosch was momentarily taken aback.

'I called you Chief.'

'Oh, good. Because I was wondering if there was some confusion here over the line of command in this room. Is there, Detective?'

Bosch looked away and out the window again. He could feel his face turning red and it upset him to give himself away.

'No,' he said.

'Good,' Irving said without a trace of tension. 'Then I am going to leave you with Captain Garwood. He will bring you up to speed on what has been accomplished so far. When he is done, we will talk about how we are going to set this case up.'

He turned to the door but Bosch stopped him.

'One more thing, Chief.'

Irving turned back to him. Bosch had recovered his composure now. He looked calmly at the deputy chief.

'You know we are going to be looking hard at cops on this. Lots of them. We'll have to go through all of the lawyer's cases, not just the Black Warrior thing. So I just need to know up front – we all need to – do you and the police chief want the chips to fall where they fall or …'

He didn't finish and Irving said nothing.

'I want to protect my people,' Bosch said. 'This kind of case … we just need to be clear about everything up front.'

Bosch was taking a gamble saying it in front of Garwood and the others. It would likely anger Irving again. But Bosch took the shot because he wanted Irving to answer him in front of Garwood. The captain was a powerful man in the department. Bosch wanted him to know that his team would be following the directives of the highest command, just in case the chips fell close to some of Garwood's people.

Irving looked at him for a long moment before finally speaking.

'Your insolence is noted, Detective Bosch.'

'Yes, sir. But what's the answer?'

'Let them fall, Detective. Two people are dead that should not be dead. It does not matter who they were. They should not be dead. Do your best work. Use all your skills. And let the chips fall.'

Bosch nodded once. Irving turned and glanced quickly at Garwood before leaving the room.

4

'Harry, you have a smoke?'

'Sorry, Cap, I'm trying to quit.'

'Me, too. I guess all that really means is that you borrow 'em rather than buy 'em.'

Garwood stepped away from the corner and blew out his breath. With his foot he moved a stack of boxes away from the wall and sat down on them. He looked old and tired to Bosch but then he had looked that way twelve years before when Bosch had gone to work for him. Garwood didn't raise any particular feelings in Bosch. He had been the aloof sort of supervisor. Didn't socialize with the squad after hours, didn't spend much time out of his office and in the bullpen. At the time, Bosch thought maybe that was good. It didn't engender a lot of loyalty from Garwood's people, but it didn't create any enmity either. Maybe that was how Garwood had lasted in the spot for so long.

'Well, it looks like we really got our tit in the wringer this time,' Garwood said. He then looked at Rider and added, 'Excuse the saying, Detective.'

Bosch's pager sounded and he quickly pulled it off his belt, disengaged the beep and looked at the number. It was not his own number as he had hoped it would be. He recognized it as the home number of Lieutenant Grace Billets. She probably wanted to know what was going on. If Irving had been as circumspect with her as he had been with Bosch on the phone, then she knew next to nothing.

'Important?' Garwood asked.

'I'll take care of it later. You want to talk in here or should we go out to the train?'

'Let me tell you what we have first. Then it's your scene to do with what you want.'

Garwood reached into the pocket of his coat, took out a softpack of Marlboros and began opening it.

'I thought you asked me for a smoke,' Bosch said.

'I did. This is my emergency pack. I'm not supposed to open it.'

It made little sense to Bosch. He watched as Garwood lit a cigarette and then offered the pack to Bosch. Harry shook his head. He put his hands in his pockets to make sure he wouldn't take one.

'This going to bother you?' Garwood asked, holding up the cigarette, a taunting smile on his face.

'Not me, Cap. My lungs are probably already shot. But these guys …'

Rider and Edgar waved it off. They appeared as impatient as Bosch did in getting to the story.

'Okay, then,' Garwood finally said. 'This is what we know. Last run of the night. Man named Elwood … Elwood … hold on a sec.'

He pulled a small pad from the same pocket he had replaced the cigarette package in and looked at some writing on the top page.

'Eldrige, yeah, Eldrige. Eldrige Peete. He was running the thing by himself – it only takes one person to run the whole operation – it's all computer. He was about to close her down for the night. On Friday nights the last ride is at eleven. It was eleven. Before sending the top car down for the last ride he goes out, gets on it, closes and locks the door. Then he comes back in here, puts the command on the computer and sends it down.'

He referred to the pad again.

'These things have names. The one he sent down is called Sinai and the one he brought up was Olivet. He says they're named after mountains in the Bible. It looked to him when Olivet got up here that the car was empty. So he goes out to lock it up – 'cause then he has to send them one more time and the computer stops them side by side in the middle of the track for overnight. Then he's done and out of here.'

Bosch looked at Rider and made a signal as if writing on his palm. She nodded and took her own pad and a pen out of the bulky purse she carried. She started taking notes.

'Only Elwood, I mean, Eldrige, he comes out to lock up the car and he finds the two bodies onboard. He backs away, comes in here and calls the police. With me?'

'So far. What next?'

Bosch was already thinking of the questions he would have to ask Garwood and then probably Peete.

'So we're covering for Central dicks and the call eventually comes to me. I send out four guys and they set up the scene.'

'They didn't check the bodies for ID?'

'Not right away. But there was no ID anyway. They were going by the book. They talked to this Eldrige Peete and they went down the steps and did a search for casings and other than that held tight until the coroner's people arrived and did their thing. Guy's wallet and watch are missing. His briefcase, too, if he was carrying one. But they got an ID off a letter the stiff had in his pocket. Addressed to Howard Elias. Once they found that, my guys took a real good look at the stiff and could tell it was Elias. They then, of course, called me and I called Irving and he called the chief and then it was decided to call you.'

He had said the last part as if he had been part of the decision process. Bosch glanced out the window. There was still a large number of detectives milling about.

'I'd say those first guys made more than just a call to you, Captain,' Bosch said.

Garwood turned to look out the window as if it had

never occurred to him that it was unusual to see as many as fifteen detectives at a murder scene.

'I suppose,' he said.

'Okay, what else?' Bosch said. 'What else did they do before they figured out who it was and that they weren't long for the case?'

'Well, like I said, they talked to this fellow Eldrige Peete and they searched the areas outside the cars. Top and bottom. They—'

'Did they find any of the brass?'

'No. Our shooter was careful. He picked up all the casings. We do know that he was using a nine, though.'

'How?'

'The second victim, the woman. The shot was through and through. The slug hit a steel window bracket behind her, flattened and fell on the floor. It's too mashed for comparison but you can still tell it was a nine. Hoffman said if he was guessing he'd say it was a federal. You'll have to hope for a better lead from the autopsies as far as ballistics go. If you ever get that far.'

Perfect, Bosch thought. Nine was a cop's caliber. And stopping to pick up the shells, that was a smooth move. You didn't usually see that.

'The way they see it,' Garwood continued, 'Elias got it just after he stepped onto the train down there. The guy comes up and shoots him in the ass first.'

'The ass?' Edgar said.

'That's right. The first shot is in the ass. See, Elias is just stepping on so he's a couple steps up from the sidewalk level. The shooter comes up from behind and holds the gun out – it's at ass level. He sticks the muzzle in there and fires off the first cap.'

'Then what?' Bosch asked.

'Well, we think Elias goes down and sort of turns to see who it is. He raises his hands but the shooter fires again. The slug goes through one of his hands and hits him in the face, right between the eyes. That's probably your cause-of-death shot right there. Elias drops back down. He's facedown now. The shooter steps into the car and puts one more in the back of his head, point-blank. He then looks up and sees the woman, maybe for the first time. He hits her from about five feet. One in the chest, through and through, and she's gone. No witness. The shooter gets the wallet and watch off Elias, picks up his shells and is gone. A few minutes later Peete brings the car up and finds the bodies. You now know what I know.'

Bosch and his partners were quiet a long moment. The scenario Garwood had woven didn't sit right with Bosch but he didn't know enough about the crime scene yet to challenge him on it.

'The robbery look legit?' Bosch finally asked.

'It did to me. I know the people down south aren't going to want to hear that but there it is.'

Rider and Edgar were silent stones.

'What about the woman?' Bosch asked. 'Was she robbed?'

'Doesn't look like it. I kind of think the shooter didn't want to come onto the train. Anyway, the lawyer was the one in the thousand-dollar suit. He'd be the target.'

'What about Peete? Did he hear the shots, a scream, anything?'

'He says no. He says the generator for the electric is right below the floor here. Sounds like an elevator running all day long so he wears earplugs. He never heard anything.'

Bosch stepped around the cable wheels and looked at the train operator's station. For the first time he saw that mounted above the cash register was a small video display box with a split screen showing four camera views of Angels Flight – from a camera in each of the train cars and from above each terminus. On one corner of the screen he could see a long shot of the inside of Olivet. The crime scene techs were still working with the bodies.

Garwood came around the other side of the cable wheels.

'No luck there,' he said. 'The cameras are live only, no tape. They are so the operator can check to make sure everyone is aboard and seated before starting the train.'

'Did he—'

'He didn't look,' Garwood said, knowing Bosch's questions. 'He just checked through the window, thought the car was empty and brought it up so he could lock it up.'

'Where is he?'

'At Parker. Our offices. I guess you'll have to come over and talk to him for yourself. I'll keep somebody with him until you make it by.'

'Any other witnesses?'

'Not a one. Eleven o'clock at night down here, the place is pretty dead. The Grand Central Market closes up at seven. There's nothing else down there except some office buildings. A couple of my guys were getting ready to go into those apartments next door here to knock on doors. But then they got the ID and sort of backed away.'

Bosch paced around in a small area of the room and thought. Very little had been done so far and the discovery of the murders was already four hours old. This bothered him even though he understood the reason behind the delay.

'Why was Elias on Angels Flight?' he asked Garwood. 'They figure that out before backing away?'

'Well, he must've wanted to go up the hill, don't you think?'

'Come on, Captain, if you know, why not save us the time?'

'We don't know, Harry. We ran a DMV check, he lives out in Baldwin Hills. That's a long way from Bunker Hill. I don't know why he was coming up here.'

'What about where he was coming from?'

'That's a little easier. Elias's office is just over on Third. In the Bradbury Building. He was probably coming from there. But where he was going ...'

'Okay, then what about the woman?'

'She's a blank. My guys hadn't even started with her when we were told to pull back.'

Garwood dropped his cigarette to the floor and crushed it with his heel. Bosch took it as a signal that the briefing was about over. He decided to see if he could get a rise out of him.

'You pissed off, Captain?'

'About what?'

'About being pulled off. About your people being on the suspect list.'

A small smile played on Garwood's thin lips.

'No, I'm not angry. I see the chief's point.'

'Are your people going to cooperate with us on this?'

After some hesitation Garwood nodded.

'Of course. The quicker they cooperate, the quicker you will clear them.'

'And you'll tell them that?'

'That's exactly what I'll tell them.'

'We appreciate that, Captain. Tell me, which one of your people do you think could have done this?'

The lips curled into a full smile now. Bosch studied Garwood's cigarette-yellowed teeth and for a moment was glad he was trying to quit.

'You're a clever guy, Harry. I remember that.'

He said nothing else.

'Thanks, Captain. But do you have an answer to the question?'

Garwood moved to the door and opened it. Before leaving he turned and looked back at them, his eyes traveling from Edgar to Rider to Bosch.

'It wasn't one of mine, Detectives. I guarantee it. You'll be wasting your time if you look there too long.'

'Thanks for the advice,' Bosch said.

Garwood stepped out, closing the door behind him.

'Jeez,' Rider said. 'It's like Captain Boris Karloff or something. Does that guy only come out at night?'

Bosch smiled and nodded.

'Mr Personality,' he said. 'So, what do you think so far?'

'I think we're at ground zero,' Rider said. 'Those guys didn't do jack before getting the hook.'

'Yeah, well, Robbery-Homicide, what do you want?' Edgar said. 'They aren't known for tap dancing. They back the tortoise over the hare any day of the week. But if you ask me, we're fucked. You and me, Kiz, we can't win on this one. Blue race, my ass.'

Bosch stepped toward the door.

'Let's go out and take a look,' he said, cutting off discussion of Edgar's concerns. He knew they were valid but for the moment they only served to clutter their mission. 'Maybe we'll get a few ideas before Irving wants to talk again.'

5

The number of detectives outside the station had finally begun to decrease. Bosch watched as Garwood and a group of his men crossed the plaza toward their cars. He then saw Irving standing to the side of the train car talking to Chastain and three detectives. Bosch didn't know them but assumed they were IAD. The deputy chief was animated in his discussion but kept his voice so low that Bosch couldn't hear what he was saying. Bosch wasn't sure exactly what the IAD presence was all about, but he was getting an increasingly bad feeling about it.

He saw Frankie Sheehan hanging back behind Garwood and his group. He was about to leave but was hesitating. Bosch nodded at him.

'I see what you mean now, Frankie,' he said.

'Yeah, Harry, some days you eat the bear …'

'Right. You taking off?'

'Yeah, the cap told us all to get out of here.'

Bosch stepped over and kept his voice low.

'Any ideas I could borrow?'

Sheehan looked at the train car as if considering for the first time who might have killed the two people inside it.

'None other than the obvious and I think that will be a waste of time. But then again, you have to waste it, right? Cover all the bases.'

'Yeah. Anybody you think I should start with?'

'Yeah, me.' He smiled broadly. 'I hated the douche bag. Know what I'm gonna do? I'm going now to try and find an all-night liquor store and buy the best Irish whiskey they got. I'm going to have a little celebration, Hieronymus. Because Howard Elias was a mother-fucker.'

Bosch nodded. With cops the word *motherfucker* was rarely used. It was heard a lot by them but not used. With most cops it was reserved as being the worst thing you could say about someone. When it was said it meant one thing; that the person had crossed the righteous, that the person had no respect for the keepers of the law and therefore the rules and bounds of society. Cop killers were always motherfuckers, no questions asked. Defense lawyers got the call, most of the time. And Howard Elias was on the motherfucker list, too. Right at the top.

Sheehan gave a little salute and headed off across the plaza. Bosch turned his attention toward the interior of the train while he put on rubber gloves. The lights were back on and the techs were finished with the laser. Bosch knew one of them, Hoffman. He was working with a trainee Bosch had heard about but not met. She was an attractive Asian woman with a large bust. He had overheard other detectives in the squad room discussing her attributes and questioning their authen-ticity.

'Gary, is it cool to come in?' Bosch asked, leaning in through the door.

Hoffman looked up from the tackle box in which he kept his tools. He was organizing things and was about to close it.

'It's cool. We're wrapping up. This one yours, Harry?'

'It is now. Got anything good for me? Gonna make my day?'

Bosch stepped into the car, followed by Edgar and Rider. Since the car was on an incline, the floor was actually a series of steps down to the other door. The seats also were on graduated levels on either side of the center aisle. Bosch looked at the slatted bench seats and suddenly remembered how hard they had been on his skinny behind as a boy.

''Fraid not,' Hoffman said. 'It's pretty clean.'

Bosch nodded and moved down a few more steps to the first body. He studied Catalina Perez the way someone might study a sculpture in a museum. There was no feeling for the object in front of him as human. He was studying details, gaining impressions. His eyes fell to the bloodstain and the small tear the bullet had made in the T-shirt. The bullet had hit the woman dead center. Bosch thought about this and envisioned the gunman in the doorway of the train twelve feet away.

'Hell of a shot, huh?'

It was the tech Bosch didn't know. He looked at her and nodded. He had been thinking the same thing, that the shooter was someone with some expertise in firearms.

'Hi, I don't think we've met. I'm Sally Tam.'

She put out her hand and Bosch shook it. It felt weird. They were both wearing rubber gloves. He told her his name.

'Oh,' she said. 'Somebody was just talking about you. About the hard-boiled eggs case.'

'It was just luck.'

Bosch knew he was getting a longer ride out of that case than he deserved. It was all because a *Times* reporter had heard about it and written a story that exaggerated Bosch's skills to the point where he seemed like a distant relative of Sherlock Holmes.

Bosch pointed past Tam and said he needed to get by to take a look at the other body. She stepped to the side and leaned back and he slid by, careful not to allow himself to rub against her. He heard her introducing herself to Rider and Edgar. He dropped into a crouch so he could study the body of Howard Elias.

'Is this still as is?' he asked Hoffman, who was

squatting next to his tackle box near the feet of the dead man.

'Pretty much. We turned him to get into his pockets but then put him back. There are some Polaroids over on that seat behind you if you want to double-check. Coroner's people took those before anybody touched him.'

Bosch turned and saw the photos. Hoffman had been right. The body was in the same position in which it had been found.

He turned back to the body and used both hands to turn the head so that he could study the wounds. Garwood's interpretation had been correct, Bosch decided. The entry wound at the back of the head was a contact wound. Though partially obscured by blood that had matted the hair, there were still powder burns and stippling visible in a circular pattern around the wound. The face shot, however, was clean. This did not refer to the blood – there was a good amount of that. But there were no powder burns on the skin. The bullet to the face had come from a distance.

Bosch picked up the arm and turned the hand so he could study the entry wound in the palm. The arm moved easily. Rigor mortis had not yet begun – the cool evening air was delaying this process. There was no discharge burn on the palm. Bosch did some computing. No powder burns on the palm meant the firearm was at least three to four feet away from the hand when the bullet was discharged. If Elias had his arm extended with his palm out, then that added another three feet.

Edgar and Rider had made their way to the second body. Bosch could feel their presence behind him.

'Six to seven feet away, through the hand and still right between the eyes,' he said. 'This guy can shoot. Better remember that when we take him down.'

Neither of them answered. Bosch hoped they picked up on the confidence in his last line as well as the warning. He was about to place the dead man's hand down on the floor when he noticed the long scratch mark on the wrist and running along the side of the palm. He guessed the wound had occurred when Elias's watch had been pulled off. He studied the wound closely. There was no blood in the track. It was a clean white laceration along the surface of the dark skin, yet it seemed deep enough to have drawn blood.

He thought about this for a moment. There were no shots to the heart, only to the head. The blood displacement from the wounds indicated the heart had continued to pump for at least several seconds after Elias had gone down. It would seem that the shooter would have yanked the watch off Elias's wrist very quickly after the shooting – there was obviously no reason to hang around. Yet, the scratch on the hand had not bled. It was as if it had occurred well after the heart had stopped pumping.

'What do you think about the lead enema?' Hoffman asked, interrupting Bosch's thoughts.

As Hoffman got out of the way, Bosch stood and gingerly stepped around the body until he was down by the feet. He crouched again and looked at the third bullet wound. Blood had soaked the seat of the pants. Still, he could see the tear and tight burn pattern where the bullet went through the cloth and into Howard Elias's anus. The weapon had been pressed in deep at the point where the seams of the pants were joined and then fired. It was a vindictive shot. More than a coup de grâce, it showed anger and hatred. It contradicted the cool skill of the other shots. It also told Bosch that Garwood had been wrong about the shooting sequence. Whether the captain had been intentionally wrong, he didn't know.

He stood up and backed to the rear door of the car so that he was in the spot where the shooter had probably stood. He surveyed the carnage in front of him once more and nodded to no one in particular, just trying to commit it all to memory. Edgar and Rider were still between the bodies and making their own observations.

Bosch turned around and looked down the tracks to the turnstile station below. The detectives he had seen before were gone. Now a lone cruiser sat down there and two patrol officers guarded the lower crime scene.

Bosch had seen enough. He made his way past the bodies and carefully around Sally Tam again and up onto the platform. His partners followed, Edgar moving by Tam more closely than he had to.

Bosch stepped away from the train car so they could huddle together privately.

'What do you think?' he said.

'I think they're real,' Edgar said, looking back toward Tam. 'They've got that natural slope to them. What do you think, Kiz?'

'Funny,' Rider said, not taking the bait. 'Can we talk about the case, please?'

Bosch admired how Rider took Edgar's frequent comments and sexual innuendo without more than a sarcastic remark or complaint fired back at him. Such comments could get Edgar in serious trouble but only if Rider made a formal complaint. The fact that she didn't indicated either she was intimidated or she could handle it. She also knew that if she went formal, she'd get what cops called a 'K-9 jacket,' a reference to the city jail ward where snitches were housed. Bosch had once asked her in a private moment if she wanted him to talk to Edgar. As her supervisor he was legally responsible for resolving the problem but he knew that if he talked to Edgar, then Edgar would know he had gotten to her. Rider knew this as well. She had thought about all of this for a few moments and told Bosch to let things alone. She said she wasn't intimidated, just annoyed on occasion. She could handle it.

'You go first, Kiz,' Bosch said, also ignoring Edgar's comment, even though he privately disagreed with his conclusion about Tam. 'Anything catch your eye in there?'

'Same as everybody else, I guess. Looks like the victims were not together. The woman either got on ahead of Elias or was about to get off. I think it's pretty clear Elias was the primary target and she was just an also-ran. The shot up the ass tells me that. Also, like you said in there, this guy was a hell of a shot. We're looking for someone who's spent some time at the range.'

Bosch nodded.

'Anything else?'

'Nope. It's a pretty clean scene. Nothing much to work with.'

'Jerry?'

'Nada. What about you?'

'Same. But I think Garwood was telling us a story. His sequence was for shit.'

'How?' Rider said.

'The shot up the pipe was the last one, not the first. Elias was already down. It's a contact wound and the entry is in the underside, where all the seams of the pants come together. It would be hard to get a muzzle up there if Elias was standing – even if he was up a step from the shooter. I think he was already down when the shooter popped that cap.'

'That changes things,' Rider said. 'Makes the last one a "fuck you" shot. The shooter was angry at Elias.'

'So he knew him,' Edgar said.

Bosch nodded.

'And you think Garwood knew this and was just trying to steer us wrong by planting the suggestion?' Rider asked. 'Or do you think he just missed it?'

'What I know about Garwood is that he is not a stupid man,' Bosch said. 'He and fifteen of his men were about to be pulled into federal court on Monday by Elias and dragged right through the shit. He knows any one of those boys might possibly be capable of this. He was protecting them. That's what I think.'

'Well, that's bullshit. Protecting a killer cop? He should be—'

'*Maybe* protecting a killer cop. We don't know. He didn't know. I think it was probably a just-in-case move.'

'Doesn't matter. If that's what he was doing, he shouldn't have a badge.'

Bosch didn't say anything to that and Rider wasn't placated. She shook her head in disgust. Like most cops in the department, she was tired of fuck-ups and cover-ups, of the few tainting the many.

'What about the scratch on the hand?'

Edgar and Rider looked at him with arched eye-brows.

'What about it?' Edgar said. 'Prob'ly happened when the shooter pulled off the watch. One of those with the expanding band. Like a Rolex. Knowing Elias, it was prob'ly a Rolex. Makes a nice motive.'

'Yeah, if it was a Rolex,' Bosch said.

He turned and looked out across the city. He doubted Elias wore a Rolex. For all of his flamboyance, Elias was the kind of lawyer who also knew the nuances of his profession. He knew that a lawyer wearing a Rolex might turn jurors off. He wouldn't wear one. He would have a nice and expensive watch, but not one that advertised itself like a Rolex.

'What, Harry?' Rider said. 'What about the scratch?'

Bosch looked back at them.

'Well, whether it was a Rolex or a high-priced watch or not, there's no blood in the scratch.'

'Meaning?'

'There is a lot of blood in there. The bullet wounds bled out, but there was no blood in the scratch. Meaning I don't think the shooter took the watch. That scratch was made after the heart stopped. I'd say long after. Which means it was made after the shooter left the scene.'

Rider and Edgar considered this.

'Maybe,' Edgar finally said. 'But that vascular system shit is hard to nail down. Even the coroner isn't gonna be definitive on that.'

'Yeah,' Bosch said, nodding. 'So call it gut instinct. We can't take it to court but I know the shooter didn't take the watch. Or probably the wallet, for that matter.'

'So what are you saying?' Edgar asked. 'Somebody else came along and took it?'

'Something like that.'

'You think it was the guy who ran the train – the one who called it in?'

Bosch looked at Edgar but didn't answer him. He hiked his shoulders.

'You think it was one of the RHD guys,' Rider whispered. 'Another just-in-case move. Send us down the robbery path, just in case it was one of their own.'

Bosch looked at her a moment, thinking about how to respond and how thin the ice was where they now stood.

'Detective Bosch?'

He turned. It was Sally Tam.

'We're clear and the coroner's people want to bag 'em and tag 'em if that's okay.'

'Fine. Hey, listen, I forgot to ask, did you get anything with the laser?'

'We got a lot. But probably nothing that will help. A lot of people ride that car. We probably got passengers, not the shooter.'

'Well, you'll run them anyway, right?'

'Sure. We'll put everything through AFIS and DOJ. We'll let you know.'

Bosch nodded his thanks.

'Also, did you collect any keys from the guy?'

'We did. They're in one of the brown bags. You want them?'

'Yeah, we're probably going to need them.'

'Be right back.'

She smiled and went back to the train car. She seemed too cheerful to be at a crime scene. Bosch knew that would wear off after a while.

'See what I mean?' Edgar said. 'They gotta be real.'

'Jerry,' Bosch said.

Edgar raised his hands in surrender.

'I'm a trained observer. Just filing a report.'

'Well, you better keep it to yourself,' Bosch whispered. 'Unless you want to file it with the chief.'

Edgar turned just in time to see Irving come up to them.

'Well, initial conclusions, Detectives?'

Bosch looked at Edgar.

'Jerry? What were you just saying you observed?'

'Uh, well, uh, at the moment we're still kind of thinking about all we saw in there.'

'Nothing that doesn't really jibe with what Captain Garwood told us,' Bosch said quickly, before Rider could say anything that would reveal their true conclusions. 'At least, preliminarily.'

'What next, then?'

'We've got plenty to do. I want to talk to the train operator again and we've got to canvass that residential building for wits. We've got next-of-kin notification and we've got to get into Elias's office. When is that help you promised us going to show up, Chief?'

'Right now.'

Irving raised an arm and beckoned Chastain and the three others he stood with. Bosch had known that was probably what they were doing at the scene but seeing Irving waving them over still put a tight feeling in his chest. Irving was well aware of the animosity between IAD and the rank and file, and the enmity that existed between Bosch and Chastain in particular. To put them together on the case told Bosch that Irving wasn't as interested in finding out who killed Howard Elias and

Catalina Perez as he had outwardly expressed. This was the deputy chief's way of appearing to be conscientious but actually working to cripple the investigation.

'Are you sure you want to do this, Chief?' Bosch asked in an urgent whisper as the IAD men approached. 'You know Chastain and I don't—'

'Yes, it is how I want to do it,' Irving said, cutting Bosch off without looking at him. 'Detective Chastain headed up the internal review of the Michael Harris complaint. I think he is an appropriate addition to this investigation.'

'What I'm saying is that Chastain and I have a history, Chief. I don't think it's going to work out with—'

'I do not care if you two do not like each other. Find a way to work together. I want to go back inside now.'

Irving led the entourage back into the station house. It was close quarters. No one said anything by way of a greeting to one another. Once inside, they all looked expectantly at Irving.

'Okay, we are going to set some ground rules here,' the deputy chief began. 'Detective Bosch is in charge of this investigation. The six of you report to him. He reports to me. I do not want any confusion about that. Detective Bosch runs this case. Now I have arranged for you to set up an office in the conference room next to my office on the sixth floor at Parker Center. There will be added phones and a computer terminal in there by Monday morning. You men from IAD, I want you to be primarily used in the areas of interviewing police officers, running down alibis, that part of the investigation. Detective Bosch and his team will handle the traditional elements of homicide investigation, the autopsy, witness interviews, that whole part of it. Any questions so far?'

The room went stone silent. Bosch was quietly seething. It was the first time he had thought of Irving as a hypocrite. The deputy chief had always been a hard-ass but ultimately a fair man. This move was different. He was maneuvering to protect the department when the rot they were seeking might be inside it. But what Irving didn't know was that Bosch had accomplished everything in his life by channeling negatives into motivation. He vowed to himself that he would clear the case in spite of Irving's maneuvers. And the chips would fall where they would fall.

'A word of warning about the media. It will be all over this case. You are not to be distracted or deterred. You are not to talk to the media. All such communications will come through my office or Lieutenant Tom O'Rourke in media relations. Understood?'

The seven detectives nodded.

'Good. That means I will not have to fear picking the *Times* up off the driveway in the morning.'

Irving looked at his watch and then back at the group.

'I can control you people but not the coroner's people or anyone else who learns about this through official channels in the next few hours. I figure by ten hundred the media will be all over this with full knowledge of the victims' identities. So I want a briefing in the conference room at ten hundred. After I am up-to-date I will brief the chief of police and one of us will address the media with the bare minimum of information we wish to put out. Any problem with that?'

'Chief, that barely gives us six hours,' Bosch said. 'I don't know how much more we'll know by then. We've got a lot of leg-work to do before we can sit down and start sifting through—'

'That is understood. You are to feel no pressure from the media. I do not care if the press conference is merely to confirm who is dead and nothing else. The media will not be running this case. I want you to run with it full bore, but at ten hundred I want everyone back at my conference room. Questions?'

There were none.

'Okay, then I will turn it over to Detective Bosch and leave you people to it.'

He turned directly to Bosch and handed him a white business card.

'You have all my numbers there. Lieutenant Tulin's as well. Anything comes up that I should know about, you call me forthwith. I do not care what time it is or where you are at. You call me.'

Bosch nodded, took the card and put it in his jacket pocket.

'Go to it, people. As I said before, let the chips fall where they may.'

He left the room and Bosch heard Rider whisper, 'Yeah, right.'

Bosch turned and looked at the faces of the new team, coming to Chastain's last.

'You know what he's doing, don't you?' Bosch said. 'He thinks we can't work together. He thinks we'll be like those fighting fish that you put in the same bowl and they go nuts trying to get at each other. Meantime, the case is never cleared. Well, it's not going to happen. Anything anybody in here's ever done to me or anyone else, forget about it. I let it go. This case is the thing. There are two people in that train that somebody blew away without so much as a second thought. We're going to find that person. That's all I care about now.'

He held Chastain's eyes until he finally saw a slight nod of agreement. Bosch nodded back. He was sure all the others had seen the exchange. He then took out his notebook and opened it to a fresh page. He handed it to Chastain.

'Okay, then,' he said. 'I want everybody to write down their names followed by their home and pager numbers. Cell phones, too, if you got 'em. I'll make a list up and everybody will get copies. I want everybody in communication. That's the trouble with these big gang bangs. If everybody isn't on the same wavelength, something can slip through. We don't want that.'

Bosch stopped and looked at the others. They were all watching him, paying attention. It seemed that for the moment the natural animosities were relaxed, if not forgotten.

'Okay,' he said. 'This is how we're going to break this down from here on out.'

6

One of the men from IAD was a Latino named Raymond Fuentes. Bosch sent him along with Edgar to the address on Catalina Perez's identification cards to notify her next of kin and to handle the questions about her. It was most likely the dead-end part of the investigation – it seemed apparent that Elias was the primary target – and Edgar tried to protest. But Bosch cut him off. The explanation he would share privately with Edgar later was that he needed to spread the IAD men out in order to give him better control of things. So Edgar went with Fuentes. And Rider was sent with a second IAD man, Loomis Baker, to interview Eldrige Peete at Parker Center and then bring him back to the scene. Bosch wanted the train operator at the scene to go over what he had seen and to operate the train as he had before discovering the bodies.

That left Bosch, Chastain and the last IAD man, Joe Dellacroce. Bosch dispatched Dellacroce to Parker Center as well, to draw up a search warrant for Elias's office. He then told Chastain that the two of them would go to Elias's home to make the death notification to his next of kin.

After the group split up, Bosch walked to the crime scene van and asked Hoffman for the keys found on the body of Howard Elias. Hoffman looked through the crate he had placed his evidence bags in and came out with a bag containing a ring with more than a dozen keys on it.

'From the front pants pocket, right side,' Hoffman said.

Bosch studied the keys for a moment. There seemed to be more than enough keys for the lawyer's home, office and cars. He noticed that there was a Porsche key on the ring as well as a Volvo key. He realized that when the investigators finished the current crop of tasks, one assignment he would have to make would be to put someone on locating Elias's car.

'Anything else in the pockets?'

'Yeah. In the left front he had a quarter.'

'A quarter.'

'Costs a quarter to ride Angels Flight. That's probably what that was for.'

Bosch nodded.

'And in the inside coat pocket was a letter.'

Bosch had forgotten that Garwood had mentioned the letter.

'Let's see that.'

Hoffman looked through his crate again and came up with a plastic evidence bag. Inside it was an envelope. Bosch took it from the crime scene tech and studied it without removing it. The envelope had been addressed to Elias's office by hand. There was no return address. On the left lower corner the sender had written PERSONAL & CONFIDENTIAL. Bosch tried to read the postmark but the light was bad. He wished he still carried a lighter.

'It's your neck of the woods, Harry,' Hoffman said. 'Hollywood. Mailed Wednesday. He probably got it Friday.'

Bosch nodded. He turned the bag over and looked at the back of the envelope. It had been cleanly cut open along the top. Elias or his secretary had opened it, probably at his office, before he had put it into his pocket. There was no way of knowing if the contents had been examined since.

'Anybody open it?'

'We didn't. I don't know what happened before we got here. I understand that the first detectives saw the name on there and then recognized the body. But I don't know if they actually looked at the letter.'

Bosch was curious about the contents of the envelope but knew it wasn't the right time or place to open it.

'I'm going to take this, too.'

'You got it, Harry. Let me just get you to sign it out. And the keys, too.'

Bosch waited while Hoffman got a chain-of-evidence form out of his kit. He squatted down and put the envelope and keys into his briefcase. Chastain came over, ready to leave the scene.

'You want to drive or you want me to?' Bosch said as he snapped his case closed. 'I've got a slick. What have you got?'

'I still have a plain jane. Runs like dogshit but at least I don't stand out like dogshit on the street.'

'That's good. You got a bubble?'

'Yes, Bosch, even IAD guys have to respond to calls now and then.'

Hoffman held a clipboard and pen out to Bosch and he signed his initials next to the two pieces of crime scene evidence he was taking with him.

'Then you drive.'

They started walking across California Plaza to where the cars were parked. Bosch pulled his pager off his belt and made sure it was running properly. The battery light was still green. He hadn't missed any pages. He looked up at the tall towers surrounding them, wondering if they could possibly interfere with a page from his wife, but then he remembered the page from Lieutenant Billets had come through earlier. He clipped the pager back to his belt and tried to think about something else.

Following Chastain's lead they came to a beat-up maroon LTD that was at least five years old and about as impressive looking as a Pinto. At least, Bosch thought, it isn't painted black and white.

'It's unlocked,' Chastain said.

Bosch went to the passenger side door and got in the car. He got his cell phone out of his briefcase and called the central dispatch center. He asked for a Department of Motor Vehicles run on Howard Elias and was given the dead man's home address as well as his age, driving record and the plate numbers of the Porsche and Volvo registered in his and his wife's names. Elias had been forty-six. His driving record was clean. Bosch thought that the lawyer was probably the most cautious driver in the city. The last thing Elias probably ever wanted to do was draw the attention of an LAPD patrol cop. It made driving a Porsche seem almost a waste.

'Baldwin Hills,' he said after closing the phone. 'Her name is Millie.'

Chastain started the engine, then plugged the flashing emergency light – the bubble – into the lighter and put it on the dashboard. He drove the car quickly down the deserted streets toward the 10 Freeway.

Bosch was silent at first, not sure how to break the ice with Chastain. The two men were natural enemies. Chastain had investigated Bosch on two different occasions. Both times Bosch was grudgingly cleared of any wrongdoing, but only after Chastain was forced to back off. It seemed to Bosch that Chastain had a hard-on for him that felt close to a vendetta. The IAD detective seemed to take no joy in clearing a fellow cop. All he wanted was a scalp.

'I know what you are doing, Bosch,' Chastain said once they got onto the freeway and started west.

Bosch looked over at him. For the first time he considered how physically similar they were. Dark hair going gray, full mustache beneath dark brown-black eyes, a lean, almost wiry build. Almost mirror images, yet Bosch had never considered Chastain to be the kind of physical threat that Bosch knew he projected himself.

Chastain carried himself differently. Bosch had always carried himself like a man afraid of being cornered, like a man who wouldn't allow himself to be cornered.

'What? What am I doing?'

'You're thinning us out. That way you have better control.'

He waited for Bosch to reply but only got silence.

'But eventually, if we're going to do this thing right, you are going to have to trust us.'

After a pause, Bosch said, 'I know that.'

Elias lived on Beck Street in Baldwin Hills, a small section of upper-middle-class homes south of the 10 Freeway and near La Cienega Boulevard. It was an area known as the black Beverly Hills – a neighborhood where affluent blacks moved when they did not wish to have their wealth take them out of their community. As Bosch considered this he thought that if there was anything that he could like about Elias, it was the fact that he didn't take his money and move to Brentwood or Westwood or the real Beverly Hills. He stayed in the community from which he had risen.

With little middle-of-the-night traffic and Chastain cruising on the freeway at ninety, they got to Beck Street in less than fifteen minutes. The house was a large brick colonial with four white columns holding up a two-story portico. It had the feeling of a Southern plantation and Bosch wondered if it was some kind of statement being made by Elias.

Bosch saw no lights from behind any of the windows and the hanging light in the portico was dark as well. This didn't sit right with him. If this was Elias's home, why wasn't a light left on for him?

There was a car in the circular driveway that was neither a Porsche nor a Volvo. It was an old Camaro with fresh paint and chromed wheels. To the right of the house there was a detached two-car garage but its door was closed. Chastain pulled into the drive and stopped behind the Camaro.

'Nice car,' Chastain said. 'Tell you what, I wouldn't leave a car like that out overnight. Even in a neighborhood like this. Too close to the jungle.'

He turned the car off and reached to open his door.

'Let's wait a second here,' Bosch said.

He opened his briefcase, got out the phone and called dispatch again. He asked for a double check on the address for Elias. They had the right place. He then asked the dispatcher to run the plate on the Camaro. It came back registered to a Martin Luther King Elias, age eighteen. Bosch thanked the dispatcher and clicked off.

'We got the right place?' Chastain asked.

'Looks like it. The Camaro must be his son's. But it doesn't look like anyone was expecting dad to come home tonight.'

Bosch opened his door and got out, Chastain doing the same. As they approached the door Bosch saw the dull glow of a bell button. He pushed it and heard the sharp ringing of a chime inside the quiet house.

They waited and pushed the bell button two more times before the portico light came on above them and a woman's sleepy but alarmed voice came through the door.

'What is it?'

'Mrs Elias?' Bosch said. 'We're police. We need to talk to you.'

'Police? What for?'

'It's about your husband, ma'am. Can we come in?'

'I need some identification before I open this door.'

Bosch took out his badge wallet and held it up but then noticed there was no peephole.

'Turn around,' the woman's voice said. 'On the column.'

Bosch and Chastain turned and saw the camera mounted on one of the columns. Bosch walked up to it and held up his badge.

'You see it?' he said loudly.

He heard the door open and turned around. A

woman in a white robe with a silk scarf wrapped around her head looked out at him.

'You don't have to yell,' she said.

'Sorry.'

She stood in the one-foot opening of the door but made no move to invite them in.

'Howard is not here. What do you want?'

'Uh, can we come in, Mrs Elias? We want—'

'No, you can't come in my house. My home. No policeman has ever been in here. Howard wouldn't have it. Neither will I. What do you want? Has something happened to Howard?'

'Uh, yes, ma'am, I'm afraid. It would really be better if we—'

'Oh my God!' she shrieked. 'You killed him! You people finally killed him!'

'Mrs Elias,' Bosch started, wishing he had better prepared himself for the assumption he should have known the woman would make. 'We need to sit down with you and—'

Again he was cut off, but this time it was by an unintelligible, animal-like sound from deep in the woman. Its anguish was resonant. The woman bowed her head and leaned into the door jamb. Bosch thought she might fall and made a move to grab her shoulders. The woman recoiled as if he were a monster reaching out to her.

'No! No! Don't you touch me! You – you murderers! Killers! You killed my Howard. Howard!'

The last word was a full-throated scream that seemed to echo through the neighborhood. Bosch looked behind him, half-expecting to see the street lined with onlookers. He knew he had to contain the woman, get her inside or at least quiet. She was moving into a full-fledged wail now. Meantime, Chastain just stood there, paralyzed by the scene unfolding before him.

Bosch was about to make another attempt to touch

the woman when he saw movement from behind her and a young man grabbed hold of her from behind.

'Ma! What? What is it?'

The woman turned and collapsed against the young man.

'Martin! Martin, they killed him! Your father!'

Martin Elias looked up over his mother's head and his eyes burned right through Bosch. His mouth formed the horrible *Oh* of shock and pain that Bosch had seen too many times before. He suddenly realized his mistake. He should have made this call with either Edgar or Rider. Rider, probably. She would have been a calming influence. Her smooth demeanor and the color of her skin would have done more than Bosch and Chastain combined.

'Son,' Chastain said, coming out of his inertia. 'We need to settle down a bit here and go inside to talk about this.'

'Don't you call me son. I'm not your goddamn son.'

'Mr Elias,' Bosch said forcefully. Everyone, including Chastain, looked at him. He then continued, in a calmer, softer voice. 'Martin. You need to take care of your mother. We need to tell you both what has happened and to ask you a few questions. The longer we stand here cursing and yelling, the longer it will be before you can take care of your mother.'

He waited a moment. The woman turned her face back into her son's chest and began to cry. Martin then stepped back, pulling her with him, so that there was room for Bosch and Chastain to enter.

For the next fifteen minutes Bosch and Chastain sat with the mother and son in a nicely furnished living room and detailed what was known of the crime and how the investigation would be handled. Bosch knew that to them it was like a couple of Nazis announcing they would investigate war crimes, but he also knew that it was important to go through the routine, to do his best to assure the victim's family that the investigation would be thorough and aggressive.

'I know what you said about it being cops,' Bosch said in summation. 'At the moment we don't know that. It is too early in the investigation to know anything about a motive. We are in a gathering phase at this time. But soon we'll move to the sifting phase and any cop who might have had even a remote reason to harm your husband will be looked at. I know there will be many in that category. You have my word that they will be looked at very closely.'

He waited. The mother and son were huddled together on a couch with a cheerful floral pattern. The son kept closing his eyes like a child hoping to ward off a punishment. He was flagging under the weight of what he had just been told. It was finally hitting home that he would not see his father again.

'Now, we know this is an awful time for you,' Bosch said softly. 'We would like to put off any kind of prolonged questioning so that you have time to yourselves. But there are a few questions that would help us right now.'

He waited for an objection but none came. He continued.

'The main one is that we can't figure out why Mr Elias was on Angels Flight. We need to find out where he was—'

'He was going to the apartment,' Martin said, without opening his eyes.

'What apartment?'

'He kept an apartment near the office so he could just stay over on court days or when he was busy getting ready for trial.'

'He was going to stay there tonight?'

'Right. He'd been staying there all week.'

'He had depos,' the wife said. 'With the police. They were coming in after work so he was staying late at the office. Then he would just go over to the apartment.'

Bosch was silent, hoping either one of them would add something more about the arrangement but nothing else was said.

'Did he call you and tell you he was staying over?' he asked.

'Yes, he always called.'

'When was this? This last time, is what I mean.'

'Earlier today. He said he'd be working late and needed to get back into it on Saturday and Sunday. You know, preparing for the trial on Monday. He said he would try to be home on Sunday for supper.'

'So you weren't expecting him to be home here tonight.'

'That's right,' Millie Elias said, a note of defiance in her voice as if she had taken the tone of Bosch's question to mean something else.

Bosch nodded as if to reassure her that he was not insinuating anything. He asked the specific address of the apartment and was told it was in a complex called The Place, just across Grand Street from the Museum of Modern Art. Bosch took out his notebook and wrote it down, then kept the notebook out.

'Now,' he said, 'Mrs Elias, can you remember more specifically when it was you last spoke to your husband?'

'It was right before six. That is when he calls and tells me, otherwise I have to figure out what's for supper and how many I'm cooking for.'

'How about you, Martin? When did you last speak to your father?'

Martin opened his eyes.

'I don't know, man. Couple days ago, at least. But what's this got to do with anything? You *know* who did it. Somebody with a badge did this thing.'

Tears finally began to slide down Martin's face. Bosch wished he could be somewhere else. Anywhere else.

'If it was a cop, Martin, you have my word, we will find him. He won't get away with it.'

'Sure,' Martin replied, without looking at Bosch. 'The man gives us his word. But who the hell is the man?'

The statement made Bosch pause a moment before continuing.

'A few more questions,' he finally said. 'Did Mr Elias have an office here at home?'

'No,' the son said. 'He didn't do his work here.'

'Okay. Next question. In recent days or weeks, had he mentioned any specific threat or person who he believed wanted to harm him?'

Martin shook his head and said, 'He just always said that it was the cops who would get him someday. It was the cops ...'

Bosch nodded, not in agreement but in his understanding of Martin's belief.

'One last question. There was a woman who was killed on Angels Flight. It looks like they were not together. Her name was Catalina Perez. Does that name mean anything to either of you?'

Bosch's eyes moved from the woman's face to her son's. Both stared blankly and shook their heads.

'Okay then.'

He stood up.

'We will leave you alone now. But either myself or other detectives will need to speak with you again. Probably later on today.'

Neither the mother nor son reacted.

'Mrs Elias, do you have a spare photo of your husband we could borrow?'

The woman looked up at him, her face showing confusion.

'Why do you want a picture of Howard?'

'We may need to show people in the course of the investigation.'

'Everybody already knows Howard, what he looks like.'

'Probably, ma'am, but we might need a photo in some cases. Do you—'

'Martin,' she said, 'go get me the albums out of the drawer in the den.'

Martin left the room and they waited. Bosch took a business card from his pocket and put it down on the wrought iron-and-glass coffee table.

'There's my pager number if you need me or if there is anything else I can do. Is there a family minister you would like us to call?'

Millie Elias looked up at him again.

'Reverend Tuggins over at the AME.'

Bosch nodded but immediately wished he hadn't made the offer. Martin came back into the room with a photo album. His mother took it and began to turn through the pages. She began to weep silently again at the sight of so many pictures of her husband. Bosch wished he had put off getting the photo until the follow-up interview. Finally, she came upon a close-up shot of Howard Elias's face. She seemed to know it would be the best photo for the police. She carefully removed it from the plastic sleeve and handed it to Bosch.

'Will I get that back?'

'Yes, ma'am, I'll see that you do.'

Bosch nodded and was about to make his way to the door. He was wondering if he could just forget about calling Reverend Tuggins.

'Where's my husband?' the widow suddenly asked.

Bosch turned back.

'His body is at the coroner's office, ma'am. I will give them your number and they will call you when it is time for you to make arrangements.'

'What about Reverend Tuggins? You want to use our phone?'

'Uh, no, ma'am. We'll contact Reverend Tuggins from our car. We can see ourselves out now.'

On the way to the door, Bosch glanced at the collection of framed photographs that hung on the wall in the entrance hallway. They were photos of Howard Elias with every notable black community leader in the city as well as many other celebrities and national leaders. There he was with Jesse Jackson, with Congresswoman Maxine Waters, with Eddie Murphy. There was a shot of Elias flanked by Mayor Richard Riordan on one side and City Councilman Royal Sparks on the other. Bosch knew that Sparks had used outrage over police misconduct to forge his rise in city politics. He would miss having Elias around to keep the fire fanned, though Bosch also knew that Sparks would now use the lawyer's murder to any advantage he could. Bosch wondered how it was that good and noble causes often seemed to bring slick opportunists to the microphones.

There were also family photos. Several depicted Elias and his wife at social functions. There were shots of Elias and his son – one of them on a boat, both holding up a black marlin and smiling. Another photo showed them at a firing range posing on either side of a paper target with several holes shot through it. The target depicted Daryl Gates, a former police chief whom Elias had sued numerous times. Bosch remembered that the targets, created by a local artist, were popular toward the end of Gates's tumultuous stewardship of the department.

Bosch leaned forward to study the photo and see if he could identify the weapons Elias and his son held but the photo was too small.

Chastain pointed to one of the photos, which showed Elias and the chief of police at some formal affair, supposed adversaries smiling at the camera.

'They look cozy,' he whispered.

Bosch just nodded and went out through the door.

Chastain pulled the car out of the driveway and headed down out of the hills and back to the freeway. They were silent, both absorbing the misery they had just brought to a family and how they had received the blame for it.

'They always shoot the messenger,' Bosch said.

'I think I'm glad I don't work homicide,' Chastain replied. 'I can deal with cops being pissed at me. But that, that was bullshit.'

'They call it the dirty work – next-of-kin notification.'

'They ought to call it something. Fucking people. We're trying to find out who killed the guy and they're saying it was us. You believe that shit?'

'I didn't take it literally, Chastain. People in that position are entitled to a little slack. They're hurting, they say things, that's all.'

'Yeah, you'll see. Wait until you see that kid on the six o'clock news. I know the type. You won't have much sympathy then. Where are we going anyway, back to the scene?'

'Go to his apartment first. You know Dellacroce's pager number?'

'Not offhand, no. Look at your list.'

Bosch opened his notebook and looked up the pager number Dellacroce had written down. He punched the number into his phone and made the page.

'What about Tuggins?' Chastain asked. 'You call him, you give him the head start on getting the south end ready to rock and roll.'

'I know. I'm thinking.'

Bosch had been thinking about that decision since the moment Millie Elias had mentioned the name Tuggins. As with many minority communities, pastors carried as much weight as politicians when it came to shaping that community's response to a social, cultural or political cause or event. In the case of Preston Tuggins, he carried even more. He headed a group of associated ministers and together they were a force, a major media-savvy force that could hold the whole community in check – or unleash it like an earthquake. Preston Tuggins had to be handled with utmost care.

Bosch dug through his pocket and pulled out the card Irving had given him earlier. He was about to call one of the numbers on it when the phone rang in his hand.

It was Dellacroce. Bosch gave him the address of Elias's apartment at The Place and told him to draw up an additional search warrant. Dellacroce cursed because he had already wakened a judge to fax him the office search warrant. He would now have to do it again.

'Welcome to homicide,' Bosch said as he clicked off.

'What?' Chastain said.

'Nothing. Just bullshit.'

Bosch punched in Irving's number. The deputy chief answered after one ring, giving his full name and rank. It seemed odd to Bosch that Irving seemed fully alert, as if he had not been asleep.

'Chief, it's Bosch. You said to call if—'

'It's no problem, Detective. What is it?'

'We just made notification. To Elias's wife and son. Uh, she wanted me to call her minister.'

'I don't see the problem.'

'The minister is Preston Tuggins and I thought maybe somebody a little further up the ladder might be better making—'

'I understand. It was good thinking. I will have it taken care of. I think perhaps the chief will want to handle that. I was just about to call him anyway. Anything else?'

'Not at this time.'

'Thank you, Detective.'

Irving hung up. Chastain asked what he said and Bosch told him.

'This case … ,' Chastain said. 'I have a feeling things are going to get hairy.'

'Say that again.'

Chastain was about to say something else but Bosch's pager sounded. He checked the number. Again it wasn't a call from home but Grace Billets's second page. He had forgotten to call her earlier. He called now and the lieutenant answered after one ring.

'I wondered if you were going to call me back.'

'Sorry. I sort of got tied up, then I forgot.'

'So what's going on? Irving wouldn't tell me who was dead, just that RHD and Central couldn't handle it.'

'Howard Elias.'

'Oh, shit … Harry … I'm sorry it's you.'

'It's okay. We'll make out.'

'Everybody will be watching you. And if it's a cop … it's a no-win situation. Do you get any sense from Irving, does he want to go at it balls to the wall?'

'Mixed signals.'

'You can't talk freely?'

'Right.'

'Well, I'm getting mixed signals here, too. Irving told me to take your team off the rotation but he said it would only be until Friday. Then I'm supposed to talk to Irving about it. Now that I know who is dead, I think the translation of that is that you have till then before he probably ships you back to Hollywood and you have to take Howard Elias back here with you and work it when you can.'

Bosch nodded but didn't say anything. It went with the other moves Irving had made. The deputy chief had created a large team to work the case, but it looked as though he was only giving them a week to work it full-time. Maybe he hoped that the media glare would drop off to a more manageable level by then and the case could eventually disappear into the unsolved files. But Bosch thought Irving was kidding himself if he thought that.

He and Billets talked for a few minutes more before Billets finally signed off with a warning.

'Watch yourself, Harry. If a cop did this, one of those RHD guys …'

'What?'

'Just be careful.'

'I will.'

He closed the phone and looked out the windshield. They were almost to the 110 transition. They would be back at California Plaza soon.

'Your lieutenant?' Chastain asked.

'Yeah. She just wanted to know what was going on.'

'So what's the deal with her and Rider? They still munching each other's pie on the side?'

'It's none of my business, Chastain. And none of yours.'

'Just asking.'

They rode in silence for a while. Bosch was annoyed by Chastain's question. He knew it was the IAD detective's way of reminding Bosch that he knew secrets, that he might be out of his element when it came to straight homicide investigation but he knew secrets about cops and should not be taken lightly. Bosch wished he hadn't made the call to Billets while Chastain was in the car.

Chastain seemed to sense his misstep and broke the silence by trying some harmless banter.

'Tell me about this hard-boiled eggs caper I keep hearing people talk about,' he said.

'It was nothing. Just a case.'

'I missed the story in the paper, I guess.'

'Just a piece of luck, Chastain. Like we could use on this case.'

'Well, tell me. I want to know – especially now that we're partnering up, Bosch. I like stories about luck. Maybe it will rub off.'

'It was just a routine call out on a suicide. Patrol called us to come out and sign off on it. Started when a mother got worried about her daughter because she hadn't shown up at the airport up in Portland. She was supposed to fly up there for a wedding or something and never showed up. The family was left waiting at the airport. Anyway, the mother called up and asked for a drive-by check of the daughter's apartment. A little place over on Franklin near La Brea. So a blue suit went by, got the manager to let him in and they found her. She had been dead a couple of days – since the morning she was supposed to have flown up to Portland.'

'What did she do?'

'It was made to look like she took some pills and then cut her wrists in the bathtub.'

'Patrol said suicide.'

'That's the way it was supposed to look. There was a note. It was torn out of a notebook and it said things about life not being what she expected and about being lonely all the time and stuff. It was kind of a ramble. Very sad, actually.'

'So? How'd you figure it out?'

'Well, we were – Edgar was with me, Rider had court – we were about to close it out. We had looked around the place and found nothing really wrong – except for the note. I couldn't find the notebook that the page had been torn out of. And that didn't sit right. I mean, it didn't mean she didn't kill herself, but it was a loose end, you know? A *what is wrong with this picture* sort of thing.'

'Okay, so you thought somebody was in there and took the notebook?'

'Maybe. I didn't know what to think. I told Edgar to take another look around and this time we switched and searched through things the other guy had searched the first time.'

'And you found something Edgar had missed.'

'He didn't miss it. It just didn't register with him. It did with me.'

'What was it already?'

'In her refrigerator there was a shelf for the eggs. You know, like little indentations that you sit the eggs in?'

'Right.'

'Well, I noticed on some of the eggs she had written a date. All the same date. It was the same day she was flying up to Portland.'

Bosch looked over at Chastain to see if there was a reaction. The IAD man had a confused look on his face. He didn't get it.

'They were hard-boiled eggs. The ones with dates on them had been hard-boiled. I took one over to the sink and cracked it. It was hard-boiled.'

'Okay.'

He still didn't get it.

'The date on the eggs was probably the date she had boiled them,' Bosch said. 'You know, so she could tell the boiled ones from the others and she'd know how old they were. And it just hit me then. You don't boil a bunch of eggs so they're ready for when you want them and then go kill yourself. I mean, what's the point?'

'So it was a hunch.'

'More than that.'

'But you just knew. Homicide.'

'It changed things. We started to look at things differently. We began a homicide investigation. It took a few days but we got it. Friends told us about some guy who was giving her trouble. Harassing her, stalking her because she turned him down on a date. We asked around the apartment and we started looking at the apartment manager.'

'Shit, I shoulda guessed it was him.'

'We talked to him and he fucked up just enough for us to convince a judge to sign a search warrant. In his place we found the notebook that the supposed suicide note had been torn from. It was like a diary where she wrote down her thoughts and things. This guy found a page where she was talking about life being bad and knew he could use it as a suicide note. We found other stuff that was hers.'

'Why'd he keep the stuff?'

'Because people are stupid, that's why, Chastain. You

want clever killers, watch TV. He kept the stuff because he never thought we'd think it wasn't a suicide. And because he was in the notebook. She wrote about him stalking her, about how she was sort of flattered and scared of him at the same time. He probably got off on reading it. He kept it.'

'When's the trial?'

'Couple months.'

'Sounds like a slam dunk.'

'Yeah, we'll see. So was O.J.'

'What did he do, drug her somehow, then put her in the tub and cut her?'

'He was letting himself in her apartment when she was out. There was stuff in the diary about her thinking someone had been creepin' her place. She was a runner – did three miles a day. We think that was when he liked to go in. She had prescription painkillers in the medicine cabinet – she got hurt playing racketball a couple years before. We think he took the pills on one of his visits and dissolved them in orange juice. The next time he went in he poured it into the juice bottle in her fridge. He knew her habits, knew that after jogging she liked to sit on the steps out front, drink her juice and cool down. She may have realized she had been drugged and looked around for help. It was him who came. He took her back inside.'

'He rape her first?'

Bosch shook his head.

'He probably tried but he couldn't get it up.'

They drove in silence for a few moments.

'You're cool, Bosch,' Chastain said. 'Nothing gets by you.'

'Yeah, I wish.'

7

Chastain parked the car in the passenger loading zone in front of the modern high-rise building called The Place. Before they were out of the car the night doorman came through the glass entrance to either greet them or tell them to move. Bosch got out and explained that Howard Elias had been murdered less than a block away and that they needed to check his apartment to make sure there were no additional victims or someone needing help. The doorman said no problem but wanted to go along. Bosch told him in a tone that invited no debate to wait in the lobby for other officers who would be arriving.

Howard Elias's apartment was on the twentieth floor. The elevator moved quickly but the silence between Bosch and Chastain made the trip seem longer.

They found their way to 20E and Bosch knocked on the door and rang the doorbell on the wall next to it. After getting no response, Bosch stooped and opened his briefcase on the floor, then took the keys out of the evidence bag Hoffman had given him earlier.

'You think we ought to wait on the warrant?' Chastain asked.

Bosch looked up at him as he closed the briefcase and snapped the locks.

'No.'

'That was a line of bullshit you gave the doorman, that people maybe needed help.'

Bosch stood up and started trying keys in the door's two locks.

'Remember what you said before about me eventually having to trust you? This is where I start to trust you, Chastain. I don't have the time to wait on a warrant. I'm going in. A homicide case is like a shark. It's gotta keep moving or it drowns.'

He turned the first lock.

'You and your fucking fish. First fighting fish, now a shark.'

'Yeah, you keep sticking around, Chastain, you might even learn how to catch something.'

Just as he said the line he turned the second lock. He looked at Chastain and winked, then opened the door.

They entered a medium-sized living room with expensive leather furnishings, cherrywood bookcases, and windows and a balcony with an expansive southern view across downtown and the civic center. The place was neatly kept except for sections of Friday morning's *Times* spread across the black leather couch and an empty coffee mug on the glass-topped coffee table.

'Hello?' Bosch called out, just to be sure the place was empty. 'Police. Anyone home?'

No answer.

Bosch put his briefcase down on the dining room table, opened it and took a pair of latex gloves out of a cardboard box. He asked Chastain if he wanted a pair but the IAD man declined.

'I'm not going to be touching anything.'

They separated and began moving through the apartment on a quick initial survey. The rest of the place was as neat as the living room. It was a two-bedroom and had a master suite with its own balcony facing west. It was a clear night. Bosch could see all the way to Century City. Past those towers the lights dropped off in Santa Monica to the sea. Chastain came into the bedroom behind him.

'No home office,' he said. 'The second bedroom looks like a guest room. Maybe for stashing witnesses.'

'Okay.'

Bosch scanned the contents of the top of the bureau. There were no photos or anything of a strong personal nature. Same with the small tables on either side of the bed. It looked like a hotel room and in a way it was – if Elias only used it for overnight stays while readying cases for court. The bed was made and this stood out to Bosch. Elias was in the middle of preparations for a major trial, working day and night, yet he had stopped to make his bed that morning when supposedly it would just be he returning at the end of the day. No way, Bosch thought. Either he made the bed because there would be someone else in the apartment or someone else made the bed.

Bosch ruled out a maid because a maid would have picked up the strewn newspaper and the empty coffee cup in the living room. No, it was Elias who had made the bed. Or someone who was with him. It was gut instinct based on his long years of delving into human habits, but at that moment Bosch felt reasonably sure that there now was another woman in the mix.

He opened the drawer of the bed table where a phone sat and found a personal phone book. He opened it and flipped through the pages. There were many names he recognized. Most were lawyers Bosch had heard about or even knew. He stopped when he came across one name. Carla Entrenkin. She, too, was an attorney specializing in civil rights cases – or had been until a year earlier, when the Police Commission appointed her inspector general of the Los Angeles Police Department. He noted that Elias had her office and home number listed. The home number was in darker, seemingly more recent, ink. It looked to Bosch as though the home number had been added well after the business number had been recorded in the book.

'Whaddaya got?' Chastain said.

'Nothing,' Bosch answered. 'Just a bunch of lawyers.'

He closed the phone book as Chastain stepped over to look. He tossed it back in the drawer and closed it.

'Better leave it for the warrant,' he said.

They conducted a casual search of the rest of the apartment for the next twenty minutes, looking in drawers and closets, under beds and couch cushions, but not disturbing anything they found. At one point Chastain called out from the bathroom off the master bedroom.

'Got two toothbrushes here.'

'Okay.'

Bosch was in the living room, studying the books on shelves. He saw one he had read years before, *Yesterday Will Make You Cry* by Chester Himes. He felt Chastain's presence and turned around. Chastain stood in the hallway leading to the bedrooms. He was holding a box of condoms up for Bosch to see.

'These were hidden in the back of a shelf under the sink.'

Bosch didn't respond. He just nodded.

In the kitchen there was a wall-mounted telephone with an answering machine. There was a flashing light on it and the digital display showed there was one message waiting to be played. Bosch pushed the playback button. It was a woman's voice on the message.

'Hey, it's me. I thought you were going to call me. I hope you didn't fall asleep on me.'

That was it. After the message, the machine reported that the call had come in at 12:01 A.M. Elias was already dead by then. Chastain, who had come into the kitchen from the living room when he heard the voice, just looked at Bosch and hiked his shoulders after the message was played. Bosch played it again.

'Doesn't sound like the wife to me,' Bosch said.

'Sounds white to me,' Chastain said.

Bosch thought he was right. He played the message one more time, this time concentrating on the tone of the woman's voice. There was a clear sense of intimacy in the voice. The time of the call and the woman's

67

assumption that Elias would know her voice supported this conclusion as well.

'Condoms hidden in the bathroom, two toothbrushes, mystery woman on the phone,' Chastain said. 'Sounds like we got a girlfriend in the works. That could make things interesting.'

'Maybe,' Bosch said. 'Somebody made the bed this morning. Any female stuff in the medicine cabinet?'

'Nothing.'

Chastain went back to the living room. After Bosch was finished in the kitchen, he felt he had seen enough for the time being and slid open the glass door leading from the living room to the balcony. He leaned on the iron railing and checked his watch. It was 4:50. He then pulled the pager off his belt to make sure he hadn't turned it off by mistake.

The pager was on, the battery not dead. Eleanor had not tried to reach him. He heard Chastain come out onto the balcony behind him. Bosch spoke without turning to look at him.

'Did you know him, Chastain?'

'Who, Elias? Yeah, sort of.'

'How?'

'I've worked cases he later went to court on. I got subpoenaed and deposed. Plus, the Bradbury. He's got his office there, we've got offices there. I'd see him every now and then. But if you're asking if I played golf with the guy, the answer is no. I didn't know him like that.'

'The guy made a living suing cops. When he got into court he always seemed to have real good information. Inside stuff. Some say better stuff than he should have had access to through legal discovery. Some say he might've had sources inside—'

'I wasn't a snitch for Howard Elias, Bosch,' Chastain said, his voice tight. 'And I don't know anyone in IAD who was. We investigate cops. *I* investigate cops. Sometimes they deserve it and sometimes it turns out

68

they don't. You know as well as I do that there has to be somebody to police the police. But snitching to the likes of Howard Elias and his bunch, that's the lowest of the low, Bosch. So fuck you very much for asking.'

Bosch looked at him now, studying the way the anger was moving into his dark eyes.

'Just asking,' he said. 'Had to know who I am dealing with.'

He looked back out across the city and then down to the plaza below. He saw Kiz Rider and Loomis Baker crossing toward Angels Flight with a man Bosch assumed was Eldrige Peete, the train operator.

'All right, you asked,' Chastain said. 'Can we get on with it now?'

'Sure.'

They were silent during the elevator ride down. It wasn't until they were in the lobby that Bosch spoke.

'You go on ahead,' he said. 'I'm gonna see if there's a can around here. Tell the others I'll be right there.'

'Sure.'

The doorman had overheard the exchange from his little lobby desk and told Bosch the rest room was around the corner behind the elevators. Bosch headed that way.

In the rest room Bosch put his briefcase on the sink counter and got his phone out. He called his house first. When the machine picked up he punched in the code to play all new messages. Only his own message played back to him. Eleanor hadn't got it.

'Shit,' he said as he hung up.

He then called information and got the number for the Hollywood Park poker room. The last time Eleanor had not come home she had told him she was playing cards there. He called the number and asked for the security office. A man identifying himself as Mr Jardine answered and Bosch gave his name and badge number. Jardine asked him to spell his name and give the number again. He was obviously writing it down.

'Are you in the video room?'

'Sure am. What can I do for you?'

'I'm looking for somebody and there is a good chance she is at one of your tables right now. I was wondering if you could look at the tubes for me.'

'What's she look like?'

Bosch described his wife but could not give any description on clothes because he had not checked the closets at the house. He then waited two minutes while Jardine apparently studied the video screens connected to the surveillance cameras in the poker room.

'Uh, if she's here, I'm not seeing her,' Jardine finally said. 'We don't have very many women in here this time of night. And she doesn't match the ones we've got. I mean, she could have been in here earlier, maybe one or two o'clock. But not now.'

'Okay, thanks.'

'Hey, you got a number? I'll take a walk around the place, call you back if I see anything.'

'I'll give you my pager. But if you see her, don't approach her. Just give me a page.'

'Will do.'

After giving the man his pager number and hanging up, Bosch thought about the card clubs in Gardena and Commerce but decided not to call. If Eleanor was going to stay local she would have gone to Hollywood Park. If she didn't go there she'd go to Vegas or maybe the Indian place in the desert near Palm Springs. He tried not to think about that and focused his mind back on the case.

Bosch next called the district attorney's night switchboard after getting the number out of his phone book. He asked to be connected to the on-call prosecutor and was eventually connected to a sleepy attorney named Janis Langwiser. She happened to be the same prosecutor who had filed charges in the so-called hard-boiled eggs case. She had recently moved over from the city attorney's office and it had been the first time Bosch had worked with her. He had enjoyed her sense of humor and enthusiasm for her job.

'Don't tell me,' she said, 'you've got a scrambled eggs case this time? Or better yet, the western omelet case.'

'Not quite. I hate to pull you out of bed but we're going to need somebody to come out and give us a little guidance on a search we'll be doing pretty soon.'

'Who's dead and where's the search?'

'Dead is Howard Elias, Esquire, and the search is going to be in his office.'

She whistled into the phone and Bosch had to hold it away from his ear.

'Wow,' she said, now fully alert. 'This is going to be ... well, something. Tell me the general details.'

He did and when he was finished Langwiser, who lived thirty miles north in Valencia, agreed to meet the search team at the Bradbury in one hour.

'Until then, take things very carefully, Detective Bosch, and don't go into the office until I am there.'

'Will do.'

It was a little thing but he liked her calling him by his title. It was not because she was a good deal younger than he was. It was because so often prosecutors treated him and other cops without respect, as simply tools for them to use whatever way they wanted in prosecuting a case. He was sure Janis Langwiser would be no different as she became more seasoned and cynical, but at least for now she outwardly showed him small nuances of respect.

Bosch disconnected and was about to put the phone away when he thought of something else. He called information again and asked for the home listing for Carla Entrenkin. He was connected to a recording that told him the number was unlisted at the customer's request. It was what he had expected to hear.

As he crossed Grand Street and California Plaza to Angels Flight, Bosch again tried not to think of Eleanor and where she might be. But it was hard. It hurt his heart when he thought about her being out there somewhere alone, searching for something he obviously couldn't give her. He was beginning to feel his marriage would be doomed if he didn't soon figure out what it was she needed. When they had married a year ago, he had found a feeling of contentment and peace that he had never experienced before. For the first time in his life he felt there was someone to sacrifice for – everything if needed. But he had come to the point where he was acknowledging to himself that it was not the same for her. She was not content or complete. And it made him feel awful and guilty and a small bit relieved, all at the same time.

Again he tried to concentrate on other things, on the case. He knew he needed to put Eleanor aside for the time being. He started thinking about the voice on the phone, the condoms hidden in the bathroom cabinet and the bed that had been neatly made. He thought about how Howard Elias could come to have the unlisted home telephone number of Carla Entrenkin in the drawer next to his bed.

8

Rider was standing next to a tall black man with graying hair just outside the door to the Angels Flight station house. They were sharing a smile about something when Bosch walked up.

'Mr Peete, this is Harry Bosch,' Rider said. 'He's in charge of this investigation.'

Peete shook his hand.

'Worst thing I ever saw in m'life. Worst thing.'

'I'm sorry you had to witness this, sir. But I'm glad you are willing to help us out. Why don't you go in and have a seat inside. We'll be with you in a few minutes.'

When Peete was inside Bosch looked at Rider. He didn't have to speak.

'Same as Garwood said. He didn't hear anything and he didn't see a lot until the car came up and he went to lock it up for the night. He didn't see anybody hanging around down there, as if they were waiting for anyone, either.'

'Any chance he's just playing deaf and dumb?'

'My gut says no. I think he's legit. He didn't see it or hear it go down.'

'He touch the bodies?'

'No. You mean the watch and wallet? I doubt it was him.'

Bosch nodded.

'Mind if I ask him a couple follow-ups?'

'Be my guest.'

Bosch walked into the little office and Rider followed. Eldrige Peete was sitting at the lunch table, holding the phone to his ear.

'I gotta go, hon,' he said when he saw Bosch. 'The policeman wants to talk to me.'

He hung up.

'My wife. She's wondering when I'm coming home.'

Bosch nodded.

'Mr Peete, did you go into the train after you saw the bodies in there?'

'No, sir. Uh, they looked pretty dead to me. I saw a lot of blood. I thought I should leave it all alone for the authorities.'

'Did you recognize either of those people?'

'Well, the man I couldn't rightly see, but I thought it might be Mr Elias just on account of the nice suit and how he looked. Now, the woman, I recognized her, too. I mean, I didn't know her name or nothin' but she got on the train a few minutes before and went on down.'

'You mean she went down first?'

'Yes, sir, she went down. She also a regular like Mr Elias. 'Cept she ride maybe only one time a week. On Fridays, like last night. Mr Elias, he ride more.'

'Why do you think she went down the hill but didn't get off the train?'

Peete stared at him blankly, as if surprised by such an easy question.

''Cause she got shot.'

Bosch almost laughed but kept it to himself. He wasn't being clear enough with the witness.

'No, I mean before she was shot. It seems as though she never got up. As if she was on the bench and had been waiting to go back up when the shooter arrived behind the other passenger who was getting on.'

'I surely don't know what she was doing.'

'When exactly did she go down?'

'The ride right before. I sent Olivet down and that lady was on it. This was five, six minutes to 'leven. I sent Olivet down and I just let her sit down there till 'leven and then I brought her up. You know, last ride. When she came up, those people were dead on there.'

Peete's apparent ascribing of the female gender to the train was confusing to Bosch. He tried to make it clear.

'So you sent Olivet down with the woman on it. Then five, six minutes later she is still on the train car when you bring it up. Is that right?'

'Right.'

'And during that five or six minutes that Olivet was sitting down there, you weren't looking down there?'

'No, I was counting the money outta the register. Then when it was 'leven 'clock I went out and locked up Sinai. Then I brought Olivet on up. That's when I found them. They were dead.'

'But you didn't hear anything from down there? No shots?'

'No, like I told the lady – Miss Kizmin – I wear ear-plugs on account of the noise underneath the station. Also, I was countin' the money. It's mostly all quarters. I run 'em through the machine.'

He pointed to a stainless-steel change counter next to the cash register. It looked like the machine put the quarters into paper rolls containing ten dollars. He then stamped his foot on the wood floor, indicating the machinery below. Bosch nodded that he understood.

'Tell me about the woman. You said she was a regular?'

'Yeah, once a week. Fridays. Like maybe she have a little job up here in the apartments, cleanin' or somethin'. The bus runs down there on Hill Street. I think she caught it down there.'

'And what about Howard Elias?'

'He a regular, too. Two, three times a week, all different times, sometimes late like last night. One time I was locking up and he was down there callin' up to me. I made a 'ception. I brought him up on Sinai. I was bein' nice. At Christmas time he gave me a little envelope. He was a nice man, 'membering me like that.'

'Was he always alone when he rode the train?'

The old man folded his arms and thought about this for a moment.

'Mostly, I think.'

'You remember him ever being with somebody else?'

'I think one or two times I remember him bein' with somebody. I can't rightly remember who it was.'

'Was it a man or woman?'

'I don't know. I think it mighta been a lady but I'm not gettin' a picture, know what I mean?'

Bosch nodded and thought about things. He looked at Rider and raised his eyebrows. She shook her head. She had nothing more to ask.

'Before you go, Mr Peete, can you turn everything on and let us ride down?'

'Sure. Whatever you and Miss Kizmin need.'

He looked at Rider and bowed his head with a smile.

'Thank you,' Bosch said. 'Then let's do it.'

Peete moved to the computer keyboard and began typing in a command. Immediately the floor began to vibrate and there was a low-pitched grinding sound. Peete turned to them.

'Anytime,' he said above the din. Bosch waved and headed out to the train car. Chastain and Baker, the IAD man who had been paired with Kizmin Rider, were standing at the guard rail, looking down the track.

'We're going down,' Bosch called over. 'You guys coming?'

Without a word they fell in behind Rider and the four detectives stepped onto the train car called Olivet. The bodies had long been removed and the evidence technicians cleared out. But the spilt blood was still on the wood floor and the bench where Catalina Perez had sat. Bosch moved down the steps, careful to avoid stepping in the maroon pool that had leaked from Howard Elias's body. He took a seat on the right side.

The others sat on benches further up the train, away from where the bodies had fallen. Bosch looked up at the station house window and waved. Immediately the car jerked and began its descent. And immediately Bosch again recalled riding the train as a kid. The seat was just as uncomfortable as he remembered it.

Bosch didn't look at the others as they rode. He kept looking out the lower door and at the track as it went underneath the car. The ride lasted no longer than a minute. At the bottom he was the first off. He turned and looked back up the tracks. He could see Peete's head silhouetted in the station house window by the overhead light inside.

Bosch did not push through the turnstile, as he could see black fingerprint powder on it and didn't want to get it on his suit. The department did not consider the powder a hazard of the job and would not repay a dry cleaning bill if he got it on himself. He pointed the powder out to the others and climbed over the turnstile.

He scanned the ground on the off chance something would catch his eye but there was nothing unusual. He was confident that the area had already been gone over by the RHD detectives anyway. Bosch had primarily come down to get a firsthand look and feel for the place. To the left of the archway was a concrete staircase for when the train wasn't running or for those who were afraid to ride the incline railroad. The stairs were also popular with weekend fitness enthusiasts who ran up and down them. Bosch had read a story about it a year or so back in the *Times*. Next to the stairs a lighted bus stop had been cut into the steep hill. There was a glass fiberglass sunshade over a double-length bench. The side partitions were used to advertise films. On the one Bosch could see there was an ad for an Eastwood picture called *Blood Work*. The movie was based on a true story about a former FBI agent Bosch was acquainted with.

Bosch thought about whether the gunman could have

waited in the bus shelter for Elias to walk up to the Angels Flight turnstile. He decided against it. The shelter was lit by an overhead light. Elias would have had a good view of whoever sat in there as he approached the train. Since Bosch thought it was likely that Elias knew his killer, he didn't think the shooter would have waited out in the open like that.

He looked at the other side of the archway where there was a heavily landscaped ten-yard strip between the train entrance and a small office building. Bushes crowded thickly around an acacia tree. Bosch wished he hadn't left his briefcase up in the station house.

'Anybody bring a flashlight?' he asked.

Rider reached into her purse and brought out a small penlight. Bosch took it and headed into the bushes, putting the light on the ground and studying his pathway in. He found no obvious sign that the killer had waited in here. There was trash and other debris scattered in behind the bushes but none of it appeared to be fresh. It looked like a place where homeless people had stopped to look through trash bags they had picked up from somewhere else.

Rider made her way into the bushes.

'Find anything?'

'Nothing good. I'm just trying to figure out where this guy would have hidden from Elias. This could have been as good a spot as any. Elias wouldn't see him, he'd come out after Elias walked by, move up behind him at the train car.'

'Maybe he didn't need to hide. Maybe they walked here together.'

Bosch looked at her and nodded.

'Maybe. As good as anything I'm coming up with in here.'

'What about the bus bench?'

'Too open, too well lighted. If it was someone Elias had reason to fear, he'd've seen him.'

'What about a disguise? He could have sat in the bus stop in a disguise.'

'There's that.'

'You've already considered all of this but you let me go on talking, saying things you already know.'

He didn't say anything. He handed the flashlight back to Rider and headed out of the bushes. He looked over at the bus stop once more and felt sure he was right in his thinking. The bus stop hadn't been used. Rider came up next to him and followed his gaze.

'Hey, did you know Terry McCaleb over at the bureau?' she asked.

'Yeah, we worked a case once. Why, you know him?'

'Not really. But I've seen him on TV. He doesn't look like Clint Eastwood, if you ask me.'

'Yeah, not really.'

Bosch saw Chastain and Baker had crossed the street and were standing in the hollow created by the closed roll-up doors at the entrance of the huge Grand Central Market. They were looking at something on the ground.

Bosch and Rider walked over.

'Got something?' Rider asked.

'Maybe, maybe not,' Chastain said.

He pointed to the dirty, worn tiles at his feet.

'Cigarette butts,' Baker said. 'Five of them – same brand. Means somebody was waiting here a while.'

'Could have been a homeless,' Rider said.

'Maybe,' Baker replied. 'Could've been our shooter.'

Bosch wasn't that impressed.

'Any of you smokers?' he asked.

'Why?' Baker asked.

'Because then you'd see what this probably is. What is it you see when you go in the front doors at Parker Center?'

Chastain and Baker looked puzzled.

'Cops?' Baker tried.

'Yeah, but cops doing what?'

'Smoking,' Rider said.

'Right. No smoking in public buildings anymore, so the smokers gather round the front doors. This market is a public facility.'

He pointed at the cigarette butts crushed on the tiles.

'It doesn't necessarily mean somebody was waiting there a long time. I think it means somebody in the market came out five times during the day for smokes.'

Baker nodded but Chastain refused to acknowledge the deduction.

'Still could be our guy,' he said. 'Where else did he wait, the bushes over there?'

'He could have. Or like Kiz said, maybe he didn't wait. Maybe he walked right up to the train with Elias. Maybe Elias thought he was with a friend.'

Bosch reached into his jacket pocket and took out a plastic evidence bag. He handed it to Chastain.

'Or maybe I'm all wrong and you're all right. Bag 'em and tag 'em, Chastain. Make sure they get to the lab.'

A few minutes later Bosch was finished with his survey of the lower crime scene. He got on the train, picked up his briefcase where he had left it and moved up the stairs to one of the benches near the upper door. He sat down heavily, almost dropping onto the hard bench. He was beginning to feel fatigue take over and wished he had gotten some sleep before Irving's call had come. The excitement and adrenaline that accompany a new case caused a false high that always wore off quickly. He wished he could have a smoke and then maybe a quick nap. But only one of the two was possible at the moment, and he would have to find an all-night market to get the smokes. Again he decided against it. For some reason he felt that his nicotine fast had become part of his vigil for Eleanor. He thought that if he smoked all would be lost, that he would never hear from her again.

'What are you thinking, Harry?'

He looked up. Rider was in the doorway of the train, coming aboard.

'Nothing. Everything. We're really just getting started on this. There's a lot to do.'

'No rest for the weary.'

'Say that again.'

His pager sounded and he grabbed it off his belt with the urgency of a man who has had one go off in a movie theater. He recognized the number on the display but couldn't remember where he had seen it before. He took the phone out of his briefcase and punched it in. It was the home of Deputy Chief Irvin Irving.

'I spoke with the chief,' he said. 'He'll handle Reverend Tuggins. He's not to be your concern.'

Irving put a sneer into the word *Reverend*.

'Okay. He isn't.'

'So where are we?'

'We're still at the scene, just finishing up. We need to canvass the building over here for witnesses, then we'll clear out. Elias kept an apartment downtown. That was where he was headed. We need to search that and his office as soon as the search warrants are signed.'

'What about next of kin on the woman?'

'Perez should be done by now, too.'

'Tell me how it went at the Elias home.'

Since Irving had not asked before, Bosch assumed he was asking now because the chief of police wanted to know. Bosch quickly went over what had happened and Irving asked several questions about the reaction of Elias's wife and son. Bosch could tell he asked them from the standpoint of public relations management. He knew that, just as with Preston Tuggins, the way in which Elias's family reacted to his murder would have a direct bearing on how the community reacted.

'So it does not at this time sound as though we can enlist the widow or the son in helping us contain things, correct?'

'As of now, that's correct. But once they get over the

initial shock, maybe. You also might want to talk to the chief about calling the widow personally. I saw his picture on the wall in the house with Elias. If he's talking to Tuggins, maybe he could also talk to the widow about helping us out.'

'Maybe.'

Irving switched gears and told Bosch that his office's conference room on the sixth floor of Parker Center was ready for the investigators. He said that the room was unlocked at the moment but in the morning Bosch would be given keys. Once the investigators moved in, the room was to remain locked at all times. He said that he would be in by ten and was looking forward to a more expanded rundown of the investigation at the team meeting.

'Sure thing, Chief,' Bosch said. 'We should be in from the canvass and the searches by then.'

'Make sure you are. I'll be waiting.'

'Right.'

Bosch was about to disconnect when he heard Irving's voice.

'Excuse me, Chief?'

'One other matter. I felt because of the identity of one of the victims in this case that it was incumbent upon me to notify the inspector general. She seemed – how do I put this – she seemed acutely interested in the case when I explained the facts we had at that time. Using the word acutely is probably an understatement.'

Carla Entrenkin. Bosch almost cursed out loud but held it back. The inspector general was a new entity in the department: a citizen appointed by the Police Commission as an autonomous civilian overseer with ultimate authority to investigate or oversee investigations. It was a further politicizing of the department. The inspector general answered to the Police commission which answered to the city council and the mayor. And there were other reasons Bosch almost cursed as well. Finding Entrenkin's name and private number in

Elias's phone book bothered him. It opened up a whole set of possibilities and complications.

'Is she coming out here to the scene?' he asked.

'I don't think so,' Irving said. 'I waited to call so that I could say the scene was clearing. I saved you that headache. But don't be surprised if you hear directly from her in the daylight.'

'Can she do that? I mean, talk to me without going through you? She's a civilian.'

'Unfortunately, she can do whatever she wants to. That is how the Police Commission set up the job. So what it means is that this investigation, wherever it goes, it better be seamless, Detective Bosch. If it is not, we will be hearing from Carla Entrenkin about it.'

'I understand.'

'Good, then all we need is an arrest and all will be fine.'

'Sure, Chief.'

Irving disconnected without acknowledging. Bosch looked up. Chastain and Baker were stepping onto the train.

'There's only one thing worse than having the IAD tagging along on this,' he whispered to Rider. 'That's the inspector general watching over our shoulders.'

Rider looked at him.

'You're kidding? Carla I'mthinkin' is on this?'

Bosch almost smiled at Rider's use of the nickname bestowed on Entrenkin by an editorialist in the police union's *Thin Blue Line* newsletter. She was called Carla I'mthinkin' because of her tendency toward slow and deliberate speech whenever addressing the Police Commission and criticizing the actions or members of the department.

Bosch would have smiled but the addition of the inspector general to the case was too serious.

'Nope,' he said. 'Now we got her, too.'

9

At the top of the hill they found Edgar and Fuentes had
returned from notifying Catalina Perez's family of her
death, and Joe Dellacroce had returned from Parker
Center with completed and signed search warrants.
Court-approved searches were not always needed for
the home and business of the victim of a homicide. But
it made good sense to get warrants in high-profile cases.
Such cases attracted high-profile attorneys if they
eventually resulted in arrest. These attorneys invariably
created their high profiles by being thorough and good
at what they did. They exploited mistakes, took the
frayed seams and loose ends of cases and ripped open
huge holes – often big enough for their clients to escape
through. Bosch was already thinking that far ahead. He
knew he had to be very careful.

Additionally, he believed a warrant was particularly
necessary to search Elias's office. There would be
numerous files on police officers and cases pending
against the department. These cases would most likely
proceed after being taken on by new attorneys, and
Bosch needed to balance the preservation of attorney-
client privacy with the need to investigate the killing of
Howard Elias. The investigators would no doubt need
to proceed carefully while handling these files. It was
the reason he had called the district attorney's office
and asked Janis Langwiser to come to the scene.

Bosch approached Edgar first, taking him by the arm
and nudging him over to the guardrail overlooking the

steep drop-off to Hill Street. They were out of earshot of the others.

'How'd it go?'

'It went the way they all go. About a million other places I'd rather be than watching the guy get the news. Know what I mean?'

'Yeah, I know. You just tell him or did you ask him some questions?'

'We asked, but we didn't get very many answers. The guy said his wife was a housecleaner and she had a gig somewhere over here. She took the bus over. He couldn't give an address. Said his wife kept all of that stuff in a little notebook she carried.'

Bosch thought for a moment. He didn't remember any notebook in the evidence inventory. Balancing his briefcase on the guardrail, he opened it and took out the clipboard on which he had the accumulated paperwork from the crime scene. On top was the yellow copy of the inventory Hoffman had given him before he had left. It listed Victim #2's belongings but there was no notebook.

'Well, we'll have to check with him again later on. We didn't get any notebook.'

'Well, send Fuentes back. The husband didn't speak English.'

'All right. Anything else?'

'No. We did the usual checklist. Any enemies, any problems, anybody giving her trouble, anybody stalking her, so on and so forth. Nada. The husband said she wasn't worried about anything.'

'Okay. What about him?'

'He looked legit. Like he got hit in the face with the big frying pan called bad luck. You know?'

'Yeah, I know.'

'Hit hard. And there was as much surprise there as anything else.'

'Okay.'

Bosch looked around to make sure they were not being overheard. He spoke low to Edgar.

'We're going to split up now and go with the searches. I want you to take the apartment Elias kept over at The Place. I was—'

'So that's where he was going.'

'Looks like it. I was just up there with Chastain, did a drive-by. I want you to take your time this time. I also want *you* to start in his bedroom. Go to the bed and take the phone book out of the top drawer of the table with the phone on it. Bag it and seal it so nobody can look at it until we get everything back to the office.'

'Sure. How come?'

'I'll tell you later. Just get to it before anybody else. Also, take the tape from the phone machine in the kitchen. There's a message we want to keep.'

'Right.'

'Okay then.'

Bosch stepped away from the guardrail and approached Dellacroce.

'Any problems with the paper?'

'Not really – except for waking the judge twice.'

'Which judge?'

'John Houghton.'

'He's okay.'

'Well, it didn't sound like he appreciated having to do everything twice.'

'What did he say about the office?'

'Had me add in a line about preserving the sanctity of attorney-client privilege.'

'That's it? Let me see.'

Dellacroce took the search warrants out of the inside pocket of his suit jacket and handed Bosch the one for the office at the Bradbury. Bosch scanned through the stock wording on the first page of the declaration and got to the part Dellacroce had talked about. It looked okay to him. The judge was still allowing the search of the office and the files, but was simply saying that any privileged information gleaned from the files must be germane to the murder investigation.

'What he's saying is that we can't go through the files and turn what we get over to the city attorney's office to help defend those cases,' Dellacroce said. 'Nothing goes outside our investigation.'

'I can live with that,' Bosch said.

He called everybody into a huddle. He noticed Fuentes was smoking and tried not to think about his own desire for a cigarette.

'Okay, we've got the search warrants,' he said. 'This is how we're gonna split it up. Edgar, Fuentes and Baker, you three take the apartment. I want Edgar on lead. The rest of us will go to the office. You guys on the apartment, I also want you to arrange for interviews of all the doormen in the building. All shifts. We need to find out as much about this guy's routines and personal life as we can. We're thinking there may be a girlfriend somewhere. We need to find out who that was. Also, on the key chain there is a key to a Porsche and a Volvo. My guess is Elias drove the Porsche and it's probably in the parking garage at the apartment building. I want you to take a look at that, too.'

'The warrants don't specify a car,' Dellacroce protested. 'Nobody told me about a car when I was sent to work up the warrants.'

'Okay, then just find the car, check it out through the windows and we'll get a search warrant if you see something and think it is necessary.'

Bosch was looking at Edgar as he said this last part. Edgar almost imperceptibly nodded, meaning that he understood that Bosch was telling him to find the car and to simply open it and search it. If anything of value to the investigation was found, then he would simply back out, get a warrant and they would act as if they had never been in the car in the first place. It was standard practice.

Bosch looked at his watch and wrapped it up.

'Okay, it's five-thirty now. We should be done with the searches by eight-thirty max. Take anything that even looks of interest and we'll sift through it all later. Chief Irving has set up the command post for this investigation in the conference room next to his office at Parker. But before we go back there, I want to meet everybody right back here at eight-thirty.'

He pointed up to the tall apartment building overlooking Angels Flight.

'We'll canvass this building then. I don't want to wait until later, have people get out for the day before we can get to them.'

'What about the meeting with Deputy Chief Irving?' Fuentes asked.

'That's set for ten. We should make it. If we don't, don't worry about it. I'll take the meeting and you people will proceed. The case comes first. He'll go along with that.'

'Hey, Harry?' Edgar said. 'If we get done before eight-thirty, all right if we get breakfast?'

'Yes, it's all right, but I don't want to miss anything. Do not hurry the search just so you can get pancakes.'

Rider smiled.

'Tell you what,' Bosch said. 'I'll make sure we have doughnuts here at eight-thirty. If you can, just wait until then. Okay, so let's do it.'

Bosch took out the key ring they had taken from the body of Howard Elias. He removed the keys to the apartment and the Porsche key and gave them to Edgar. He noted that there were still several keys on the ring that were unaccounted for. At least two or three would be to the office and another two or three for his home in Baldwin Hills. That still left four keys and Bosch thought about the voice he had heard on the answering machine. Maybe Elias had keys to a lover's home.

He put the keys back in his pocket and told Rider and Dellacroce to drive cars down the hill and over to the Bradbury. He said he and Chastain would take the train down and walk over, making a check of the sidewalks Elias would have covered between his office building and the lower Angels Flight terminus. As the detectives broke up and headed toward their assignments, Bosch went to the station window and looked in on Eldrige Peete. He was sitting on the chair by the cash register, earplugs in place and his eyes closed. Bosch rapped gently on the window but the train operator was startled anyway.

'Mr Peete, I want you to send us down once more and then you can close up, lock up and go home to your wife.'

'Okay, whatever you say.'

Bosch nodded and turned to head to the train, then he stopped and looked back at Peete.

'There's a lot of blood. Do you have someone who is going to clean up the inside of the train before it opens tomorrow?'

'Don't worry, I'll get that. I've got a mop and bucket back here in the closet. I called my supervisor. Before you got here. He said I gotta clean Olivet up so she's ready to go in the morning. We start at eight Satadays.'

Bosch nodded.

'Okay, Mr Peete. Sorry you have to do that.'

'I like to keep the cars clean.'

'Also, down at the bottom, they left fingerprint dust all over the turnstile. It's nasty stuff if you get that on your clothes.'

'I'll get that, too.'

Bosch nodded.

'Well, thanks for your help tonight. We appreciate it.'

'Tonight? Hell, it's morning already.'

Peete smiled.

'I guess you're right. Good morning, Mr Peete.'

'Yeah, not if you ask them two that were on the train.'

Bosch started away and then once more came back to the man.

'One last thing. This is going to be a big story in the papers. And on TV. I'm not telling you what to do but you might want to think about taking your phone off the hook, Mr Peete. And maybe not answering your door.'

'I gotcha.'

'Good.'

'I'm gonna sleep all day, anyway.'

Bosch nodded to him one last time and got on the train. Chastain was already on one of the benches near the door. Bosch walked past him and again went down the steps to the end where Howard Elias's body had fallen. He was careful again not to step in the pooled and coagulated blood.

As soon as he sat down the train began its descent. Bosch looked out the window and saw the gray light of dawn around the edges of the tall office buildings to the east. He slumped on the bench and yawned deeply, not bothering to raise a hand to cover his mouth. He wished he could turn his body and lie down. The bench was hard, worn wood but he had no doubts that he would quickly fall into sleep and that he would dream about Eleanor and happiness and places where you did not have to step around the blood.

He dropped the thought and brought his hand up and all the way into the pocket of his jacket before he remembered there were no cigarettes to be found there.

10

The Bradbury was the dusty jewel of downtown. Built more than a century before, its beauty was old but still brighter and more enduring than any of the glass-and-marble towers that now dwarfed it like a phalanx of brutish guards surrounding a beautiful child. Its ornate lines and glazed tile surfaces had withstood the betrayal of both man and nature. It had survived earthquakes and riots, periods of abandonment and decay, and a city that often didn't bother to safeguard what little culture and roots it had. Bosch believed there wasn't a more beautiful structure in the city – despite the reasons he had been inside it over the years.

In addition to holding the offices for the legal practice of Howard Elias and several other attorneys, the Bradbury housed several state and city offices on its five floors. Three large offices on the third floor were leased to the LAPD's Internal Affairs Division and used for holding Board of Rights hearings – the disciplinary tribunals police officers charged with misconduct must face. The IAD had leased the space because the rising tide of complaints against officers in the 1990s had resulted in more disciplinary actions and more BORs. Hearings were now happening every day, sometimes two or three running at a time. There was not enough space for this flow of misconduct cases in Parker Center. So the IAD had taken the space in the nearby Bradbury.

To Bosch, the IAD was the only blemish on the building's beauty. Twice he had faced Board of Rights hearings in the Bradbury. Each time he gave his testimony, listened to witnesses and an IAD investigator – once it had been Chastain – report the facts and findings of the case, and then paced the floor beneath the atrium's huge glass skylight while the three captains privately decided his fate. He had come out okay after both hearings and in the process had come to love the Bradbury with its Mexican tile floors, wrought-iron filigree and suspended mail chutes. He had once taken the time to look up its history at the Los Angeles Conservancy offices, and found one of the more intriguing mysteries of Los Angeles: the Bradbury, for all its lasting glory, had been designed by a $5-a-week draftsman. George Wyman had no degree in architecture and no prior credits as a designer when he drew the plans for the building in 1892, yet his design would see fruition in a structure that would last more than a century and cause generations of architects to marvel. To add to the mystery, Wyman never again designed a building of any significance, in Los Angeles or anywhere else.

It was the kind of mystery Bosch liked. The idea of a man leaving his mark with the one shot he's given appealed to him. Across a whole century, Bosch identified with George Wyman. He believed in the one shot. He didn't know if he'd had his yet – it wasn't the kind of thing you knew and understood until you looked back over your life as an old man. But he had the feeling that it was still out there waiting for him. He had yet to take his one shot.

Because of the one-way streets and traffic lights Dellacroce and Rider faced, Bosch and Chastain got to the Bradbury on foot before them. As they approached the heavy glass doors of the entrance, Janis Langwiser got out of a small red sports car that was parked illegally at the curb out front. She was carrying a leather bag on a shoulder strap and a Styrofoam cup with the tag of a tea bag hanging over the lip.

'Hey, I thought we said an hour,' she said good-naturedly.

Bosch looked at his watch. It was an hour and ten minutes since they had talked.

'So you're a lawyer, sue me,' he said, smiling.

He introduced Chastain and gave Langwiser a more detailed rundown on the investigation. By the time he was finished, Rider and Dellacroce had parked their cars in front of Langwiser's car. Bosch tried the doors to the building but they were locked. He got out the key ring and hit the right key on the second try. They entered the atrium of the building and each of them involuntarily looked up, such was the beauty of the place. Above them the atrium skylight was filled with the purples and grays of dawn. Classical music played from hidden speakers. Something haunting and sad but Bosch couldn't place it.

'Barber's "Adagio,"' Langwiser said.

'What?' Bosch said, still looking up.

'The music.'

'Oh.'

A police helicopter streaked across the skylight, heading home to Piper Tech for change of shift. It broke the spell and Bosch brought his eyes down. A uniformed security guard was walking toward them. He was a young black man with close-cropped hair and startling green eyes.

'Can I help you people? The building's closed right now.'

'Police,' Bosch said, pulling out his ID wallet and flipping it open. 'We've got a search warrant here for suite five-oh-five.'

He nodded to Dellacroce, who removed the search warrant from his coat pocket once again and handed it to the guard.

'That's Mr Elias's office,' the guard said.

'We know,' Dellacroce said.

'What's going on?' the guard asked. 'Why do you have to search his place?'

'We can't tell you that right now,' Bosch said. 'We need you to answer a couple questions, though. When's your shift start? Were you here when Mr Elias left last night?'

'Yeah, I was here. I work a six-to-six shift. I watched them leave about eleven last night.'

'Them?'

'Yeah, him and a couple other guys. I locked the door right after they went through. The place was empty after that – 'cept for me.'

'Do you know who the other guys were?'

'One was Mr Elias's assistant or a whatchamacallit.'

'Secretary? Clerk?'

'Yeah, clerk. That's it. Like a young student who helped him with the cases.'

'You know his name?'

'Nah, I never asked.'

'Okay, what about the other guy? Who was he?'

'Don't know that one.'

'Had you seen him around here before?'

'Yeah, the last couple nights they left together. And a few times before that I think I saw him going or coming by hisself.'

'Did he have an office here?'

'No, not that I know of.'

'Was he Elias's client?'

'How would I know?'

'A black guy, white guy?'

'Black.'

'What did he look like?'

'Well, I didn't get a real good look at him.'

'You said you've seen him around here before. What did he look like?'

'He was just a normal-looking guy. He ...'

Bosch was growing impatient but wasn't sure why.

94

The guard seemed to be doing the best he could. It was routine in police work to find witnesses unable to describe people they had gotten a good look at. Bosch took the search warrant out of the guard's hand and handed it back to Dellacroce. Langwiser asked to see it and began reading it while Bosch continued with the guard.

'What's your name?'

'Robert Courtland. I'm on the waiting list for the academy.'

Bosch nodded. Most security guards in this town were waiting for a police job somewhere. The fact that Courtland, a black man, was not already in the academy told Bosch that there was a problem somewhere in his application. The department was going out of its way to attract minorities to the ranks. For Courtland to be wait-listed there had to be something. Bosch guessed he had probably admitted smoking marijuana or didn't meet the minimum educational requirements, maybe even had a juvenile record.

'Close your eyes, Robert.'

'What?'

'Just close your eyes and relax. Think of the man you saw. Tell me what he looks like.'

Courtland did as he was told and after a moment came up with an improved but still sketchy description.

'He's about the same height as Mr Elias. But he had his head shaved. It was slick. He got one of them soul chips, too.'

'Soul chip?'

'You know, like a little beard under his lip.'

He opened his eyes.

'That's it.'

'That's it?' Bosch said in a friendly, cajoling tone. 'Robert, how're you going to make it into the cops? We need more than that. How old was this guy?'

'I don't know. Thirty or forty.'

'That's a help. Only ten years' difference. Was he thin? Fat?'

'Thin but with muscles. You know, the guy was built.'

'I think he's describing Michael Harris,' Rider said.

Bosch looked at her. Harris was the plaintiff in the Black Warrior case.

'It fits,' Rider said. 'The case starts Monday. They were probably working late, getting ready for court.'

Bosch nodded and was about to dismiss Courtland when Langwiser suddenly spoke while still reading the last page of the search warrant.

'I think we have a problem with the warrant.'

Now everyone looked at her.

'Okay, Robert,' Bosch said to Courtland. 'We'll be all right from here. Thanks for your help.'

'You sure? You want me to go up with you, unlock the door or something?'

'No, we have a key. We'll be all right.'

'Okay, then. I'll be in the security office around behind the stairs if you need anything.'

'Thanks.'

Courtland started walking back the way he had come but then stopped and turned around.

'Oh, you know, all five of you better not take the elevator up at once. That's probably too much weight on that old thing.'

'Thanks, Robert,' Bosch said.

He waited until the guard had gone around the staircase and was out of sight before turning back to Langwiser.

'Miss Langwiser, you probably haven't gone out on too many crime scenes before,' he said. 'But here's a tip, never announce that there is a problem with a search warrant in front of somebody who isn't a cop.'

'Oh, shit, I'm sorry. I didn't—'

'What's wrong with the warrant?' Dellacroce said, his voice showing he was upset by the apparent challenge to his work. 'The judge didn't see anything wrong with it. The judge said it was fine.'

Langwiser looked down at the three-page warrant in her hand and waved it, its pages fluttering like a falling pigeon.

'I just think that with a case like this we better be damn sure of what we're doing before we go in there and start opening up files.'

'We have to go into the files,' Bosch said. 'That's where most of the suspects will be.'

'I understand that. But these are confidential files relating to lawsuits against the police department. They contain privileged information that only an attorney and his client should have. Don't you see? It could be argued that by opening a single file you've violated the rights of Elias's clients.'

'All we want is to find the man's killer. We don't care about his pending cases. I hope to Christ that the killer's name isn't in those files and that it isn't a cop. But what if it is and what if in those files Elias kept copies or notes on threats? What if through his own investigations he learned something about somebody that could be a motive for his killing? You see, we need to look at the files.'

'All of that is understandable. But if a judge later rules the search was inappropriate you won't be able to use anything you find up there. You want to run that risk?'

She turned away from them and looked toward the door.

'I have to find a phone and make a call about this,' she said. 'I can't let you open that office yet. Not in good conscience.'

Bosch blew out his breath in exasperation. He silently chastised himself for calling in a lawyer too soon. He should have just done what he knew he had to do and dealt with the consequences later.

'Here.'

He opened his briefcase and handed her his cell phone. He listened as she called the DA's office switchboard and asked to be connected to a prosecutor named David Sheiman, who Bosch knew was the supervisor of the major crimes unit. After she had Sheiman on the line she began summarizing the situation and Bosch continued to listen to make sure she had the details right.

'We're wasting a lot of time standing around, Harry,' Rider whispered to him. 'You want Edgar and me to pick up Harris and have a talk with him about last night?'

Bosch almost nodded his approval but then hesitated as he considered the possible consequences.

Michael Harris was suing fifteen members of the Robbery-Homicide Division in a highly publicized case set to begin trial on Monday. Harris, a car-wash employee with a record of burglary and assault convictions, was seeking $10 million in damages for his claims that members of the RHD had planted evidence against him in the kidnapping and murder of a twelve-year-old girl who was a member of a well-known and wealthy family. Harris claimed the detectives had abducted, held and tortured him over a three-day period in hopes of drawing a confession from him as well as learning the location of the missing girl. The lawsuit alleged that the detectives, frustrated by Harris's unwillingness to admit his part in the crime or lead them to the missing girl, pulled plastic bags over Harris's head and threatened to suffocate him. He further claimed that one detective pushed a sharp instrument – a Black Warrior Number 2 pencil – into his ear, puncturing the ear drum. But Harris never confessed and on the fourth day of the interrogation the girl's body was found decomposing in a vacant lot just one block from his apartment. She had been sexually assaulted and strangled.

The murder became one more in a long line of crimes that gripped public attention in Los Angeles.

The victim was a beautiful blonde, blue-eyed girl named Stacey Kincaid. She had been spirited from her bed while she slept in her family's large and seemingly safe Brentwood home. It was the kind of crime that sent a chilling message across the city: Nobody is safe.

As horrible as it was in itself, the murder of the little girl was exponentially magnified by the media. Initially, this was because of who the victim was and where she came from. She was the stepdaughter of Sam Kincaid, scion of a family that owned more automobile dealerships in Los Angeles County than it was possible to count on two hands. Sam was the son of Jackson Kincaid, the original 'car czar,' who had built the family business from a single Ford dealership his father had passed on to him after World War II. Like Howard Elias after him, Jack Kincaid had seen the merit in local television marketing and in the 1960s became a fixture of late-night TV advertising. On camera, he showed a folksy charm, exuding honesty and friendship. He seemed as reliable and trustworthy as Johnny Carson and he was in the living rooms and bedrooms of Los Angeles just as often. If Los Angeles was seen as an 'autotopia' then Jack Kincaid was certainly seen as its unofficial mayor.

Off camera, the car czar was a calculating businessman who always played both sides of politics and mercilessly drove competitors out of business or at least away from his dealerships. His dynasty grew rapidly, his car lots spreading across the southern California landscape. By the 1980s Jack Kincaid's reign was done and the moniker of car czar was turned over to his son. But the old man remained a force, though a mostly unseen one. And this was never more clear than when Stacey Kincaid disappeared and old Jack returned to TV, this time to appear on newscasts and put up a million-dollar reward for her safe return. It was another surrealistic episode in Los Angeles murder lore. The old man everyone had grown up with on TV was back on once again and tearfully begging for his granddaughter's life.

It was all for naught. The reward and the old man's tears became moot when the girl was found dead by passersby in the vacant lot close to Michael Harris's apartment.

The case went to trial based solely on evidence consisting of Harris's fingerprints being found in the bedroom from which the girl had been abducted and the proximity of the body's disposal to his apartment. The case held the city rapt, playing live every day on *Court TV* and local news programs. Harris's attorney, John Penny, a lawyer as skilled as Elias when it came to manipulating juries, mounted a defense that attacked the body's disposal location as coincidental and the fingerprints – found on one of the girl's schoolbooks – as simply being planted by the LAPD.

All the power and money the Kincaids had amassed over generations was no match against the tide of anti-police sentiment and the racial underpinnings of the case. Harris was black, the Kincaids and the police and prosecutors on the case were white. The case against Harris was tainted beyond repair when Penny elicited what many perceived as a racist comment from Jack Kincaid during testimony about his many dealerships. After Kincaid detailed his many holdings, Penny asked why one of the dealerships was not in South Central Los Angeles. Without hesitation and before the prosecutor could object to the irrelevant question, Kincaid said he would never place a business in an area where the inhabitants had a propensity to riot. He said he made the decision after the Watts riots of 1965 and it was confirmed after the more recent riots of 1992.

The question and answer had little if anything to do with the murder of a twelve-year-old girl but proved to be the pivotal point in the trial. In later interviews jurors said Kincaid's answer was emblematic of the city's deep racial gulf. With that one answer sympathy swayed from the Kincaid family to Harris. The prosecution was doomed.

The jury acquitted Harris in four hours. Penny then turned the case over to his colleague, Howard Elias, for civil proceedings and Harris took his place next to Rodney King in the pantheon of civil rights victims and heroes in South L.A. Most of them deserved such honored status, but some were the creations of lawyers and the media. Whichever Harris was, he was now seeking his payday – a civil rights trial in which $10 million would be just the opening bid.

Despite the verdict and all the attached rhetoric, Bosch didn't believe Harris's claims of innocence or police brutality. One of the detectives Harris specifically accused of brutality was Bosch's former partner, Frankie Sheehan, and Bosch knew Sheehan to be a total professional when dealing with suspects and prisoners. So Bosch simply thought of Harris as a liar and murderer who had walked away from his crime. He would have no qualms about rousting him and taking him downtown for questioning about Howard Elias's murder. But Bosch also knew as he stood there with Rider that if he now brought Harris in, he would run the risk of compounding the alleged wrongs already done to him – at least in the eyes of much of the public and the media. It was a political decision as much as a police decision that he had to make.

'Let me think about this for a second,' he said.

He walked off by himself through the atrium. The case was even more perilous than he had realized. Any misstep could result in disaster – to the case, to the department, to careers. He wondered if Irving had realized all of this when he had chosen Bosch's team for the case. Perhaps, he thought, Irving's compliments were just a front for a real motive – leaving Bosch and his team dangling in the wind. Bosch knew he was now venturing into paranoia. It was unlikely that the deputy chief could have come up with such a plan so quickly.

Or that he would even care about Bosch's team with so much else at stake.

Bosch looked up and saw the sky was much brighter now. It would be a sunny and hot day.

'Harry?'

He turned. It was Rider.

'She's off.'

He walked back to the group and Langwiser handed him his phone.

'You're not going to like this,' she said. 'Dave Sheiman wants to bring in a special master to look at the files before you do.'

'Special master?' Dellacroce asked. 'What the hell is that?'

'It's an attorney,' Langwiser said. 'An independent attorney appointed by a judge who will oversee the files. He will be hired to protect the rights of those clients while still giving you people what you need. Hopefully.'

'Shit,' Bosch said, his frustration finally getting the better of him. 'Why don't we just stop the whole thing now and drop the damn case? If the DA's office doesn't care about us clearing it then we won't care either.'

'Detective Bosch, you know it's not like that. Of course we care. We just want to be safe. The warrant you have is still good for searching the office. Sheiman said you can even go through completed case files – which I am sure you need to look at as well. But the special master will have to come in and look at all pending files first. Remember, this person is not an adversary to you. He will give you everything you are entitled to see.'

'And when will that be? Next week? Next month?'

'No. Sheiman is going to go to work on that this morning. He'll call Judge Houghton, apprise him of the situation, and see if he has any recommendations for a special master. With any luck, the appointment will be made today and you'll have what you need from the files this afternoon. Tomorrow, at the very latest.'

'Tomorrow at the latest is too late. We need to keep moving on this.'

'Yeah,' Chastain chimed in. 'Don't you know an investigation is like a shark? It's got to keep—'

'All right, Chastain,' Bosch said.

'Look,' Langwiser said. 'I'll make sure Dave understands the urgency of the situation. In the meantime you'll just have to be patient. Now do you want to keep standing down here talking about it or do you want to go up and do what we can in the office?'

Bosch looked at her for a long moment, annoyed by her chiding tone. The moment ended when the phone in his hand rang. It was Edgar and he was whispering. Bosch held a hand over his ear so he could hear.

'I didn't hear that. What?'

'Listen, I'm in the bedroom. There's no phone book in the bed table. I checked both bed tables. It's not here.'

'What?'

'The phone book, it's not here, man.'

Bosch looked at Chastain, who was looking back at him. He turned and walked away, out of earshot of the others. Now he whispered to Edgar.

'You sure?'

''Course I'm sure. I woulda found it if it was here.'

'You were first in the bedroom?'

'Right. First one in. It's not here.'

'You're in the bedroom to the right when you come down the hall.'

'Yeah, Harry. I'm in the right place. It's just not here.'

'Shit.'

'What do you want me to do?'

'Nothing. Continue the search.'

Bosch flipped the phone closed and put it in his pocket. He walked back to the others. He tried to act calm, as if the call had only been a minor annoyance.

'Okay, let's go up and do what we can up there.'

They moved to the elevator, which was an open wrought-iron cage with ornate flourishes and polished brass trim.

'Why don't you take the ladies up first,' Bosch said to Dellacroce. 'We'll come up after. That ought to distribute the weight pretty evenly.'

He took Elias's key ring out of his pocket and handed it to Rider.

'The office key should be on there,' he said. 'And never mind about that other thing with Harris for the time being. Let's see what we've got in the office first.'

'Sure, Harry.'

They got on and Dellacroce pulled the accordion gate closed. The elevator rose with a jerking motion. After it was up one floor and those on it could not see them, Bosch turned to Chastain. The anger and frustration of everything going wrong flooded him then. He dropped his briefcase and with both hands grabbed Chastain by the collar of his jacket. He roughly pushed him against the elevator cage and spoke in a low, dark voice that was full of rage.

'Goddammit, Chastain, I'm only asking this one time. Where's the fucking phone book?'

Chastain's face flushed crimson and his eyes grew wide in shock.

'What? What the fuck are you talking about?'

He brought his hands up to Bosch's and tried to free himself but Bosch maintained the pressure, leaning all of his weight into the other man.

'The phone book in the apartment. I know you took it and I want it back. Right the fuck now.'

Finally, Chastain tore himself loose. His jacket and shirt and tie were wrenched askew. He stepped away from Bosch as if he was scared and adjusted himself. He then pointed a finger at him.

'Stay away from me! You're fucking nuts! I don't have any phone book. You had it. I saw you put it in the goddamn drawer next to the bed.'

Bosch took a step toward him.

'You took it. When I was on the bal—'

'I said stay away! I didn't take it. If it's not there, then somebody came in and took it after we left.'

Bosch stopped. It was an obvious explanation but it hadn't even entered his mind. He had automatically thought of Chastain. He looked down at the tiles, embarrassed by how he'd let an old animosity cloud his judgment. He could hear the elevator gate opening on the fifth floor. He raised his eyes, fixed Chastain with a bloodless stare and pointed at his face.

'I find out otherwise, Chastain, I promise I'll take you apart.'

'Fuck you! I didn't take the book. But I am going to take your badge for this.'

Bosch smiled but not in a way that had any warmth.

'Go ahead. Write your ticket, Chastain. Anytime you can *take* my badge you can have it.'

11

The others were inside Howard Elias's law offices by the time Bosch and Chastain made it up to the fifth floor. The office was essentially three rooms: a reception area with a secretary's desk, a middle room where there was a clerk's desk and two walls of file cabinets, and then the third and largest room, Elias's office.

As Bosch and Chastain moved through the offices the others stood silently and didn't look at them. It was clear that they had heard the commotion in the lobby as they had taken the elevator up. Bosch didn't care about that. He had already put the confrontation with Chastain behind him and was thinking about the search. He was hoping something would be found in the office that would give the investigation a focus, a specific path to follow. He walked through the three rooms making general observations. In the last room he noticed that through the windows behind Elias's large polished wood desk he could see the huge face of Anthony Quinn. It was part of a mural depicting the actor with arms outstretched on the brick wall of a building across the street from the Bradbury.

Rider came into the office behind him. She looked out the window, too.

'You know every time I'm down here and see that I wonder who that is.'

'You don't know?'

'César Chávez?'

'Anthony Quinn. You know, the actor.'

He got a nonresponse from her.

'Before your time, I guess. The mural is called the Pope of Broadway, like he's watching over all the homeless around here.'

'Oh, I see.' She didn't sound impressed. 'How you want to do this?'

Bosch was still staring at the mural. He liked it, even though he had a hard time seeing Anthony Quinn as a Christlike figure. But the mural seemed to capture something about the man, a raw masculine and emotional power. Bosch stepped closer to the window and looked down. He saw the forms of two homeless people sleeping beneath blankets of newspapers in the parking lot beneath the mural. Anthony Quinn's arms were outstretched over them. Bosch nodded. The mural was one of the little things that made him like downtown so much. Just like the Bradbury and Angels Flight. Little pieces of grace were everywhere if you looked.

He turned around. Chastain and Langwiser had entered the room behind Rider.

'I'll work in here. Kiz and Janis, you two take the file room.'

'And what?' Chastain said. 'Me and Del get the secretary's desk?'

'Yeah. While you're going through it, see if you can come up with her name and the name of the intern or clerk. We'll need to talk to them today.'

Chastain nodded but Bosch could see he was annoyed about getting the weakest assignment.

'Tell you what,' Bosch added, 'why don't you go out first and see if you can find some boxes. We're going to be taking a lot of files out of here.'

Chastain left the office without a word. Bosch glanced at Rider and saw her give him a look that told him he was acting like an asshole.

'What?'

'Nothing. I'll be in the file room.'

She left then, leaving just Langwiser and Bosch.

'Everything okay, Detective?'

'Everything's fine. I'm going to get to work now. Do what I can until we hear about your special master.'

'Look, I'm sorry. But you called me out here to advise you and this is what I advise. I still think it is the right way to go.'

'Well, we'll see.'

For most of the next hour Bosch methodically went through Elias's desk, studying the man's belongings, appointment calendar and paperwork. Most of his time was spent reading through a series of notebooks in which Elias had kept reminders to himself, lists of things to do, pencil drawings and general notes from phone calls. Each notebook was dated on the outside cover. It appeared that Elias filled the pages of one book every week or so with his voluminous notations and doodles. Nothing in the books jumped out at Bosch as being pertinent to the investigation. But he also knew that so little about the circumstances of Elias's murder was known that something seeming unimportant in the notebooks at the moment might become important later.

Before starting to page through the most recent notebook, Bosch was interrupted by another call from Edgar.

'Harry, you said there was a message on the phone machine?'

'That's right.'

'There ain't now.'

Bosch leaned back in Elias's chair and closed his eyes.

'Goddammit.'

'Yeah, it's been cleared. I dicked around with it and it's not a tape. Messages are stored on a microchip. The chip was cleared.'

'Okay,' Bosch replied, angrily. 'Continue the search. When you're done, talk to the security people about who's been in and out of that place. See if they've got any video points in the lobby or parking garage. Somebody went in there after I left.'

'What about Chastain? He was with you, wasn't he?'

'I'm not worried about Chastain.'

He flipped the phone closed and got up and went to the window. He hated the feeling growing inside – that he was being worked by the case, rather than the other way around.

He blew out his breath and went back to the desk and the last notebook that Howard Elias had kept. As he paged through, he came across repeated notes regarding someone referred to as 'Parker.' Bosch did not believe this to be a person's real name, but rather a code name for a person inside Parker Center. The notations were mostly lists of questions Elias apparently intended to ask 'Parker,' as well as what looked like notes on conversations with this person. They were mostly in abbreviated form or the lawyer's own version of shorthand and therefore difficult to decipher. But in other instances the notes were clear to Bosch. One notation clearly indicated to Bosch that Elias had a deeply connected source inside Parker Center.

Parker:
Get all 51s – unsustained
1. Sheehan
2. Coblenz
3. Rooker
4. Stanwick

Bosch recognized the names as belonging to four RHD detectives who were among the defendants in the Black Warrior case. Elias wanted the 51 reports – or citizen complaint files – on the four detectives. More specifically, Elias wanted the unsustained files, meaning he was interested in complaints against the four that had been investigated by the IAD but not substantiated. Such unsustained complaints were removed from officers' personnel files as a matter of department policy and were therefore out of reach of a subpoena from a lawyer like Elias. The notation in the notebook told Bosch that Elias somehow knew that there were unsubstantiated prior complaints against the four and that he had a source in Parker Center who had access to the old files on those complaints. The first assumption was not a major leap; all cops had unsubstantiated complaints. It was part of being a cop. But someone with access to that sort of file was different. If Elias had such a source, it was a well-placed source.

One of the last references to Parker in the notebook appeared to be notes of a conversation, which Bosch assumed to have been a phone call to Elias at his desk. It appeared that Elias was losing his source.

Parker won't
jeopardy/exposure
force the issue?

Parker won't what? Bosch wondered. Turn over the files Elias wanted? Did Parker believe that getting the files to Elias would expose him as a source? There wasn't enough there for him to make a conclusion. There wasn't enough for him to understand what 'force the issue' meant either. He wasn't sure what any of the notes might have to do with the killing of Howard Elias. Nevertheless, Bosch was intrigued. One of the department's most vocal and successful critics had a mole inside Parker Center. There was a traitor inside the gate and it was important to know this.

Bosch put the last notebook into his briefcase and wondered if the discoveries he had made through the notes, particularly about Elias's source inside the department, now placed him in the area Janis Langwiser feared might be an infringement of attorney-client privilege. After mulling it over for a few moments he decided not to go out into the file room and ask her for an interpretation. He moved on with the search.

Bosch turned the chair to a side desk that had a

personal computer and laser printer set up on it. The machines were off. There were two small drawers in this desk. The top contained the computer keyboard while the bottom contained office supplies with a single manila file on top. Bosch took out the file and opened it. It contained a color printout of a photo of a partially nude woman. The printout had two crease marks indicating it had been folded at one time. The photo itself did not have the technical quality of those in skin magazines found on the newstand. There was an amateurish, badly lit quality to it. The woman in the picture was white and had short, white-blonde hair. She wore thigh-high leather boots with three-inch heels and a G-string, nothing else. She stood with her rear to the camera, one foot up on a chair, her face turned mostly away. There was a tattoo of a ribbon and bow at the center of the small of her back. Bosch also saw at the bottom of the picture a notation that had been printed by hand.

http://www.girlawhirl.com/gina

Bosch knew little about computers but he knew enough to understand he was looking at an Internet address.

'Kiz?' he called.

Rider was the resident computer expert on his team. Before coming to Hollywood Homicide she had worked a fraud unit in Pacific Division. A lot of the work she had done was on computers. She walked in from the file room and he waved her over to the desk.

'How is it going out there?'

'Well, we're just stacking files. She won't let me look through anything until we hear from the special master. I hope Chastain brings back a lot of boxes because we have a – what is that?'

She was looking at the open file and the printout of the blonde woman.

'It was in the drawer. Take a look. It's got an address on it.'

Rider came around the desk and looked down at the printout.

'It's a web page.'

'Right. So how do we get to it and take a look?'

'Let me get in there.'

Bosch got up and Rider sat in front of the computer. Bosch stood behind the chair and watched as she turned the computer on and waited for it to boot up.

'Let's see what Internet provider he's got,' she said. 'Did you see any letterhead around?'

'What?'

'Letterhead. Stationery. Sometimes people put their E-mail address on it. If we know Elias's E-mail address we're halfway there.'

Bosch understood now. He hadn't seen any letterhead during his search.

'Hold on.'

He went out to the reception room and asked Chastain, who was sitting behind the secretary's desk, if he'd seen any stationery. Chastain opened a drawer and pointed to an open box of letterhead stationery. Bosch grabbed a page off the top. Rider had been correct. Elias's E-mail address was printed beneath his postal address on the top center of the page.

Helias@lawyerlink.net

Bosch took the page with him back to Elias's office. When he got there he saw Rider had closed the file that contained the printout of the blonde woman. Bosch realized it must have been embarrassing to her.

'I got it,' he said.

She looked at the page Bosch placed on the desk next to the computer.

'Good. That's the user name. Now we just need his password. He's got the whole computer password protected.'

'Shit.'

'Well,' she said as she began typing, 'most people choose something pretty easy – so even they won't forget.'

She stopped typing and watched the screen. The cursor had turned into an hourglass as it worked. A message then printed across the screen informing Rider she had used an improper password.

'What did you use?' Bosch asked.

'His DOB. You did next of kin, right? What was his wife's name?'

'Millie.'

Rider typed it in and after a few seconds got the same rejection message.

'What about his son?' Bosch asked. 'His name was Martin.'

Rider didn't type anything.

'What's the matter?'

'A lot of these password gates give you three strikes. If you don't get in on the third one they go into automatic lockdown.'

'Forever?'

'No. For however long Elias would have set it at. Could be fifteen minutes or an hour or even longer. Let's think about this for a—'

'V-S-L-A-P-D.'

Rider and Bosch turned. Chastain was in the doorway.

'What?' Bosch asked.

'That's the password. V-S-L-A-P-D. As in Elias versus the LAPD.'

'How do you know that?'

'The secretary wrote it down on the underside of her blotter. Guess she's got to use the computer, too.'

Bosch studied Chastain for a moment.

'Harry?' Rider said. 'Should I?'

'Give it a shot,' Bosch said, still looking at Chastain. He then turned and watched as his partner typed in the password. The hourglass blinked on and then the screen changed and icon symbols began appearing on a field of blue sky and white clouds.

'We're in,' Rider said.

Bosch glanced back at Chastain.

'Good one.'

He then looked back at the screen and watched as Rider hit keys and maneuvered through the icons, files and programs, all of it meaning little to Bosch and reminding him that he was an anachronism.

'You really ought to learn this stuff, Harry,' Rider said, seeming to know his thoughts. 'It's easier than it looks.'

'Why should I when I've got you? What are you doing anyway?'

'Just having a look around. We'll have to talk to Janis about this. There are a lot of file names corresponding with cases. I don't know if we should open them before—'

'Don't worry about it for now,' Bosch interjected. 'Can you get on the Internet?'

Rider made a few more moves with the mouse and then typed the user name and password into blanks on the screen.

'I'm running lawyerlink,' she said. 'Hopefully the same passwords work and we'll be able to go to that naked lady's web page.'

'What naked lady?' Chastain said.

Bosch picked the file off the desk and handed it unopened to Chastain. He opened it, glanced at the photo and smirked.

Bosch looked back at the screen. Rider was on lawyerlink, using Elias's user name.

'What's that address?'

Chastain read it off to her as she typed. She then hit the enter key and they waited.

'What this is is a singular web page address within a

larger web site,' she said. 'What we'll get here is the Gina page.'

'You mean that's her name? Gina?'

'Looks like it.'

As she said this the photo from the printout appeared on the screen. Beneath it was information on what the woman in the photo provided and how to contact her.

I am Mistress Regina. I am a lifestyle dominatrix providing elaborate bondage, humiliation, forced feminization, slave training and golden blessings. Other torments available upon request. Call me now.

Below the block of information there was a phone number, a pager number and an E-mail address. Bosch wrote these down in a notebook he took from his pocket. He then looked back at the screen and saw there was also a blue button with the letter A on it. He was about to ask Rider what the button meant when Chastain made a disdainful sound with his mouth. Bosch turned and looked at him and the Internal Affairs man shook his head.

'The bastard was probably getting his rocks off on his knees with this broad,' Chastain said. 'I wonder if Reverend Tuggins and his pals down at the SCCA knew about that.'

He was referring to an organization called the South Central Churches Association, a group which Tuggins headed and which always seemed to be at Elias's beck and call when he needed to show the media an image of South Central outrage in regard to alleged police misconduct.

'We don't know that he ever even met the woman yet, Chastain,' Bosch said.

'Oh, he met her. Why else did he have this laying around? I tell you, Bosch, if Elias was into rough trade like that, there's no telling where that could've led. It's a righteous avenue of investigation and you know it.'

'Don't worry, we'll be checking everything out.'

'You're damn right we will.'

'Uh,' Rider said, interrupting. 'There's an audio button.'

Bosch looked at the screen. Rider had the arrow poised over the blue button.

'What do you mean?' he asked.

'I think we can actually hear Mistress Regina.'

She clicked the arrow on the button. The computer then downloaded an audio program and started playing it. A dark and heavy voice came from the computer's speaker.

'This is Mistress Regina. If you come to me I will find the secret of your soul. Together, we will reveal the true subservience through which you will know your rightful identity and attain the release you can find nowhere else. I will mold you into my own. I will own you. I am waiting. Call me now.'

They were all silent for a long moment. Bosch looked at Chastain.

'Does it sound like her?'

'Like who?'

'The woman on tape at the apartment.'

Chastain suddenly realized the possibility and was silent as he thought about this.

'What tape?' Rider asked.

'Can you play it again?' Bosch asked.

Rider clicked the audio button again and asked about the tape once more. Bosch waited until the replay was over.

'A woman left a message on the phone at Elias's apartment. It wasn't his wife. But I don't think it was this voice either.'

He looked at Chastain once more.

'I don't know,' Chastain said. 'Could be. We'll be able to do a comparison in the lab if we need to.'

Bosch hesitated, studying Chastain for any indication that he knew the phone message had been erased. He saw nothing.

'What?' Chastain said, uneasy under Bosch's stare.
'Nothing,' Bosch said.

He turned back and looked at the computer screen.
'You said this was part of a larger web site,' he said to
Rider. 'Can we look at that?'

Rider didn't answer. She just went to work on the
keyboard. In a few moments the screen changed and
they were looking at a graphic which showed a woman's
stocking-clad leg bent at the knee and reaching across
the screen. Below this it said:

WELCOME TO GIRLAWHIRL
A directory of intimate, sensual and erotic services
in southern California

Below this was a table of contents by which the user
could choose listings of women offering a variety of
services, from sensual massage to evening escort to
female domination. Rider clicked the mouse on this last
offering and a new screen was revealed featuring boxes
with the names of mistresses followed by an area code
prefix.

'It's a goddamn Internet whorehouse,' Chastain said.
Bosch and Rider said nothing. Rider moved the
arrow onto the box marked *Mistress Regina*.

'This is your directory,' she said. 'You choose which
page you want and click.'

She clicked the mouse and the Regina page appeared
again.

'He chose her,' Rider said.

'A white woman,' Chastain said. There was glee in
his voice. 'Golden blessings from a white woman. I bet
they aren't going to be too pleased about that on the
South Side, either.'

Rider turned around and looked sharply at Chastain.
She was about to say something when her eyes widened
and looked past the IAD detective. Bosch noticed this
and turned. Standing in the doorway of the office was
Janis Langwiser. Next to her was a woman Bosch

recognized from her newspaper photos and television appearances. She was an attractive woman with the smooth coffee-and-cream skin of mixed races.

'Wait a minute,' Bosch said to Langwiser. 'This is a crime investigation. She can't come in here and—'

'Yes, Detective Bosch, she can,' Langwiser said. 'Judge Houghton just appointed her special master on the case. She'll be reviewing the files for us.'

With that the woman Bosch recognized stepped fully into the room, smiled but not warmly and held her hand out to him in order to shake his.

'Detective Bosch,' she said. 'It's good to meet you. I hope we will be able to work together on this. I'm Carla Entrenkin.'

She waited a beat but no one responded. She continued.

'Now the first thing I am going to need is for you and all of your people to vacate these premises.'

12

Outside the front doors of the Bradbury the detectives walked empty-handed to their cars. Bosch was still angry but was cooler now. He walked slowly, allowing Chastain and Dellacroce to get to their car first. As he watched them drive off on their way back up Bunker Hill to California Plaza he opened the passenger door of Kiz's slickback but didn't get in. He bent down and looked in at her as she pulled the seat belt across her lap.

'You go on up, Kiz. I'll meet you up there.'

'You're going to walk it?'

Bosch nodded and looked at his watch. It was eight-thirty.

'I'll take Angels Flight. It should be running again. When you get up there you know what to do. Start everybody knocking on doors.'

'Okay, see you up there. You going to go back up and talk to her again?'

'Entrenkin? Yeah, I think so. Do you still have Elias's keys?'

'Yeah.' She dug them out of her purse and handed them to Bosch. 'Is there something I should know about?'

Bosch paused for a moment.

'Not yet. I'll see you up there.'

Rider started the car. She looked over at him again before putting it into drive.

'Harry, you okay?'

'Yeah, I'm fine.' He nodded. 'It's just the case. First

we got Chastain – asshole's always been able to get to me. Now we've got Carla I'mthinkin. It's bad enough we knew she'd be watching the case. Now she's a part of it. I don't like politics, Kiz. I just like putting cases together.'

'I'm not talking about all of that. It's like you've been walking on the sun since we met this morning to pick up the cars in Hollywood. You want to talk about it?'

He almost nodded.

'Maybe later, Kiz,' he said instead. 'We got work to do right now.'

'Whatever, but I'm about to get worried about you, Harry. You need to be straight. If you're distracted, then we're distracted and we aren't going to get anywhere on this thing. That'd be okay most days but on this one you just said it yourself, we're under the glass.'

Bosch nodded again. Her having picked up on his personal turmoil was a testament to her skill as a detective – reading people was always more important than reading clues.

'I hear you, Kiz. I'll straighten up.'

'I copy that.'

'I'll see you up there.'

He slapped the roof of the car and watched her drive off, knowing this would be the time he would normally put a cigarette in his mouth. He didn't. Instead he looked down at the keys in his hand and thought about his next move and how he had to be very careful.

Bosch went back into the Bradbury and as he rode the slow-moving elevator back up he tumbled the keys in his hand and thought about Entrenkin's three separate entries into the case. First as a curious listing in Elias's now missing phone book, then in her capacity as inspector general and now finally a full entrance as a player, the special master who would decide what in Elias's files the investigators would be allowed to see.

Bosch didn't like coincidences. He didn't believe in

them. He needed to know what Entrenkin was doing. He believed he had a good idea what that was and intended to confirm it before going any further with the case.

After being delivered to the top floor, Bosch pushed the button that would send the elevator back down to the lobby and got off. The door to Elias's offices was locked and Bosch knocked sharply on the glazed glass, just below the lawyer's name. In a few moments Janis Langwiser opened it. Bosch could see Carla Entrenkin standing a few feet behind her.

'Forget something, Detective Bosch?' Langwiser asked.

'No. But is that your little foreign job down there in the no-park zone? The red one? It was about to get towed. I badged the guy and told him to give me five minutes. But he'll be back.'

'Oh, shit!' She glanced back at Entrenkin as she headed out the door. 'I'll be right back.'

As she moved by him Bosch stepped into the office and closed the door behind him. He then locked it and turned back to Entrenkin.

'Why did you lock that?' she asked. 'Please leave it open.'

'I just thought it might be better if I said what I want to say without anybody interrupting us.'

Entrenkin folded her arms across her chest as if bracing for an attack. He studied her face and got the same vibe he had gotten before, when she had told them all they had to leave. There was a certain stoicism there, propping her up despite some clear pain beneath. She reminded Bosch of another woman he knew only from TV: the Oklahoma law school teacher who was brutalized in Washington by the politicians a few years before during the confirmation of a Supreme Court justice.

'Look, Detective Bosch, I really don't see any other way around this. We have to be careful. We have to think about the case as well as the community. The people have to be reassured that everything possible is being done – that this won't be swept under in the manner they have seen so many times before. I want—'

'Bullshit.'

'Excuse me?'

'You shouldn't be on this case and we both know it.'

'That's what is bullshit. I have the trust of this community. You think they will believe anything you say about this case? Or Irving or the police chief?'

'But you don't have the trust of the cops. And you've got one big conflict of interest, don't you, Inspector General?'

'What are you saying? I think it was rather wise of Judge Houghton to choose me to act as special master. As inspector general I already have a degree of civilian oversight on the case. This just streamlines things instead of adding another person to the mix. He called me. I didn't call him.'

'I'm not talking about that and you know it. I'm talking about a conflict of interest. A reason you shouldn't be anywhere near this case.'

Entrenkin shook her head in an I-don't-understand gesture but her face clearly showed she feared what Bosch knew.

'You know what I'm saying,' Bosch said. 'You and him. Elias. I was in his apartment. Must've been just before you got there. Too bad we missed each other. We could've settled all of this then.'

'I don't know what you're talking about but I was just led to believe by Miss Langwiser that you people waited on warrants before entering his apartment and the office. Are you telling me that is not true?'

Bosch hesitated, realizing he had made a mistake. She could now turn his move away or back on him.

'We had to make sure no one was hurt or in need of help in the apartment,' he said.

'Sure. Right. Just like the cops who jumped the fence

at O.J. Simpson's house. Just wanting to make sure everybody was okay.'

She shook her head again.

'The continued arrogance of this department amazes me. From what I had heard about you, Detective Bosch, I expected more.'

'You want to talk about arrogance? You were the one who went in there and removed evidence. The inspector general of the department, the one who polices the police. Now you want to—'

'Evidence of what? I did no such thing!'

'You cleared your message off the phone machine and you took the phone book with your name and numbers in it. I'm betting you had your own key and garage pass. You came in through the garage and nobody saw you. Right after Irving called to tell you Elias was dead. Only Irving didn't know that you and Elias had something going on.'

'That's a nice story. I'd like to see you try to prove any of it.'

Bosch held his hand up. On his palm were Elias's keys.

'Elias's keys,' he said. 'There's a couple on there that don't fit his house or his apartment or his office or his cars. I was thinking of maybe pulling your address from DMV and seeing if they fit your door, Inspector.'

Entrenkin's eyes moved quickly away from the keys. She turned and walked back into Elias's office. Bosch followed and watched as she slowly walked around the desk and sat down. She looked as if she might cry. Bosch knew he had broken her with the keys.

'Did you love him?' he asked.

'What?'

'Did you love—'

'How dare you ask me that?'

'It's my job. There's been a murder. You're involved.'

She turned away from him and looked to her right. She was staring through the window at the painting of

Anthony Quinn. Again, the tears appeared to be barely holding back.

'Look, Inspector, can we try to remember one thing? Howard Elias is dead. And believe it or not, I want to get the person who did it. Okay?'

She nodded tentatively. He continued, talking slowly and calmly.

'In order to get this person, I'm going to need to know everything I can about Elias. Not just what I know from television and newspapers and other cops. Not just from what's in his files. I've got to know—'

Out in the reception area someone tried the locked door and then knocked sharply on the glass. Entrenkin got up and went to the door. Bosch waited in Elias's office. He listened as Entrenkin answered the door and spoke to Langwiser.

'Give us a few minutes, please.'

She closed the door without waiting for a response, locked it again and came back to Elias's office, where she took the seat behind the desk. Bosch spoke to her in a voice low enough not to be heard outside of the office.

'I've got to know it all,' he said. 'We both know you are in a position to help. So can't we come to some sort of truce here?'

The first tear fell down Entrenkin's cheek, soon followed by another on the other side. She leaned forward and began opening drawers in the desk.

'Bottom left,' Bosch said from memory of his inventory of the desk.

She opened the drawer and removed the box of tissues. She placed it on her lap, took one tissue and dabbed at her cheeks and eyes. She began to speak.

'It's funny how things change so quickly ...'

A long silence went by.

'I knew Howard superficially for a number of years. When I was practicing law. It was strictly professional, mostly "How are you"s in the hallways of the federal building. Then when I was appointed inspector general,

I knew it was important that I knew the critics of the police department as well as I knew the department. I arranged to meet Howard. We met right here – him sitting right here … It went from there. Yes, I loved him …'

This confession brought more tears and she pulled out several tissues to take care of them.

'How long were you two … together?' Bosch asked.

'About six months. But he loved his wife. He wasn't going to leave her.'

Her face was dry now. She returned the tissue box to its drawer and it seemed as though the clouds that had crossed her face moments before were gone. Bosch could see she had changed. She leaned forward and looked at him. She was all business.

'I'll make a deal with you, Detective Bosch. But only with you. Despite everything … I think if you give me your word then I can trust you.'

'Thank you. What is your deal?'

'I will only talk to you. In return I want you to protect me. And by that I mean keep the source of your information confidential. You don't have to worry, nothing I tell you would be admitted in court anyway. You can keep everything I tell you in background. It may help you, it may not.'

Bosch thought about this for a moment.

'I should be treating you as a suspect, not a source.'

'But you know in your gut that it wasn't me.'

He nodded.

'It wasn't a woman's murder,' he said. 'It's got male written all over it.'

'It's got cop written on it, too, doesn't it?'

'Maybe. That's what I'm going to find out – if I could just get to the case and not have to worry about the community and Parker Center politics and everything else.'

'Then do we have an agreement?'

'Before making any agreement like that I have to

know something first. Elias had a source inside Parker. Somebody with high access. Somebody who could get him unsustained IAD files. I need—'

'It wasn't me. Believe me, I may have crossed a line when I began a relationship with him. That was my heart, not my head. But I didn't cross the line you are talking about. Never in a hundred years. Contrary to what most of your fellow officers think, my goal is to save and improve the department. Not destroy it.'

Bosch looked at her blankly. She took it as disbelief.

'How would I get him files? I am public enemy number one in that department. If I went in to get files, or even just made a request for them, the word would spread around that building and out into the ranks faster than an earthquake wave.'

Bosch studied her defiant face. He knew she was right. She wouldn't make much of a deep cover source. He nodded.

'Then we have an agreement?' she asked.

'Yes. With one asterisk.'

'And what is that?'

'If you lie one time to me and I find out about it, all bets are off.'

'That is more than acceptable to me. But we can't talk now. I want to finish the files so that you and your people can pursue all leads. Now you know why I want this case solved not only for the sake of the city but for myself. What do you say we meet later? When the files are done.'

'Fine with me.'

As Bosch crossed Broadway fifteen minutes later he could see the garage doors of the Grand Central Market had been rolled up. It was years since he had been in the market, maybe decades. He decided to cut through it to Hill Street and the Angels Flight terminus.

The market was a huge conglomeration of food booths, produce stalls and butcher shops. Vendors sold cheap trinkets and candy from Mexico. And though the doors had just opened and there were more sellers readying for the day than buyers inside, the overwhelming smell of oil and fried food already hung heavy in the air. As he made his way through Bosch picked up pieces of conversations, delivered in staccato snippets of Spanish. He saw a butcher carefully placing the skinned heads of goats on ice in his refrigerated display case next to the neat rows of sliced oxtail. At the far end old men sat at picnic tables, nursing their cups of thick, dark coffee and eating Mexican pastries. Bosch remembered his promise to Edgar to bring doughnuts before they began the canvass. He looked around and found no doughnuts but bought a bag of *churros*, the crisp-fried dough sticks with cinnamon sugar that were the Mexican alternative.

As he came out on the Hill Street side of the market he glanced to his right and saw a man standing in the spot where Baker and Chastain had found the cigarette butts hours earlier. The man had a blood-stained apron wrapped around his waist. He wore a hair net. He snaked his hand in underneath the apron and came out with a pack of smokes.

'Got that right,' Bosch said out loud.

He crossed the street to the Angels Flight arch and waited behind two Asian tourists. The train cars were passing each other at the midpoint on the tracks. He checked the names painted above the doors of each car. Sinai was going up and Olivet was coming down.

A minute later, Bosch followed the tourists as they stepped onto Olivet. He watched as they unknowingly sat on the same bench where Catalina Perez had died about ten hours earlier. The blood had been cleaned away, the wood too dark and old to reveal any stain. He didn't bother telling them the recent history of their spot. He doubted they understood his language anyway.

Bosch took the spot where he had sat before. He yawned again the moment the weight was off his feet.

The car jerked and started its ascent. The Asians started taking photos. Eventually they got around to using sign language to ask Bosch to take one of their cameras and take photos of them. He obliged, doing his part for the tourist trade. They then quickly took the camera back and moved to the other end of the car.

He wondered if they had sensed something about him. A danger or maybe a sickness in him. He knew that some people had that power, that they could tell these things. With him, it would not be difficult. It was twenty-four hours since he had slept. He rubbed a hand across his face and it felt like damp stucco. He leaned forward, elbows on his knees, and felt the old pain that he had hoped would never be in his life again. It had been a long time since he had felt so alone, since he had felt like such an outsider in his own city. There was a tightness in his throat and chest now, a feeling of claustrophobia like a shroud about him, even in the open air.

Once more he got the phone out. He checked the battery display and found it almost dead. Enough juice for one more call if he was lucky. He punched in the number for home and waited.

There was one new message. Fearing the battery wouldn't hold, he quickly punched in the playback code and held the phone back up to his ear. But the voice he heard was not Eleanor's. It was the sound of a voice distorted by cellophane wrapped around the receiver and then perforated with a fork.

'Let this one go, Bosch,' the voice said. 'Any man who stands against cops is nothing but a dog and deserves to die like a dog. You do the right thing. You let it go, Bosch. You let it go.'

13

Bosch got to Parker Center twenty-five minutes before he was to meet with Deputy Chief Irving to update him on the investigation. He was alone, having left the other six members of the Elias team to conclude the canvass of the apartment building next to Angels Flight and then to pursue their next assignments. Stopping at the front counter he showed his badge to the uniformed officer and he told the man that he was expecting some information to be called in anonymously to the front desk within the next half-hour. He asked the officer to relay the information to him immediately in Chief Irving's private conference room.

Bosch then took an elevator up to the third floor rather than the sixth, where Irving's office was located. He went down the hall to the Robbery-Homicide Division squad room and found it empty except for four detectives he had called earlier. They were Bates, O'Toole, Engersol and Rooker – the four detectives who had originally handled the call out to the Angels Flight murder scene. They looked suitably bleary-eyed, having been up half the night before the case was turned over to Bosch and his squad. Bosch had rousted them from sleep at nine and given them a half hour to meet him at Parker Center. It had been easy enough to get them in so quickly. Bosch had told them their careers depended on it.

'I don't have a lot of time,' Bosch began as he walked down the main aisle between the rows of desk, locking eyes with the four. Three of the detectives were standing around Rooker, who was seated at his desk. This was a clear giveaway. Whatever decisions had been made out at the scene, when it was only the four of them, Bosch was sure were made by Rooker. He was leader of the pack.

Bosch stayed standing, stopping just outside the informal grouping of the other four. He started telling the story, using his hands in an informal manner, almost like a television news reporter, as if to underline that it was simply a story he was telling, not the threat that he was actually delivering.

'The four of you get the call out,' he said. 'You get out there, push the uniforms back and make a perimeter. Somebody checks the stiffs and lo and behold the DL says one of them is Howard Elias. You then put—'

'There was no driver's license, Bosch,' Rooker said, interrupting. 'Didn't the cap tell you that?'

'Yeah, he told me. But now I'm telling the story. So listen up, Rooker, and shut up. I'm trying to save your ass here and I don't have a lot of time to do it.'

He waited to see if anybody wanted to say anything more.

'So like I said,' he began again, looking directly at Rooker, 'the DL identifies one of the stiffs as Elias. So you four bright guys put your heads together and figure there's a good chance that it was a cop who did this. You figure Elias got what he had coming and more power to the badge who had the guts to put him down. That's when you got stupid. You decided to help out this shooter, this murderer, by staging the robbery. You took off—'

'Bosch, you are full—'

'I said shut up, Rooker! I don't have the time to hear a bunch of bullshit when you know it went down just like I said. You took off the guy's watch and his wallet. Only you fucked up, *Rooker*. You scratched the guy's wrist with the watch. *Post*mortem wound. It's going to come up on the autopsy and that means you four are going to go down the toilet unless it gets contained.'

He paused, waiting to see if Rooker had anything to say now. He didn't.

'Okay, sounds like I have your attention. Anybody want to tell me where the watch and wallet are?'

Another pause while Bosch looked at his watch. It was a quarter to ten. The four RHD men said nothing.

'I didn't think so,' Bosch said, looking from face to face. 'So this is what we're going to do. I meet with Irving in fifteen minutes to give him the overview. He then holds the press conference. If the front desk downstairs doesn't get a call with information as to the location of the gutter or trash can or whatever place this stuff was stashed, then I tell Irving the robbery was staged by people at the crime scene and it goes from there. Good luck to you guys then.'

He scanned their faces again. They showed nothing but anger and defiance. Bosch expected nothing less.

'Personally, I wouldn't mind it going that way, seeing you people get what you got coming. But it will fuck the case – put hair on the cake, taint it beyond repair. So I'm being selfish about it and giving you a chance it makes me sick to give.'

Bosch looked at his watch.

'You've got fourteen minutes now.'

With that he turned and started heading back out through the squad room. Rooker called after him.

'Who are you to judge, Bosch? The guy was a dog. He deserved to die like a dog and who gives a shit? You should do the right thing, Bosch. Let it go.'

As if it was his intention all along, Bosch casually turned behind an empty desk and came back up a smaller aisle toward the foursome. He had recognized the phrasing of the words Rooker had used. His demeanor disguised his growing rage. When he got back to the group, he broke their informal circle and leaned over Rooker's desk, his palms down flat on it.

'Listen to me, Rooker. You call my home again – whether it's to warn me off or to just tell me the weather – and I'll come looking for you. You won't want that.'

Rooker blinked but then raised his hands in surrender.

'Hey, man, I don't know what the fuck you're talk—'

'Save it for somebody you can convince. At least you could've been a man and skipped the cellophane. That's coward shit, boy.'

Bosch had hoped that when he got to Irving's conference room there would be at least a few minutes for him to look at his notes and put his thoughts together. But Irving was already seated at the round table, his elbows on the polished surface and the fingertips of both hands touching and forming a steeple in front of his chin.

'Detective, have a seat,' he said as Bosch opened the door. 'Where are the others?'

'Uh,' Bosch said, putting his briefcase down flat on the table. 'They're still in the field. Chief, I was just going to drop my case off and then run down to get a cup of coffee. Can I get you something?'

'No, and you do not have time for coffee. The media calls are starting. They know it was Elias. Somebody leaked. Probably in the coroner's office. So it's about to get crazy. I want to hear what is happening, starting right now. I have to brief the police chief, who will lead a press conference that has been scheduled for eleven. Sit down.'

Bosch took a seat opposite Irving. He had worked a case out of the conference room once before. That seemed like a long time ago but he remembered it as the time he had earned Irving's respect and probably as much trust as the deputy chief was willing to give to anyone else who carried a badge. His eyes moved across the surface of the table and he saw the old cigarette scar that he had left during the investigation of the Concrete Blonde case. That had been a difficult case but it seemed almost routine beside the investigation he was involved in now.

'When are they coming in?' Irving asked.

He still had his fingers together like a steeple. Bosch had read in an interrogation manual that such body language denoted a feeling of superiority.

'Who?'

'The members of your team, Detective. I told you I wanted them here for the briefing and then the press conference.'

'Well, they're not. Coming in. They are continuing the investigation. I thought that it didn't make sense that all seven of us should just drop things to come in here when one of us could easily tell you the status of things.'

Bosch watched angry flares of red explode high on Irving's cheeks.

'Once again we seem to have either a communication problem or the chain of command remains unclear to you. I specifically told you to have your people here.'

'I must've misunderstood, Chief,' Bosch lied. 'I thought the important thing was the investigation. I remembered that you wanted to be brought up to date, not that you wanted everybody here. In fact, I doubt there is enough room in here for everybody. I—'

'The point is I wanted them here. Do your partners have phones?'

'Edgar and Rider?'

'Who else?'

'They have phones but they're dead. We've been running all night. Mine's dead.'

'Then page them. Get them in here.'

Bosch slowly got up and headed to the phone which was on top of the storage cabinet that ran along one wall of the room. He called Rider and Edgar's pagers, but when he punched in the return number he added an extra seven at the end. This was a long-standing code they used. The extra seven – as in code seven, the radio call for out of service – meant they should take their time in returning the pages, if they returned them at all.

'Okay, Chief,' Bosch said. 'Hopefully, they'll call in. What about Chastain and his people?'

'Never mind them. I want your team back here by eleven for the press conference.'

Bosch moved back to his seat.

'How come?' he asked, though he knew exactly why. 'I thought you said the police chief was going—'

'The chief will lead it. But we want to have a show of force. We want the public to know we have top-notch investigators on this case.'

'You mean top-notch *black* investigators, don't you?'

Bosch and Irving held hard stares for a moment.

'Your job, Detective, is to solve this case and solve it as quickly as you can. You are not to concern yourself with other matters.'

'Well, that's kind of hard to do, Chief, when you are pulling my people out of the field. Can't solve anything quickly if they've got to be here for every dog and pony show you people cook up.'

'That is enough, Detective.'

'They *are* top-notch investigators. And that's what I want to use them for. Not as cannon fodder for the department's race relations. They don't want to be used that way, either. That in itself is ra—'

'*Enough*, I said! I do not have time to debate racism, institutional or otherwise with you, Detective Bosch. We are talking about public perceptions. Suffice it to say that if we mishandle this case or its perceptions from the outside, this city could be burning again by midnight.'

Irving paused to look at his watch.

'I meet the police chief in twenty minutes. Could you please begin to enlighten me with the accomplishments of the investigation up to this point?'

Bosch reached over and opened his briefcase. Before he could reach for his notebook the phone on the cabinet rang. He got up and went to it.

'Remember,' Irving said, 'I want them here by eleven.'

Bosch nodded and picked up the phone. It wasn't Edgar or Rider and he had not expected that it would be.

'This is Cormier downstairs in the lobby. This Bosch?'

'Yeah.'

'You just got a message here. Guy wouldn't give a name. He just said to tell you that what you need is in a trash can in the MetroLink station, First and Hill. It's in a manila envelope. That's it.'

'Okay, thanks.'

He hung up and looked at Irving.

'It was something else.'

Bosch sat back down and took his notebook out of his briefcase along with the clipboard with the crime scene reports, sketches and evidence receipts attached to it. He didn't need any of it to summarize the case but he thought it might be reassuring to Irving to see the accumulation of paper the case was engendering.

'I'm waiting, Detective,' the deputy chief said by way of prompting him.

Bosch looked up from the paperwork.

'Where we are is pretty much point zero. We have a good idea what we have. We don't have much of a handle on the who and why.'

'Then what have we got, Detective?'

'We're going with Elias being the primary target in what looks an outright assassination.'

Irving brought his head down so that his clasped hands hid his face.

'I know that's not what you want to hear, Chief, but if you want the facts, that's what the facts point to. We have—'

'The last thing Captain Garwood told me was that it looked like a robbery. The man was wearing a thousand-dollar suit, walking through downtown at eleven o'clock at night. His watch and wallet are missing. How can you discount the possibility of a robbery?'

Bosch leaned back and waited. He knew Irving was venting steam. The news Bosch was giving him was guaranteed to put ulcers on his ulcers once the media picked it up and ran.

'The watch and wallet have been located. They weren't stolen.'

'Where?'

Bosch hesitated, though he had already anticipated the question. He hesitated because he was about to lie to a superior on the behalf of four men who did not deserve the benefit of the risk he was taking.

'In his desk drawer at the office. He must've forgotten them when he closed up and headed to his apartment. Or maybe he left them on purpose in case he got robbed.'

Bosch realized he would still need to come up with an explanation in his reports when the autopsy on Elias revealed the postmortem scratches on his wrist. He would have to write it off as having occurred while the body was being manipulated or moved by the investigators.

'Then perhaps it was an armed robber who shot Elias when he did not turn over a wallet,' Irving said, oblivious to Bosch's internal discomfort. 'Perhaps it was a robber who shot first and searched for valuables second.'

'The sequence and manner of the shots suggests otherwise. The sequence suggests a personal tie – rage transmitted from one person to Elias. Whoever did this knew Elias.'

Irving put his hands down on the table and leaned a few inches toward its center. He seemed impatient when he spoke.

'All I am saying is that you cannot completely eliminate these other possible scenarios.'

'That might be true but we're not pursuing those scenarios. I believe it would be a waste of time and I don't have the manpower.'

'I told you I wanted a thorough investigation. I want no stone unturned.'

'Well, we'll get to those stones later. Look, Chief, if you are focusing on this so you can tell the media it might be a robbery, then fine, say it might be. I don't care about what you tell the media. I'm just trying to tell you where we stand and where we're going to be looking.'

'Fine. Proceed.'

He waved a hand in a dismissive gesture.

'We need to look at the man's files and draw up lists of potential suspects. The cops who Elias really nailed in court or vilified in the media over the years. Or both. The grudges. And the cops he would have tried to nail beginning Monday.'

Irving showed no reaction at all. It seemed to Bosch he was already thinking about the next hour, when he and the police chief would go out on a cliff and address the media about such a dangerous case.

'We are being handicapped,' Bosch continued. 'Carla Entrenkin has been appointed by the warrants judge as a special master to oversee the protection of Elias's clients. She's in his office right now and won't let us in.'

'I thought you said you found the man's wallet and watch in the office.'

'I did. That was before Carla showed up and kicked us out.'

'How did she get appointed?'

'She says the judge called her, thought she'd be perfect. She and a deputy from the DA are there. I'm hoping to get the first batch of files this afternoon.'

'Okay, what else?'

'There's something you should know. Before Carla

made us leave, we came across a couple things of interest. The first is some notes Elias kept at his desk. I read through them and there were indications that he had a source in here. Parker Center, I mean. A good source, somebody who apparently knew how to find and get access to old files – unsubstantiated IAD investigations. And there were indications of a dispute. The source either couldn't or wouldn't provide something Elias wanted on the Black Warrior thing.'

Irving went quiet for a second, staring at Bosch, processing. When he spoke again his voice was more distant still.

'Was this source identified?'

'Not in what I saw, which wasn't a lot. It was coded.'

'What was it that Elias wanted? Could it be related to the killings?'

'I don't know. If you want me to pursue it as a priority I will. I was thinking that other things would be the priority. The cops he dragged into court in the past, the ones he was going to pull in starting Monday. Also, there was a second thing we found in the office before we got kicked out.'

'What was that?'

'It actually branches into two more avenues of investigation.'

He quickly told Irving about the photo printout of Mistress Regina and the indication that Elias might have been involved in what Chastain had called rough trade. The deputy chief seemed to take a keen interest in this aspect of the investigation and asked Bosch what his plans were in regard to pursuing it.

'I'm planning on attempting to locate and interview the woman, see if Elias ever actually had any contact with her. After that, we see where it goes.'

'And the other branch of investigation this leads to?'

'The family. Whether it was this Regina woman or not, it looks like Elias was a philanderer. There are enough indications in his downtown apartment to suggest this. So if the wife knew about all of this, then we have a motivation right there. Of course, I'm just talking right here. At the moment we have nothing that indicates she even knew, let alone arranged or carried out the kill. It also flies in the face of the psychological read on the killings.'

'Which is what?'

'It doesn't look like the dispassionate work of a hired killer. There is a lot of rage in the killing method. It looks to me like the killer knew Elias and hated him – at least at the moment of the shooting. I would also say it looks like it was a man.'

'How so?'

'The shot up the ass. It was vindictive. Like a rape. Men rape, women don't. So my gut instinct tells me this clears the widow. But my instincts have been wrong. It's still something we have to follow up on. There's the son, too. Like I told you before, he reacted pretty hot when we gave them the news. But we don't really know what his relationship with his father was like. We do know that the kid has been around weapons – we saw a picture in the house.'

Irving pointed a finger of warning at Bosch.

'You be careful with the family,' he said. 'Very careful. That has to be handled with a lot of finesse.'

'It will be.'

'I do not want that blowing up in our faces.'

'It won't.'

Irving checked his watch once more.

'Why have your people not answered the pages?'

'I don't know, Chief. I was just thinking the same thing.'

'Well, page them again. I need to meet with the chief. At eleven I want you and your team in the press conference room.'

'I'd rather get back to work on the case. I've got—'

'That is a direct order, Detective,' Irving said as he

stood. 'No debate. You won't have to answer questions but I want your people on hand.'

Bosch picked up the clipboard and threw it back into his open briefcase.

'I'll be there,' he said, though Irving was already through the door.

Bosch sat for a few minutes thinking. He knew Irving would now repackage the information he had given him and deliver it to the police chief. They would put their heads together and then reshape it once more before delivering it to the media.

He looked at his watch. He had a half hour until the press conference. He wondered if that was time enough to get over to the Metrolink station, find Elias's wallet and watch and get back in time. He had to make sure he recovered the dead lawyer's property, particularly because he had already told Irving it was in his possession.

Finally, he decided that there wasn't enough time to do it. He decided to use the time to get coffee and to make a phone call. He walked to the cabinet once more and called his house. Once more the machine picked up. Bosch hung up after hearing his own voice saying no one was home.

14

Bosch decided he would be too nervous waiting until after the press conference and drove over to the MetroLink station at First and Hill. It was only three minutes away and he was pretty sure he could make it back to Parker Center for the start of the press conference. He parked illegally at the curb in front of the entrance to the subway platform. It was one of the few good things about driving a slickback; there was no need to worry about parking tickets. As he got out he removed the baton from the sleeve in the car's door.

He trotted down the escalator and spotted the first trash can next to the automatic doors at the entrance to the station. The way he figured it, Rooker and his partner had left the Angels Flight crime scene with the stolen property and stopped at the first spot they knew they would find a trash can. One waited up top with the car while the other ran down the stairs to get rid of the wallet and watch. So Bosch was confident this first trash can would be the one. It was a large, white rectangular receptacle with the MetroLink symbol painted on its sides. A blue hood on top housed the push door. Bosch quickly lifted it off and looked down. The receptacle was full but there was no manila envelope visible in the debris at top.

Bosch put the hood on the ground and used the baton to stir through the detritus of discarded newspapers, fast-food wrappers and garbage. The can smelled as though it had not been emptied in days, cleaned in months. He came across an empty purse and one old shoe. As he used the baton like an oar to dig deeper, he began to worry that one of the homeless men who populated downtown had beaten him to the can and found the watch and wallet first.

Near the bottom, just before he gave up to try one of the cans further into the station, he saw an envelope smeared with catsup and fished it out with two fingers. He tore it open, careful to take most of the catsup with the discarded end, and looked inside at a brown leather wallet and a gold Cartier watch.

Bosch used the escalator on the way up but this time was content to just ride as he looked in the envelope. The watchband was also gold or gold plated and was the accordion style that slipped over the wrist and hand. Bosch bounced the envelope a bit in his hand in order to move the watch without touching it. He was looking for any fragments of skin that might be caught in the band. He saw nothing.

Once he was back inside the slickback he put on gloves, took the wallet and watch out of the torn envelope and threw the envelope over the seat and to the floor in the back. He then opened the wallet and looked through its partitions. Elias had carried six credit cards in addition to identification and insurance cards. There were small studio-posed photos of his wife and son. In the billfold section there were three credit card receipts and a blank personal check. There was no currency.

Bosch's briefcase was on the seat next to him. He opened it and took out the clipboard, then flipped through it until he found the victim's property report. It detailed everything taken from each victim. Only a quarter had been found in Elias's pockets at the time they were searched by a coroner's assistant.

'You pricks,' Bosch said out loud as he realized that whoever took the wallet had decided to keep whatever cash had been in it. It was unlikely that Elias had been walking to his apartment with only the quarter it would cost him to ride Angels Flight.

Once more he wondered why he was sticking his neck out for people who didn't deserve it. He tried to dismiss the thought, knowing that it was too late to do anything about it, but he couldn't. He was a coconspirator now. Bosch shook his head in disgust with himself, then put the watch and wallet into separate plastic evidence bags after labeling each one with a white sticker on which he wrote the case number, the date and a time of 6:45 A.M. He then wrote a brief description of each item and the drawer of Elias's desk in which it was found, initialed the corner of each sticker and put the bags into his briefcase.

Bosch looked at his watch before starting the car. He had ten minutes to make it to the press conference room. No sweat.

There were so many members of the media attending the press conference that several were standing outside the door to the police chief's press room, unable to find space inside. Bosch pushed and excused and squeezed his way through them. Inside, he saw the back stage was lined wall to wall with television cameras on tripods, their operators standing behind them. He quickly counted twelve cameras and knew that the story would soon go national. There were eight television stations carrying local news in Los Angeles, including the Spanish-language channel. Every cop knew that if you saw more than eight camera crews at a scene or a press conference then you were talking network attention. You were working something huge, something dangerous.

In the middle of the room, every folding chair was taken by a reporter. There were close to forty, with the TV people clearly identifiable in their nice suits and makeup and the print and radio people just as recognizable as the ones wearing jeans and with ties pulled loose at the neck.

Bosch looked to the front stage and saw a flurry of activity around the podium, which had the LAPD chief's badge affixed. Sound men were taping their equipment to the ever-widening tree of microphones on the podium. One of them was standing directly behind the podium and giving a voice check. Behind and to the side of the podium stood Irving, conferring in whispers with two men in uniform, both wearing lieutenant's stripes. Bosch recognized one of them as Tom O'Rourke, who worked in the media relations unit. The other Bosch did not recognize but assumed he was Irving's adjutant, Michael Tulin, whose call had awakened Bosch just hours earlier. A fourth man stood on the other side of the podium by himself. He wore a gray suit and Bosch had no idea who he was. There was no sign of the police chief. Not yet. The police chief did not wait for the media to get ready. The media waited for him.

Irving spotted Bosch and signaled him to the front stage. Bosch walked up the three steps and Irving put a hand on his shoulder to usher him into a private huddle out of earshot of the others.

'Where are your people?'

'I haven't heard back from them.'

'That is not acceptable, Detective. I told you to get them in here.'

'All I can say, Chief, is that they must be in the middle of a sensitive interview and didn't want to break the momentum of the situation to call back on my pages. They are reinterviewing Elias's wife and his son. It takes a lot of finesse, especially in a case like—'

'I am not interested in that. I wanted them here, period. At the next press conference you have them here or I will split your team up and send you to three divisions so far apart you will have to take a vacation day to have lunch together.'

Bosch studied Irving's face for a moment.

'I understand, Chief.'

'Good. Remember it. Now we are about to get started here. O'Rourke is going now to get the chief and escort him in. You will not be answering any questions. You do not have to worry about that.'

'Then why am I here? Can I go?'

Irving looked as though he was finally about to curse for the first time in his career, maybe his life. His face was turning red and the muscles of his powerful jaw were at full flex.

'You are here to answer any questions from me or the chief of police. You can leave when I dismiss you.'

Bosch raised his arms in a hands-off fashion and took a step back against the wall to wait for the show to begin. Irving stepped away and conferred briefly with his adjutant and then walked over to the man in the suit. Bosch looked out into the audience. It was hard to see because the overhead TV lights were on. But past the glare he managed to pick out a few faces he knew either personally or from TV. When his eyes finally came to Keisha Russell's he attempted to look away before the *Times* reporter saw him but was too late. Their eyes briefly caught and held, then she nodded once, almost unnoticeably. Bosch did not nod back. He didn't know who might pick up on it. It was never good to acknowledge a reporter in public. So he just held her gaze for a few moments longer and then looked away.

The door to the side of the stage opened and O'Rourke came through and turned so that he could then hold the door open for the chief of police, who entered the room wearing a charcoal gray suit and with a somber look on his face. O'Rourke stepped to the podium and leaned down to the microphone tree. He was much taller than the police chief, for whom the microphones had been set.

'Everybody ready?'

Though a couple of cameramen from the back called out, '*No*' and '*Not yet*,' O'Rourke ignored them.

'The chief has a brief statement about today's events and then he'll field a few questions. But only general details of the case will be released at this time because of the ongoing investigation. Deputy Chief Irving is also here to field questions. Let's maintain some order and we'll get through this quickly and smoothly and everybody will get what they need. Chief?'

O'Rourke stepped aside and the chief of police stepped to the podium. He was an impressive man. Tall, black and handsome, he had spent thirty years on the job in the city and was a skilled media man. He was, however, new to the chief's post, chosen for the job just the summer before after his predecessor, an overweight outsider with no feel for the department and little feel for the community, was dumped in favor of the insider who was striking enough to play himself in a Hollywood movie. The chief gazed out silently at the faces in the room for a moment. The vibe Bosch picked up was that this case and how he handled it would be the chief's first, true test in the job. He was sure the chief had picked up the vibe as well.

'Good morning,' the chief finally said. 'I have disturbing news to report today. The lives of two citizens were taken late last night here in downtown. Catalina Perez and Howard Elias were riding separately on the Angels Flight railroad when they were each shot and killed shortly before eleven o'clock. Most people in this city know of Howard Elias. Revered or not, he was a man who nevertheless was a part of our city, who helped mold our culture. On the other hand, Catalina Perez, like so many of us, was not a famous person or a celebrity. She was just struggling to make a living so that she and her family – a husband and two young children – could live and prosper. She worked as a housekeeper. She worked long days and nights. She was going home to her family when she was slain. I am simply here this morning to assure our citizens that these two murders will not go unanswered or forgotten. You can be assured that we will be working tirelessly on this investigation until we achieve justice for Catalina Perez and Howard Elias.'

Bosch had to admire what the chief was doing. He was packaging both victims as a set, making it seem implausible that Elias was the sole target and Perez just an unlucky traveler in the crossfire. He was slickly attempting to portray them as equal victims of the senseless and often random violence that was the city's cancer.

'At this point, we can't go into too many details because of the investigation. But it can be said that there are leads being followed and we have every belief and hope that the killer or killers will be identified and brought to justice. In the meantime, we ask that the good citizens of Los Angeles remain calm and allow us to do our job. What we need to guard against at this time is jumping to conclusions. We don't want anyone to get hurt. The department, either through me or Deputy Chief Irving or the media relations office, will be providing regular updates on the progress of the case. Information will be provided when it can be released without being detrimental to the investigation or eventual prosecution of suspects.'

The chief took a half step back from the podium to look at O'Rourke, a signal that he was finished. O'Rourke made a move toward the podium but before he had raised a foot there was a loud chorus from the audience of reporters yelling, 'Chief!' And above this din came the deeply resonant voice of one reporter, a voice recognizable to Bosch and everyone else with a television as belonging to Channel 4's Harvey Button.

'Did a cop kill Howard Elias?'

The question caused a momentary pause, then the chorus continued. The chief stepped back to the podium and raised his hands as if trying to calm a pack of dogs.

'Okay, hold on a second. I don't want everybody yelling at me. One at a—'

'Did a cop do this, Chief? Can you answer that or not?'

It was Button again. This time the other reporters remained silent and in doing so fell in behind him, their silence demanding that the chief address the question. It was, after all, the key question. The entire press conference boiled down to one question and one answer.

'At this time,' the chief said, 'I cannot answer that. The case is under investigation. Of course, we all know Howard Elias's record with this department. It would not be good police work if we did not look at ourselves. And we will do that. We are in the process of doing that. But at this point we—'

'Sir, how can the department investigate itself and still have credibility with the community?'

Button again.

'That's a good point, Mr Button. First off, the community can be assured that this investigation will reach its fruition no matter where it leads. The chips will fall where they may. If a police officer is responsible then he or she will be brought to justice. I guarantee it. Secondly, the department is being aided in this investigation by Inspector General Carla Entrenkin, who as you all know is a civilian observer who reports directly to the police commission, the city council and mayor.'

The chief raised his hand to cut off another question from Button.

'I'm not finished, Mr Button. As I said, lastly I would like at this time to introduce Assistant Special Agent in Charge Gilbert Spencer from the Los Angeles field office of the Federal Bureau of Investigation. I have discussed this crime and this investigation with Mr Spencer at length and he has agreed to bring the bureau in to help us. Beginning tomorrow, FBI agents will be working side by side with LAPD detectives in a group effort to bring this investigation to a swift and successful conclusion.'

Bosch tried to show no response as he listened to the chief announce the FBI involvement. He was not shocked by it. He realized it was a good move by the chief and might buy some time in the community. It might even get the case solved, though that was probably a secondary condition in the chief's decision making. He was primarily trying to put out fires before they started. The bureau was a pretty good hose with which to do that. But Bosch was annoyed that he had been left out of the loop and was finding out about the bureau's entry into his case at the same time as Harvey Button and everybody else. He glanced over at Irving, who picked it up on his radar and looked back. They traded glares until Irving looked away to the podium as Spencer took a position behind the microphones.

'I don't have much to say yet,' the bureau man said. 'We will be assigning a team to the investigation. These agents will work with the LAPD detectives and it is our belief that together we will break this case quickly.'

'Will you be investigating the officers in the Black Warrior case?' a reporter called out.

'We will be taking a look at everything but we are not going to be sharing our investigative strategy at this time. From this point, all media inquiries and releases will be handled through the LAPD. The bureau will—'

'Under what authority is the FBI entering the case?' Button asked.

'Under civil rights codes the bureau has the authority to open an investigation to determine if an individual's rights have been violated under color of law.'

'The color of law?'

'By an officer of the law. I am going to turn this over to …'

Spencer stepped back from the podium without

finishing. He clearly didn't enjoy being in the glare of the media's headlights. The police chief stepped back into place and introduced Irving, who then moved behind the podium and began reading a press release which contained more details of the crime and the investigation. It was still just the basics, nothing anybody could do much with. The statement also mentioned Bosch by name as the detective in charge of the investigation. It also explained why potential conflict of interest with the RHD and scheduling problems with Central Division detectives required a team from Hollywood Division to run the case. Irving then said he could field a few questions, reminding the reporters once again that he would not compromise the investigation by revealing vital information.

'Can you talk more about the focus of the investigation?' a reporter called out ahead of the others.

'The focus is wide-ranging,' Irving said. 'We are looking at everything from police officers who might have held a grudge against Howard Elias to the possibility of the killings being part of a robbery. We—'

'A follow-up,' another reporter barked, knowing that you had to get your question in before the subject finished the last one or you'd never be heard in the ensuing cacophony. 'Was there anything at the crime scene to indicate a robbery?'

'We are not going to discuss details of the crime scene.'

'My information is that there was no watch or wallet on the body.'

Bosch looked at the reporter. He was not a TV man. Bosch could tell that by his rumpled suit. And it did not appear that he was from the *Times* because Keisha Russell was already in the room. Bosch didn't know who he was but he had obviously been leaked the information on the watch and wallet.

Irving paused as if deciding on how much to reveal. 'Your information is correct but incomplete. Mr Elias apparently left his watch and wallet in his desk when he left his office last night. The property was found there today. Of course, that does not preclude attempted robbery as a motive for this crime but it is too early in the investigation and we know too little to make such an assumption at this time.'

Keisha Russell, ever the cool one, had not joined the shouting for attention. She sat calmly with her hand raised, waiting for the others to run out of things to ask and for Irving to call on her. After Irving fielded a few more repetitive questions from the TV people he finally called on her.

'You said Mr Elias's property was found in his office today. Have you searched his office and, if so, what if anything is being done to safeguard the attorney-client privilege that Mr Elias shared with his clients, all of whom are suing the agency that conducted the search of the office.'

'Good question,' Irving replied. 'We have not conducted a full search of the victim's office for the very reason you just mentioned. That is where Inspector General Entrenkin comes into play. She is reviewing files in the victim's office and will turn them over to investigators after she has vetted them for any sort of sensitive information that could possibly fall under attorney-client privilege. This review process was ordered earlier today by the judge who issued search warrants for Howard Elias's office. My understanding is that the watch and wallet were found in or on the victim's desk, very much as if he had simply forgotten them last night when he left work. Now I think that will wrap things up here. We have an investigation to focus on. When there are any further updates we will—'

'One last one,' Russell called out. 'Why has the department gone to twelve and twelves?'

Irving was about to answer but then looked back at the chief of police, who nodded and stepped back to the podium.

'We want to be ready for any eventuality,' he said. 'Going to twelve-hour shifts puts more officers on the street at any given time. We believe the citizens of this city will remain calm and give us time to conduct our investigation, but as a safety precaution I have instituted a readiness plan that includes all officers working twelve hours on and twelve hours off until further notice.'

'Is this the civil disorder response plan that was drawn up after the last riots?' Russell asked. 'When the department was caught flat-footed because it had no plan?'

'It is the plan drawn in 1992, yes.'

He was about to step away from the podium when Russell tossed another curveball.

'Then you are expecting violence.'

It was said as a statement, not a question. The chief returned to the microphones.

'No, Miss, uh, Russell, I am not expecting that. As I said, this is merely precautionary. I am expecting the citizens of this community to act in a calm and responsible manner. Hopefully, the media will act in the same way.'

He waited for one more response from Russell but this time got none. O'Rourke moved forward and leaned in front of the chief to get to the microphones.

'Okay, that's it. There will be copies of Chief Irving's statement down in media relations in about fifteen minutes.'

As the reporters slowly filed out of the room Bosch kept his eyes on the man who had asked the question about the wallet and watch. He was curious to know who he was and what news outlet he worked for. At the logjam at the door the confluence of people brought the man side by side with Button and they started talking. Bosch thought this was odd because he had never seen a print reporter give a TV reporter the time of day.

'Detective?'

Bosch turned. The chief of police was standing to his side with his hand out. Bosch instinctively shook it. He had spent nearly twenty-five years in the department to the chief's thirty, yet they had never crossed paths close enough to speak to each other, let alone shake hands.

'Chief.'

'Good to meet you. I want you to know how much we are counting on you and your team. If you need anything don't hesitate to contact my office or to go through Deputy Chief Irving. Anything.'

'Well, at the moment I think we're okay. I appreciate the heads-up on the bureau, though.'

The chief hesitated but only for a moment, apparently discarding Bosch's gripe as unimportant.

'That couldn't be helped. I wasn't sure the bureau was going to become involved until shortly before we started the press conference.'

The chief turned and looked for the FBI man. Spencer was talking with Irving. The chief signaled them over and introduced Bosch to Spencer. Bosch thought he caught a glimmer of disdain on Spencer's face. Bosch did not have a positive record over the years in his dealings with the FBI. He had never dealt directly with Spencer but if he was assistant special agent in charge of the L.A. field office, then he had probably heard of Bosch.

'How are we going to work this, gentlemen?' the chief asked.

'I'll have my people assembled and here at eight tomorrow morning, if you like,' Spencer said.

'Excellent. Chief Irving?'

'Yes, that will be fine. We will be working out of the conference room next to my office. I'll have our team there at eight, we can go over what we've got and take it from there.'

Everybody nodded except for Bosch. He knew he had no say in the matter.

They broke up and headed toward the door the chief

had come through. Bosch found himself next to O'Rourke. He asked him if he knew who the reporter was who asked about the watch and wallet.

'Tom Chainey.'

It almost rang a bell with Bosch but not quite.

'He's a reporter?'

'Not really. He was with the *Times* a lot of years ago but now he's TV. He's Harvey Button's producer. He's not pretty enough to go on camera. So they pay him a ton of money to get scoops for Harvey and to tell him what to say and ask. To make him look good. Harvey's got the face and that voice. Chainey's got the brains. Why do you ask? Is there something I can do for you?'

'No. I was just wondering.'

'You mean the question about the wallet and the watch? Well, like I said, Chainey's been around. He's got sources. More than most.'

They moved through the doorway and Bosch turned left to head back to Irving's conference room. He wanted to leave the building but didn't want to wait for an elevator with all of the reporters.

Irving was waiting for him in the conference room. He was sitting in the same spot he had taken before.

'Sorry about the bureau deal,' he said. 'I did not know about it until right before. It was the chief's idea.'

'So I heard. It's probably the smart play.'

He was quiet for a moment, waiting for Irving to make the next move.

'So what I want you to do is have your team finish up the interviews they are involved in now, then everybody gets a good night's sleep, because tomorrow it all starts again.'

Bosch had to stop himself from shaking his head no.

'You mean just shelve everything until the bureau shows up? Chief, this is a homicide – a double homicide. We can't just shut it down and start over tomorrow.'

'I am not talking about shutting anything down. I

said finish up what you have going at the moment. Tomorrow we will retrench and regroup and create a new battle plan. I want your people fresh and ready to run.'

'Fine. Whatever.'

But Bosch had no intention of waiting for the bureau. His intention was to continue the investigation, drive it forward and then follow where it led. It didn't matter what Irving said.

'Can I get a key to this room?' Bosch asked. 'We should get the first batch of files from Entrenkin in a little while. We need a secure place for them.'

Irving shifted his weight and reached into his pocket. He removed a key that was unattached to a ring and slid it across the table. Bosch picked it up and started working it onto his own key ring.

'So how many people have a copy of this?' he said. 'Just so I know.'

'You don't have to worry, Detective. No one will be going into this room who is not a member of the team or does not have my permission.'

Bosch nodded even though Irving had not answered his question.

15

As Bosch stepped through the glass doors of Parker Center he saw the beginning of the manufacturing and packaging of a media event. Spread out across the front plaza were a half dozen television crews and reporters ready to transmit stand-up reports as lead-in on the footage from the press conference. Out at the curb was the microwave forest – a line of TV trucks with their microwave transmitters raised high and ready. It was a Saturday, normally the slowest news day of the week. But the murder of Howard Elias was big. The guaranteed lead story and then some. A Saturday morning assignment editor's dream come true. The local stations were going to go live at noon. And then it would begin. The news of Elias's murder would blow through the city like the hottest Santa Ana wind, setting nerves on edge and possibly turning silent frustrations into loud and malevolent actions. The department – and the city, for that matter – was relying on how these young and beautiful people interpreted and delivered the information they had been given. The hope was that their reports would not fan the already smoldering tensions in the community. The hope was that they would show restraint and integrity and common sense, that they would simply report the known facts without any speculation or editorial twisting of the knife. But Bosch knew those hopes had about as much chance as Elias had when he stepped onto Angels Flight little more than twelve hours before.

Bosch took an immediate left and headed to the

employee parking lot, careful not to walk into view of any of the cameras. He didn't want to be on the news unless absolutely necessary.

He successfully avoided detection and got to his car. Ten minutes later he parked illegally in front of the Bradbury, pulling in behind yet another TV truck. He looked around as he got out but didn't see the news crew. He guessed that they had walked over to the Angels Flight terminus to tape footage for the story.

After taking the old elevator up to the top floor Bosch pulled back the gate and stepped out onto the landing only to be met by Harvey Button, his producer and a cameraman. There was an uneasy silence as he tried to move around them. Then the producer spoke.

'Uh, Detective Bosch? I'm Tom Chainey from Channel Four.'

'Good for you.'

'I was wondering if we could talk for a few moments about the—'

'No, we can't talk. Have a nice day.'

Bosch managed to get around them and started toward Elias's office. Chainey spoke to his back.

'You sure? We're picking up a lot of information and it would probably do us both a lot of good if we could get it confirmed. We don't want to cause you any problems. It would be better if we could work as a team. You know.'

Bosch stopped and looked back at him.

'No, I don't know,' he said. 'If you want to put unconfirmed information on the air, that's your choice. But I'm not confirming anything. And I already have a team.'

He turned without waiting for a reply and headed toward the door with Howard Elias's name on it. He heard nothing else from Chainey or Button.

When he walked into the office he found Janis Langwiser sitting behind the secretary's desk, looking through a file. Next to the desk there were three cardboard boxes full of files that weren't there before. Langwiser looked up.

'Detective Bosch.'

'Hey. These boxes for me?'

She nodded.

'The first batch. And, hey, that wasn't very nice what you did before.'

'What?'

'Telling me my car was being towed. That was a lie, wasn't it?'

Bosch had completely forgotten.

'Uh, no, not really,' he said. 'You were in a tow-away zone. They would've gotten you.'

He smiled when he knew she knew it was a bullshit cover-up. His face started turning red.

'Look, I had to talk to Inspector Entrenkin alone. I'm sorry.'

Before she could say anything, Carla Entrenkin looked in from the room next door. She, too, was holding a file in her hand. Bosch pointed to the three boxes on the floor.

'Looks like you're making some progress.'

'I hope so. Can I talk to you for a moment in here?'

'Sure. But first, did Channel Four come in here and try to talk to you two?'

'They did,' Langwiser said. 'And Channel Nine was here before them.'

'Did you talk to them?'

Langwiser's eyes darted momentarily toward Entrenkin and then down at the floor. She said nothing.

'I gave a brief statement,' Entrenkin said. 'Something innocuous, just explaining my role. Can we talk in here?'

She stepped back from the doorway and Bosch entered the file room. There was another cardboard box on the desk that was half full of files. Entrenkin closed the door after Bosch entered. She then threw the file she was holding on the clerk's desk, folded her arms and put a stern expression on her face.

'What is it?' Bosch asked.

'Tom Chainey just told me that it was announced at the press conference that How— uh, Mr Elias had left his wallet and watch in his office, in his desk. And I thought that when you people were asked to leave this morning it was clear that—'

'I'm sorry. I forgot.'

Bosch put his briefcase down on the desk and opened it. He lifted out the evidence bags containing the wallet and watch.

'I had already bagged them and put them in my case before you came in this morning. I forgot about it and left with them. You want me to put it all back where I found it?'

'No. I just wanted an explanation. And I'm not sure I believe the one you just offered.'

There was a long silence while they stared at each other.

'Was that all you wanted to talk to me about?' Bosch finally asked.

She turned back to the desk and the file she had been looking through.

'I thought our relationship would be better than this.'

'Look,' Bosch said as he closed the briefcase. 'You've got your secrets. You've got to give me mine. The bottom line is Howard Elias wasn't robbed. So we move on from there. Okay?'

'If you are telling me that there were people involved in this investigation who were attempting to tamper with evidence, then—'

'I'm not telling you anything.'

He saw anger flare in her eyes.

'They shouldn't be a part of this department. You know that.'

'That's another battle for another day. I've got more import—'

'You know there are some people who might think there is nothing more important than a police department in which there is no question about the integrity of its members.'

'Sounds like you're giving a press conference, Inspector. I'm going to take those files now. I'll be back for the next batch later.'

He started to turn back to the front room.

'I just thought you were different, that's all,' she said.

He turned back to her.

'You don't know if I'm different because you don't know the first thing about me. I'll talk to you later.'

'There's something else missing.'

Bosch stopped and looked back at her.

'What?'

'Howard Elias was a consummate note taker. He kept a spiral notebook on his desk or with him all the time. His last notebook is missing. You know where that is?'

Bosch came back to the desk and reopened his briefcase. He took the notebook out and tossed it down.

'You won't believe me but I had already put that in my briefcase when you came in and kicked us out.'

'Matter of fact, I do believe you. Did you read it?'

'Parts of it. Also before you showed up.'

She looked at him for a long moment.

'I'll look through it and if it is okay you will have it back later today. Thank you for returning it.'

'You're welcome.'

By the time Bosch got to Philippe's the Original, the others were already there and eating. They had one of the long tables in the back room and were by themselves. He decided to take care of business before waiting in one of the lines at the counter to order.

'How'd it go?' Rider asked as he stepped over the bench and sat next to her.

'Well, I think I definitely was a little too pale for Irving's liking.'

'Well, fuck him,' Edgar said. 'I didn't sign up for this shit.'

'Me, too,' Rider said.

'What are you talking about?' Chastain asked.

'Race relations,' Rider said. 'Typical you can't figure that out.'

'Hey, I—'

'Never mind,' Bosch interjected. 'Let's talk about the case, okay? You first, Chastain. Did you finish the apartment building?'

'Yeah, we finished. Nothing.'

'Except we found out about the woman,' Fuentes said.

'Oh, yeah, right.'

'What woman?'

'The other victim. Catalina Perez. Hold a second.'

Chastain reached down to the bench next to him and came up with a legal tablet. He flipped to the second page and looked at the notes.

'Apartment nine-oh-nine. Perez was the cleaning woman. Came every Friday night. So that's where she was coming from.'

'But she was going up,' Bosch said. 'She didn't work till eleven?'

'No, this is the deal. She works six to ten-thirty, then takes Angels Flight down to the bus stop, catches the bus and goes home. Only on the way down she must've looked in her purse and noticed her notebook, where she keeps her schedule and phone numbers, is missing. She took it out in the apartment last night because her employer, a Mr D. H. Reilly, changed his phone number and gave her the new one. Only she left the notebook on his kitchen table. She had to go back for it so she'd know her schedule. This lady ...'

He reached to the bench again and pulled up the notebook. It was in a plastic evidence bag.

'... I mean, I looked at the schedule. She worked her tail off. She's got gigs every day and a lot of nights. This

Reilly guy said Friday nights was the only regular night he could get her for. She did a good job …'

'So she was going back up to get her book when she got popped,' Edgar said.

'Looks that way.'

'The old I-O-I-A,' Rider said in a singsong way that was not mirthful in any way.

'What's that?' Chastain asked.

'Nothing.'

They were all silent for a long moment. Bosch was thinking about how leaving that notebook behind had cost Catalina Perez her life. He knew that what Rider had said referred to the inequities of it all – the phrase she began using after a year on the homicide squad to sum up the bad breaks, coincidences and twists of fate that often left people dead.

'Okay, good,' Bosch finally said. 'We now know what everybody was doing on that train. The rest of the building was clean?'

'Nobody heard a thing, nobody saw a thing,' Chastain said.

'You get everybody?'

'No response at four apartments. But they were all on the other side, away from Angels Flight.'

'All right, let those go for now. Kiz, you talk to the wife and son again?'

Rider was chewing her last bite of French dip sandwich and held her finger up until she swallowed.

'Yeah, separately and together. Nothing pulled my trigger. They're both pretty much convinced a cop did it. I didn't—'

'Of course they are,' Chastain interjected.

'Let her talk,' Bosch said.

'I didn't pick up any feel that they knew much about his cases or possible threats. He didn't even keep a home office. I touched on Elias's fidelity and Millie said she believed he was faithful. She said it like that. She "believed." Something about it sounds wrong. I think if there was no doubt she would say he "was" faithful, not that she "believed" he was faithful, know what I mean?'

'So you think she knew?'

'Maybe. But I also think that if she knew then she was the type that would put up with it. There was a lot of social standing in being Howard Elias's wife. Lot of wives in that position make choices. They look the other way on some things to keep the image intact, to keep the life they have intact.'

'What about the son?'

'I think he believed his father was a god. He's hurting.'

Bosch nodded. He respected Rider's interviewing skills. He had seen her in action and knew she was empathic. He also knew he had used her in a way not so dissimilar to the way Irving had wanted to use her during the press conference. He had sent her to do the follow-up interviews because he knew she would be good at it. But also because she was black.

'You ask them the A question?'

'Yeah. They were both at home last night. Neither went out. They're each other's alibi.'

'Great,' Chastain said.

'Okay, Kiz,' Bosch said. 'Anybody else got something they want to bring up?'

Bosch leaned forward on the table so he could look down his side and see every face. No one said anything. He noticed everybody had finished eating their sandwiches.

'Well, I don't know if you've heard anything about the press conference, but the chief called in the cavalry. Tomorrow morning the bureau enters the case. We have a meet at eight in Irving's conference room.'

'Shit,' Chastain said.

'What the hell are they going to do that we can't?' Edgar asked.

'Probably nothing,' Bosch said. 'But his announcing it at the press conference will probably go a long way toward keeping the peace. At least, for now. Anyway, let's worry about that tomorrow when we see how things shake out. We still have the rest of today. Irving gave me an unofficial cease and desist until the agents show up but that's bullshit. I say we keep working.'

'Yeah, we don't want the shark to drown, do we?' Chastain said.

'That's right, Chastain. Now, I know nobody's had much sleep. My thinking is that some of us keep working and knock off early, some of us go home, take a nap and come back in fresh tonight. Any problem with that?'

Again no one said anything.

'All right, this is how we break it up. I've got three boxes of files from Elias's office in my trunk. I want you IAD guys to take them and go back to Irving's conference room. You take the files, pull out names of cops and anybody else to be checked out. I want a chart made up. When we get legit alibis we scratch the names off the chart and move on. I want this ready by the time the bureau arrives tomorrow. When you have it done, then you guys can knock off for the night.'

'And what are you going to be doing?' Chastain asked.

'We're going to run down Elias's secretary and his clerk. Then after that, I'm going home to take a nap. Hopefully. Then tonight we're going to talk to Harris and chase down that Internet thing. I want to know what that's all about before the bureau comes in.'

'You better be careful with Harris.'

'We will. That's one reason we're waiting until tonight. We play it right and the media doesn't even find out we talked to the guy.'

Chastain nodded.

'What about these files you're giving us, they old or new?'

'They're old ones. Entrenkin started on the closed cases.'

'When are we going to see the Black Warrior file? That's the one. The rest of this is bullshit.'

'Hopefully, I'll be picking that up later today. But the rest isn't bullshit. We have to look at every damn file in that office. Because the one we skip is likely to be the one some lawyer shoves up our ass in trial. You understand that? Don't skip anything.'

'I got it.'

'Besides, what do you care so much about the Black Warrior file for? You cleared those guys on it, right?'

'Yeah, so?'

'So what are you going to find in the file other than what you already know? You think you missed something, Chastain?'

'No, but ...'

'But what?'

'It's the case of the moment. I think there's gotta be something there.'

'Well, we'll see. All in good time. For now stick to the old files and don't skip anything.'

'I told you, we won't. It's just a pain in the ass to know you're wasting time.'

'Welcome to homicide.'

'Yeah, yeah.'

Bosch reached into his pocket and pulled out a small brown bag. It contained several copies of the key Irving had given him that he had had made in Chinatown on his way to the restaurant. He turned the bag over on the center of the table and keys clattered onto the table.

'Everybody take a key. They'll open the door to Irving's conference room. Once the files are in there I want the room locked at all times.'

Everybody reached to the center of the table and took a key except Bosch. He had already put the original on his key ring. He stood up and looked at Chastain.

'Let's go get those files out of my car.'

16

The interviews with the secretary and the clerk were so uneventful that Bosch wished the detectives could have spent the time in their beds sleeping. Tyla Quimby, the secretary, had been out with the flu and holed up in her home in the Crenshaw district for the last week. She had no knowledge of Howard Elias's activities during the days before his death. Aside from exposing Bosch, Edgar and Rider to the flu, she gave the detectives very little. She explained that Elias kept his case strategies and other aspects of his work largely to himself. Her role was primarily opening mail, answering phones, handling walk-in visitors and clients, and paying the office expenses through a small operating account Elias put money into each month. As far as the phone traffic went, she said Elias had a direct private phone line in his office that over the years had become widely known among friends and associates as well as some reporters and even enemies. So she was of little use as far as helping them determine whether Elias had been specifically threatened in the weeks before his murder. The investigators thanked her and left her home, hoping they would not fall victim to her illness.

The clerk, John Babineux, was an equal disappointment. He was able to confirm that it had been he and Michael Harris who had worked until late Friday with Elias. But Babineux said that Harris and Elias had been behind closed doors most of the evening. Babineux, as it turned out, had graduated from the USC law school three months before and was studying for the bar exam at night while clerking for Elias by day. He did his studying in Elias's offices at night because it allowed him access to the law books he needed for memorizing case law and penal codes. It obviously was a better study environment than the crowded apartment near USC he shared with two other law students. Shortly before eleven he had walked out with Elias and Harris because he had felt he had done enough studying for one night. He said he and Harris walked to their cars in a nearby pay lot while Elias walked up Third Street alone toward Hill Street and Angels Flight.

Like Quimby, Babineux described Elias as secretive about his cases and preparation for trial. The clerk said that his responsibility in the last week of work had largely been preparing the transcripts of the many pretrial depositions taken in the Black Warrior case. His job was to download the transcripts and related material onto a laptop computer which would then be taken to court and accessed by Elias when he needed specific references to evidence and testimony during trial.

Babineux could give the detectives no information about specific threats to Elias – at least none that the attorney was taking seriously. He described Elias as extremely upbeat in recent days. He said Elias wholeheartedly believed that he was going to win the Black Warrior case.

'He said it was a slam dunk,' Babineux told the three detectives.

As Bosch drove up Woodrow Wilson Drive toward home he thought about the two interviews and wondered why Elias had been so secretive about the case he was bringing to trial. This didn't fit with his past history of press leaks and sometimes full-scale press conferences as a primary strategy. Elias was being uncharacteristically quiet, yet he was confident in his case, enough to call it a slam dunk.

Bosch hoped the explanation of this would be revealed when he got the Black Warrior file from Entrenkin, hopefully in a few hours. He decided to put thoughts of it aside until then.

Immediately Eleanor came to mind. He thought about the closet in the bedroom. He purposely hadn't checked it before, not sure how he would react if he found she had taken her clothes. He decided he needed to do that now, to get it over with. It would be a good time to do it. He was too tired now to do anything other than crash down onto his bed, regardless of what he found.

But as he came around the last curve he saw Eleanor's car, the beat-up Taurus, parked at the curb in front of their house. She had left the carport open for him. He felt the muscles in his neck and shoulders begin to relax. The tightness in his chest began to ease. She was home.

The house was quiet when he entered. He put his briefcase down on one of the dining room chairs and started stripping off his tie as he moved into the living room. He then moved down the short hallway and looked into the bedroom. The curtains were drawn and the room was dark except for the outline of exterior light around the window. He saw Eleanor's still form under the covers on the bed. Her brown hair was splayed over the pillow.

He moved into the bedroom and quietly took off his clothes, draping them over a chair. He then went back down the hallway to the guest bathroom to take a shower without waking her up. Ten minutes later he slid into the bed next to her. He was on his back, looking through the darkness to the ceiling. He listened to her breathing. He didn't hear the slow, measured breaths of her sleeping that he was used to.

'You awake?' he whispered.

'Mmm-hmm.'

He waited a long moment.

'Where were you, Eleanor?'

'Hollywood Park.'

Bosch didn't say anything. He didn't want to accuse her of lying. Maybe Jardine, the security guy, had simply missed her during his survey of the video screens. He stared at the ceiling, wondering what to say next.

'I know that you called there looking for me,' Eleanor said. 'I knew Tom Jardine in Las Vegas. He used to work at the Flamingo. He lied when you called. He came to me first.'

Bosch closed his eyes and remained silent.

'I'm sorry, Harry, I just didn't want to have to deal with you then.'

'Deal with me?'

'You know what I mean.'

'Not really, Eleanor. How come you didn't answer my message when you got home?'

'What message?'

Bosch realized he had played the message back himself earlier. There wouldn't have been a flashing light on the machine. She would not have heard the message.

'Never mind. When did you get home?'

She lifted her head off the pillow to look at the glowing numbers on the bedside clock.

'Couple hours ago.'

'How'd you do?'

He didn't really care. He just wanted her to keep talking to him.

'All right. Came out a little ahead but I messed up. I missed a big one.'

'What happened?'

'I went with a long shot when I should've stuck with a sure thing.'

'What do you mean?'

'I was dealt a pair of aces but I also had four clubs – ace, three, four, five. So on the draw I broke the pair of aces. I discarded the ace of hearts and went for the deuce, the two of clubs to make the straight flush. They keep a progressive bonus pot going for a straight flush. It was up to about three thousand dollars. That's what I was going for.'

'So what happened?'

'I didn't get the deuce. I didn't even get a club to make a flush. What I got was the ace of spades.'

'Damn.'

'Yeah, I threw down an ace only to get an ace. I stayed in with that but didn't come close. Three tens won it – the pot was about three hundred. So if I had kept the ace of hearts I would have ended up with three aces and been the winner. I blew it. That's when I left.'

Bosch didn't say anything. He thought about the story and wondered if she was trying to say something else. Tossing the ace of hearts, aiming for the bigger pot, failing.

After a few minutes of silence, Eleanor spoke again.

'Were you out on a case? You hadn't been in the bed. I could tell.'

'Yeah, I got a call out.'

'I thought you weren't up on rotation.'

'It's a long story and I don't feel like talking about it. I want to talk about us. Tell me what's going on, Eleanor. We can't … this isn't right. Some nights I don't even know where you are or if you are all right. Something's wrong or missing and I don't know what it is.'

She turned and moved under the covers until she was next to him. She put her head down on his chest and brought her hand up to caress the scar on his shoulder.

'Harry …'

He waited but she didn't say anything. She moved over on top of him then and started a gentle rocking motion with her hips.

'Eleanor, we need to talk about this.'

He felt her finger glide across his lips, telling him not to speak

They made love slowly, Bosch's mind a jumble of conflicting thoughts. He loved her, more than he had ever loved anyone. He knew she loved him in some way. Having her in his life had made him feel whole. But at some point he could tell that Eleanor had realized she did not have that feeling. For her there was something missing and the realization that they were on separate planes brought Bosch down as low as he had ever felt.

The feeling of doom had fallen upon the marriage then. During the summer he had caught a series of time-consuming investigations, including a case requiring him to make a week-long trip to New York. While he was gone she went to the poker room at Hollywood Park for the first time. It was out of the boredom of being left alone and the frustration at her lack of success in finding an acceptable job in Los Angeles. She had returned to the cards, doing what she had done when Bosch had found her, and it was at those blue felt tables that she found the thing that was missing.

'Eleanor,' he said when they were finished making love, his arms wrapped around her neck. 'I love you. I don't want to lose you.'

She smothered his mouth with a long kiss and then whispered, 'Go to sleep, darling. Go to sleep.'

'Stay with me,' he said. 'Don't move away until I'm asleep.'

'I won't.'

She held him tighter and he tried for the moment to let everything go. Just for a while, he decided. He would take it all up later. But for now he would sleep.

In a few minutes he was gone, deep into a dream in which he was riding Angels Flight up the tracks to the top of the hill. As the other car came down and passed, he looked in through the windows and saw Eleanor sitting alone. She wasn't looking back at him.

Bosch awoke in a little over an hour. The room was

darker, as the light from outside was no longer directly on the windows. He looked around and saw Eleanor was gone from the bed. He sat up and called her name, his voice reminding him of how he had answered the phone that morning.

'I'm here,' she called from the living room.

Bosch pulled on his clothes and left the bedroom. Eleanor was sitting on the couch, wearing the bathrobe he had bought for her at the hotel in Hawaii where they had gone after getting married in Las Vegas.

'Hey,' he said. 'I thought … I don't know.'

'You were talking in your sleep. I came out here.'

'What did I say?'

'My name, a few other things that didn't make sense. Something about a fight. Angels fighting.'

He smiled and nodded and sat down in the chair on the other side of the coffee table.

'*Flight*, not fight. You ever been on Angels Flight in downtown?'

'No.'

'It's two train cars. When one goes up the hill, the other goes down. They pass in the middle. I dreamed I was going up and you were in the car going down. We passed in the middle but you wouldn't look at me … What do you think it means, that we're going different ways?'

She smiled sadly.

'I guess it means you're the angel. You were going up.'

He didn't smile.

'I have to go back in,' he said. 'This one's going to take up my life for a while. I think.'

'You want to talk about it? Why were you called out?'

He ran the case down for her in about ten minutes. He always liked telling her about his cases. He knew it was a form of ego gratification, but sometimes she made a suggestion that helped or a comment that let him see something he had missed. It was many years since she had been an FBI agent. It was a part of her life that was a distant memory. But he still respected her investigative logic and skills.

'Oh, Harry,' she said when he was done telling the story. 'Why is it always you?'

'It's not always me.'

'Seems like it is. What are you going to do?'

'Same as I always do. I'm going to work the case. All of us are. There's a lot there to work with – they just have to give us the time with it. It's not going to be a quick turn.'

'I know you, they'll throw every roadblock they can think of in front of you. It does no one any good to hook somebody up and bring them in on this. But you'll be the one to do it. You'll bring somebody in no matter if it makes every cop in every division despise you.'

'Every case counts, Eleanor. Every person. I despise people like Elias. He was a suckerfish – making his life off bullshit cases against cops just trying to do their jobs. For the most part, at least. Every now and then he had a legitimate case, I guess. But the point is nobody should get away with what they did. Even if it's a cop who did it. It's not right.'

'I know, Harry.'

She looked away from him, out through the glass doors and past the deck. The sky was turning red. The lights of the city were coming on.

'What's your cigarette count?' he asked just to be saying something.

'I had a couple. You?'

'Still at zero.'

He had smelled the smoke in her hair earlier. He was glad she hadn't lied.

'What happened over at Stocks and Bonds?'

He'd been hesitant about asking. He knew that whatever had happened during the interview had been what sent her to the poker room.

'Same as the others. They'll call if something comes up.'

'I'll go over and talk to Charlie next time I'm at the station.'

Stocks and Bonds was a storefront bail bond agency across from the Hollywood station on Wilcox. Bosch had heard they were looking for a skip tracer, preferably female because a good portion of the bail jumpers out of Hollywood station were prostitutes and a female tracer stood a better chance of running them down. He had gone over and talked to the owner, Charlie Scott, about it and he had agreed to consider Eleanor for the job. Bosch was honest about her background, both good and bad. Former FBI agent on the plus side, convicted felon being the minus. Scott said he didn't believe the criminal record would be a problem – the position did not require a state private investigator's license, which Eleanor could not qualify for with a record. The problem was that he liked his tracers to be armed – especially a woman – when they went looking for bail jumpers. Bosch didn't share the concern. He knew that most skip tracers were unlicensed to carry weapons but did so anyway. The true art of the craft, though, was never get close enough to your quarry to make having or not having a weapon a question. The best tracers located their quarry from a safe distance and then called the cops in to make the pickup.

'Don't talk to him, Harry. I think he was just trying to do you a favor but reality hit him between when he told you to send me in and when I arrived. Just let it go.'

'But you'd be good at that.'

'That's beside the point.'

Bosch stood up.

'I've got to get ready.'

He went into the bedroom and stripped off his clothes, took another shower and then dressed in a fresh suit. Eleanor was in the same position on the couch when he came back out to the living room.

'I don't know when I'll be back,' he said, not looking at her. 'We've got a lot to do. Plus the bureau's coming in tomorrow.'

'The bureau?'

'Civil rights. The chief made the call.'

'He thinks it will keep things calm down south.'

'He hopes.'

'Do you have a name of who is coming over?'

'Not really. There was an assistant SAC at the press conference today.'

'What was his name?'

'Gilbert Spencer. But I doubt he'll be involved anymore.'

Eleanor shook her head.

'He's after my time. He probably just came for the show.'

'Yeah. He's supposed to send a team over tomorrow morning.'

'Good luck.'

He looked at her and nodded.

'I don't have the number yet. If you need me just use the pager.'

'Okay, Harry.'

He stood there for a few moments before finally asking her what he wanted to ask all along.

'Are you going to go back?'

She looked back out through the doors.

'I don't know. Maybe.'

'Eleanor …'

'Harry, you have your addiction. I have mine.'

'What's that mean?'

'You know that feeling you get when you pull up on a new case? That little thrill you get when you're back in the hunt? You know what I'm talking about. Well, I don't have that anymore. And the closest thing I've found to it is when I pick those five cards up off the felt and see what I've got. It is hard to explain and even harder to understand, but I feel like I'm alive again then, Harry. We're all junkies. It's just different drugs. I wish I had yours, but I don't.'

Bosch just stared at her a moment. He wasn't sure he could say anything without his voice betraying him. He moved to the door, looking back at her once he had it open. He moved through it but then stepped back.

'You break my heart, Eleanor. I always hoped that I could make you feel alive again.'

Eleanor closed her eyes. She looked as though she might cry.

'I'm so sorry, Harry,' she whispered. 'I should never have said that.'

Bosch stepped silently through the door and closed it behind him.

17

Bosch was still feeling emotionally bruised when he got to Howard Elias's office a half hour later. The door was locked and he knocked. He was about to use the keys to open it when he saw movement behind the glazed glass. Carla Entrenkin opened the door and allowed him in. He could tell by the way she appraised him that she noticed he was wearing a different suit.

'I got to take a little break,' he said. 'I think we'll be working a good part of the night. Where's Miss Langwiser?'

'We finished and I sent her home. I said I would wait for you. It's only been a few minutes.'

She led him back to Elias's office and took the seat behind the huge desk. Bosch could see Anthony Quinn through the window though it was getting dark out. He also saw that there were six file cartons on the floor in front of the desk.

'Sorry you were waiting,' he said. 'I thought you were going to page me when you were done.'

'I was about to. I was just sitting here thinking ...'

Bosch looked at the boxes.

'This is the rest?'

'That's it. Those six are more closed cases. These back here are current cases.'

She rolled her chair back and pointed to the floor behind the desk. Bosch stepped over and looked down. There were two more full boxes.

'This is mostly Michael Harris stuff. Most of it is the police file and depo transcripts. There are also files on lawsuits that haven't proceeded past the initial claims. And there is a file containing general threats and crank mail – I mean unrelated specifically to the Harris case. Mostly just anonymous stuff from racist cowards.'

'Okay. What are you not giving me?'

'I'm holding back only one file. It was his working file. It contains notes on strategy in the Harris case. I don't think you should have that. I believe it goes directly to attorney-client privilege.'

'Strategy?'

'Basically, it's a trial map. Howard liked to chart his trials. He once told me he was like a football coach who designs the plays and what order he will call them in before the game even starts. Howard always knew exactly where he wanted to go during trial. The trial map showed his strategy, what witness came when, when each piece of evidence was to be introduced, things like that. He had the first few questions for every one of his witnesses already written. And he also had his opening statement outlined and in the file.'

'Okay.'

'I can't give it to you. It was the heart of his case and I think whoever the attorney is who inherits the case will want to follow the map. It was a brilliant plan. Therefore, the LAPD shouldn't have it.'

'You think he was going to win?'

'Definitely. I take it you don't?'

Bosch sat down in one of the chairs in front of the desk. Despite having taken the nap, he was still tired and feeling it.

'I don't know the particulars of the case,' he said. 'All I know is Frankie Sheehan. Harris accused him of some of that stuff – you know, with the plastic bag. And I know that's not Frankie.'

'How can you be sure?'

'I can't, I guess. But we go back. Sheehan and I were partners one time. It was a long time ago but you still know people. I know him. I can't see him doing these things. I can't see him letting anybody else do it, either.'

'People change.'

Bosch nodded.

'They do. But usually not at the core.'

'The core?'

'Let me tell you a story. One time Frankie and I brought this kid in. A carjacker. His deal was that first he'd steal a car, any shit can off the street, then he'd go out driving and looking for something nice, something he could take to a chop shop and get a decent amount of bread for. When he saw what he wanted he'd come up behind and at a stop light he'd hit the back end. You know, like a little fender bender, not enough to do much damage. Then the owner of the Mercedes or the Porsche or whatever it was would get out to check. The jacker would get out and just jump into the target car and take off. The owner and the stolen shit can were left behind.'

'I remember when carjacking was the big fad.'

'Yeah, some fad. This guy'd been doing this about three months and making a good amount of money at it. Then one time he hits the back of a Jaguar XJ6 too hard. The little old lady who was driving wasn't wearing her seat belt. She weighs about ninety pounds and she is thrown into the steering wheel. Hits it hard. No air bag. It crushes one lung and sends a rib through the other. She's sittin' there fillin' up with blood and dying when this kid comes up, opens the door and just yanks her out of the car. He leaves her lying on the street and drives off with the Jag.'

'I remember that case. What was that, ten years ago? The media went nuts on it.'

'Yeah. Carjack homicide, one of the first ones. And that's where me and Frankie came in. It was a hot case and we were under pressure. We finally got a line on the kid through a chop shop that Burglary-Auto Theft took down in the Valley. This kid lived over in Venice and when we went to pick him up he saw us coming. Fired a three fifty-seven through the front door after Frankie knocked. Missed him by an inch. Frankie had longer hair back then. The bullet actually went through his hair. The kid went through the back door and we chased him through the neighborhood, calling for backup on our handhelds as we ran. The radio calls brought the media out – helicopters, reporters, everything.'

'You got him, right? I remember.'

'We chased him almost all the way through Oakwood. We finally got him in an abandoned house, a shooting gallery. The hypes went scattering and he stayed inside. We knew he had the gun and he had already taken a shot at us. We could've gone in there and blown his shit away and there wouldn't have been a question. But Frankie went in first and talked the kid out. It was just him and me and the kid in there. Nobody would've known or questioned what had happened. But Frankie, he didn't think like that. He told the kid he knew the lady in the Jag was an accident, that he didn't mean to kill anybody. He told him he still had a chance at life. Fifteen minutes earlier the kid tried to kill Frankie, now Frankie was trying to save the kid's life.'

Bosch stopped for a moment, remembering the moments in the abandoned house.

'The kid finally stepped out of a closet, holding his hands up. He still had the gun in his hand. It would have been so easy … and so right. But it was Frankie's call. He was the one who almost took the bullet. But he just went over and took the gun from the kid and cuffed him. End of story.'

Entrenkin considered the story for a long moment before responding.

'So what you are saying is that because he spared one black man that he could have easily gotten away with killing, then he would not have tried to suffocate another black man nearly a decade later.'

Bosch shook his head and frowned.

'No, I'm not saying that. I'm saying that that was just one of the times I saw Frank Sheehan's core. It was when I knew what he was made of. And that's why I know the Harris thing is bullshit. He would never have planted evidence on the guy, he would never have pulled a bag over his head.'

He waited for her to say something but she didn't.

'And I never said anything about the carjacker being black. That had nothing to do with it. That's just something you bring to the story yourself.'

'I think it was an obvious part that you left out. Maybe if it had been a white boy in that abandoned house you would never even have thought about what you could have gotten away with.'

Bosch stared at her a long moment.

'No, I don't think so.'

'Well, it's not worth arguing about. You left something else out of the story, didn't you?'

'What?'

'A few years later your buddy Sheehan *did* use his gun. And he put a bunch of bullets into a black man named Wilbert Dobbs. I remember that case, too.'

'That was a different story and a righteous shoot. Dobbs was a murderer who drew down on Sheehan. He was cleared by the department, the DA, everybody.'

'But not a jury of his peers. That was one of Howard's cases. He sued your friend and he won.'

'It was bullshit. The case went to trial a few months after the Rodney King thing. There was no way a white cop who had shot a black man was going to get a clean verdict in this town back then.'

'Be careful, Detective, you're revealing too much of yourself.'

'Look, what I said was the truth. Deep down, you

know it was the truth. How come the moment the truth might be uncomfortable people raise the race card?'

'Let's just drop this, Detective Bosch. You have your belief in your friend and I admire that. I guess we'll see what happens when the lawyer who inherits this case from Howard brings it to trial.'

Bosch nodded and was thankful for the truce. The accusatory discussion had made him feel uncomfortable.

'What else have you held back?' he asked, to try to move on.

'That's pretty much it. Spent all day in here to basically hold one file back.'

She blew her breath out and suddenly seemed very tired.

'You doing okay?' he asked.

'Fine. I think it was good for me to stay busy. I haven't had much time to think about what has happened. I'm sure I will tonight.'

Bosch nodded.

'Any more reporters come around?'

'A couple. I gave them a sound bite and they went on their merry way. They all think the city's going to cut loose over this.'

'What do you think?'

'I think if a cop did this, there's no telling what's going to happen. And if a cop didn't do it, there will be people who just won't believe it. But you already know that.'

Bosch nodded.

'One thing you should know about the trial map.'

'What's that?'

'Despite what you said about Frank Sheehan a moment ago, Howard was out to prove Harris innocent.'

Bosch hiked his shoulders.

'I thought he already was in the criminal trial.'

'No, he was found not guilty. There's a difference.

Howard was going to prove his innocence by proving who did it.'

Bosch stared at her a long moment, wondering how he should proceed.

'Does it say in that trial map who that was?'

'No. Like I said, there was just an outline of the opener. But it's in there. He was going to tell the jury that he would deliver the murderer to them. Those were his words. "Deliver the murderer to you." He just didn't write who that was. It would have been a bad opener, if he did. It would give it away to the defense and make for an anticlimactic moment later in trial when he revealed who this person was.'

Bosch was silent as he thought about this. He didn't know how much weight to give what she had told him. Elias was a showman, in and out of court. Revealing a killer in court was Perry Mason stuff. It almost never happened.

'I'm sorry but I probably shouldn't have told you that,' she said.

'Why did you?'

'Because if others knew this was his strategy, it could have been a motive.'

'You mean the real killer of that little girl came back to kill Elias.'

'That's a possibility.'

Bosch nodded.

'Did you read the depos?' he asked.

'No, not enough time. I'm giving all depositions to you because the defense – in this case the city attorney's office – would have been furnished copies. So I'm not giving you something you wouldn't already have access to.'

'What about the computer?'

'I looked through it very quickly. It appears to be depositions and other information out of the public file. Nothing privileged.'

'Okay.'

Bosch started to get up. He was thinking about how many trips down to the car it would take him to move the files.

'Oh, one other thing.'

She reached down to the box on the floor and came up with a manila file. She opened it on the desk, revealing two envelopes. Bosch leaned over the desk to see.

'This was in the Harris stuff. I don't know what it means.'

Both envelopes were addressed to Elias at his office. No return addresses. Both were postmarked Hollywood, one mailed five weeks earlier and the other three weeks earlier.

'There's a single page with a line in each. Nothing that makes sense to me.'

She started opening one of the envelopes.

'Uh … ,' Bosch began.

She stopped, holding the envelope in her hand.

'What?'

'I don't know. I was thinking about prints.'

'I already handled these. I'm sorry.'

'Okay, go ahead, I guess.'

She finished opening the envelope, unfolded the page on the desk and turned it so Bosch could read it. There was one typed line at the top of the page.

dot the i humbert humbert

'Humbert Humbert … ,' Bosch said.

'It's the name of a character from literature – or what some people consider literature,' Entrenkin said. '*Lolita*, by Nabokov.'

'Right.'

Bosch noticed that a notation had been written in pencil at the bottom of the page.

#2 – 3/12

'That was probably Howard's marking,' Entrenkin said. 'Or someone in his office.'

She opened the next envelope, the more recently mailed of the two, and unfolded the letter. Bosch leaned over again.

license plates prove his innocense

'Looks to me like they're obviously from the same person,' Entrenkin said. 'Also, notice that *innocence* is spelled wrong.'

'Right.'

There was also a pencil notation at the bottom of the page.

#3 – 4/5

Bosch pulled his briefcase up onto his lap and opened it. He took out the evidence envelope that contained the letter Elias had been carrying in his inside suit pocket when gunned down.

'Elias was carrying this when he … when he got on Angels Flight. I forgot that the crime scene people gave it to me. It might be good if you are here observing when I open it. It's got the same postmark as those two. It was mailed to him Wednesday. This one I want to preserve for prints.'

He took a pair of rubber gloves out of the cardboard dispenser in his case and put them on. He then carefully removed the letter and opened it. He unfolded a piece of paper similar to the first two. Again there was one line typed on the page.

he knows you know

As Bosch stared at the page he felt the slight flutter in his heart that he knew came with the surge of adrenaline.

'Detective Bosch, what does this mean?'

'I don't know. But I sure wish I had opened it sooner.'

There was no pencil notation on the bottom of the third page. Elias hadn't gotten around to it, apparently.

'It looks like we're missing one,' Bosch said. 'These are marked two and three and this one came after – this one would be four.'

'I know. But I haven't found anything that would be number one. Nothing in the files. Maybe he threw it out, not realizing it meant something until the second one came.'

'Maybe.'

He thought about the letters for a moment. He was mostly going on instinct and premonition, but he felt the charge sustaining in his blood. He felt he had found his focus. This exhilarated him but at the same time he also felt a bit foolish at having unknowingly carried such a potentially key piece of the case around in his briefcase now for about twelve hours.

'Did Howard ever talk to you about this case?' he asked.

'No, we never talked about each other's work,' Entrenkin said. 'We had a rule. You see, we knew that what we were doing was ... something that wouldn't be understood – the inspector general with one of the department's most vocal and well-known critics.'

'Not to mention him being married and all.'

Her face turned hard.

'Look, what is wrong with you? One minute we're getting along fine and maybe making some progress on this and the next you just want to antagonize me.'

'What's wrong is that I wish you would save the we-knew-it-was-wrong sermon for somebody else. I find it hard to believe you two didn't talk about the LAPD when you were alone up in that apartment.'

Bosch saw pure fire in her eyes.

'Well, I don't give a good goddamn what you find hard to believe, Detective.'

'Look, we made our deal. I'm not going to tell anyone. If I make trouble for you, you can make trouble for me. If I did tell even my partners, you know what they'd say? They'd say I was crazy for not treating you as a suspect. That's what I should be doing but I'm not. I'm flying on pure instinct and that can be scary. So to make up for it I'm looking for any edge or piece of luck or help I can get.'

She was silent a moment before responding.

'I appreciate what you are doing for me, Detective. But I am not lying to you. Howard and I never spoke in detail about his cases or my work with the department. *Never* in detail. The one thing I remember him saying about the Harris case is so vague as to defy interpretation. But if you must know what it was, I will tell you. He told me to brace myself because he was going to blow the department and a few of the city's big shots out of the water on this one. I didn't ask him what he meant.'

'And when was that?'

'That was Tuesday night.'

'Thank you, Inspector.'

Bosch got up and walked around a bit. He found himself at the window staring out at Anthony Quinn in shadows. He looked at his watch and saw it was almost six. He was supposed to rendezvous with Edgar and Rider at seven at the Hollywood station.

'You know what this means, don't you?' he asked, without turning back to Entrenkin.

'What does it mean?'

He turned to her.

'That if Elias was on to something and got close to identifying the killer – the real killer – then it wasn't a cop who put him down.'

She thought a moment and said, 'You're only looking at it from one side.'

'What's the other?'

'Say he was about to go to trial and pull the real killer out of his hat. Conclusively. That would put the lie to the police evidence, wouldn't it? So proving Harris innocent would at the same time prove the cops framed him. If the real killer knew Howard was on to him, yes he could have come after him. But say a cop knew that Howard was going to prove that that cop framed Harris, he could have come at him, too.'

Bosch shook his head.

'It's always the cops with you. Maybe the frame was in place before the cops even showed up.'

He shook his head again, more emphatically, as if warding off a thought.

'I don't know what I'm saying. There was no frame. It's too farfetched.'

Entrenkin watched him for a long moment.

'Whatever you say, Detective. Just never say I didn't warn you.'

Bosch ignored her statement. He looked at the boxes on the floor. For the first time he noticed a two-wheeled trolley leaning against the wall near the door. Entrenkin followed his eyes to it.

'I called the security guy and told him we needed to move some boxes. He brought it up.'

Bosch nodded.

'I guess I better get this stuff to my car. Do you still have the search warrant or did Miss Langwiser take it? I need to fill out the receipt.'

'I have it and I've already catalogued the files. You just need to sign it.'

Bosch nodded and walked over to the trolley. He remembered something and turned back to her.

'What about the file we were looking at when you came in this morning? With the photo in it.'

'What about it? It's in the box there.'

'Well, I mean … uh … what do you think?'

'I don't know what to think about it. If you're asking me if I believed Howard Elias was involved with that woman I would say no.'

'We asked his wife today if it was possible he was having an affair and she said no, it was not possible.'

'I get your point. But I still think it's impossible. Howard was a well-known man in this city. First of all, he would hardly have to pay for sex. And secondly, he was smart enough to know that he would be vulnerable to extortion from these people if they recognized him.'

'Then what was the file doing in his desk?'

'Like I said, I don't know. It had to be part of a case but I don't know which one. I looked at every file in the office today and didn't find anything that connects to it.'

Bosch just nodded. His mind was already off the file and back on the mystery letters, the last one in particular. His take on it was that it was a warning to Elias. Someone had discovered that the lawyer was in possession of a dangerous piece of information. Bosch was feeling more certain that the investigation, the true investigation, should stem from that note.

'Do you mind if I put on the television now?' Entrenkin said. 'It's six. I want to watch the news.'

Bosch came out of his reverie.

'Sure. Turn it on.'

She moved to a large oak cabinet against the wall opposite the desk and opened the doors. Inside the cabinet were two shelves, each containing a television. Elias apparently liked to watch more than one TV at a time. Probably, Bosch guessed, so he had a better chance of catching all his appearances on newscasts.

Entrenkin hit the power on both sets. As the picture came into focus on the top set, Bosch saw a reporter standing in front of a strip shopping center in which three or four stores were ablaze. Several yards behind the reporter, firefighters worked to contain the blaze but it looked to Bosch as though the buildings were beyond being saved. They were already gutted.

'It's happening,' he said.

'Not again,' Entrenkin said, her voice a scared plea.

18

Bosch turned on KFWB on the car radio while driving into Hollywood. The radio reports were more conservative than the TV news at six. This was because the radio report contained only words, not images.

The bottom-line news was that there was a fire in a strip mall on Normandie, just a few blocks from the intersection of Florence, the intersection that was the flashpoint of the 1992 riots. At that moment it was the only fire burning in South L.A. and there was not yet any confirmation that the fire was an arson linked to protest or anger over the murder of Howard Elias. But every news channel that Bosch and Entrenkin had checked in the office was broadcasting from the mall. Flames filled the screens and the image projected was clear: Los Angeles was burning once again.

'Fucking TV,' he said. 'Excuse my language.'

'What about TV?'

It was Carla Entrenkin. She had talked her way into being taken along for the interview with Harris. Bosch hadn't put up much of a protest. He knew she might help put Harris at ease, if he knew who she was. Bosch knew it was important that Harris be willing to talk to them. He might be the only one to whom Howard Elias had confided the identity of Stacey Kincaid's murderer.

'Overreacting as usual,' Bosch said. 'One fire and they're all there, showing the flames. You know what that does? That's like throwing gasoline on it. It will spread now. People will see that in their living rooms and go outside to see what is happening. Groups will form, things will be said and people won't be able to back down from their anger. One thing will lead to another and we'll have our media-manufactured riot.'

'I give the people a little more credit than that,' Entrenkin responded. 'They know not to trust the TV. Civil unrest occurs when the feelings of overwhelming powerlessness hit critical mass. It has nothing to do with television. It has to do with society not addressing the essential needs of overlooked people.'

Bosch noted that she called it civil unrest instead of rioting. He wondered if calling a riot a riot had become politically incorrect.

'It's about hope, Detective,' she continued. 'Most of the people in the minority communities of Los Angeles have no power, have no money, have no voice. They subsist on hope for these things. And Howard Elias was hope for many of them. A symbol of hope for a day when things will be equal, when their voice will be heard. Of a day when they need not fear the police officers in their community. When you take hope away it leaves a void. Some people fill that up with anger and with violence. To simply blame it on the media is wrong. It's much deeper than that.'

Bosch nodded.

'I understand,' he said. 'At least I think I do. But all I'm saying is the media don't help any by exaggerating things.'

Entrenkin now nodded to his point.

'Somebody once called the media the merchants of chaos.'

'Yeah, well, they got that right.'

'It was Spiro Agnew. Right before he resigned.'

Bosch had no answer for that and decided to drop the conversation. He got his cell phone out of the charger on the floor between the seats and called his home. There was no answer except for the machine and he left a message asking Eleanor to call him. He tried not to show outwardly that he was upset. He called information and got the number for the Hollywood Park poker room again. He called the number, asked for Jardine, the security man, and he was transferred through.

'This is Jardine.'

'This is Detective Bosch from last night. I—'

'She never showed up, pal. At least not on my wa—'

'You can save it, *pal*. She told me that you and she go back to the Flamingo. I understand what you did and it's cool. But I know she's back there now and I want you to give her a message. Tell her to call me on my cell phone as soon as she takes a break. Tell her it's an emergency. You got that, Mister Jardine?'

Bosch stressed the word *mister* so that maybe Jardine would realize he was making a mistake screwing with the LAPD.

'Yeah,' Jardine said. 'I got it.'

'Good.'

Bosch clicked off.

'You know what I remember most about ninety-two?' Entrenkin said. 'One image. A photo that was in the *Times*. The caption was something like "Father and Son Looters" and the picture showed a man leading his four- or five-year-old son out of the smashed-in door of a K-mart or something. And you know what each one was carrying, what they had looted?'

'What?'

'Each one had taken one of those Thigh-Master things. You know, that ridiculous exercise contraption that some television star from the eighties sold late at night on TV.'

Bosch shook his head at the inanity of her image.

'They saw it on TV and so they thought it was valuable,' he said. 'Like Howard Elias.'

She didn't respond and he realized he had been out of line, even if he believed there was something valid in what he had said.

'Sorry ...'

They drove in silence for a few minutes before Bosch spoke again.

'You know what my image is of ninety-two?'

'What?'

'I was assigned to Hollywood Boulevard. And, as you know, we weren't really supposed to do anything unless we saw people in danger of physical harm. Essentially, this meant that if the looters were orderly about it, we basically weren't going to stop them. It made no – anyway, I was on the Boulevard and I remember a lot of weird things. The Scientologists surrounding their buildings, standing practically shoulder to shoulder and carrying broomsticks, ready to make a stand if needed. The guy who ran the Army surplus store near Highland was in full combat infantry dress and carrying a sniper rifle over his shoulder. He was marching back and forth in front of his store like he was at the gate at Benning ... People get crazy, the good and the bad. It's day of the locusts.'

'Well, aren't you the well-read detective, Detective Bosch.'

'Not really. I once lived with a woman who taught junior lit at Grant High in the Valley. It was one of the books she taught. I read it then. Anyway, the image that sticks with me from ninety-two is Frederick's of Hollywood.'

'The lingerie place?'

Bosch nodded.

'I pulled up there and the place was swarming. Multiracial, multiage, people who had just lost it. They cleaned that place out in about fifteen minutes. I mean, everything. When they were done I walked in there and there was nothing left. They even stole the manikins. Absolutely nothing but the hangers left on the floor and the chrome display racks ... and the thing is, all it had been was *underwear*. Four cops get off for beating the shit out of Rodney King on video and people respond by going nuts and stealing underwear. It was so surreal that that's what comes into my head when people bring up the riots. I remember walking around in that empty store.'

'It didn't matter what they took. They were acting out frustrations. It's like the Thigh-Masters. That father and son didn't care what they took. The important thing was that they took something, that in some way they made a statement. They had no use for those things but by taking them they were showing The Man. That's the lesson the father taught his son.'

'It still doesn't make—'

Bosch's phone rang and he opened it. It was Eleanor. 'You winning?' he asked.

He said it with a happy inflection and then immediately realized he had said it in such a way so that his passenger might not surmise what was really going on with his marriage. At once he felt embarrassed and guilty that he would even let what Entrenkin thought or interpreted enter into his relationship with Eleanor.

'Not yet. I just got here.'

'Eleanor, I want you to go home.'

'Harry, we're not going to talk about this now. I—'

'No, I'm not talking about all of that. I think the city … have you watched the news?'

'No. I've been coming here.'

'Well, it doesn't look good. The media's lighting the match, Eleanor. And if something happens and the city goes, you're not in a good place to be.'

Bosch took a furtive glance at Entrenkin. He knew he was acting out white paranoia in front of her. Hollywood Park was in Inglewood, a primarily black community. He wanted Eleanor back at their home in the hills where it was safe.

'Harry, I think you're being paranoid. I'll be fine.'

'Eleanor, why take the—'

'Harry, I have to go. They're holding my chair. I'll call you later.'

She hung up then and Bosch said good-bye to a dead line. He dropped the phone onto his lap.

'For what it's worth,' Entrenkin said, 'I think you're being paranoid.'

'That's what she said.'

'I'll tell you right now there are as many blacks as whites, maybe even more, who don't want to see it happen again. Give them the benefit of the doubt, Detective.'

'I guess I don't have a choice.'

The Hollywood Station seemed deserted when Bosch and Entrenkin arrived. There were no patrol cars in the rear lot and when they came through the back door the rear hallway, usually abuzz with activity, was empty. Bosch stuck his head through the open door of the watch office and saw a lone sergeant at a desk. A television mounted on the wall was on. There were no flames on the screen. It showed a news anchor in a studio. The graphic hanging over his shoulder was a photo of Howard Elias. The volume was too low for Bosch to hear what was being said.

'How we doing?' Bosch said to the sergeant.

'Hanging in. For now.'

Bosch knocked twice on the door and headed down the hallway to the detective bureau, Entrenkin following. Rider and Edgar were already there. They had rolled the television out of the lieutenant's office and were watching the same news report. They saw Bosch and Entrenkin and the surprise registered on their faces.

Bosch introduced Entrenkin to Edgar, who had not been in Elias's office that morning. He then asked what the latest news was.

'The city's holding tight, it looks like,' Edgar said. 'Couple fires and that's it. Meantime, they're pretty much making Elias into Saint Howard. Not much said about what an opportunistic asshole he was.'

Bosch glanced at Entrenkin. She showed nothing.

'Well, let's turn it off,' he said. 'We have to talk.'

Bosch brought his partners up to date and showed them the three anonymous notes that had been mailed to Elias. He explained Entrenkin's presence and said he wanted to try to get Harris's cooperation and at the same time eliminate him as a potential suspect in the killings.

'Do we even know where Harris is?' Edgar asked. 'He hasn't shown up on TV that I've seen. Maybe he doesn't even know about Elias.'

'Well, we'll find out. His current address and phone number were in Elias's files. Looks like Elias was putting him up, probably trying to keep him out of trouble before the trial. He's close by – if he's home.'

Bosch got out his notebook and got the phone number. He went to his desk and called it. A man answered.

'Can I speak to Harry?' Bosch said good-naturedly.

'No Harry here, man.'

The phone was hung up.

'Well, somebody's home,' Bosch said to the others. 'Let's go.'

They drove in one car. Harris currently lived in an apartment on Beverly Boulevard near the CBS complex. Elias had put him into a large complex that wasn't luxurious but was more than nice. And downtown was a straight shot down Beverly.

There was a security door but Harris's name was not on the list of occupants next to the door phone. Bosch had the apartment number but this did not mean anything. The phone codes following occupants' names did not correspond with apartment numbers for security reasons. Bosch called the code number for the building's manager but got no answer.

'Look at this,' Rider said.

She pointed to a listing for E. Howard. Bosch shook his shoulders as if to say it was worth a try and punched in the number. A male voice answered and Bosch thought it was the same voice that had answered his earlier call from the station.

'Michael Harris?'

'Who is it?'

'LAPD. We need to ask you some questions. I—'

'No fucking way. Not without my lawyer here, you don't.'

He hung up. Bosch immediately called back.

'What the fuck you want?'

'In case you don't know it yet, your lawyer is dead. That's why we are here. Now, listen and don't hang up. I have Inspector General Carla Entrenkin here with me. You know who she is? She's going to make sure you are treated well. We just need to—'

'She the watchdog lady, 'sposed to tell when the LAPD is runnin' roughshod?'

'That's her. Hold on.'

Bosch stepped to the side and handed the phone to Entrenkin.

'Tell him he's safe.'

She took the phone, giving Bosch a look that said she now realized why he allowed her to come along. She spoke into the phone while looking at him.

'Michael, this is Carla Entrenkin. You don't have to worry. No one is here to harm you. We need to ask you about Howard Elias, that is all.'

If Harris said anything to her Bosch didn't hear it. The door lock buzzed and Edgar pulled it open. Entrenkin hung up the phone and they all went in.

'The guy's a mutt,' Edgar said. 'I don't know why we're treating him like a saint.'

Entrenkin gave Edgar her look then.

'Yes, you do, Detective Edgar.'

Edgar was sufficiently cowed by her tone.

When Harris opened the door of his fourth-floor apartment he was holding a gun at his side.

'A'right, this is my home,' he announced. 'I don't

mean to be threatenin' anybody but I need this for my pers'nal comfort and protection. Otherwise, you ain't comin' in the place, know what I mean?'

Bosch looked at the others, got no read, and looked back at Harris. He tried to contain his fury. Despite what Entrenkin had told him earlier, he still had little doubt that Harris was the murderer of a child. But he knew that what was important at the moment was the current investigation. He had to put his enmity for the man aside in order to extract whatever information he had.

'All right,' he said. 'But you keep that weapon low and at your side. You point it at one of us and we're going to have a big problem. We understand each other?'

'Oh, we understand.'

Harris backed away from the door and let them in by pointing the weapon toward the living room.

'Remember, keep that thing down,' Bosch said sternly.

Harris dropped the gun to his side and they all entered. The apartment was furnished with rental stuff – puffy couch and matching chairs in light blue, cheap faux wood tables and shelves. Pastoral prints were on the walls. There was a cabinet with a television in it. The news was on.

'Have a seat, ladies and gentlemen.'

Harris took one of the big chairs, slumping in it so that the back rose above his head, giving him the appearance of sitting on a throne. Bosch stepped over and turned the television off, then introduced everybody and showed his badge.

'It figure the white man in charge,' Harris said.

Bosch ignored it.

'I take it you know that Howard Elias was murdered last night?' he asked.

''Course I know. Been sittin' here watchin' it all got-damned day.'

'Then why'd you say you wouldn't talk to us without your lawyer if you knew your lawyer was dead?'

'I got more than one lawyer, dumbshit. I also got a crim'nal lawyer and I got a entertainment lawyer. I got lawyers, don't worry. And I'll get another to take Howie's place. I'm gonna need 'em, man, 'specially after they start cuttin' up in South Central. I'mma have my own riot like Rodney. That'll put me on top.'

Bosch could barely follow Harris's line of thought but he understood enough to know Harris was on a power trip at his own community's expense.

'Well, let's talk about your late lawyer, Howard Elias. When was the last time you saw him?'

'Last night, but you already know that, right Chet?'

'Till when?'

'Till we walked out the muthafuckin' door. Are you throwin' down on me, man?'

'What?'

'You in-ter-OH-gating me, man?'

'I'm trying to find out who killed Elias.'

'You did that. You people got him.'

'Well, that's a possibility. That's what we're trying to find out.'

Harris laughed as if what Bosch had said was absurd.

'Yeah, you know that thing they say about the kettle and the pot, that's what that is.'

'We'll see. When did you two part company? You and Howard Elias.'

'When he went to his apartment and I went home.'

'Which was when?'

'I don't know, Chet. Quarter to eleven, eleven a'clock. I don't wear a watch. People tell me the time when I want to know it. They say on the news he got his ass shot at eleven, so we left quarter of.'

'Had he mentioned any threats? Was he afraid of anyone?'

'He wasn't afraida shit. But he knew he was a dead man.'

'What do you mean?'

'You people is what I mean. He knew you would come gunnin' for him someday. Somebody finally did. Prob'ly come for me, too, one day. Tha's why as soon as I get my money I'm splittin' this place. All you cops can have it. And that's all I got to say, Chet.'

'Why do you call me that?'

'Because that's what you are. You're a Chet, Chet.'

Harris's smile was a challenge. Bosch held his gaze for a moment, then turned to Entrenkin and nodded. She took it from there.

'Michael, do you know who I am?'

'Sure, I seen ya on the TV. Just like Mr Elias. I know you.'

'Then you know I am not a police officer. My job is to make sure the police officers in this city are honest and do their jobs the way they should be done.'

Harris snickered.

'You got a lot a work 'head you, lady.'

'I know that, Michael. But the reason I am here is to tell you that I think these three detectives want to do what is right. They want to find the person who killed Howard Elias, whether it is a cop or not. And I want to help them. You should want to help as well. You owe Howard that much. So will you please answer a few more questions?'

Harris looked around the room and at the gun in his hand. It was a Smith & Wesson 9 millimeter with a satin finish. Bosch wondered if Harris would have brandished it in front of them if he knew the murder weapon was a nine. Harris shoved the weapon into the crack between the seat cushion and the arm of the big chair.

'Okay, I guess. But not Chet. I don' talk to white cops or Tom boys. You ask me.'

Entrenkin looked back at Bosch and then back to Harris.

'Michael, I want the detectives to ask the questions.

They are better at it than me. But I think it's okay for you to answer.'

Harris shook his head.

'You don't unnerstand, lady. Why should I help these fuckers? These people tortured me for no fucking reason. I ain't got forty percent of my hearing because of the L-A-P-D. I ain't *cop*-erating. Now if you got a question, then *you* ask it.'

'Okay, Michael, that's fine,' Carla said. Tell me about last night. What did you and Howard work on?'

'We worked on my testimony. Only you know how the cops call it testi-*lying* on account they never tell the damn truth when it comes to the brothers? Well, I call it my testi-*money* cause the LAPD is going to pay my ass for framin' me and then fuckin' with me. Damn right.'

Bosch picked up the questioning as though Harris had never said he wouldn't speak to him. 'Did Howard tell you that?'

'Sure did, Mr Chet.'

'Did he say he could prove it was a frame?'

'Yeah, 'cause he knew who really done the murder a that little white girl and then put her in the lot near my place. An' it wudn't me. He was goin' to court Monday to start to zonerate me completely and get my money, my man Howard.'

Bosch waited a beat. The next question and answer would be crucial.

'Who?'

'Who what?'

'Who really did the murder? Did he tell you?'

'Nope. He said I didn't need to know. Said it was dangerous to know that shit. But I bet it's in there in his files. He ain't gonna get away again.'

Bosch glanced at Entrenkin.

'Michael, I spent all day with the files. Yes, there are indications that Howard knew who killed Stacey Kincaid but no name was recorded anywhere. Are you sure he never told you a name or gave you any indication of who this person was?'

Harris was momentarily nonplussed. He evidently realized that if Elias went down with the murderer's name kept to himself, his case might have gone down a few notches as well. He would always carry the stigma of being a murderer who got off because a slick defense lawyer knew how to play a jury.

'Goddamn,' he said.

Bosch came over and sat on the corner of the coffee table, so that he could be close to Harris.

'Think hard,' he said. 'You spent a lot of time with him. Who would it be?'

'I don't know,' Harris said defensively. 'Whyn't you ask Pelfry about it, man?'

'Who is Pelfry?'

'Pelfry's his leg man. His investigator.'

'You know his whole name?'

'I think it's somethin' like Jenks or somethin'.'

'Jenks?'

'Yeah, Jenks. Tha's what Howard call him.'

Bosch felt a finger poke his shoulder and he turned to see Entrenkin give him a look. She knew who Pelfry was. He could let it go. Bosch stood up and looked down at Harris.

'You came back here last night after you left Elias?'

'Yeah, sure. Why?'

'Anybody with you? You call anybody?'

'What the fuck is this? You're throwin' down on me, man.'

'It's routine. Relax. We ask everybody where they've been. Where were you?'

'I was here, man. I was beat. I came home and got in my bed. Ain't nobody with me.'

'Okay. Mind if I have a look at your pistola for a second?'

'Jesus Christ, I shoulda known you people weren't on the level. Got-damn.'

He pulled the gun out from the side of the chair cushion and handed it to Bosch. Bosch kept his eyes on Harris's until the gun was safely in his hand. He then studied the weapon and smelled the barrel. He smelled no oil or burned gunpowder. He ejected the cartridge and thumbed out the top bullet. It was a Federal, full metal jacket. A very popular brand and make of ammunition, Bosch knew, and possibly the same brand used in the Angels Flight murders. They wouldn't know until the autopsies. He looked back down at Harris.

'You're a convicted felon, Mr Harris. You realize it is a crime for you to have this weapon?'

'Not in my house, man. I need protection.'

'Anywhere, I'm afraid. This could send you back to prison.'

Harris smiled at him. Bosch could see one of his incisors was gold with a star etched on the front.

'Then take me away, man.'

He raised his arms, offering his wrists for the handcuffs.

'Take me away and watch this muthafuckin' place burn, baby, burn.'

'No. Actually I was thinking of cuttin' you a break, seeing how you've been so helpful tonight. But I'm going to have to keep the weapon. I'd be committing a crime if I left it here with you.'

'Be my guess, Chet. I can always get what I need from my car. Know what I mean?'

He said *Chet* the way some white people say the word *nigger*.

'Sure. I know what you mean.'

They waited for the elevator in silence. Once they were inside and descending Entrenkin spoke.

'Does that gun match?'

'It's the same kind. Ammo might be the same. We'll have the lab check it, but I sort of doubt he would have kept it around if he killed Elias with it. He's not that stupid.'

'What about his car? He said he could get anything from his car.'

'He didn't mean his car car. He meant his crew. His people. Together they're a car, driving somewhere together. It's a saying that comes from county lockup. Eight people to a cell. They call them cars. What about Pelfry? You know him?'

'Jenkins Pelfry. He's a PI. An independent. I think he's got an office over in the Union Law Center in downtown. A lot of the civil rights lawyers use him. Howard was using him on this.'

'We have to talk to him then. Thanks for telling us.'

There was annoyance in Bosch's voice. He looked at his watch. He figured it was too late to try to run down Pelfry.

'Look, it's in the files I gave you,' Entrenkin protested. 'You didn't ask me about it. How was I to know to tell you?'

'You're right. You didn't know.'

'If you want, I could put a call—'

'No, that's okay. We've got it from here, Inspector. Thanks for your help with Harris. We probably wouldn't have gotten up there to see him without you along.'

'You think he had anything to do with the murders?'

'I'm not thinking anything yet.'

'I seriously doubt he's involved.'

Bosch just looked at her, hoping his eyes conveyed that he believed she was treading into areas where she had neither expertise nor a mandate to be.

'We'll give you a ride back,' he said. 'Your car at the Bradbury?'

She nodded. They were crossing the lobby to the doors.

'Detective, I want to be kept apprised of the case and any significant developments.'

'Fine. I'll talk to Chief Irving in the morning and see how he wants to do that. He might prefer to keep you informed himself.'

'I don't want the whitewashed version. I want to hear it from you.'

'Whitewashed? You think that whatever I tell you won't be *white*washed? I'm flattered, Inspector.'

'A poor choice of words. But my point being I would rather hear it from you than after it has been processed by the department's management.'

Bosch looked at her as he held the door.

'I'll remember that.'

19

Kiz Rider had run the telephone number from the Mistress Regina web page through the criss-cross directory contained on a CD-ROM in the squad room computer. The phone was assigned to an address on North Kings Road in West Hollywood. This did not mean that the address would be where they would find the woman, however. Most prostitutes, late-night masseuses and so-called exotic entertainers used elaborate call-forwarding systems to make it hard for law enforcement agencies to find them.

Bosch, Rider and Edgar pulled to the curb at the intersection of Melrose and Kings and Bosch used his phone to call the number. A woman answered after four rings. Bosch went into his act.

'Mistress Regina?'

'Yes, who is this?'

'My name is Harry. I was wondering if you were available tonight?'

'Have we had a session before?'

'No. I saw your web page and thought ...'

'Thought what?'

'I thought I might want to try a session.'

'How advanced are you?'

'I don't under—'

'What are you into?'

'I'm not sure yet. I'd like to try it out.'

'You know there is no sex, right? No physical contact. I play mind games with people. Nothing illegal.'

'I understand.'

'Do you have a secure phone number that I can call you back at?'

'What do you mean secure?'

'I mean no pay phones!' she said harshly. 'You have to give me a real number.'

Bosch gave her his cell phone number.

'Okay. I'll call you back in one minute. Be there.'

'I will.'

'I will ask for three-six-seven. That is you. You are not a person to me. You do not have a name. You are simply a number.'

'Three-six-seven. I understand.'

He closed the phone and looked at his partners.

'We'll know if it worked in about a minute.'

'You sounded nice and subservient, Harry,' Rider said.

'Thank you. I try my best.'

'You sounded like a cop to me,' Edgar said.

'We'll see.'

Bosch turned the car on, just to be doing something. Rider yawned and then he had to. Then Edgar joined in.

The phone rang. It was Mistress Regina. She asked for him by number.

'You can come to me in one hour. I require a donation of two hundred dollars for a one-hour session. Cash only and in advance. Is that understood?'

'Yes.'

'Yes what?'

'Uh, yes, Mistress Regina.'

'That's very good.'

Bosch looked over at Rider, who was in the front passenger seat, and winked. She smiled back at him.

Regina gave the address and apartment number. Bosch turned the overhead light on and looked over at Rider's notes. The address he had just been given was the same one Rider had but the apartment number was different. He told Regina he would be there and they ended the call.

'It's a go. But not for an hour. She uses a different apartment in the same building.'

'We gonna wait?' Edgar asked.

'Nope. I want to get home and get some sleep.'

Bosch turned the car onto Kings Road and cruised a half block up until they found the address. It was a small apartment building made of wood and stucco. There was no parking anywhere so he pulled into a red zone in front of a fireplug and they got out. He didn't really care if Regina had a front apartment and saw the slickback. They weren't coming to make an arrest. All they wanted was information.

Apartments six and seven were in the back of the building anyway. Their doors were side by side. Bosch guessed the woman who called herself Mistress Regina lived in one apartment and worked in the other. They knocked on the work door.

And got no answer.

Edgar hit the door again, harder, and this time kicked it a couple times as well. Finally, a voice was heard from the other side.

'What is it?'

'Open up. Police.'

Nothing.

'Come on, Regina, we need to ask you some questions. That's all. Open the door or we'll have to break the lock. Then what are you gonna do?'

It was a baseless threat. Bosch knew he had no legal power to do anything if she didn't want to open her door.

Finally, Bosch heard the locks turning and the door opened to reveal the angry face of the woman Bosch recognized from the photo print he had found in Howard Elias's office.

'What do you want? Let me see some ID.'

Bosch badged her.

'Can we come in?'

'You're LAPD? This is West Hollywood, Mister. You're off your turf.'

She pushed the door closed but Edgar reached a strong arm up and stopped it. He pushed it all the way back open and stepped in, a mean look on his face.

'Don't you be closing the door on my face, Mistress Regina.'

Edgar said her name in a tone that indicated that he was subservient to no one. Regina stepped back to allow him space to enter. Bosch and Rider followed him in. They stepped into a dimly lit landing with stairs going up and down from it. Bosch looked down the stairs to his left and saw they retreated into complete darkness. The stairs going up led to a lighted room. He moved to them and started up.

'Hey, you can't just barge in here like this,' Regina said, but the protest was leaving her voice. 'You need a warrant.'

'We don't need anything, Mistress Regina, you invited us in. I'm Harry – or make that three-six-seven. We just talked on the phone, remember?'

She followed them up the stairs. Bosch turned and got his first full look at her. She was wearing a sheer black robe over a leather corset and black silk underwear. She wore black stockings and spike-heeled shoes. Her makeup consisted of dark eye liner and glaring red lipstick. It was a sad caricature of a depressing male fantasy.

'Been a long time since Halloween,' Bosch said. 'Who are you supposed to be?'

Regina ignored the question.

'What are you doing here?'

'We have questions. Sit down. I want to show you a picture.'

Bosch pointed to a black leather couch and the woman reluctantly went to it and sat down. He put his briefcase down on the coffee table and opened it. He nodded slightly to Edgar and started looking for the photo of Elias.

'Hey, where's he going?' Regina cried.

Edgar had moved to another set of stairs that led up to a loft.

'He's insuring our safety by making sure you don't have anybody hiding in the closet,' Bosch said. 'Now take a look at this picture, please.'

He slid the photo across the table and she looked at it without touching it.

'Recognize him?'

'What is this?'

'Do you recognize him?'

'Of course.'

'He a client?'

'Look, I don't have to tell you a fucking thing about—'

'IS HE A CLIENT?' Bosch yelled, silencing her.

Edgar came down from the loft and moved across the living room. He glanced into the alcove kitchen, saw nothing that interested him and went down the stairs to the landing. Bosch then heard his steps on the lower staircase as he descended into the darkness below.

'No, he isn't a client, okay? Now, will you please leave?'

'If he isn't a client then how do you recognize him?'

'What are you talking about? Haven't you been watching TV today?'

'Who is he?'

'He's that guy, the one that got killed on—'

'Harry?'

It was Edgar from below.

'What?'

'I think you ought to come down here a sec.'

Bosch turned to Rider and nodded.

'Take over, Kiz. Talk to her.'

Bosch went down the steps and made the turn in the landing. There was now a glowing red light emanating from the room below. As he came down Bosch saw Edgar was wide-eyed.

'What is it?'

'Check this out.'

As they crossed the room Bosch saw that it was a bedroom. One wall was completely mirrored. Against the opposite wall was a raised hospital-style bed with what looked like plastic sheets and restraints buckled across it. Next to it was a chair and a floor lamp with a red bulb in it.

Edgar led him into a walk-in closet. Another red bulb glowed from the ceiling. There was nothing hanging on the clothes rods running down either side of the closet. But a naked man stood spread-eagled on one side of the closet, his arms up and wrists handcuffed to the clothing rod. The cuffs were gold-plated and had ornate designs on them. The man was blindfolded and had a red ball gag in his mouth. There were red welts caused by fingernail scratches running down his chest. And between his legs a full liter bottle of Coke dangled at the end of a leather strap that was tied in a slipknot around the head of his penis.

'Jesus,' Bosch whispered.

'I asked him if he needed help and he shook his head no. I think he's her customer.'

'Take the gag out.'

Bosch pulled the blindfold up on the man's forehead while Edgar pulled out the gag. The man immediately jerked his face to the right and tried to turn away. He moved his arm and tried to use it to block the view of his face, but his cuffed wrist prevented him from hiding. The man was in his mid-thirties with a good build. It seemed as though he could certainly defend himself against the woman upstairs. If he wanted to.

'Please,' he said in a desperate voice. 'Leave me alone. I'm fine. Just leave me alone.'

'We're the police,' Bosch said. 'Are you sure?'

'Of course, I'm sure. You think if I needed help I

wouldn't ask for it? I don't need you here. This is completely consensual and nonsexual. Just leave us alone.'

'Harry,' Edgar said, 'I think we ought to just step the fuck back out of here and forget we ever saw this guy.'

Bosch nodded and they stepped out of the closet. He looked around the room and saw that the chair had clothes draped over it. He went to them and checked the pockets of the pants. He pulled out the wallet and walked to the floor lamp, where he opened it and studied the driver's license in the red glow. He felt Edgar come up behind him and look over his shoulder.

'Recognize the name?'

'No, do you?'

Bosch shook his head and closed the wallet. He walked back and returned it to the pocket of the pants.

Rider and Regina were silent as they came back up the steps. Bosch studied Regina and thought he saw a look of pride and a slight smile on her face. She knew that what they had seen down there had shocked them. He glanced at Rider and saw that she, too, had registered the looks on their faces.

'Everything okay?' she asked.

'Everything's fine,' he said.

'What is it?'

Bosch ignored the question and looked at the other woman.

'Where are the keys?'

She put a little pout on her face and reached into her bra. Her hand came out with the tiny cuff key and she held it out to him. Bosch took it and handed it to Edgar.

'Go down and cut him loose. If he wants to stay after that, that's his business.'

'Harry, he said he—'

'I don't care what he said. I said cut him loose. We aren't going to leave here with some guy in shackles down there.'

Edgar went down the stairs while Bosch stared at Regina.

'That's what you get two hundred dollars an hour for?'

'Believe me, they get their money's worth. And, you know, they all come back for more. Hmm, I wonder what it is about men? Maybe you should try me sometime, Detective. Might be kind of fun.'

Bosch stared a long time before breaking away and looking at Rider.

'What've you got, Kiz?'

'Her real name is Virginia Lampley. She says she knows Elias from TV, not as a client. But she says Elias's investigator was here a few weeks ago, asking questions just like us.'

'Pelfry? What did he ask?'

'A bunch of bullshit,' Regina said before Rider could answer. 'He wanted to know if I knew anything about that little girl that was murdered last year. The daughter of the car czar from TV. I told him I didn't know why the hell he was asking me about that. What would I know about it? He tried to get rough but I got rough right back. I don't let men fuck with me. He left. I think somebody put you on the same wild goose chase he was on.'

'Maybe,' Bosch said.

There was silence for a moment. Bosch was distracted by what he had seen in the closet. He couldn't think of what else to ask.

'He's staying.'

It was Edgar. He came up the stairs and handed the cuff key back to Regina. She took it and made a big production out of returning it to her bra, looking at Bosch all the while.

'All right, let's go,' Bosch said.

'Are you sure you don't want to stay for a Coke, Detective?' Virginia Lampley asked, a clever smile on her face.

'We're going,' Bosch said.

They went silently down the steps to the door, Bosch the last in line. On the landing he looked down into the dark room. The glow of the red light was still there and Bosch could see the faint outline of the man sitting on the chair in the corner of the room. His face was in darkness but Bosch could tell the man was looking up at him.

'Don't worry, Detective,' Regina said from behind him. 'I'll take good care of him.'

Bosch turned and looked at her from the door. That smile of hers was back.

20

On the way back to the station Rider repeatedly asked exactly what they had seen in the lower room but neither Bosch nor Edgar told her more than the basic fact that one of Mistress Regina's clients was shackled in the closet. Rider knew there was more to it and kept pressing but she got nowhere.

'The man down there is not important,' Bosch finally said as a means of ending that part of the discussion. 'We still don't know what Elias was doing with her picture and web address. Or for that matter, why he sent Pelfry to her.'

'I think she was lying,' Edgar said. 'She knows the whole story.'

'Maybe,' Bosch said. 'But if she knows the story, why keep it secret now that Elias is dead?'

'Pelfry is the key,' Rider said. 'We should run him down right now.'

'No,' Bosch said. 'Not tonight. It's late and I don't want to talk to Pelfry until we've gone through Elias's files and know what's in them. We master the files, then we brace Pelfry about Mistress Regina and everything else. First thing tomorrow.'

'What about the FBI?' Rider asked.

'We meet the FBI at eight. I'll figure something out by then.'

They drove the rest of the way in silence. Bosch dropped them off at their cars in the Hollywood station parking lot and reminded them to be at Parker Center at eight the following morning. He then parked his slickback but didn't turn in the key because the file cartons from Elias's office were still in the trunk. After locking the car he went to his own car.

He checked the clock as he was pulling out onto Wilcox and saw it was ten-thirty. He knew it was late but he decided to make one last call before going home. As he drove through Laurel Canyon to the Valley, he kept thinking about the man in the walk-in closet and how he had turned his face away, wishing not to be seen. Working homicide for so many years, Bosch could not be surprised anymore by the horrors people inflicted on each other. But the horrors people saved for themselves were a different story.

He took Ventura Boulevard west to Sherman Oaks. It was a busy Saturday night. On the other side of the hill the city could be a tinderbox of tensions but on the main drag in the Valley the bars and coffee shops seemed full. Bosch saw the red-coated valets running to get cars in front of Pinot Bistro and the other upscale restaurants that lined the boulevard. He saw teenagers cruising with the top down. Everyone was oblivious to the seething hatred and anger that churned in other parts of the city – beneath the surface like an undiscovered fault line waiting to open up and swallow all above.

At Kester he turned north and then made a quick turn into a neighborhood of tract houses sandwiched between the boulevard and the Ventura Freeway. The houses were small and with no distinct style. The hiss of the freeway was always present. They were cops' houses except they cost between four and five hundred thousand dollars and few cops could afford them. Bosch's old partner Frankie Sheehan had bought early and bought well. He was sitting on a quarter of a million dollars in equity. His retirement plan, if he made it to retirement.

Bosch pulled to the curb in front of Sheehan's house and left the car running. He got out his phone, looked up Sheehan's number in his phone book, and made the call. Sheehan picked up after two rings, his voice alert. He'd been awake.

'Frankie, it's Harry.'

'My man.'

'I'm out front. Why don't you come out and we'll take a drive.'

'Where to?'

'It doesn't matter.'

Silence.

'Frankie?'

'Okay, give me a couple minutes.'

Bosch put the phone away and reached into his coat pocket for a smoke that wasn't there.

'Damn,' he said.

While he waited he thought about the time he and Sheehan were looking for a drug dealer suspected of having wiped out a rival's operation by going into a rock house with an Uzi and killing everyone in it – six people, customers and dealers alike.

They'd repeatedly pounded on the door of the suspect's apartment but no one answered. They were thinking about their options when Sheehan heard a tiny voice from inside the apartment saying, 'Come in, come in.' They knocked on the door once again and called out that it was the police. They waited and listened. Again the voice called out, 'Come in, come in.'

Bosch tried the knob and it turned. The door was unlocked. Assuming combat stance they entered the apartment only to find it empty – except for a large green parrot in a cage in the living room. And lying right there in full view on a kitchen table was an Uzi submachine gun broken down and ready for cleaning. Bosch walked over to the door and knocked on it once again. The parrot called out, 'Come in, come in.'

A few minutes later, when the suspect returned from the hardware store with the gun oil he needed to finish his work on the Uzi, he was arrested. Ballistics matched the gun to the killings and he was convicted after a judge refused to throw out the fruits of the search. Though the defendant claimed the entry of the apartment was without permission and unlawful, the judge ruled that Bosch and Sheehan were acting in good faith when they acted on the invitation from the parrot. The case was still winding its way through the nation's appellate courts, while the killer remained in jail.

The Jeep's front passenger door opened and Sheehan got into the car.

'When did you get this ride?' he asked.

'When they made me start driving a slickback.'

'Oh, yeah, forgot about that.'

'Yeah, you RHD bigshots don't have to worry about that shit.'

'So, what's up? You got your ass out in the wind on this case, don't you?'

'Yeah, it's out there. How're Margaret and the girls doing?'

'They're all fine. What are we doing? Riding, talking, what?'

'I don't know. Is that Irish place still over on Van Nuys?'

'No, that one's gone. Tell you what, go on up to Oxnard and go right. There's a little sports bar down there.'

Bosch pulled away from the curb and started following the directions.

'I was just thinking about the Polly-wants-an-Uzi case,' he said.

Sheehan laughed.

'That one still cracks me up. I can't believe it's shot the rapids this far. I hear the douche bag's down to one last shot – El Supremo Court.'

'It'll make it. It woulda got shot down by now if it wasn't going to fly – no pun intended.'

'Well, what's it been, eight years? We got our money's worth, even if they do kick him loose.'

'Yeah, six murders, eight years. Sounds fair.'

'Six douche bags.'

'You still like saying douche bag, don't you?'

'Yeah, I'm partial to it. So you didn't come over the hill to talk about parrots and douche bags and old times, did you?'

'No, Frankie. I need to ask you about the Kincaid thing.'

'Why me?'

'Why do you think? You were lead detective.'

'Everything I know is in the files. You should be able to get them. You're lead on Elias.'

'I got 'em. But the files don't always have everything in them.'

Sheehan pointed to a red neon sign and Bosch pulled over. There was a parking place at the curb right outside the bar's door.

'This place is always pretty dead,' Sheehan said. 'Even Saturday nights. I don't know how the guy makes it by. Must be taking numbers or selling weed on the side.'

'Frankie,' Bosch said, 'between you and me, I gotta know about the fingerprints. I don't want to be chasing my tail out there. I mean, I got no reason to doubt you. But I want to know if you heard anything, you know what I mean?'

Sheehan got out of the Cherokee without a word and walked to the door. Bosch watched him go in and then got out himself. Inside, the place was just about empty. Sheehan was sitting at the bar. The bartender was drawing a beer off the tap. Bosch took the stool next to his former partner and said, 'Make it two.'

Bosch took out a twenty and put it on the bar. Sheehan still hadn't looked at him since he had asked the question.

The bartender put down the frosted mugs on napkins that advertised a Superbowl party almost three months before. He took Bosch's twenty and went down to the cash register. In unison Bosch and Sheehan took long pulls on their drinks.

'Ever since O.J.,' Sheehan said.

'What's that?'

'You know what I'm talking about. Ever since the Juice, nothing is solid anymore. No evidence, no cop, nothing. You can take anything you want into a courtroom and there still will be somebody who can tear it to shreds, drop it on the floor and piss on it. Everybody questions everything. Even cops. Even partners.'

Bosch took more of his beer before saying anything.

'I'm sorry, Frankie. I got no reason to doubt you or the prints. It's just that weeding through this Elias stuff, it looks like he was going into court next week with the idea of proving who killed the girl. And he wasn't talking about Harris. Somebody—'

'Who?'

'I don't know. But I'm trying to look at it from his side of things. If he had somebody other than Harris, then how the hell did these prints end up on—'

'Elias was a fucking mutt. And as soon as they get him in the ground I'm gonna go out there one night and do my granddaddy's Irish jig on his grave. Then I'm gonna piss on it and never think about Elias again. All I can say is that it's too fucking bad that Harris wasn't with him on that train. Goddamned murderer. That would have been hitting the quinella, the both of them being put down together.'

Sheehan held his glass up in a toast to Elias's killer and then took a deep swallow. Bosch could almost feel the hate radiating from him.

'So nobody fucked with the scene,' Bosch said. 'The prints are legit.'

'Fucking A legit. The room was sealed by patrol. Nobody went in until I got there. I then watched over everything – we were dealing with the Kincaid family and I knew what that meant. The car czar and heavy contributor to local political coffers. I was on the straight and narrow with everything. The prints were on her schoolbook – a geography book. SID got four fingers on one side and a thumb on the other – as if he had picked the book up by the binding. Those prints were perfect. The guy must've been sweating like a pig when he left 'em because they were grade A perfect.'

He drained his glass and then held it up so the bartender would see he needed a refill.

'I can't believe you can't smoke anymore in a fucking bar in this city,' Sheehan said. 'Fucking douche bags.'

'Yeah.'

'Anyway, we ran everything and Harris pops up. Ex-con, did time for assault, burglary, he's got about as much a legitimate reason for his prints being in her room as I have a chance of winning the lottery – and I don't fucking play. So bingo, we got our man. We go hook him up. Remember, at that time the girl's body hadn't turned up. We were operating on the belief she might still be alive somewhere. We were wrong but we didn't know it at the time. So we hook him up, bring him downtown and put him in the room. Only this motherfucker won't tell us the time of day. Three days and we get nothing. We never even took him to a cell at night. He was in that room seventy-two straight hours. We worked in teams and in shifts and we could not crack his egg. Never gave us jack shit. I tell you what, I'd like to kill the fuck, but I gotta respect him for that. He was the best I ever went against.'

Sheehan took a double gulp from his new beer. Bosch was still only halfway through his first. He was content to let Sheehan talk and tell the story at his own pace without interrupting him with questions.

'On the last day some of the guys lost it a little bit. Did things.'

Bosch closed his eyes. He had been wrong about Sheehan.

'Me, too, Harry.'

He said it matter of factly, as if it felt good to finally say it out loud. He drank more of his beer, turned on his stool and looked about the bar as if seeing it for the first time. There was a TV mounted in a corner. It was tuned to ESPN.

'We're off the record here, right, Harry?'

'Sure.'

Sheehan turned back and leaned toward Bosch in a conspiratorial sort of way.

'What Harris says happened … happened. But that doesn't excuse what he did. He rapes and strangles that little girl; we stick a pencil in his ear. Big fucking deal. He gets off and I'm the new Mark Fuhrman – a racist cop who planted evidence. I just wish somebody could tell me how the fuck I could've planted those prints?'

He was getting loud. Luckily, only the bartender was noticing.

'I know,' Bosch said. 'I'm sorry, man. I shouldn't have asked.'

Sheehan went on as if he hadn't heard Bosch.

'I guess I always carried around a set of throw-down prints that belonged to a douche bag I wanted to send away. I then put them on the book – don't ask me how – and *voilà*, we got our douche bag. Only why would I pick Harris to pin it on? I never knew the mutt or had anything to do with him. And there's nobody on this planet that can prove I did because it's not there to be proved.'

'You're right.'

Sheehan shook his head and looked down into his beer.

'I quit caring about shit when that jury came in and said not guilty. When they said I was guilty … when they believed that man instead of us.'

Bosch remained silent. He knew that Sheehan had to say his piece.

'We're losing the battle, man. I see that now. It's all a game. The fucking lawyers, what they can do to you.

To the evidence. I give up, Harry. I really do. I already decided. It's twenty-five and out for me. I got eight more months and I'm counting the fuckers down. I'm gonna punch out, move on up to Blue Heaven and leave this toilet for all the douche bags.'

'I think that's a good idea, Frankie,' Bosch said quietly.

He couldn't think of what else he could say. He was hurt and stunned by his friend's lapse into a complete state of hate and cynicism. He understood it but was simply surprised by the complete toll it had taken. He was also disappointed in himself and privately embarrassed at how wholeheartedly he had defended Sheehan to Carla Entrenkin.

'I remember on that last day,' Sheehan said. 'I was in there with him. In the room. And I got so fucking angry I just wanted to take my gun out and blow his shit away. But I knew I couldn't. Because he knew where she was. He had the girl!'

Bosch just nodded.

'We had tried everything and got nothing. He broke us before we could break him. It got down to where I was just begging him to tell us. It was embarrassing, Harry.'

'And what did he do?'

'He just stared at me as if I wasn't there. He said nothing. He did nothing. And then … then the anger just came over me like … like I don't know what. Like it was a bone caught in my throat. Like it never had before. There was a trash can in the corner of the room. I went over and pulled the bag out and just pulled it right down over his fucking head. And I grabbed it around his neck and I held it and I held it and …'

Sheehan started crying and trying to finish.

'… and they … they had to pull me off of him.'

He put his elbows on the bar and pressed the heels of his palms into his eyes. For a long time he didn't move.

Bosch saw a drop fall from his chin and into his beer. He reached over and put his hand on his old partner's shoulder.

'It's okay, Frankie.'

Without moving his hands away from his face, Sheehan spoke.

'You see, Harry, I became the very thing that I spent all these years hunting. I wanted to kill him right there and then. I would have if my guys hadn't come in. I'm never going to be able to forget that.'

'It's okay, man.'

Sheehan drank some beer and seemed to recover somewhat.

'After I did what I did, that opened the door. The other guys, they did that thing with the pencil – popped his fucking ear drum. We all became monsters. Like Vietnam, going wild in the villages. We probably would've killed the guy but you know what saved him? The girl. Stacey Kincaid saved him.'

'How's that?'

'They found the body. We got the word and went out to the scene. We left Harris in a cell. Alive. He was lucky the word came when it did.'

He stopped to take another gulp of beer.

'I went out there – just a block from Harris's place. She was pretty much decomposed, the young ones go fast. But I remember how she looked. Like a little angel, her arms out like she was flying ...'

Bosch remembered the pictures from the newspapers. Stacey Kincaid had been a pretty little girl.

'Harry, leave me alone now,' Sheehan said quietly. 'I'm going to walk back.'

'No, let me give you a ride.'

'No thanks. I'm walking.'

'You sure you're all right?'

'I'm fine. Just a little worked up. That's all. This is going to stay between us, right?'

'Till the end, man.'

Sheehan tried a weak smile. But he still didn't look at Bosch.

'Do me one favor, Hieronymus.'

Bosch remembered when they had been a team. They only used their formal names, Hieronymus and Francis, when they were talking seriously and from the heart.

'Sure, Francis. What?'

'When you catch the guy who did Elias, I don't care if it's a cop or not, shake his hand for me. You tell him he's my hero. But tell him he missed a good chance. Tell him he should've gotten Harris, too.'

A half hour later Bosch opened the door to his home. He found his bed empty. But this time he was too tired to stay awake waiting for Eleanor. He started stripping off his clothes and thinking about his plans for the next day. He finally sat down on the bed ready for sleep and reached for the light. The moment he was in darkness, the phone rang.

He turned the light back on and picked up the phone.

'You bastard.'

A woman's voice – familiar, but he couldn't place it.

'Who is this?'

'Carla Entrenkin, who do you think? Do you really think I wouldn't know what you did?'

'I don't know what you're talking about. What happened?'

'I just watched Channel 4. Your buddy Harvey Button.'

'What did he have?'

'Oh, he blew it up real big. Let's see if I can quote him correctly. "A link between Elias and an Internet prostitution ring was found in Elias's office, a source close to the investigation says. It is believed by this source that Elias may have had liaisons with at least one

of the women who advertised her services as a dominatrix on the web site." I think that about sums it up. I
hope you are happy.'

'I didn't—'

'Don't bother.'

She hung up. Bosch sat there a long time thinking
about what she had said.

'Chastain, you asshole,' he said out loud.

He turned out the light again and dropped back on
the bed. He was soon asleep and having the same dream
again. He was riding Angels Flight, going up. Only now
there was a little blonde girl seated across the aisle from
him. She looked at him with sad and empty eyes.

21

Bosch had a surprise waiting for him when he pushed the supply cart stacked with file boxes through the door of Deputy Chief Irving's conference room. It was quarter to eight on Sunday morning. There were six FBI agents already crowded into the room and waiting. The surprise was the lead agent who stepped over to Bosch, his hand out and a smile on his face.

'Harry Bosch,' the man said.

'Roy Lindell,' Bosch replied.

Bosch pushed the cart over to the table and took the man's hand.

'You're on this? What happened to OC?'

'Organized crime was getting boring. Especially after the Tony Aliso case. Hard to top that one, don't you think?'

'Yeah.'

A couple of years earlier they had worked the Aliso murder – the 'Trunk Music' case, according to the local media. Bosch and Lindell had started out as adversaries, but by the time the case was concluded in Las Vegas there was a respect between the two that certainly wasn't shared between the two agencies they worked for. Bosch immediately took Lindell's assignment to the Elias case as a good sign.

'Listen,' Lindell said, 'I think we have a few minutes. You want to grab a cup of coffee and talk about things?'

'Sounds like a plan.'

As they walked down the hall to the elevator they

were met by Chastain, who was heading to the conference room. Bosch introduced Lindell.

'You guys going for coffee? I'll come with you.'

'No, that's okay,' Bosch said. 'We've got some stuff to talk about ... and I don't want it coming out of Harvey Button's mouth on the news later. Know what I mean?'

'I don't know what you're talking about, Bosch.'

Bosch said nothing. Chastain looked at Lindell and then back at Bosch.

'Never mind the coffee,' he said. 'I don't need artificial stimulants, anyway.'

When they were alone at the elevator lobby Bosch warned Lindell about Chastain.

'He's leaking,' he said. 'You see Channel Four last night?'

'The Internet dominatrix thing?'

'Yeah. Six people knew about that. Me, my two partners, Chastain, Carla Entrenkin and Deputy Chief Irving. I can vouch for my partners and I doubt Entrenkin would leak anything negative about Elias. Either Irving or Chastain talked to Harvey Button. My bet is on Chastain. Irving's been trying to put a clamp on things from the start.'

'Well, was the story bullshit or what?'

'Looks that way. We can't make a connection. Whoever leaked it did it to smear Elias, even things up a bit.'

'I'll watch him. But you know sometimes leaks aren't from the obvious source.'

The elevator opened and Lindell stepped on, leaving Bosch standing there thinking about Irving and whether it was possible that he was the leak.

'You coming?' Lindell asked.

Bosch stepped onto the elevator and pushed the button for the third floor.

'You check the news this morning?' Lindell asked. 'How's it going out there?'

'So far so good. A couple fires last night, but that was about it. No looting and it's pretty quiet now. Supposed to be rain coming in by tomorrow. Maybe that will help.'

They went into the cafeteria and took their coffees to a table. Bosch checked his watch and saw it was five before eight. He looked at Lindell.

'So?'

Lindell laughed.

'So what the fuck. We going to divvy this up or what?'

'Yeah. I got a deal for you, Roy. A good deal.'

'Let's hear it.'

'You can have it. I'll step back and let you run the show. I just want one thing. I want my team to run with the original case. Stacey Kincaid. We'll take the original murder book and review everything RHD did on the case. Then we'll take everything Elias did and go from there.'

Lindell's eyes narrowed their focus as he wondered what this meant. Bosch continued.

'It looks like Elias's plan was to go into court this week and try to prove that Michael Harris didn't kill her. He was going to name her killer and—'

'Who?'

'That's the million-dollar question. We don't know. He was keeping it in his head instead of his files. But that's why I want the case. Because if he had a bead on somebody, that somebody's a pretty good suspect for the Angels Flight murders.'

Lindell looked down at his smoking coffee and was quiet a long moment.

'Sounds like lawyer bullshit to me. Grandstanding. How was he gonna find the killer if you guys on the PD didn't? That is, if the killer really wasn't Michael Harris, like every cop and white person in this town believes.'

Bosch hiked his shoulders.

'Even if he was wrong – even if he was going to name somebody as a smoke screen, it could have made him a target.'

He purposely wasn't telling Lindell everything – particularly about the mystery notes. He wanted the FBI agent to think that Bosch's team would be chasing rainbows while he would be commanding the real investigation.

'So you run with that and I chase down bad cops, is that the deal?'

'Pretty much. Chastain should have a head start for you. First of all, he's the most familiar with the Black Warrior thing. He handled the IAD investigation on it. And—'

'Yeah, but he cleared everybody on it.'

'Maybe he messed up. Or maybe he was told to clear everybody.'

Lindell nodded that he understood the suggestion.

'Also, his crew was supposedly going through Elias's files yesterday and making a list. And I just brought in five more boxes of files. From all of that you'll get a list of guys to talk to. I think you're in good shape.'

'If I'm in such great shape why are you giving this side of things to me?'

''Cause I'm a nice guy.'

'Bosch, you're holding out.'

'I just have a hunch, that's all.'

'That what, Harris really was framed?'

'I don't know. But something wasn't right with the case. I want to find out what it was.'

'So meantime I'm stuck with Chastain and his crew.'

'Yup. That's the deal.'

'Well, what am I going to do with them? You just told me Chastain's a leak.'

'Send them out for coffee and then run away and hide.'

Lindell laughed.

'This is what I would do,' Bosch then added on a

serious note. 'I'd put two of them on Elias and two on Perez. You know, doing the paper, managing the evidence, taking the autopsies – which will probably be today anyway. That will keep them busy and out of your way. Regardless of whether it's them or not, you've got to put at least one body on Perez. We've treated her as an also-ran, which she obviously was. But you gotta do the due diligence on it or it can come back on you if you ever go to court and the lawyer asks why Perez wasn't pursued as the primary target.'

'Right, right. We gotta cover all the bases.'

'Right.'

Lindell nodded but said nothing further.

'So come on, do we have a deal?' Bosch prompted.

'Yeah. Sounds like a plan to me. But I want to know what you and your people are doing. You keep in touch.'

'You got it. Oh, and by the way, one of the IAD guys is a Spanish speaker. Fuentes. Put him on Perez.'

Lindell nodded and pushed back from the table. He left his coffee cup there, untouched. Bosch took his with him.

On his way through the anteroom to Irving's conference room, Bosch noticed that the deputy chief's adjutant was not at his desk. He saw a telephone message pad on the blotter and reached down and grabbed it as he passed by. He put it in his pocket and entered the conference room.

Bosch's partners and the IAD men were now in the conference room. Irving was there also. It was very crowded. After some brief introductions the floor was turned over to Bosch, who briefed the newcomers and Irving on the investigation up to that point. He left out specific details about the visit to Virginia Lampley's apartment, making that part of the investigation appear to be at a dead end. He also made no mention at all of his barroom talk with Frankie Sheehan. When he was done he nodded to Irving, who then took the floor.

Bosch moved over to the wall and leaned next to a bulletin board Irving had apparently had installed for the investigators to use.

Irving began speaking of the political tensions surrounding the case like a storm pressure cell. He mentioned that protest marches were scheduled that day in front of three of the South End police stations and at Parker Center. He said City Councilman Royal Sparks and Reverend Preston Tuggins were scheduled to be guests that morning on a local meet-the-press type of television show called *Talk of L.A.* He said the chief of police had met with Tuggins and other South Central church leaders the night before to call in markers and urge them to call for calm and restraint from the pulpits during the morning's services.

'We are sitting on a powder keg here, people,' Irving said. 'And the way to defuse it is to solve this case one way or the other … quickly.'

While he talked, Bosch took out the phone message pad and wrote on it. He then checked the room to make sure all eyes were on Irving and quietly tore off the top sheet. He reached over and tacked it to the bulletin board and then nonchalantly moved inch by inch down the wall and away from the board. The sheet he had put on the board had Chastain's name on it. In the message section it said: 'Harvey Button called, said thanks for the tip. Will call back later.'

Irving wound up his comments with a mention about the Channel 4 story.

'Someone in this room leaked information to a television reporter yesterday. I am warning you people that we will not have this. That one story was your grace period. One more leak and you people will be the ones under investigation.'

He looked around the room at the LAPD faces, to make sure the message was clear.

'Okay, that is it,' he finally said. 'I will leave you to it.

Detective Bosch, Agent Lindell? I would like to be briefed at noon on our progress.'

'No problem, Chief,' Lindell said before Bosch could respond. 'I will be talking to you then.'

Fifteen minutes later Bosch was walking down the hallway to the elevators again. Edgar and Rider were following behind.

'Harry, where are we going?' Edgar asked.

'We'll work out of Hollywood station.'

'What? Doing what? Who is going to run the show?'

'Lindell. I made a deal. He runs the show. We do something else.'

'Suits me,' Edgar said. 'Too many agents and too much brass around here anyway.'

Bosch got to the elevators and pushed the call button.

'What exactly are we doing, Harry?' Rider asked.

He turned and looked at them.

'Starting over,' he said.

22

The squad room was completely empty, which was unusual, even for a Sunday. Under the twelve-and-twelve readiness plan all detectives not assigned to time-critical investigations were to be in uniform and out on the street. The last time such deployment had been instituted was after a major earthquake had rocked the city in 1994. The Elias murder was a social rather than a geologic cataclysm, but its magnitude was just as great.

Bosch carried the box containing Elias's files on the Black Warrior case to what they called the homicide table, a raft of desks pushed up against each other to create a huge boardroom-like table. The section that belonged to team one, Bosch's team, was at the end, near an alcove of file cabinets. He put the box in the middle, where his team's three desks conjoined.

'Dig in,' he said.

'Harry … ,' Rider said, not happy with his lack of direction.

'Okay, listen, this is what I want. Kiz, you're going to be master of the ship. Jerry and I will work the field.'

Rider groaned. Master of the ship meant that she was to be the keeper of the facts. She was to become familiar with all facets of the files, a walking compendium of the details of the investigation. Since they were starting off with an entire carton of files, this was a lot of work. It also meant she would not be doing much, if anything, in the way of field investigation. And no detective wants to be stuck in a windowless and empty office all day.

'I know,' Bosch said. 'But I think you are best for it. We've got a ton of stuff here and your mind and your computer will be best for keeping track of it.'

'Next time I get the field.'

'There might not be a next time if we don't do something this time. Let's see what we got here.'

They spent the next ninety minutes going through Elias's files on the Harris case, pointing out specific items to each other when they seemed to warrant attention, other times tossing files back into the box when their importance was not apparent.

Bosch spent his time with the investigative files that Elias had subpoenaed from the LAPD. He had a copy of the entire RHD murder book. Reading the daily investigative summaries turned in by Sheehan and other RHD detectives, Bosch noted that the case seemed initially to be lacking a focus. Stacey Kincaid had been taken from her room in the night, her abductor jimmying the lock on a bedroom window with a screwdriver and then grabbing the girl while she slept. Initially suspecting an inside job, the detectives interviewed the gardeners, the pool man, a local maintenance man, a plumber who had been in the house two weeks earlier, as well as the sanitation men and postal workers who had the route that included the Kincaids' home in Brentwood. Teachers, janitors and even fellow students from Stacey's private school in West Hollywood were interviewed. But the wide net being thrown by Sheehan and his cohorts was pulled in after the lab came up with the fingerprint match between the missing girl's schoolbook and Michael Harris. The case then shifted to a complete focus on locating Harris, taking him into custody and then attempting to make him confess to what he had done with the girl.

The second section of the file also dealt with the crime scene investigation and efforts to connect Harris to the body through scientific analysis and technology. This proved to be a dead end. The girl's body had been found by two homeless men in a vacant lot. The body was naked and badly decomposed after four days. It had apparently been washed after her death and therefore was lacking any significant microscopic evidence that could be analyzed and connected to Harris's apartment or car. Though the girl appeared to have been raped, no bodily fluids belonging to her attacker were recovered. Her clothes were never found. The ligature that had been used to strangle her had been cut away by her killer and that, too, was never found. In the end, the only evidence that connected Harris to the crime was his fingerprints on the book in Stacey's bedroom and the disposal of the body in the vacant lot less than two blocks from his apartment.

Bosch knew that was usually more than enough to win a conviction. He had worked cases in which convictions were won with less evidence. But that was before O.J. Simpson, before juries looked at police in Los Angeles with suspicious and judging eyes.

Bosch was writing a list of things to do and people to be interviewed when Edgar cried out.

'Yahtzee!'

Bosch and Rider looked at him and waited for an explanation.

'Remember the mystery notes?' Edgar said. 'The second or third one said license plates prove he's innocent?'

'Wait a second,' Bosch said.

He opened his briefcase and took out the file containing the notes.

'The third one. "License plates prove his innocense." Came in April five. Innocence spelled wrong.'

'Okay, here's Elias's file on subpoena returns. Got one here dated April fifteen for Hollywood Wax and Shine. That's where Harris worked before they arrested him. It seeks – quote – "copies of all records and receipts of customer orders and billings containing license plate numbers of said customers between the dates of April one and June fifteen of last year." It's gotta be what the note was talking about.'

Bosch leaned back in his chair to think about this. 'This is a subpoena return, right? It was approved.'

'Right.'

'Well, April one and June fifteen, that's seventy-five days. There—'

'Seventy-six days,' Rider corrected.

'Seventy-six days. That would be a lot of receipts. We got none here and there weren't any in the office I saw. There should be boxes of receipts.'

'Maybe he returned them,' Edgar said.

'You said he subpoenaed copies.'

Edgar hiked his shoulders.

'Another thing, why those days?' Bosch asked. 'The murder of the girl was July twelve. Why not subpoena the receipts right up until then?'

'Because he knew what he was looking for,' Rider said. 'Or knew within the parameters of those dates.'

'Knew what?'

They dropped into silence. Bosch's mind was running the puzzle but coming up empty. The license plate clue was still as mysterious as the Mistress Regina lead. Then by joining the two mysteries he came up with something.

'Pelfry again,' he said. 'We need to talk to him.'

He stood up.

'Jerry, get on the phones. See if you can run down Pelfry and set up an interview for as soon as you can get it. I'm going out back for a few minutes.'

Normally, when Bosch told his partners he was going out back it meant he was going outside the building to have a smoke. As he walked toward the rear doorway, Rider called after him.

'Harry, don't do it.'

He waved without turning back.

'Don't worry, I'm not.'

Out in the lot Bosch stood and looked around. He knew he had done some of his best analytical thinking while standing outside smoking. He hoped he could put something together now, without the aid of a smoke. He looked into the sand jar that the station's smokers used and saw a half-smoked cigarette protruding from the sand. There was lipstick on it. He decided he wasn't that desperate yet.

He thought about the mystery notes. He knew because of postmarks and the markings made on the notes by Elias that they had numbers two, three and four, but not the first note. The meaning of the fourth note – the warning Elias was carrying with him – was obvious. The third note they now had a line on, thanks to the subpoena return Edgar had come across. But the second note – Dot the i humbert humbert – still made no sense to Bosch.

He looked at the cigarette protruding from the sand again but once more dismissed it. He remembered he carried no matches or lighter anyway.

It suddenly occurred to him that the one other piece of the puzzle that seemed to stand out as making no sense, at least so far, was the Mistress Regina connection – whatever that was.

Bosch turned and quickly headed back into the station. Edgar and Rider had their heads down and into the paperwork when he came to the table. Bosch immediately began looking through the stacks of files.

'Who has the Mistress Regina file?'

'Over here,' Edgar said.

He handed over the file and Bosch opened it and took out the photo printout of the dominatrix. He then put it down next to one of the mystery notes and tried to make a comparison between the printing on the note and the printing below the photo – the web page address. It was impossible for him to determine if the same hand had printed both lines. He was no expert and there were no obvious anomalies in the printing to make a comparison easy.

When Bosch took his hand off the printout, its top and bottom edges rose an inch off the desk, telling him that at one time the page had been folded top and bottom, as if to be placed in an envelope.

'I think this is the first note,' he said.

Bosch had often found that when he made a logic breakthrough it was like clearing a clog in a drain. The pipe was open and other breaks soon came. It happened now. He saw what he could have and maybe should have seen all along.

'Jerry, call Elias's secretary. Right now. Ask her if he had a color printer in the office. We should have seen this – *I* should have seen it.'

'Seen what?'

'Just make the call.'

Edgar started looking through a notebook for a phone number. Rider got up from her spot and came around next to Bosch. She looked down at the printout. She was now riding on Bosch's wave. She saw where he was going.

'This was the first one,' Bosch said. 'Only he didn't keep the envelope because he probably thought it was crank mail.'

'But it probably was,' Edgar said, the phone to his ear. 'We were there, the woman didn't know the man and didn't know what the hell we—'

He stopped and listened when his line was picked up.

'Mrs Quimby? It is Detective Edgar from yesterday? I have one quick question for you. Do you know if there was a color printer in the office? A printer that could print out stuff from one of the computers. In color.'

He waited and listened, his eyes on Bosch and Rider.

'Thank you, Mrs Quimby.'

He hung up.

'No color printer.'

Bosch nodded and looked down at the printout of Mistress Regina.

'We should have picked up on this yesterday,' Rider said.

Bosch nodded and started to ask Edgar if he had contacted Pelfry, the private investigator, when his pager went off. He cut it off and pulled it off his belt. It was his home number. Eleanor.

'Yeah, I talked to him,' Edgar said. 'He'll meet us at noon at his office. I didn't mention anything about receipts or this Regina. I just said we needed to talk.'

'Okay.'

Bosch picked up his phone and punched in his home number. Eleanor answered after three rings. She sounded either sleepy or sad.

'Eleanor.'

'Harry.'

'Everything all right?'

He slid back into his seat and Rider went back to hers.

'I'm fine ... I just ...'

'When did you get in?'

'A little while ago.'

'Did you win?'

'I didn't really play. After you called me there last night ... I left.'

Bosch leaned forward and put an elbow on the table, a hand against his forehead.

'Well ... where'd you go?'

'A hotel ... Harry, I just came back for some clothes and things. I ...'

'Eleanor?'

There was a long silence on the phone. Bosch heard Edgar say he was going to get some coffee in the watch office. Rider said she'd go along, even though Bosch knew she didn't drink coffee. She had an assortment of herbal teas she kept in the drawer of her desk.

'Harry, it's not right,' Eleanor said.

'What are you talking about, Eleanor?'

Another long moment of silence went by before she answered.

'I was thinking about that movie we saw last year. About the *Titanic*.'

'I remember.'

'And the girl in that. She fell in love with that boy, that she only met right there on the boat. And it was … I mean, she loved him so much. So much that at the end she wouldn't leave. She didn't take the lifeboat so she would be with him.'

'I remember, Eleanor.'

He remembered her crying in the seat next to him and his smiling and not being able to understand how a film would affect her in such a way.

'You cried.'

'Yes. It's because everybody wants that kind of love. And, Harry, you deserve that from me. I—'

'No, Eleanor, what you give me is more than—'

'She jumped from a lifeboat *back* onto the *Titanic*, Harry.' She laughed a little bit. But it sounded sad to Bosch. 'I guess nobody can ever top that.'

'You're right. Nobody can. That's why it was a movie. Listen … you are all I've ever wanted, Eleanor. You don't have to do anything for me.'

'Yes, I do. I do … I love you, Harry. But not enough. You deserve better.'

'Eleanor, no … please. I …'

'I'm going to go away for a while. Think about things.'

'Will you wait there? I'll be home in fifteen minutes. We can talk about—'

'No, no. That's why I paged. I can't do this in person.'

He could tell she was crying.

'Well, I'm coming up there.'

'I won't be here,' she said urgently. 'I packed the car before I paged you. I knew you'd try to come.'

Bosch put his hand over his eyes. He wanted to be in darkness.

'Where will you be?'

'I'm not sure.'

'Will you call?'

'Yes, I'll call.'

'Are you all right?'

'I'm ... I'll be fine.'

'Eleanor, I love you. I know I never said that enough but I—'

She made a shushing sound in the phone and he stopped.

'I love you, Harry, but I have to do this.'

After a long moment, during which he felt a deep tearing inside, he said, 'Okay, Eleanor.'

The silence that followed was as dark as the inside of a coffin. His coffin.

'Good-bye, Harry,' she finally said. 'I'll see you.'

She hung up. Bosch took his hand away from his face and the phone from his ear. In his mind he saw a swimming pool, its surface as smooth as a blanket on a bed. He remembered a time long before when he had been told his mother was dead and that he was alone in the world. He ran to that pool and dove beneath the calm surface, into its warm water. At the bottom, he screamed until his air was gone and his chest ached. Until he had to choose between staying there and dying, or going up and life.

Bosch now longed for that pool and its warm water. He wanted to scream until his lungs burst inside him.

'Everything okay?'

He looked up. It was Rider and Edgar. Edgar carried a steaming cup of coffee. Rider had a look that said she was concerned or maybe even scared by the look she was seeing on Bosch's face.

'Everything's cool,' Bosch said. 'Everything's fine.'

23

They had ninety minutes to kill before the meeting with Pelfry. Bosch told Edgar to drive over to Holly-wood Wax and Shine, on Sunset not far from the station. Edgar pulled to the curb and they sat there watching. Business was slow. Most of the men in orange coveralls who dried and polished the cars for minimum wage and tips were sitting around, drying rags draped over their shoulders, waiting. Most of them stared balefully at the slickback as if the police were to blame.

'I guess people aren't that interested in having their cars washed when they might end up turned over or torched,' Edgar said.

Bosch didn't answer.

'Bet they all wish they were in Michael Harris's shoes,' Edgar continued, staring back at the workers. 'Hell, *I'd* trade three days in an interview room and pencils in my ears to be a millionaire.'

'So then you believe him,' Bosch said.

Bosch hadn't told him about Frankie Sheehan's barroom confession. Edgar was quiet a moment and then nodded.

'Yeah, Harry, I guess I sort of do.'

Bosch wondered how he had been so blind as to not even have considered that the torturing of a suspect could be true. He wondered what it was about Edgar that made him accepting of the suspect's story over the cops'. Was it his experience as a cop or as a black man? Bosch assumed it had to be the latter and it depressed him because it gave Edgar an edge he could never have.

'I'm gonna go in, talk to the manager,' Bosch said. 'Maybe you should stay with the car.'

'Fuck that. They won't touch it.'

They got out and locked the car.

As they walked toward the store Bosch thought about the orange coveralls and wondered if it was coincidence. He guessed that most of the men working at the car wash were ex-cons or fresh out of county lockup – institutions in which they also had to wear orange coveralls.

Inside the store Bosch bought a cup of coffee and asked for the manager. The cashier pointed down a hallway to an open door. On the way down the hall, Edgar said, 'I feel like a Coke but I don't think I can drink a Coke after what I saw last night in that bitch's closet.'

A man was sitting at a desk in the small, windowless office with his feet up on one of the open drawers. He looked up at Bosch and Edgar and said, 'Yes, Officers, what can I do for you?'

Bosch smiled at the man's deduction. He knew he had to be part businessman, part parole officer. Most of the polishers were ex-cons. It was the only job they could get. That meant the manager had seen his share of cops and knew how to pick them out. Either that or he saw them pull up in the slickback.

'We're working a case,' Bosch began. 'The Howard Elias case.'

The manager whistled.

'A few weeks ago he subpoenaed some of your records. Receipts with license plate numbers on them. You know anything about that?'

The manager thought about it for a few moments.

'All I know is that I was the one who had to go through everything and get it copied for his guy.'

'His guy?' Edgar asked.

'Yeah, what do you think, a guy like Elias comes get

244

the stuff himself? He sent somebody. I got his card here.'

He lowered his feet to the floor and opened the desk's pencil drawer. There was a stack of business cards with a rubber band around it. He took it off and looked through the cards and chose one. He showed it to Bosch.

'Pelfry?' Edgar asked.

Bosch nodded.

'Did his guy say exactly what they were looking for in all that stuff?' he asked.

'I don't know. You'd have to ask them. Or, I mean, ask Pelfry.'

'Did Pelfry come back with the stuff yet?'

'No, it was copies, anyway. I mean, he came back but not to bring back the receipts.'

'Then why'd he come back?' Edgar asked.

'He wanted to see one of Michael Harris's old time cards. From when he worked here.'

'Which one?' Edgar asked, a tone of urgency in his voice.

'I don't remember, man. I gave him a copy. You go talk to him and maybe he—'

'Did he have a subpoena for the time card?' Bosch asked.

'No, he just asked for it, you know. I said sure and got it for him. But he gave me the date and you didn't. I don't remember it. Anyway, look, if you want to ask more about this then maybe you better call our lawyer. I'm not going to get involved in talking about stuff I don't—'

'Never mind that stuff,' Bosch said. 'Tell me about Michael Harris.'

'What's to tell? I never had a problem with the guy. He was okay, then they came in and said he killed that little girl. And did things to her. It didn't seem like the guy I knew. But he hadn't been working here that long. Maybe five months.'

'Know where he was before that?' Edgar asked.

'Yeah. Up at Corcoran.'

Corcoran was a state prison near Bakersfield. Bosch thanked the manager and they left. He took a few sips of his coffee but dumped it in a trash can before getting back to the car.

While Bosch waited at the passenger door for it to be unlocked, Edgar went around to his side. He stopped before opening the door.

'Goddammit.'

'What?'

'They wrote shit on the door.'

Bosch came around and looked. Someone had used light blue chalk – the chalk used to write washing instructions on the windshields of clients' cars – to cross out the words *To protect and serve* on the driver's side front fender. Then written in large letters were the words *To murder and maim*. Bosch nodded his approval.

'That's pretty original.'

'Harry, let's go kick some ass.'

'No, Jerry, let it go. You don't want to start something. It might take three days to end it. Like last time. Like Florence and Normandie.'

Edgar sullenly unlocked the car and then opened Bosch's door.

'We're right by the station,' Bosch said after he got in. 'We can go back and spray it off. Or we can use my car.'

'I'd like to use one of those assholes' faces to clean it off.'

After they had the car cleaned up there was still time for them to drive by the lot where Stacey Kincaid's body had been found. It was off Western and was on the way downtown, where they would go to meet Pelfry.

Edgar was silent the whole way there. He had taken the vandalism of the patrol car personally. Bosch didn't mind the silence, though. He used the time to think about Eleanor. He felt guilty because deep down and despite his love for her, he knew that he was feeling a growing relief that their relationship was coming to a head, one way or the other.

'This is it,' Edgar said.

He pulled the car to the curb and they scanned the lot. It was about an acre and bordered on both sides by apartment buildings with banners announcing move-in bonuses and financing. They didn't look like places where people would want to live unless they had no choice. The whole neighborhood had a rundown and desperate feel.

Bosch noticed two old black men sitting on crates in the corner of the lot, under a sprawling and shade-giving eucalyptus tree. He opened the file he'd brought with him and studied the map that charted the location of the body. He estimated that it was less than fifty feet from where the two men were now sitting. He turned pages in the file until he found the incident report which named the two witnesses who reported finding the body.

'I'm getting out,' he said. 'I'm going to go talk to those guys.'

He got out and Edgar did, too. They crossed the lot nonchalantly and approached the two men. As they got closer, Bosch saw sleeping bags and an old Coleman camp stove. Parked against the trunk of the eucalyptus were two supermarket carts filled with clothing, bags of aluminum cans and assorted junk.

'Are you men Rufus Gundy and Andy Mercer?'

'Depends on who's doin' the askin'.'

Bosch showed his badge.

'I wanted to ask a few questions about the body you guys found here last year.'

'Yeah, what took you so long?'

'Are you Mr Gundy or Mr Mercer?'

'I'm Mercer.'

Bosch nodded.

'Why do you say we took so long? Weren't you interviewed by detectives when you found the body?'

'We was interviewed, but not by no detectives. Some wet-eared patrol boy akst us what we knew.'

Bosch nodded. He pointed to the sleeping bags and the camp stove.

'You guys live here?'

'We runnin' a piece of bad luck. We just stayin' till we on our feet again.'

Bosch knew there was nothing in the incident report about the two men living on the lot. The report said they were passing through the lot, looking for cans, when they came across her body. He thought about this and realized what had happened.

'You were living here then, weren't you?'

Neither of them answered.

'You didn't tell the cops that because you thought you might get run off.'

Still no reply.

'So you hid your sleeping bags and your stove and called it in. You told that patrol officer that you were just passing through.'

Finally, Mercer spoke.

'If'n you're so smart, how come you ain't chief yet?'

Bosch laughed.

'Because they're smart enough not to make me chief. So, tell me something, Mr Mercer and Mr Gundy. If you two were sleepin' here during nights back then, you probably would've found that body a lot sooner if it had been here the whole time she was missing, right?'

'Most likely,' Gundy said.

'So somebody probably dumped that body the night before you found it.'

'Could be,' Gundy said.

'Yeah, I'd say that was so,' Mercer added.

'With you two sleeping, what, forty, fifty feet away?'

This time they didn't verbally agree. Bosch stepped

over and dropped into a catcher's squat so he was on their eye level.

'Tell me what you men saw that night.'

'We didn't see nothin',' Gundy said adamantly.

'But we heard things,' Mercer said. 'Heard things.'

'What things?'

'A car pull up,' Mercer said. 'A door open, then a trunk. We heard somethin' heavy hit the ground. Then the trunk closed and the door, then the car drive off.'

'You didn't even look?' Edgar asked quickly. He had stepped over and was leaning over, hands on his knees. 'A body gets dumped there fifty feet away and you don't look?'

'No, we don't look,' Mercer retorted. 'People be dumpin' their garbage and whatnot in the field most every night. We never look. We keep our heads down. In the morning we look. We got some nice items time to time from what people throw away. We always wait till mornin' to check out what they throw.'

Bosch nodded that he understood and hoped Edgar would leave the men alone.

'And you never told all of this to the cops?'

'Nope,' Mercer and Gundy said in unison.

'What about anybody else? You ever told it to somebody who could verify this has been the true story all along?'

The men thought about it. Mercer was shaking his head no when Gundy nodded yes.

'The only one we told was Mr Elias's man.'

Bosch glanced at Edgar and then back at Gundy.

'Who's that?'

'His man. The investigator. We told him what we told you. He said Mr Elias was gonna use us in court one day. He said Mr Elias would be takin' care of us.'

'Pelfry?' Edgar asked. 'Was that his name?'

'Could be,' Gundy said. 'I don't know.'

Mercer didn't say anything.

'You guys read the paper today?' Bosch asked. 'See any TV news?'

'On what TV?' Mercer asked.

Bosch just nodded and stood up. They didn't even know Elias was dead.

'How long ago was that when Mr Elias's man talked to you?'

'Be about a month,' Mercer said. 'Somewhere around that.'

Bosch looked at Edgar and nodded that he was done. Edgar nodded back.

'Thanks for your help,' Bosch said. 'Can I buy you guys some dinner?'

He reached into his pocket and pulled out his money. He gave each man a ten. They thanked him politely and he walked away.

As they sped north on Western to Wilshire, Bosch started riffing on what the information from the two homeless men meant.

'Harris is clear,' he said excitedly. 'That's how Elias knew. Because the body was moved. It was dumped there three days after she was dead. And Harris was in custody when it was moved. The best alibi in the world. Elias was going to bring those two old guys into court and put the lie to the LAPD.'

'Yeah, but hold on, Harry,' Edgar said. 'It doesn't clear Harris completely. It could just mean he had an accomplice. You know, who moved the body while he was in lockup.'

'Yeah, then why dump it so close to his apartment and further implicate him? I don't think there's an accomplice. I think it was the real killer. He read in the paper or saw on TV that they had Harris as a suspect and he moved the body to his neighborhood, to be another nail in Harris's coffin.'

'What about the fingerprints? How did Harris's prints get into that nice mansion in Brentwood? Are you goin' along with them being planted by your buddy Sheehan and his team?'

'No, I'm not. There's an explanation. We just don't know it yet. It's what we ask Pel—'

There was a loud explosion as the rear window shattered and glass blasted through the car. Edgar momentarily lost control and the car swerved into the oncoming lanes. There was a chorus of angry horns as Bosch reached over and yanked the wheel right, bringing the car back across the yellow lines.

'What the fuck?' Edgar cried as he finally got the car under control and put on the brakes.

'No!' Bosch yelled. 'Keep going, keep going!'

Bosch grabbed the radio out of the recharge slot on the floor and depressed the transmit button.

'Shots fired, shots fired! Western and Olympic.'

He held the button down as he looked over the backseat and out over the trunk. His eyes scanned the rooftops and windows of the apartment buildings two blocks back. He saw nothing.

'Suspect unknown. Sniper fire on a marked investigative services unit. Request immediate backup. Request air surveillance of rooftops east and west sides of Western. Extreme caution is advised.'

He clicked off the transmit button. While the dispatch operator repeated most of what he had just said to other units, he told Edgar that they had gone far enough and that he could stop.

'I think it came from the East Side,' Bosch said to Edgar. 'Those apartments with the flat roof. I think I heard it in my right ear first.'

Edgar exhaled loudly. His hands were gripped so tight on the steering wheel now that the knuckles were as white as Bosch's.

'You know what?' he said. 'I think I'm never going to drive one of these fucking targets again.'

24

'You guys are late. I was thinkin' about goin' home, already.'

Jenkins Pelfry was a big man, with a barrel chest and a complexion so dark it was hard to make out the lines of his face. He sat on the top of a small secretary's desk in the anteroom of his office suite in the Union Law Center. There was a small television on a credenza to his left. It was tuned to a news channel. The view on the screen was from a helicopter circling a scene somewhere in the city.

Bosch and Edgar had arrived forty minutes late for their noon appointment.

'Sorry, Mr Pelfry,' Bosch said. 'We ran into a little problem on the way over. Appreciate you staying.'

'Lucky for you I lost track of the time. I was watching the tube here. Things are not looking too good at the moment. It's looking a little testy out there.'

He indicated the television with one of his huge hands. Bosch looked again and realized the scene that the helicopter was circling was the scene he and Edgar had just left – the search for the sniper who had taken the shot at their car. On the tube Bosch could see the sidewalks on Western were now crowded with people watching the cops moving from building to building. More officers were arriving on the scene and these new officers were wearing riot helmets.

'These guys oughta just get out of there. They're baitin' the crowd. This isn't good. Just back the hell out, man. Live to fight another day.'

'Tried that last time,' Edgar said. 'Didn't work.'

The three of them watched for a few more moments in silence, then Pelfry reached over and turned off the tube. He looked at his visitors.

'What can I do for you?

Bosch introduced himself and his partner.

'I suppose you know why we're here. We're working the Howard Elias case. And we know you were doin' some work for him on the Black Warrior thing. We could use your help, Mr Pelfry. If we find who did this, we maybe have a shot at cooling this place off.'

Bosch nodded at the blank tube of the television to underline his point.

'You want my help,' Pelfry said. 'Yeah, I worked for Eli – I always called him Eli. But I don't know what I can do for you.'

Bosch looked at Edgar and his partner made a subtle nod of his head.

'Mr Pelfry, our conversation here has to be kept confidential. My partner and I are following an investigative trail that indicates that whoever killed Stacey Kincaid may have also killed your employer. We think Elias got too close to the truth. If you know what he knew, then you could be in danger yourself.'

Pelfry laughed at him – a short, loud snort. Bosch looked at Edgar and then back at Pelfry.

'No offense but that's about the worst pickup line I ever heard,' Pelfry said.

'What are you talking about?'

He pointed at the television once more. Bosch noticed how white the underside of his hand was.

'I told you I been watchin' the news. Channel Four says you guys are already measuring a cell for somebody. One of your own.'

'What are you talking about?'

'They're sweatin' a suspect over at Parker right now.'

'Did they have a name?'

'They didn't say a name but they knew it. They said

it was one of the Black Warrior cops. The lead detective, in fact.'

Bosch was dumbfounded. The lead detective was Frankie Sheehan.

'That's impos— can I use your phone?'

'Help yourself. By the way, do you know you have glass in your hair?'

Bosch brushed his hand through his hair while he stepped to the desk and picked up the phone. While he punched in the number of Irving's conference room Pelfry watched. The phone was answered immediately.

'Let me talk to Lindell.'

'This is Lindell.'

'It's Bosch. What's this on Channel Four about a suspect?'

'I know. I'm checking into it. Somebody leaked. All I can say is that I updated Irving and the next thing I know it's on TV. I think he's your leak, not Chas—'

'I don't care about that. What are you saying, it's Sheehan? That's im—'

'I'm not saying that. That's the leak talking and I think the leak is the goddamned deputy chief.'

'Have you brought Sheehan in?'

'Yeah, we got him in here and we're talking to him. Strictly voluntary at this point. He thinks he can talk his way out of the box. We got all day and then some. We'll see if he can.'

'Why Sheehan? Why'd you bring him in?'

'I thought you knew. He was on top of Chastain's list this morning. Elias sued him once before. Five years ago. He shot some asshole while trying to make an arrest on a murder. Put five holes in him. The widow sued and eventually won a hundred grand – even though to me it looked like a righteous shoot. In fact your buddy Chastain was the one who investigated the shoot and cleared him.'

'I remember the case. It *was* a righteous shoot. But

that didn't matter to the jury. It was just a little while after Rodney King.'

'Okay, well before it went to trial, Sheehan threatened Elias. During a depo, in front of the lawyers, the widow and, most important, the steno girl. She got it down word for word and it was in the depo which was in the file that Chastain and his people read yesterday. The threat was that Sheehan told Elias that someday when he least expected it, Sheehan was going to come up from behind and put him down like a dog. Words to that effect. Words that describe what happened on Angels Flight pretty good.'

'Come on, that was five years ago. You've got to be kidding me.'

Bosch noticed that both Edgar and Pelfry were watching him intently.

'I know it, Bosch. But then you have this new lawsuit on the Black Warrior thing and who's the lead? Detective Frank Sheehan. On top of that, he uses a nine-millimeter Smith and Wesson. And one other thing, we pulled his file. He's qualified eleven straight years at the range as an expert marksman. And you know the kind of shooting it took on Angels Flight. You take it all into consideration and it puts him at the top of the list of people to talk to. So we're talking to him.'

'The marksman thing is bullshit. They give those pins out like candy at the range. I bet seven or eight out of every ten cops have that ribbon. And eight out of ten cops carry Smith nines. Meantime, Irving – or whoever the leak is – is throwing him to the wolves. Sacrificing him to the media so maybe he can stop the city from burning.'

'He's only a sacrifice if he didn't do it.'

There was a cynical casualness in Lindell's voice that Bosch didn't like.

'You better take it slow,' Bosch said. 'Because I guarantee you Frankie wasn't the shooter.'

'Frankie? You guys friends, are you?'

'We were partners. A long time back.'

'Well, it's funny. He doesn't seem so fond of you now. My guys tell me that the first thing he said when they knocked on his door was "Fuck Harry Bosch." He thinks you ratted him out, man. He doesn't know that we have the threat in the deposition. Or he doesn't remember it.'

Bosch put the phone down on its hook. He was in a daze. Frankie Sheehan believed that Bosch had turned their conversation of the night before against him. He believed Harry had turned him in to the bureau. It made Bosch feel worse than the knowledge that his old partner and friend now sat in an interview room fighting for his life.

'Sounds like you don't agree much with Channel Four,' Pelfry said.

'No, I don't.'

'You know something, I'ma take a wild ass guess here, but I think that glass in your hair means you're the two guys they were talkin' about on TV getting potshotted over on Western.'

'Yeah, what about it?' Edgar asked.

'Well, that's a few blocks from where that Stacey Kincaid girl ended up.'

'Yeah, so?'

'Well, if that's where you were comin' from, then I wonder if you met my two buddies, Rufus and Andy.'

'Yeah, we met 'em and we know all about the body being dumped three days late.'

'You're following my footsteps then.'

'Some of them. We visited Mistress Regina last night, too.'

Bosch was finally out of his daze but hung back and watched Edgar making progress with Pelfry.

'Then this isn't all bullshit what you said about who you think hit Eli?'

'We're here, aren't we?'

'Then what else you want to know? Eli kept his cards

close most of the time. Very close to the vest. I never knew for sure which corner of the puzzle I was working, if you know what I mean.'

'Tell us about the license plates,' Bosch said, ending his silence. 'We know you guys pulled seventy-six days' worth of receipts from Hollywood Wax. How come?'

Pelfry looked at them a long moment as if deciding something.

'Come on back,' he finally said.

He led them to the rear office.

'I didn't want you guys back here,' he said. 'But now ... '

He raised his hands to indicate the boxes covering every horizontal surface in the office. They were short boxes that normally held four six-packs of soda Stacked in them were bundled receipts with cardboard markers with dates written on them.

'Those are the receipts from Hollywood Wax?' Bosch asked.

'That's right. Eli was going to bring 'em all into court as an exhibit. I was holding 'em here till he needed 'em.'

'What exactly was he going to show with them?'

'I thought you boys knew.'

'We're a little behind you, Mr Pelfry.'

'Jenkins. Or Jenks. Most people call me Jenks. I don't know exactly what alla these receipts meant – remember what I said about Eli not showin' me all the cards in his deck – but I got an idea. See, when he su'peenied these, he gave me a list of license plate numbers on a piecea paper. He said I was to look through alla these and see if any of those numbers on the list turned up on the receipts.'

'Did you?'

'Yeah, took me the better part of a week.'

'Any matches?'

'One match.'

He went over to one of the boxes and stuck his finger

into the stack where there was a cardboard marker with the date 6/12 noted on it.

'This one.'

Pelfry pulled out a receipt and took it over to Bosch. Edgar came over and looked as well. The receipt was for a daily special. It identified the car to be washed as a white Volvo wagon. It listed the license plate number and the price of the special – $14.95 plus tax.

'This plate number was on the list Elias gave you,' Bosch said.

'That's right.'

'It was the only match you found.'

'That's what I said.'

'You know whose car this plate is from?'

'Not exactly. Eli didn't tell me to run it. But I got a guess who it belongs to.'

'The Kincaids.'

'Now you're with me.'

Bosch looked at Edgar. He could tell by his partner's face he hadn't made the leap.

'The fingerprints. To prove Harris was innocent beyond any kind of doubt, he had to explain his client's fingerprints on the victim's schoolbook. If there was no reason or possible legitimate explanation for Harris having been in the Kincaid house and touching the book, then there were two alternative reasons. One, the prints were planted by the cops. Two, Harris touched the book when it was somewhere else, outside of the girl's bedroom.'

Edgar nodded as he understood.

'The Kincaids had their car washed at Hollywood Wax and Shine, where Harris worked. The receipt proves it.'

'Right. All Elias had to do was put the book in the car.'

Bosch turned to the boxes on Pelfry's desk and ticked his finger on the cardboard marker.

'June twelve,' he said. 'That's right around the end of

the school year. Kids clear out their lockers. They take all their books home. They're not doing homework anymore so maybe the books lie around in the back of the Volvo.'

'The Volvo goes to the car wash,' Edgar said. 'I'd bet the daily special includes a vacuum, maybe some Armoral on the inside.'

'The washer – the polish man – touches the book when he's working inside the car,' Bosch added. 'There are your prints.'

'The polish man was Harris,' Edgar said. He then looked at Pelfry and said, 'The manager at the car wash said you came back to look at the time cards.'

Pelfry nodded.

'I did. I got a copy of a time card that proves Harris was working at the time that white Volvo came in and got the special. Eli asked me to go over to the car wash and try to finesse that without a su'peenie. I figure the time card was the lynch pin and he didn't want anybody to know about it.'

'Even the judge who signed the subpoenas on the case,' Bosch said. 'He must not have trusted anybody.'

'Looks like with good reason,' Pelfry said.

While Edgar asked Pelfry to show him the time card, Bosch withdrew and tried to think about this latest information. He remembered what Sheehan had said the night before about the fingerprints being so good because the person who had left them had probably been sweating. He understood now that that was not because of nervousness over the crime being committed, but because he was working at the car wash, vacuuming a car when those prints were left on that book. Michael Harris. He was innocent. Truly innocent. Bosch had not been convinced until that moment. And it was astounding to him. He wasn't a dreamer. He knew cops made mistakes and innocent people went to prison. But the mistake here was colossal. An innocent man tortured as cops tried to bully him into confessing

259

to something he had clearly not done. Satisfied they had their man, the police had dropped their investigation and let the real killer slip away – until a civil rights lawyer's investigation found him, a discovery that got the lawyer killed. The chain reaction went even further, pushing the city once more to the brink of self-destruction.

'So then, Mr Pelfry,' Bosch said, 'who killed Stacey Kincaid?'

'It's Jenks. And I don't know. I know it wasn't Michael Harris – ain't no doubt about that. But Eli didn't tell me the other part – if he knew before they got him.'

'They?' Bosch asked.

'Whatever.'

'Tell us about Mistress Regina,' Edgar said.

'What's to tell? Eli got a tip, he passed it to me. I checked the broad out and couldn't see any connection. She's just a freak – a dead end. If you guys were there, you know what I mean. I think Eli dropped it after I told him about her.'

Bosch thought a moment and shook his head.

'I don't think so. There's something there.'

'Well, if there is, he didn't tell me about it.'

In the car Bosch called Rider to check in. She said she had completed a review of the files without anything that needed immediate follow-up catching her eye.

'We're going to see the Kincaids,' Bosch said.

'How come so soon?'

'Turns out one of them was Harris's alibi.'

'What?'

Bosch explained the license plate discovery Pelfry and Elias had made.

'One out of four,' she said.

'What do you mean?'

'We now know what one out of four of the mystery notes means.'

'Yeah, I guess so.'

'I was thinking about the first two. I think they're connected and I've got an idea about "dot the i." I'm going to go online and check it out. You know what a hypertext link is?'

'I don't speak that language, Kiz. I still type with two fingers.'

'I know. I'll explain it when you get back here. Maybe I'll know if I have something.'

'Okay. Good luck.'

He was about to hang up.

'Oh, Harry?'

'What?'

'You gotta call from Carla Entrenkin. She said she needed to talk to you. I was going to give her your pager but then I thought you might not want that. She might start paging you every time she gets a wild hair.'

'That's fine. Did she leave a number?'

She gave it to him and they hung up.

'We're going to the Kincaids'?' Edgar asked.

'Yeah, I just decided. Get on the radio and run the plate on that white Volvo. See what name's on it. I've got to make a call.'

Bosch called the number Carla Entrenkin had left and she answered after two rings.

'It's Bosch.'

'Detective ...'

'You called?'

'Yes, uh, I just wanted to apologize about last night. I was upset at what I saw on the television and ... and I think I spoke too soon. I've done some checking and I think I was wrong about what I said.'

'You were.'

'Well, I'm sorry.'

'Okay, Inspector, I appreciate you calling. I better—'

'How is the investigation going?'

'It's going. Have you talked to Chief Irving?'

'Yes, I have. He told me that they are questioning Detective Sheehan.'

'Don't hold your breath on that.'

'I'm not. What about what you are pursuing? I was told you are reinvestigating the original case. The murder of Stacey Kincaid.'

'Well, we can now prove Harris didn't do it. You were right about that. Elias was going to go into court and clear him. He didn't do it. We now just have to prove somebody else did. And my money is still on that somebody being the one who also did Elias. I have to go now, Inspector.'

'Will you call me if you make significant progress?'

Bosch thought about this for a few moments. Dealing with Carla Entrenkin somehow gave him the feel of consorting with the enemy.

'Yes,' he finally said. 'I'll call if there is significant progress.'

'Thank you, Detective.'

'Don't mention it.'

25

The Los Angeles car czar and his wife now lived off Mulholland Drive in an exclusive development called The Summit. It was a gated and guarded neighborhood of side-by-side millionaires with spectacular homes that looked down from the Santa Monica Mountains and north across the basin of the San Fernando Valley. The Kincaids had moved from Brentwood to these gated hills after their daughter's murder. It was a move toward security that was too late for the little girl.

Bosch and Edgar had called ahead and were welcomed at the gatehouse. There they were given directions along a curving development road to a huge French Provincial mansion built on a piece of property that must have been the summit of The Summit. A Latina maid answered the door and led them to a living room that was bigger than Bosch's entire house. It had two fireplaces and three distinct groupings of furniture. Bosch wasn't sure what the purpose of this could be. The long northern wall of the room was almost entirely glass. It revealed an expansive view across the Valley. Bosch had a hill house but the difference in views was a couple of thousand feet in altitude and maybe ten million dollars in attitude. The maid told them that the Kincaids would be with them shortly.

Bosch and Edgar stepped to the window, which they were meant to do. The rich kept you waiting so that you could feel free to admire all that they had.

'Jetliner views,' Edgar said.

'What's that?'

'That's what they call it when you're this high up. Jetliner views.'

Bosch nodded. Edgar had sold real estate as a side job with his wife a few years back, until it threatened to turn his police work into a side job.

Bosch could see across the Valley to the Santa Susanna Mountains. He could pick out Oat Mountain above Chatsworth. He remembered going there years before on a field trip from the youth hall. The overall view, however, could not be called beautiful. A heavy layer of smog – especially for April – stretched across the Valley. They were high enough in the Kincaid house to be above it. Or so it seemed.

'I know what you're thinking. It's a million-dollar view of the smog.'

Bosch turned around. A smiling man and a blank-faced woman had entered the living room. Behind them stood a second man in a dark suit. Bosch recognized the first man from TV. Sam Kincaid, the car czar. He was smaller than Bosch expected. More compact. His deep tan was real, not television makeup, and his jet-black hair seemed legitimate. On TV it always looked like a wig. He was wearing a golf shirt like the ones he always wore on his commercials. Like the ones his father had worn when he was the one on the commercials a decade earlier.

The woman was younger than Kincaid by a few years, about forty and well preserved by weekly massages and trips to the salons down on Rodeo Drive. She looked past Bosch and Edgar to the view. She had a vague expression on her face and Bosch immediately realized that Katherine Kincaid had probably not come close to recovering from the loss of her daughter.

'But you know what?' Sam Kincaid continued, smiling. 'I don't mind seeing the smog. My family's been selling cars in this city for three generations. Since nineteen hundred and twenty-eight. That's a lot of years and a lot of cars. That smog out there reminds me of that.'

His statement sounded rehearsed, as if he used it as an opener with all of his guests. He stepped forward with his hand out.

'Sam Kincaid. And my wife, Kate.'

Bosch shook his hand and introduced himself and Edgar. The way Kincaid studied Edgar before shaking his hand made Bosch think that his partner might have been the first black man to set foot in his living room – not counting the ones who were there to serve canapés and take drink orders.

Bosch looked past Kincaid to the man still standing beneath the arch of the entryway. Kincaid noticed and made the last introduction.

'This is D.C. Richter, my chief of security,' Kincaid said. 'I asked him to come up and join us, if you don't mind.'

Bosch was puzzled by the addition of the security man but didn't say anything. He nodded and Richter nodded back. He was about Bosch's age, tall and gaunt and his short graying hair was spiked with gel. Richter also had a small earring, a thin gold hoop on his left ear.

'What can we do for you gentlemen?' Kincaid asked. 'I have to say I'm surprised by this visit. I would have guessed that with everything going on, you two would be out on the street somewhere, trying to keep down the animals.'

There was an awkward silence. Kate Kincaid looked down at the rug.

'We're investigating the death of Howard Elias,' Edgar said. 'And your daughter's.'

'My daughter's? I don't understand what you mean.'

'Why don't we sit down, Mr Kincaid?' Bosch said.

'Sure.'

Kincaid led them to one of the furniture groupings. Two couches faced each other across a glass coffee table. To one side was a fireplace Bosch could almost walk into, to the other was the view. The Kincaids sat on one couch while Bosch and Edgar took the other. Richter stood to the side and behind the couch where the Kincaids sat.

'Let me explain,' Bosch said. 'We are here to inform you that we are reopening the investigation of Stacey's death. We need to start again.'

Both Kincaids opened their mouths into small looks of puzzlement. Bosch continued.

'In the course of investigating the killing Friday night of Howard Elias we have uncovered information that we believe exonerates Michael Harris. We—'

'Impossible,' Sam Kincaid barked. 'Harris was the killer. His fingerprints were found in the house, the old house. You're going to tell me that the Los Angeles Police Department now believes its own people planted this evidence?'

'No, sir, I'm not. I'm telling you that we now have what we think is a reasonable explanation for that evidence.'

'Well, I'd love to hear it.'

Bosch took two folded pieces of paper from his jacket pocket and opened them. One was a photocopy of the car wash receipt Pelfry had found. The other was a photocopy of Harris's time card, also from Pelfry.

'Mrs Kincaid, you drive a white Volvo station wagon with license plate number one-bravo-henry-six-six-eight, correct?'

'No, that's wrong,' Richter answered for her.

Bosch looked up at him for a moment and then back at the woman.

'*Did* you drive this car last summer?'

'I drove a white Volvo station wagon, yes,' she said. 'I don't remember the license number.'

'My family owns eleven dealerships and parts of six more in this county,' her husband said. 'Chevy, Cadillac, Mazda, you name it. Even a Porsche store. But no Volvo franchise. And so what do you know, that's the car she picks. She says it's safer for Stacey and then she ends up … anyway.'

Sam Kincaid brought a hand up to cover his lip and held himself still. Bosch waited a moment before pressing on.

'Take my word for it about the plate number. The car was registered to you, Mrs Kincaid. On June twelve last year that car, the Volvo, was washed at Hollywood Wax and Shine on Sunset Boulevard. The person who took the car there asked for the daily special, which included interior vacuuming and polish. Here's the receipt.'

He leaned forward and put it on the coffee table in front of the couple. They both leaned down to look at it. Richter leaned over the back of the couch for a look.

'Does either of you remember doing that?'

'We don't wash our cars,' Sam Kincaid said. 'And we don't go to public car washes. I need a car washed I have it taken to one of my stores. I don't need to pay to—'

'I remember,' his wife said, cutting him off. 'I did it. I took Stacey to the movies at the El Capitan. Where we parked there was construction – a new roof being put on the building next to the garage. When we came out the car had something on it. Like little spots of tar that had blown onto it. It was a white car and it was very noticeable. When I paid the parking attendant I asked him where a car wash was. He told me.'

Kincaid was looking at his wife as if she had just belched at the charity ball.

'So you got the car washed there,' Bosch said.

'Yes. I remember now.'

She looked at her husband and then back at Bosch.

'The receipt says June twelve,' Bosch said. 'How long after the end of school for your daughter was that?'

'It was the next day. It was our way of kicking off the summer. Lunch and the movies. It was a movie about these two guys who can't find a mouse in their house. It was cute … The mouse got the better of them.'

Her eyes were on the memory, and on her daughter. They then focused on Bosch once more.

'No more school,' Bosch said. 'Could she have left her books from the last day in the Volvo? Maybe in the back?'

Kate Kincaid slowly nodded.

'Yes. I remember having to tell her at one point during the summer to take the books out of the car. They kept sliding around when I drove. She didn't do it. I finally took them out and put them in her room.'

Bosch leaned forward again and put the other photocopy down for them.

'Michael Harris worked at Hollywood Wax and Shine last summer. That's his time card for the week including June twelve. He worked a full day on the day you brought the Volvo in.'

Sam Kincaid leaned forward again and studied the photocopy.

'You mean all this time we've … ,' Kincaid began and then stopped. 'You're saying that he – Harris – vacuumed out the Volvo and in the process touched my stepdaughter's book? Picked it up or whatever, then the book was eventually taken to her bedroom. And after she was taken …'

'The police found the prints on it,' Bosch finished. 'Yes, that's now what we think.'

'Why didn't this come out at the trial? Why—'

'Because there was other evidence linking Harris to the murder,' Edgar said. 'The girl's – uh, Stacey – was found less than two blocks from his apartment. That was a strong tie-in. His lawyer decided the tack he had to take was to go after the cops. Taint the fingerprints by tainting the cops. He never went after the truth.'

'And neither did the cops,' Bosch said. 'They had the prints and when the body was found in Harris's neighborhood, that sealed it. You remember, the investigation was emotionally charged from the beginning.

It changed at that point when they found the body and it all tied into Harris. It changed from a search for a little girl to a prosecution of a specific target. In between it never was a search for the truth.'

Sam Kincaid seemed shell-shocked.

'All this time,' he said. 'Can you imagine the hate I have built up inside of me for this man? This hate, this utter and complete contempt, has been the only real emotion I've had for the last nine months ...'

'I understand, sir,' Bosch said. 'But we need to start over now. We need to reinvestigate the case. That was what Howard Elias was doing. We have reason to believe that he knew what I just told you. Only he also knew or had a pretty good idea who the actual killer was. We think that got him killed.'

Sam Kincaid looked surprised.

'But the TV said a little while ago that—'

'The TV's wrong, Mr Kincaid. It's wrong and we're right.'

Kincaid nodded. His eyes wandered out to the view and the smog.

'What do you want from us?' Kate Kincaid said.

'Your help. Your cooperation. I know we are hitting you out of the blue with this so we're not expecting you to drop everything. But as you can tell if you've been watching TV, time isn't something we have a lot of.'

'You have our full cooperation,' Sam Kincaid said. 'And D.C. here can do whatever you need him to do.'

Bosch looked from Kincaid to the security man and then back to Kincaid.

'I don't think that will be necessary. We just have a few more questions for right now and then tomorrow we want to come back and start the case over.'

'Of course. What are your questions?'

'Howard Elias learned what I just told you because of an anonymous note that came in the mail. Do either of you know who that could have come from? Who would

269

have known about the Volvo going to that car wash?'

There was no answer for a long time.

'Just me,' Kate Kincaid said. 'I don't know who else. I don't remember telling anyone I went there. Why would I?'

'Did you send Howard Elias the note?'

'No. Of course not. Why would I help Michael Harris? I thought he was the one who … who took my daughter. Now you tell me he is innocent and I think I believe you. But before, no, I wouldn't have lifted a finger to help him.'

Bosch studied her as she spoke. Her eyes moved from the coffee table to the view and then to her hands clasped in front of her. She didn't look at her questioner. Bosch had been reading people in interviews and interrogations for most of his adult life. In that moment he knew she had sent Elias the anonymous note. He just couldn't figure out why. He glanced up again at Richter and saw that the security man was also closely studying the woman. Bosch wondered if he was reading the same thing. He decided to move on.

'The house where this crime took place. The one in Brentwood. Who owns that now?'

'We still own it,' Sam Kincaid said. 'We're not sure what we're going to do with it. Part of us wants to get rid of it and never think of it again. But the other part … Stacey was there. She lived half of her life there …'

'I understand. What I'd like—'

Bosch's pager went off. He cut it off and continued.

'I'd like to take a look at it, at her room. Tomorrow, if possible. We'll have a search warrant by then. I know you're a busy man, Mr Kincaid. Maybe, Mrs Kincaid, you could meet me there, show me around. Show me Stacey's room. If that won't be too difficult.'

Kate Kincaid looked as if she dreaded the possibility of returning to the Brentwood house. But she nodded her head yes in a disengaged sort of way.

'I'll have D.C. drive her,' Sam Kincaid announced.

'And you can have the run of the place. And you won't need a search warrant. We give you our permission. We have nothing to hide.'

'Sir, I didn't mean to imply that you did. The search warrant will be necessary so there will be no questions later. It is more a protection for us. If something new in the house is found and leads to the real killer, we don't want that person to be able to challenge the evidence on any legal grounds.'

'I understand.'

'And we appreciate you offering the help of Mr Richter but that won't be necessary.' Bosch looked at Kate Kincaid. 'I would prefer it if just you came, Mrs Kincaid. What time would be good?'

While she thought about this Bosch looked down at his pager. The number on it was one of the homicide lines. But there was a 911 added after the phone number. It was code from Kiz Rider: Call immediately.

'Uh, excuse me,' Bosch said. 'It looks like this call is important. Do you have a phone I could use? I have a cell phone in the car but in these hills I'm not sure I'll be able to get—'

'Of course,' Sam Kincaid said. 'Use my office. Go back out to the entry hall and go left. The second door on the left. You'll have privacy. We'll wait here with Detective Edwards.'

Bosch stood.

'It's Edgar,' Edgar said.

'I'm sorry. Detective Edgar.'

As Bosch headed to the entry hall another pager sounded. This time it was Edgar's. He knew it was Rider sending the same message. Edgar looked down at his pager and then at the Kincaids.

'I better go with Detective Bosch.'

'Sounds like something big,' Sam Kincaid offered. 'Hope it's not a riot.'

'Me, too,' Edgar said.

*

Kincaid's home office would have been able to accommodate the entire Hollywood homicide squad. It was a huge room with towering ceilings and bookcases along two walls that went all the way up to the ceiling. The centerpiece of the room was a desk that would have dwarfed Howard Elias's. It looked as if you could build a nice-sized office *inside* it.

Bosch came around behind it and picked up the phone. Edgar came into the room behind him.

'You get one from Kiz?' Bosch asked.

'Yeah. Something's happening.'

Bosch punched in the number and waited. He noticed that on the desk was a gold-framed photo of Kincaid holding his stepdaughter on his lap. The girl was indeed beautiful. He thought about what Frankie Sheehan had said about her looking like an angel, even in death. He looked away and noticed the computer set up on a worktable to the right of the desk. There was a screen saver on the tube. It showed a variety of different cars racing back and forth across the screen. Edgar noticed it, too.

'The car czar,' Edgar whispered. 'More like the smog wog.'

Rider answered before the first ring was finished.

'It's Bosch.'

'Harry, did you talk to the Kincaids yet?'

'We're here now. We're in the middle of it. What's going—'

'Did you advise them?'

Bosch was silent a moment. When he spoke again his voice was very low.

'Advise them? No. What for, Kiz?'

'Harry, back out of there and come back to the station.'

Bosch had never heard Rider's voice with such a serious tone. He looked at Edgar, who just raised his eyebrows. He was in the dark.

'Okay, Kiz, we're on our way. You want to tell me why?'

'No. I have to show you. I found Stacey Kincaid in afterlife.'

26

Bosch couldn't put his finger on the look he saw on Kizmin Rider's face when he and Edgar returned to the squad room. She sat alone at the homicide table, her laptop in front of her, the glow of the screen reflecting slightly on her dark face. She looked both horrified and energized. Bosch knew the look but didn't have the words for it. She had seen something horrible but at the same time she knew she was going to be able to do something about it.

'Kiz,' Bosch said.

'Sit down. I hope you didn't leave hair on the cake with the Kincaids.'

Bosch pulled out his seat and sat down. Edgar did likewise. The phrase Rider had used referred to making a miscue that tainted a case with constitutional or procedural error. If a suspect asks for a lawyer but then confesses to a crime before the lawyer arrives, there is hair on the cake. The confession is tainted. Likewise, if a suspect is not advised of his rights before questioning, it is unlikely anything he says in that conversation can be used against him later in court.

'Look, neither one was a suspect when we walked in there,' Bosch said. 'There was no reason to advise. We told them the case was open again and asked a few basic questions. Nothing came out of any consequence anyway. We told them Harris has been cleared and that's it. What do you have, Kiz? Maybe you should just show us.'

'Okay, bring your chairs around here. I'll school you.'

They moved their chairs to positions on either side of her. Bosch checked her computer and saw the Mistress Regina web page was on the screen.

'First off, either of you guys know Lisa or Stacey O'Connor in Major Fraud downtown?'

Bosch and Edgar shook their heads.

'They're not sisters. They just have the same last name. They work with Sloane Inglert. You know who she is, right?'

Now they nodded. Inglert was a member of a new computer fraud unit working out of Parker Center. The team, and Inglert in particular, had gotten a lot of play in the media earlier that year when they bagged Brian Fielder, a hacker of international reputation who headed a crew of hackers known as the 'Merry Pranksters.' Fielder's exploits and Inglert's chase of her quarry across the Internet had played in the paper for weeks and were now destined to be filmed by Hollywood.

'All right,' Rider said. 'Well, they're friends of mine from when I worked Fraud. I called them and they were happy to come in to work this because otherwise they'd have to put on uniforms and work twelve hours tonight.'

'They came here?' Bosch asked.

'No, their office at Parker. Where the real computers are. Anyway, we talked over the phone once they got there. I told them what we had – this web address that we knew was important but at the same time didn't make any sense. I told them about going to Mistress Regina's place and I think I pretty much creeped them out. Anyway, they told me there was a good chance that what we were looking for had nothing to do with Regina herself, just her web page. They said the page could have been hijacked and that we should be looking for a hidden hypertext link somewhere in the image.'

Bosch raised his hands palms up but before he could say anything Rider kept going.

'I know, I know, talk English. I will. I just wanted to take you step by step. Do either of you know anything at all about web pages? Am I making even any basic sense here?'

'Nope,' said Bosch.

'Nada,' said Edgar.

'Okay, then I'll try to keep this simple. We start with the Internet. The Internet is the so-called information superhighway, okay? Thousands and thousands of computer systems all connected by a Telnet system. It is worldwide. On that highway are millions of turnoffs, places to go. These are whole computer networks, web sites, so on and so forth.'

She pointed to Mistress Regina on her computer screen.

'This is an individual web page that is on a web site where there are many other pages. You see this on my computer here but its home, so to speak, is on the larger web site. And that web site resides in an actual, physical piece of equipment – a computer we call the web server. Do you follow me?'

Bosch and Edgar nodded.

'So far,' Bosch said. 'I think.'

'Good. Now the web server may have many, many web sites that it manages and maintains. See, if you wanted to have a Harry Bosch web page you would go to a web server and say put my page on one of your web sites. Do you have one that features morose detectives who never say much of anything to anybody?'

That got a smile from Bosch.

'That's how it works. Often you have like-minded businesses or interests bundled on one site. That's why when you look at this site it's like Sodom and Gomorrah on the Internet. Because like-minded advertisers seek the same sites.'

'Okay,' Bosch said.

'The one thing the web server should provide is security. By that I mean security from anyone hacking in and compromising your page – altering it or crashing it. The problem is, there isn't a whole lot of security out there on these web servers. And if someone can hack into a server they can then assume site-administrator capabilities for a web site and hijack any page on the site.'

'What do you mean, hijack?' Edgar said.

'They can go to a page on the site and use it as a front for their own intentions. Think of it as it is on my screen here. They can come up behind the image you see here and add all kinds of hidden doors and commands, whatever they want. They can then use the page as a gateway to anything they want.'

'And that's what they did with her page?' Bosch asked.

'Exactly. I had O'Connor/O'Connor run a uniform resource locator. In effect they traced this page back to the web server. They checked it out. There are indeed some firewalls – security blocks – but the default passwords are still valid. They, in effect, render the firewalls invalid.'

'You lost me,' Bosch said.

'When a web server is first set up, there are default passwords necessary for first getting inside. In other words, standard log-on names and passwords. Guest/ guest, for example. Or administrator/administrator. Once the server is up and running these should be eliminated to prevent compromise but quite often it is forgotten about and these become back doors, ways to sneak in. It was forgotten here. Lisa got in using administrator/administrator. And if she was able to do it, then any hacker worth his salt could have gotten in and then hijacked the Mistress Regina page. And somebody did.'

'What did they do?' Bosch asked.

'They put in a hidden hypertext link. A hot button. When located and pushed, it will take the user to another web site all together.'

'In English,' Edgar said.

Rider thought for a moment.

'Think of it as a tall building – the Empire State building. You are on one floor. The Mistress Regina floor. And you find a hidden button on the wall. You push it and an elevator door you didn't even see before opens and you get on. The elevator takes you to another floor and opens. You step out. You are someplace completely new. But you couldn't have gotten there if you hadn't been on Mistress Regina's floor and stumbled onto that hidden button.'

'Or been told where it was,' Bosch said.

'Exactly,' Rider said. 'Those in the know can go.'

Bosch nodded at her computer.

'Show us.'

'Well, remember, the first note to Elias was the web page address and the image of Regina. The second one said, "dot the i humbert humbert." The mystery writer was simply telling Elias what to do with the web page.'

'Dot the i in Regina?' Edgar asked. 'Click the mouse on the dot?'

'That's what I thought but O'Connor/O'Connor said a hot button can only be hidden behind an image. Something about pixel redefinition that I don't need to get into.'

'So you dot the eye?' Bosch said, pointing to his eye.

'Right.'

She turned to her laptop to which she had attached a mouse. She now moved it with her hand and Bosch watched the arrow on the screen move to Mistress Regina's left eye. Rider double-clicked the mouse button and the screen went blank.

'Okay, we're on that elevator.'

After a few seconds a field of blue sky and clouds appeared on the screen. Then tiny angels with wings and halos appeared sitting on the clouds. Then a password template appeared.

'Humbert humbert,' Bosch said.

'See, Harry, you get this stuff. You're just acting like you don't.'

She typed in the name humbert in the user name and password slots and the screen went blank once again. A few seconds later there was a welcome message.

WELCOME TO CHARLOTTE'S WEB SITE

Below the message a moving cartoon image formed. A spider crawled along the bottom of the page and then began weaving a web across the screen, shooting back and forth until the web was formed. Then tiny photographic images of young girls' faces appeared in the web, as if caught there. When the image of the web and its captives was complete, the spider took a position at the top of the web.

'This is sick,' Edgar said. 'I'm getting a bad feeling here.'

'It's a pedophile site,' Rider said. With a fingernail she tapped the screen below one of the photos in the web. 'And that is Stacey Kincaid. You click on the photo you like and you get a full spread of photos and videos. It is truly, truly horrible stuff. That poor little angel, she might be better off dead.'

Rider moved the arrow to the photo of the blond girl. It was too small for Bosch to identify the girl as Stacey Kincaid. He wished he could just take Rider's word for it.

'Are you ready for this?' Rider asked. 'I can't run videos on my laptop but the photos give you the idea.'

She didn't wait for a reply and she didn't get one. She double-clicked the mouse and a new screen appeared. A photo appeared on the screen. It was a young girl standing naked in front of a hedge. She was smiling in a forced, seemingly unnatural way. Despite the smile she still had a lost-in-the-woods look on her face. Her hands were on her hips. Bosch could tell it was Stacey Kincaid. He tried to breathe but it felt like his lungs were collapsing. He folded his arms across his chest.

Rider started scrolling the screen and a series of photos came up featuring the girl in several poses by herself and then finally with a man. Only the man's naked torso was shown, never his face. The last photos were the girl and the man engaged in various sex acts. Finally, they came to the final photo. It showed Stacey Kincaid in a white dress with little semaphore flags on it. She was waving at the camera. The photo seemed somehow to be the worst one even though it was the most innocent.

'Okay, go back or forward or whatever you do to get that off there,' Bosch said.

He watched Rider move the cursor to a button below the final photo that said HOME on it. It seemed sadly ironic to Bosch that clicking HOME was the way out. Rider clicked the mouse and the screen went back to the spider's web. Bosch pulled his chair back to his spot and dropped down into it. Fatigue and depression suddenly hit him. He wanted to go home and go to sleep and forget everything he knew.

'People are the worst animals,' Rider said. 'They will do anything to each other. Just to indulge their fantasies.'

Bosch got up and walked over to one of the other nearby desks. It belonged to a burglary detective named McGrath. He opened the drawers and started looking through them.

'Harry,' Rider said, 'what are you looking for?'

'A cigarette. I thought Paul kept his smokes in his desk.'

'He used to. I told him to start taking them home with him.'

Bosch looked over at her, his hand still holding one of the drawers.

'You told him that?'

'I didn't want you slipping, Harry.'

Bosch shoved the drawer closed and came back to his chair.

'Thanks a lot, Kizmin. You saved me.'

There wasn't a drop of thanks in the tone he had used.

'You'll get through this, Harry.'

Bosch gave her a look.

'You probably haven't smoked an entire cigarette in your entire life and you're going to tell me about quitting and how I'll get through it?'

'Sorry. I'm just trying to help.'

'Like I said, thanks.'

He looked over at her computer and nodded.

'What else? What are you thinking about? How does that tie in Sam and Kate Kincaid to the point we should've advised them?'

'They had to know about this,' Rider said, amazed that Bosch didn't see what she saw. 'The man in the photos, that's got to be Kincaid.'

'Whoah!' Edgar said. 'How can you say that? You couldn't see the guy's face. We were just talking to the guy and he and his wife are still righteously fucked-up over this.'

It hit Bosch then. When he had first seen the photos on the computer he had thought they were taken by the girl's abductor.

'You're saying these photos are old,' he said. 'That she was abused before she was abducted.'

'I'm saying there probably wasn't an abduction at all. Stacey Kincaid was an abused child. My guess is that her stepfather defiled her and then probably killed her. And that doesn't happen without tacit knowledge, if not approval, by the mother.'

Bosch was silent. Rider had spoken with such fervor and even pain that he couldn't help but wonder if she was talking from some kind of personal experience.

'Look,' Rider said, apparently sensing the skepticism of her partners. 'There was a time that I thought I wanted to move into child sex crimes. This was before I put in for homicide. There was an opening on the endangered-child team in Pacific and the job was mine if I wanted it. They first sent me to Quantico for a two-week training program the bureau puts on once a year on child sex crimes. I lasted eight days. I realized I couldn't hack it. I came back and put in for homicide.'

She stopped there but neither Bosch or Edgar said anything. They knew there was more.

'But before I left,' Rider continued, 'I learned enough to know that most often sexual abuse of children comes from inside the family, relatives or close friends. The boogie monsters who climb through the window and abduct are few and far between.'

'It's still not evidence in this specific case, Kiz,' Bosch said gently. 'This could still be the rare exception. It wasn't Harris who came through the window but this guy.'

He pointed to her computer, though the images of the headless man's assault on Stacey Kincaid were thankfully not on the screen.

'Nobody came through the window,' Rider insisted.

She pulled a file over and opened it. Bosch saw it contained a copy of the protocol from the autopsy of Stacey Kincaid. She leafed through it until she came to the photos. She picked the one she wanted and handed it to Bosch. While he looked at it she started paging through the protocol.

The photo Bosch held was a shot of Stacey Kincaid's body *in situ* – the position and place where it was found. Her arms were spread wide. Sheehan had been right. Her body was darkening with interior decomposition and the face was gaunt, but there was an angelic quality to her in repose. His heart ached from looking at the photos of her tortured and now dead.

'Look at the left knee,' Rider commanded.

He did so. He saw a round dark spot that appeared to be a scab.

'A scab?'

'Right. The protocol calls it premortem by five to six days. It happened before she was abducted. So she had that scab on her knee the entire time she was with her abductor – if there really was one. In the photos on the web site, she has no scab. I can go back in and show you if you like.'

'I'll take your word for it,' Bosch said.

'Yeah,' Edgar added. 'Me, too.'

'So these photos on the web were taken well before she was supposedly kidnapped, well before she was murdered.'

Bosch nodded, then shook his head.

'What?' Rider asked.

'It's just … I don't know. Twenty-four hours ago we were working the Elias thing and thinking maybe we were looking for a cop. Now all of this …'

'It changes things all right,' Edgar said.

'Wait a minute, if that's Sam Kincaid in those pictures with her, why the hell are they still on that web site? It doesn't make sense that he would risk that.'

'I thought about that,' Rider said. 'There are two possible explanations. One being that he doesn't have editing access to the web site. In other words, he can't take those photos off without going to the site administrator, raising suspicions and exposing himself. The second possibility, and it might be a combination of both, is that he felt he was safe. Harris was fingered as the killer and whether he was convicted or not that was the end of the story.'

'It's still a risk leaving those photos out there to be seen,' Edgar said.

'Who's going to see them?' Rider asked. 'Who's going to tell?'

Her voice was too defensive. She realized this and continued in a calmer tone.

'Don't you see? The people with access to this site are pedophiles. Even if someone recognized Stacey, which is unlikely, what were they going to do? Call the police and say, "Uh, yes, I like fucking children but I don't stand for murdering them. Could you get these photos off our web site?" Not in a million years. Hell, maybe keeping the photos on there was a form of bragging. We don't even know what we have here. Maybe every girl on that site is dead.'

Her voice was growing sharper as she tried to convince them.

'Okay, okay,' Bosch said. 'You make good points, Kiz. Let's stay on our case for now. What is your theory. You think Elias got this far along and it got him killed?'

'Absolutely. We know it did. The fourth note. "He knows you know." Elias went onto the secret web site and was found out.'

'How'd they know he was in there if he had the passwords from the third note?' Edgar asked.

'Good question,' Rider replied. 'I asked the O'Connors the same thing. They did some snooping around after getting into the server. They found a cookie jar on the web site. What that means is that there is a program that captures data about each user who enters the site. It then analyzes the data to determine if someone has entered the site who should not have had access. Even if they have the passwords, their entry is still recorded and a data trail called an Internet protocol address is left behind. It's like fingerprints. The IP, or the cookie, is left on the site you enter. The cookie jar program will then analyze the IP address and match it to a list of known users. If there is no match a flag is raised. The site's manager sees the flag and can trace the intruder. Or he can set up a tripwire program that waits for a return visit from the intruder. When he comes back, the program will attach a tracer which will provide the site manager with the intruder's E-mail address. And once you have that you have the intruder cold. You can identify him then. If it looks like a cop you close the elevator – the page you hijacked and were using as a secret gateway – and you go find a new web page to hijack. But in this case it wasn't a cop. It was a lawyer.'

'And they didn't shut down,' Bosch said. 'They sent someone out to kill him.'

'Right.'

'So you think this is what Elias did,' Bosch said. 'He got these notes in the mail and followed the clues. He stumbled into this web site and set off an alarm. A flag. The response was to kill him.'

'Yes, that would be my interpretation of what we know at this point, particularly in light of the fourth note. "He knows you know."'

Bosch shook his head, confused by his own extrapolations of the story.

'I'm still not getting this. Who is the "they" we're talking about here? That I just accused of murder.'

'The group. The users of the site. The site administrator – which might possibly be Kincaid – picked up on the intruder, realized it was Elias, and dispatched someone to take care of the problem in order to fend off exposure. Whether or not he polled all members of the group first doesn't matter. They are all guilty because the web site is a criminal enterprise.'

Bosch held his hand up to slow her down.

'Slow down. We can leave the group and the bigger picture for the DA to worry about. Stay focused on the killer and Kincaid. We are assuming he was involved in all of this and somehow someone knew about it, then decided to inform Elias instead of the cops. Does that make sense?'

'Sure it does. We just don't know all the details yet. But the notes speak for themselves. They clearly indicate someone tipped Elias to the site, then later warned him that he had been found out.'

Bosch nodded and thought about this for a moment.

'Wait a minute. If he set off a flag, then didn't you just do the same?'

'No. Thanks to the O'Connors. When they were inside the server they added my IP as well as their own to the site's good guy list. No alarms. The operators and users of the site won't know we've been there unless they actually look at their good guy list and notice it has been altered. I think we've got the time to do what we need to do.'

Bosch nodded. He wanted to ask whether what the O'Connors had done had been legal but thought it best not to know.

'So who sent Elias the notes?' he asked instead.

'The wife,' Edgar said. 'I think she got an attack of the guilts and wanted to help Elias rip Sam the car czar a new asshole. She sent the notes.'

'It fits,' Rider said. 'Whoever sent the notes had knowledge of two separate things: Charlotte's Web Site and the car-wash receipts. Actually, a third thing as well: that Elias had tripped an alarm. So my vote goes with the wife, too. What was she like today?'

Bosch spent the next ten minutes updating her on their activities during the day.

'And that's just our work on the case,' Edgar added. 'Harry didn't even tell you how we got the back window of my car shot out.'

'What?'

Edgar told the story and Rider seemed mesmerized by it.

'They catch the shooter?'

'Not that we heard. We didn't wait around.'

'You know, I've never been shot at,' she said. 'Must be a rush.'

'Not the kind you want,' Bosch said. 'I still have questions about all of this Internet stuff.'

'What are they?' Rider said. 'If I can't answer, one of the O'Connors can.'

'No, not technical questions. Logic questions. I still don't understand how and why this stuff is still available for us to look at. I understand what you said about the users all being pedophiles and their seeming feeling of safety, but now we have Elias dead. If they killed him, why the hell didn't they at least move to a new gateway?'

'Maybe they are in the process of trying to do just that. Elias hasn't been dead forty-eight hours.'

'And what about Kincaid? We just told him we are reopening the case. Whether he was in danger of exposure or not, it seems he would have gotten on the computer the minute we left and either contacted the site administrator or tried to crash the site and those pictures himself.'

'Again, maybe it's in process. And even if it is, it's too late. The O'Connors backed everything onto a Zip drive. They can crash the site but we still have it. We'll be able to trace every IP address and take every one of those people – if you consider them people.'

Again the fervor and anger in her voice made Bosch wonder if something about what she had seen on the web site had touched something personal, something deep inside.

'So where do we go from here?' he asked. 'Search warrants?'

'Yep,' Rider said. 'And we bring in the Kincaids. Fuck their big mansion on the hill. We have enough already to bring them in for questioning on the child abuse. We separate them and sweat them in the rooms. We go for the wife and get a confession. Get her to waive spousal privilege and give us her husband, that rat bastard.'

'You're talking about a very powerful and politically connected family.'

'Don't tell me you're afraid of the car czar.'

Bosch checked her look to make sure she was kidding.

'I'm afraid of moving too fast and blowing it. We've got nothing that directly links anybody to Stacey Kincaid or Howard Elias. If we bring mom down here and don't turn her, then we watch the car czar drive away. That's what I'm afraid of, okay?'

Rider nodded.

'She's dying to be turned,' Edgar said. 'Why else send those notes to Elias?'

Bosch put his elbows on the desk and washed his face with his hands as he thought about things. He had to make a decision.

'What about Charlotte's Web Site?' he asked, his face still covered by his hands. 'What do we do with that?'

'We give that to Inglert and the O'Connors,' Rider said. 'They'll jump all over it. Like I said, they'll be able to trace the good guy list to the users. They'll identify them and take them down. We're talking multiple arrests of an Internet pedophile ring. That's just for starters. The DA might want to try to link them all to the homicides.'

'They're probably all over the country,' Edgar said. 'Not just L.A.'

'They might be all over the world but it won't matter. Our people will work with the bureau on it.'

More silence passed by and Bosch finally dropped his hands to the desk. He'd made his decision.

'Okay,' he said. 'You two stay here and work on the search warrants. I want them ready to go tonight, in case we decide to move. We want all weapons, computer equipment – you know what to do. I want warrants for the old house, which they still own, as well as the new house, all cars and Kincaid's office. Also, Jerry, see what you can find out about the security guy.'

'D.C. Richter, will do. What—'

'In fact, on the warrants, write up one for his car.'

'What's the PC?' Rider asked.

Bosch thought a moment. He knew what he wanted but he needed a legal means of getting there.

'Just say that as Kincaid's director of security it is believed that his vehicle may have been used in the commission of crimes relating to Stacey Kincaid.'

'That's not probable cause, Harry.'

'We stick the warrant in with the other ones,' he said.

'Maybe the judge won't care after he's read what is in them. In fact, check the judge list. Let's take these to a woman.'

Rider smiled and said, 'Aren't we sly?'

'What are you going to be doing, Harry?' Edgar asked.

'I'm going downtown to talk to Irving and Lindell, tell them what we got and see how they want to play it.'

Bosch looked at Rider and now saw disappointment.

'Harry, this isn't like you,' she said. 'You know that if you go to Irving he'll take the conservative route. He won't let us move until we've nailed down every possibility.'

Bosch nodded and said, 'Normally, that would be true. But these aren't normal times. He wants to prevent the city from burning. Going with this, and going fast, might be the way. Irving's smart enough to see that.'

'You have too much faith in human nature,' she said.

'What are you talking about?'

'The best way of cooling this city off is to arrest a cop. Irving's already down there with Sheehan in the box. He isn't going to want to hear this, Harry.'

'You think that if you arrest the car czar and say he did Elias that everybody will believe you and be cool,' Edgar added. 'You don't understand. There are people out there who *need* this to be a cop and they won't listen to anything else. Irving's smart enough to see that, too.'

Bosch thought of Sheehan downtown at Parker Center in a room. He was being measured as the department's sacrificial lamb.

'Just work on the warrants,' he said. 'I'll worry about the rest.'

27

Bosch looked out the window and down at the protestors lining the sidewalks in front of Parker Center and across Los Angeles Street. They moved in orderly lines, carrying signs that said 'JUSTICE NOW' on one side and 'JUSTICE FOR HOWARD ELIAS' on the other. The duplication of the signs attested to the careful orchestration of the protest for the benefit of the media. Bosch saw Reverend Preston Tuggins was one of the marchers. As he walked, reporters walked along with him, sticking microphones in front of him and focusing cameras at his face. Bosch didn't see any signs that said anything about Catalina Perez.

'Detective Bosch,' Deputy Chief Irving said from behind him. 'Run it down for us. You've told us what information you've accumulated. Now put it into perspective. Tell us what you think it means.'

Bosch turned around. He looked at Irving, then at Lindell. They were in Irving's office. Irving was ensconced behind his desk, sitting ramrod straight in his full uniform – an indication he would be appearing at a press conference later. Lindell sat in one of the chairs across the desk. Bosch had just recounted for them what Rider had come up with and the steps his team had taken to that point. Irving now wanted his interpretation of it all.

Bosch composed his thoughts as he stepped back to the desk and took the seat next to Lindell.

'I think Sam Kincaid killed his stepdaughter or had something to do with it. There never was an abduction.

That was the story he cooked up. Then he got lucky. He caught a big break when those fingerprints happened to point to Harris. After that was discovered he was practically home free.'

'Start at the start.'

'Okay. You start with Kincaid being a pedophile. He married Kate six years ago, probably as a cover. And to get at her daughter. The girl's body was too decomposed for the coroner to determine if there was indication of long-term sexual abuse. But I'm saying there was. And at—'

'The mother knew?'

'I don't know. She found out at some point but *when* that was is the question.'

'Go on. Sorry to interrupt.'

'Something happened last summer. Maybe the girl threatened to tell someone – her mother, if she didn't know yet, or maybe go to authorities. Or maybe Kincaid simply grew tired of her. Pedophiles target a specific age group. They're not interested in children older than their target group. Stacey Kincaid was about to turn twelve. She may have been too old for her stepfather's … tastes. If she was no longer of use to him in that way, she was only a danger to him.'

'This conversation is turning my stomach, Detective. We are talking about an eleven-year-old girl.'

'What do you want me to do about it, Chief? It's turning mine, too. I've seen the pictures.'

'Then move on please.'

'So something happened and he killed her. He hid the body and jimmied the window. He then let events take place. In the morning the mother finds her gone and calls the cops. The abduction story starts to unfold.'

'He then gets lucky,' Lindell said.

'Right. He catches a nice piece of luck. Of all the prints collected in the girl's room and the rest of the house, the computer spits out a match with Michael Harris, ex-convict and all-around dirtbag. RHD was off to the races then. Like they were wearing blinders. They dropped everything and Harris became the only focus. They picked him up and did their thing with him. Only a funny thing happened on the way to a conviction. Harris didn't confess and there was no other evidence to go with those fingerprints. Meantime, Harris's name was leaked to the media. It became known that the cops had a suspect. Kincaid found out where Harris lived – maybe he got it from a friendly cop who was just keeping the parents of the victim informed. However it happened, he knew where Harris lived. He went to the spot where he'd hidden the body and moved it. My guess is that it was in the trunk of a car all along. Probably on one of his car lots. Anyway, he took the body to Harris's neighborhood and dumped it in a trash lot a couple blocks from the suspect's apartment. When it was found the next morning, the cops finally had another piece of evidence – circumstantial as it was – to go with the fingerprints. But all Harris was was a patsy.'

'His prints had been left when he washed Mrs Kincaid's car,' Irving said.

'Right.'

'So what about Elias?' Lindell asked. 'How did he get himself killed?'

'I think Mrs Kincaid did that. By mistake. At some point since she put her daughter in the ground I think she started seeing ghosts. She was feeling guilty about her daughter and maybe tried to make it right. She knew what her husband was capable of, maybe he had even threatened her outright, so she tried to do it on the sly. She started sending anonymous letters to Elias, to help him along. It did. Elias was able to get to the secret web site, Charlotte's Web. Once he saw those pictures of the girl, he knew who the real killer probably was. He was going about it very quietly. But he was going to subpoena Kincaid and spring it on him in court. Only he made a mistake and showed his hand.

292

He left a trail on the web site. Kincaid or the operators of the site learned they had been compromised.'

'They sent out a gun,' Lindell said.

'I seriously doubt it was Kincaid himself. But probably somebody working for him. He's got a security guy working for him. We're checking him out.'

They all sat silent for a long moment. Irving clasped his hands on the desk in front of him. There was nothing on top of it. It was just polished wood.

'You have to cut Sheehan loose,' Bosch said. 'He didn't do it.'

'Don't worry about Sheehan,' Irving said. 'If he's clean he goes home. I want to know how we proceed with Kincaid. It seems so ...'

Bosch ignored his hesitancy.

'We do what we're doing,' he said. 'We get search warrants signed and ready to go. I'm supposed to meet Mrs Kincaid tomorrow morning at the old house. I go, try to play her, try to get an admission. I think she's fragile, maybe ready to be flipped. Either way, we spring the warrants. We use everybody and hit all places at once – the homes, the cars, the offices. We see what they bring. We also have to pull records on his dealerships. Find out what cars Kincaid was using back in July. Richter, too.'

'Richter?'

'He's the security guy.'

Irving got up and went to the window this time.

'You're talking about a member of a family that helped build this city,' he said. 'The son of Jackson Kincaid.'

'I know that,' Bosch replied. 'The guy's from a powerful family. He's even proprietary about the smog. He looks at it like it's a family accomplishment. But that doesn't matter, Chief. Not after what he's done.'

Irving's eyes dropped and Bosch knew he was looking down at the protest march.

'The city's held together ...'

He didn't finish. Bosch knew what he was thinking. That those people down on the sidewalks were expecting news of charges being filed – against a cop.

'Where are we with Detective Sheehan?' Irving asked.

Lindell looked at his watch.

'We've been talking to him for six hours now. When I left he had yet to say a single self-incriminating word in regard to the murder of Howard Elias.'

'He previously threatened the victim in the manner in which the victim was killed.'

'That was a long time ago. Plus, it was said in public, in front of witnesses. It's been my experience that people who make threats like that usually don't carry them out. They are blowing off steam most of the time.'

Irving nodded, his face still to the window.

'What about ballistics?' he asked.

'Nothing yet. The autopsy on Elias was supposed to start this afternoon. I sent Detective Chastain over. They'll dig the slugs out and he'll take them over to your firearms people. It will take too long to send them to my people in Washington. But remember, Chief, Sheehan volunteered his gun. He said, "Do the ballistics." Yes, he carries a nine but I kinda think he wouldn't have offered the gun if he didn't know the gun wouldn't match the bullets.'

'And his home?'

'We searched it top to bottom – again, with his permission. Nothing. No other weapons, no hate notes about Elias, nothing.'

'Alibi?'

'Only place he's hurting. He was home alone Friday night.'

'What about his wife?' Bosch asked.

'The wife and kids were up in Bakersfield,' Lindell said. 'Apparently they've been up there a good long time.'

It was one more surprise about Sheehan. Bosch wondered why Sheehan hadn't mentioned it when Bosch had asked about his family.

Irving remained silent and Lindell continued.

'I guess what I'm saying is that we can hold him and wait till tomorrow when we've got the ballistics report to clear him. Or we can hop on Harry's wagon and kick him loose now. But we keep him overnight and the expectations out on the street will just rise that much further ...'

'And if we release him without explanation we could touch off a riot,' Irving said.

Irving continued to stare at the window, brooding. This time Lindell waited.

'Kick him loose at six,' Irving finally said. 'At the five o'clock briefing I will say he is being released pending further investigation. I can hear the howls already from Preston Tuggins and his people.'

'That's not good enough, Chief,' Bosch said. 'You have to say he's clear. "Pending further investigation?" You might as well say we think he did it but we don't have the evidence to charge him yet.'

Irving wheeled from the window and looked at Bosch.

'Do not dare to tell me what is good enough, Detective. You do your job and I will do mine. Speaking of which, the briefing is in an hour. I want your two partners there for it. I am not going to stand up there with a bunch of white faces behind me and say we are letting a white cop go pending further investigation. I want your people there this time. And absolutely no excuse will be acceptable.'

'They'll be there.'

'Good. Now let's talk about what we will say to the media about the direction the investigation is heading in.'

The press conference was short. This time there was no

sign of the chief of police. It was left to Irving to explain that the investigation was continuing and widening. He also said that the police officer who had been interviewed for several hours was being released. This brought an immediate chorus of shouted questions from the reporters. Irving raised his hands as if the action might in some way control the crowd. He was wrong.

'We are not going to turn this into a shouting match,' he barked. 'I will take a handful of questions and that is it. We have an investigation to get back to. We—'

'What do you mean by released, Chief?' Harvey Button called out. 'Are you saying he has been cleared or you just don't have evidence to hold him?'

Irving looked at Button for a moment before answering.

'What I am saying is that the investigation is now moving into other areas.'

'Then Detective Sheehan has been cleared, correct?'

'I am not getting into naming people we talk to.'

'Chief, we all know the name. Why can't you answer the question?'

Bosch thought it was amusing in a cynical sort of way to watch this exchange because Lindell had convinced him it was Irving who had first leaked Frankie Sheehan's name to the media. Now the deputy chief was trying to act insulted that it was out there.

'All I am saying is that the police officer we have talked to provided satisfactory answers at this time. He is going home and that is all I am—'

'What other directions is the investigation going in?' another reporter called out.

'I cannot get into detail,' Irving said. 'Suffice it to say we will be turning over every stone.'

'Can we ask the FBI agent questions?'

Irving glanced back at Lindell, who was standing at the back of the stage next to Bosch, Edgar and Rider.

He then looked back at the crowd of lights, cameras and reporters.

'The FBI and the LAPD have decided this will best be handled by funneling information through the police department. If you have a question, ask me.'

'Are other cops being questioned?' Button called out.

Irving had to think again to make sure he put the right words in the right order.

'Yes, police officers are being questioned in a routine manner. At this point there are no police officers that we would classify as suspects.'

'Then you are saying Sheehan is not a suspect.'

Button got him. Irving knew it. He had talked himself into a logic corner. But he took the easy, if not disingenuous, way out.

'No comment.'

'Chief,' Button continued, above the din of other reporters, 'the murders are almost forty-eight hours old. Are you saying there are no solid suspects at this time?'

'We're not going to get into what suspects there may or may not be. Next.'

Irving quickly pointed to another reporter in order to steer things away from Button. The questioning went on for another ten minutes. At one point Bosch looked over at Rider and she gave him a look that said, *What are we doing here?* And Bosch returned a look that answered, *We are wasting our time.*

When it was finally over, Bosch huddled on the stage with Edgar and Rider. They had arrived from Holly-wood station just as the press conference had begun and he hadn't had time to talk to them.

'So where are we on the search warrants?' he asked.

'Almost done,' Edgar said. 'It didn't help that we had to come down here for the dog and pony show.'

'I know.'

'Harry, I thought you were going to steer us clear of this stuff,' Rider said.

'I know. It was selfish. Frankie Sheehan is a friend. What they did to him, leaking his name like that, was bullshit. I was hoping that having you two here might add some credibility to the announcement that he was being let go.'

'So you used us the way Irving wanted to yesterday,' she said. 'You wouldn't let him do it but it was okay for yourself.'

Bosch studied her face. He could tell she was genuinely angry at being used in such a way. Bosch knew that it was a betrayal. A small one in his mind, but a betrayal just the same.

'Look, Kiz, we can talk about this later. But like I said, Frankie's a friend. He's now your friend for this. And that could be valuable someday.'

He waited and watched and finally she gave a slight nod. It was over, for now.

'How much more time do you need?' he asked.

'Maybe an hour,' Edgar said. 'Then we've got to find a judge.'

'Why?' Rider said. 'What did Irving say?'

'Irving's sitting on the fence. So I want to have everything ready. I want to be able to move. Tomorrow morning.'

'Tomorrow morning's no problem,' Edgar said.

'Good. Then you two go back and finish up. Get to a judge tonight. Tomorrow we'll—'

'Detective Bosch?'

Bosch turned. Harvey Button and his producer, Tom Chainey, were standing there.

'I can't talk to you,' Bosch said.

'We understand that you have reopened the Stacey Kincaid case,' Chainey said. 'We'd like to talk to you about—'

'Who told you that?' Bosch snapped, anger quickly showing on his face.

'We have a source who—'

'Well, tell your source he's full of shit. No comment.'

A cameraman came up and poked his lens over Button's shoulder. Button raised a microphone.

'Have you exonerated Michael Harris?' Button blurted out.

'I said no comment,' Bosch said. 'Get that out of here.'

Bosch reached to the camera and put his hand over the lens. The cameraman shrieked.

'Don't touch the camera! This is private property.'

'So is my face. Get it away from me. The press conference is over.'

Bosch put his hand on Button's shoulder and forcefully ushered him off the stage. The cameraman followed. So did Chainey, but in a slow, calm way as if daring Bosch to manhandle him as well. Their eyes locked.

'Watch the news tonight, Detective,' Chainey said. 'You might find it interesting.'

'I doubt that,' Bosch said.

Twenty minutes later Bosch was sitting on an empty desk at the mouth of the hallway that led to the RHD interview rooms on the third floor. He was still thinking about the exchange he'd had with Button and Chainey and wondering what they had. He heard one of the doors open and looked up. Frankie Sheehan came down the hallway with Lindell. Bosch's old partner looked drained. His face was slack, his hair unkempt and his clothes – the same ones he had worn the night before in the bar – were disheveled. Bosch slid off the desk and stood up, ready to deflect a physical assault if need be. But Sheehan apparently read his body language and raised his hands, palms forward. He smiled crookedly.

'It's okay, Harry,' Sheehan said, his voice very tired and hoarse. 'Agent Lindell here gave me the scoop. Part of it, at least. It wasn't you who … It was myself. You know I forgot all about threatening that douche bag.'

Bosch nodded.

'Come on, Frankie,' he said. 'I'll give you a ride.'

Without thinking too much about it Bosch led him to the main elevators and they headed down to the lobby. They stood side by side, both looking up at the lighted numbers above the door.

'Sorry I doubted you, buddy,' Sheehan said quietly.

'Don't worry about it, buddy. That makes us even.'

'Yeah? How so?'

'Last night when I asked about the prints.'

'You still doubt them?'

'Nope. Not at all.'

In the lobby they went out a side door to the employee parking lot. They were about halfway to the car when Bosch heard a commotion and turned to see several reporters and cameramen moving toward them.

'Don't say anything,' Bosch said quickly. 'Don't say a word to them.'

The initial wave of reporters descended quickly and surrounded them. Bosch could see more coming.

'No comment,' Bosch said. 'No comment.'

But it wasn't Bosch they cared about. They shoved their microphones and cameras at Sheehan's face. His eyes, so tired before, seemed wild now, even scared. Bosch tried to pull his friend through the crowd and to the car. The reporters shouted their questions.

'Detective Sheehan, did you kill Howard Elias?' a woman asked, louder than the others.

'No,' Sheehan said. 'I didn't – I didn't do anything.'

'Did you previously threaten the victim?'

'Look, no comment,' Bosch said before Sheehan could react to the question. 'Do you hear that? No comment. Leave us a—'

'Why were you questioned?'

'Tell us why you were questioned, Detective.'

They were almost there. Some of the reporters had dropped off, realizing they would get nothing. But most of the cameras were staying with them. They could always use the video. Suddenly, Sheehan broke from Bosch's grip and wheeled around on the reporters.

'You want to know why I was questioned? I was questioned because the department needs to sacrifice somebody. To keep the peace. Doesn't matter who it is, as long as they fit the bill. That's where I came in. I fit the—'

Bosch grabbed Sheehan and yanked him away from the microphones.

'Come on, Frankie, forget about them.'

By moving between two parked cars they were able to cut off the clot of reporters and cameramen. Bosch pushed Sheehan quickly to his slickback and opened the door. By the time the reporters followed in single file to the car, Sheehan was inside and safe from the microphones. Bosch went around to his side and got in.

They drove in silence until they were on the 101 Freeway going north. Bosch then glanced over at Sheehan. His eyes were staring ahead.

'You shouldn't have said that, Frankie. You're fanning the fire.'

'I don't give a fuck about the fire. Not anymore.'

Silence returned. They were on the freeway cutting through Hollywood and traffic was light. Bosch could see smoke rising from a fire somewhere to the south and west. He thought about putting KFWB on the radio but decided he didn't want to know what that smoke meant.

'They give you a chance in there to call Margaret?' he asked after a while.

'Nope. They didn't give me a chance to do anything other than confess. I'm sure glad you rode into town and saved the day, Harry. I never did get told what you told 'em but whatever it was it sure saved my ass.'

Bosch knew what Sheehan was asking but he wasn't ready to tell him.

'The media's probably been out to your house,' he

said instead. 'Margaret probably got blindsided with this.'

'I got news for you, Harry. Margaret left me eight months ago. Took the girls and moved to Bakersfield. To be near her folks. There's nobody at my house.'

'Sorry, Frankie.'

'I should've told you last night when you asked about them.'

Bosch drove for a little bit, thinking about things.

'Why don't you get some stuff from your place and come stay at my house? The reporters won't find you. Until this blows over.'

'I don't know, Harry. Your house is the size of a box of Girl Scout cookies. I'm already claustrophobic from being in that room all day. Besides, I never met your wife, you know? She's not going to want some stranger sleeping on your couch.'

Bosch looked at the Capitol Records building as the freeway cut past it. It was supposed to resemble a stack of records with a phonograph stylus on top. But like most of Hollywood time had passed it by. They didn't make records anymore. Music came on compact discs. They sold record albums in secondhand stores now. Sometimes all of Hollywood seemed like a secondhand story to Bosch.

'My house got wrecked in the earthquake,' Bosch said. 'It's rebuilt now. I even have a guest room … and, Frankie, my wife left me, too.'

It felt strange to say it out loud. As if it was some form of confirmation of the death of his marriage.

'Oh, shit, Harry, you guys only got married a year or so ago. When did this happen?'

Bosch looked over at him and then back at the road.

'Recently.'

There were no reporters waiting outside Sheehan's home when they got there twenty minutes later. Bosch said he was going to wait in the car and make some calls while Sheehan got his things. When he was alone he called his house to check for messages, so he wouldn't have to play them in front of Sheehan when they got there. But there were none. He put the phone away and just sat. He wondered if his inviting Sheehan to stay at his house had been a subconscious effort to avoid facing the emptiness of the place. After a while he decided it wasn't. He had lived alone most of his life. He was used to places that were empty. He knew the real shelter of a home was inside yourself.

Light washing across the mirrors caught Bosch's eyes. He checked the side view and saw the lights of a car that was being parked against the curb a block or so back. He doubted it was a reporter. A reporter would have pulled right into Sheehan's driveway, made no effort at concealment. He started thinking about what he wanted to ask Sheehan.

A few minutes later his former partner came out of the house carrying a grocery bag. He opened the back door and tossed it in, then got in up front. He was smiling.

'Margie took all the suitcases,' he said. 'I didn't realize that till tonight.'

They took Beverly Glen up the hill to Mulholland and then took it east to Woodrow Wilson. Bosch usually loved driving Mulholland at night. The curving road, the city lights coming in and out of view. But along the way they drove by The Summit and Bosch studied the gate and thought about the Kincaids somewhere behind it in the safety of their home with jetliner views.

'Frankie, I have to ask you something,' he said.

'Shoot.'

'Back on the Kincaid thing, during the investigation, did you talk to Kincaid much? Sam Kincaid, I mean.'

'Yeah, sure. Guy like that you handled with kid gloves. Him and the old man. You be careful, else it might come back on you.'

'Yeah. So you were pretty much keeping him informed on what was happening?'

'Yeah, pretty much. What about it? You're sounding like those bureau guys who were all over me all day, Harry.'

'Sorry, just asking. Did he call you a lot or did you call him?'

'Both ways. He also had a security guy who was talking to us, staying in touch.'

'D.C. Richter?'

'Yeah, that's him. Harry, you going to tell me what's goin' on or what?'

'In a minute. Let me ask you something first. How much did you tell Kincaid or Richter about Michael Harris, you remember?'

'What do you mean?'

'Look, I'm not saying you did anything wrong. A case like that, you keep the principals involved and informed. So did you go to them and tell them you had brought Harris in on the fingerprints and, you know, that you were smoking him in the rooms?'

'Sure we did. Standard operating procedure.'

'Right. And did you tell them about who Harris was and where he came from, that sort of thing?'

'I suppose I did.'

Bosch let it go for a while. He turned onto Woodrow Wilson and drove the winding road down to the house. He pulled into the carport.

'Hey, this looks nice,' Sheehan said.

Bosch put the car into park but paused before getting out.

'Did you tell the Kincaids or Richter specifically where Harris lived?' he asked.

Sheehan looked over at him.

'What are you telling me?'

'I'm *asking* you. Did you tell any of them where Harris lived?'

'I might have. I don't remember.'

Bosch got out and headed to the kitchen door. Sheehan got his stuff out of the back seat and followed.

'Talk to me, Hieronymus.'

Bosch unlocked the door.

'I think you made a mistake.'

He went inside.

'Talk to me, Hieronymus.'

Bosch led Sheehan to the guest room and Sheehan threw his bag onto the bed. Back out in the hall Bosch pointed into the bathroom and headed back into the living room. Sheehan was silent, waiting.

'The toilet handle in that one is broken,' Bosch said, not looking at him. 'You have to hold it down the whole time it's flushing.'

He now looked at his former partner.

'We can explain Harris's fingerprints. He didn't abduct or kill Stacey Kincaid. In fact, we don't even think there was an abduction. Kincaid killed his stepdaughter. He was abusing her and killed her, then staged the abduction scene. He got lucky when the prints on the book tied in Harris. He then used it. We think it was him – or his man, Richter – who dumped the body near Harris's place because he knew where that place was. So think, Francis. I don't want probablys. I need to know if you told Kincaid or his security man where Harris lived.'

Sheehan looked dumbfounded and his eyes wandered to the floor.

'You're saying we were wrong about Harris ...'

'You guys had blinders on, man. Once those prints came up, you could only see Harris.'

Sheehan kept his eyes on the floor and slowly nodded his head.

'We all make mistakes, Frankie. Sit down and think about what I just asked. What did you tell Kincaid and at what point did you tell him? I'll be right back.'

While he left Sheehan to ponder what he had just been told, Bosch went back down the hall to his bedroom. He stepped in and looked around. It looked the same. He opened the door to the walk-in closet and hit the light. Eleanor's clothes were gone. He looked down at the floor. Her shoes had been cleared out as well. On the rug he saw a little bundle of netting tied with a blue ribbon. He bent down and picked it up. The netting was wrapped around a handful of rice. He remembered that the chapel in Las Vegas had provided the rice bundles as part of the wedding package – for tossing at the happy couple. Eleanor had kept one as a keepsake. Now Bosch wondered if she had mistakenly left it behind or had simply discarded it.

Bosch dropped the bundle into his pocket and turned off the light.

28

Edgar and Rider had rolled the television out of the lieutenant's office and were watching the news when Bosch walked into the squad room after leaving Sheehan at his house. They barely looked up to acknowledge him.

'What?' Bosch asked.

'I guess people didn't like us cutting Sheehan loose,' Edgar said.

'Sporadic looting and arson,' Rider said. 'Nothing like last time. I think we'll make it if we get through this night. We got roving platoons out there and they're coming down on anything that moves.'

'No bullshit like last time,' Edgar added.

Bosch nodded and stared at the TV for a few moments. The screen showed firefighters aiming three-inch hoses into the balling flames pouring through the roof of another strip mall. It was too late to save it. It almost seemed as though it was being done for the media.

'Urban redevelopment,' Edgar said. 'Get rid of all the strip malls.'

'Problem is, they just put strip malls back,' Rider said.

'At least they look better than before,' Edgar said. 'Real problem is the liquor stores. These things always start in the liquor stores. We put a squad out front of every liquor store, no riot.'

'Where are we on the warrants?' Bosch asked.

'We're done,' Rider said. 'We just have to take them over to the judge.'

'Who are you thinking about?'

'Terry Baker. I already called and she said she'd be around.'

'Good. Let's have a look.'

Rider got up and walked over to the homicide table while Edgar stayed behind and continued to watch the television. Stacked neatly at her spot were the search warrant applications. She handed them to Bosch.

'We've got the two houses, all cars, all offices and on Richter we have his car at the time of the killing and his apartment – we threw that in, too,' she said. 'I think we're set.'

Each petition was several pages stapled together. Bosch knew that the first two pages were always standard legalese. He skipped these and quickly read the probable cause statements of each package. Rider and Edgar had done well, though Bosch knew it was likely Rider's doing. She had the best legal mind of the team. Even the PC statements on the proposed search of Richter's apartment and car were going to fly. Using clever language and selected facts from the investigation, the PC statement said the evidence of the case indicated two suspects were involved in the disposal of Stacey Kincaid's body. And by virtue of the close employer/employee relationship that existed at the time between Sam Kincaid and D.C. Richter, Richter could be considered a second suspect. The petition asked permission to search all vehicles operated or accessible by the two men at the time of the crime. It was a carefully worded tap dance but it would work, Bosch believed. Asking to search all cars 'accessible' by the two men was a masterstroke by Rider. If approved, this essentially would allow them access to any car on any one of the car lots owned by Kincaid because he most certainly had access to those cars.

'Looks good,' Bosch said when he had finished reading. He handed the stack back to Rider. 'Let's get them signed tonight so tomorrow we can move when we want to.'

A search warrant was good for twenty-four hours following approval from a judge. In most cases it could be extended another twenty-four hours with a phone call to the signing judge.

'What about this Richter guy?' Bosch asked then. 'We get anything on him yet?'

'A little,' Edgar said.

He finally got up, turned the sound down on the television and came over to the table.

'Guy was a washout at the academy. This is way back, fall of eighty-one. He then went to one of those bullshit private eye academies in the Valley. Got his state license in eighty-four. Apparently went to work for the Kincaid family after that. He worked his way up to the top, I guess.'

'Why was he a washout?'

'We don't know yet. It's Sunday night, Harry. Nobody's over at the academy. We'll pull the records tomorrow.'

Bosch nodded.

'You check the computer, see if he's got a concealed license?'

'Oh, yeah, we did. He's got a license to carry. He's strapped.'

'With what? Tell me it's a nine.'

'Sorry, Harry. The ATF was closed tonight. We'll get that tomorrow, too. All we know now is that he's got a license to carry a concealed weapon.'

'Okay, remember that, you two. Remember how good the shooter was on Angels Flight.'

Rider and Edgar nodded.

'So you think Richter's doing Kincaid's bidding?' Rider asked.

'Probably. The rich don't get themselves dirty like that. They call the shots, they don't take 'em. Right now I like Richter.'

He looked at his partners a moment. He felt that they were very close to breaking this thing open. They'd know in the next twenty-four hours. He hoped the city could wait that long.

'What else?' he asked.

'You get Sheehan all tucked in?' Rider asked.

Bosch noted the tone of her voice.

'Yeah, he's tucked in. And, uh, look, I apologize about the press conference. Irving wanted you there but I probably could've gotten you out of it. I didn't. I know it wasn't a good move. I apologize.'

'Okay, Harry,' Rider said.

Edgar nodded.

'Anything else before we go?'

Edgar started shaking his head, then said, 'Oh, yeah. Firearms called with an FYI. They took a look at Michael Harris's gun this morning and it looks clean. They said it probably hasn't been fired or cleaned in months, judging by the dust buildup in the barrel. So he's clear.'

'They going to go ahead with it anyway?'

'That's what they were calling for. They got an ASAP from Irving to do Sheehan's gun tomorrow morning as soon as they get the slugs from the autopsy. They wanted to know if you wanted them to go ahead with Harris's piece. I told them they might as well.'

'Good. Anything else?'

Edgar and Rider shook their heads.

'Okay then,' Bosch said. 'Let's go see Judge Baker and then we'll call it a day. I have a feeling tomorrow's gonna be a long one.'

29

It had started to rain. Bosch pulled into his carport and shut off his car. He was looking forward to a couple of beers to take the caffeine edge off his nerves. Judge Baker had served them coffee while she reviewed the search warrant petitions. She had reviewed the search warrants slowly and thoroughly and Bosch had drunk two full cups. In the end, though, she had signed every warrant and Bosch didn't need the caffeine to feel jazzed. The next morning they would be 'hunting and confronting,' as Kiz Rider called it – the put-up or shut-up phase of an investigation, the point where theories and hunches culminated in hard evidence and charges. Or they disintegrated.

Bosch went in through the kitchen door. Besides the beer, he was already thinking about Kate Kincaid and how he would handle her the next day. He was looking forward to it the way a confident quarterback who has digested all the film and known strategies of the opposition looks forward to the next day's game.

The light was already on in the kitchen. Bosch put his briefcase on the counter and opened the refrigerator. There was no beer.

'Shit,' he said.

He knew there had been at least five bottles of Anchor Steam in the refrigerator. He turned and saw the five bottle caps on the counter. He started further into the house.

'Hey, Frankie!' he called. 'Don't tell me you drank everything!'

There was no reply. Bosch moved through the dining room and then the living room. The place appeared as he had left it earlier that evening, as if Sheehan had not made himself at home. He checked the rear deck through the glass doors. The light was off outside and he saw no sign of his former partner. He walked down the hallway and leaned close to the closed door of the guest room. He heard nothing. He looked at his watch. It wasn't yet eleven.

'Frankie?' he whispered.

No reply, only the sound of the rain on the roof. He knocked lightly on the door.

'Frankie?' he said louder.

Still nothing. Bosch reached to the knob and slowly opened the door. The lights were off in the room but light from the hallway cut across the bed and Bosch could see it was not occupied. He flicked the wall switch and a bed table lamp came on. The bag Sheehan had carried his belongings in was empty on the floor. His clothes had been dumped onto the bed in a pile.

Bosch's curiosity turned into a low-grade concern. He quickly moved back into the hallway and made a quick search of his own bedroom and the bathrooms. There was no sign of Sheehan.

Back in the living room Bosch paced about for a few moments wondering what Sheehan might have done. He had no car. It was unlikely he would have tried to walk down the hill into the city and where would he be going anyway? Bosch picked up the phone and hit redial to see if by chance Sheehan had called a cab. It sounded like more than seven tones to Bosch but the redial was so fast he wasn't sure. After one ring the phone was answered by the sleepy voice of a woman.

'Yes?'

'Uh, who is this, please?'

'Who is this?'

'I'm sorry. My name is Detective Harry Bosch of

the LAPD. I am trying to trace a call that was made from—'

'Harry, it's Margie Sheehan.'

'Oh … Margie …'

He realized he should have guessed Sheehan would have called her.

'What's wrong, Harry?'

'Nothing, Margie, nothing. I'm trying to find Frankie and I thought maybe he called a cab or something. I'm sorry to—'

'What do you mean, find him?'

He could read the rising concern in her voice.

'It's nothing to worry about, Margie. He was staying with me tonight and I had to go out. I just got home and he isn't here. I'm just trying to figure out where he went. He talked to you tonight?'

'Earlier.'

'How'd he seem, okay?'

'He told me what they did to him. How they're trying to blame him.'

'No, not anymore. That's why he's staying with me. We got him out of there and he's going to hide out here a few days, till it blows over. I'm really sorry that I woke—'

'He said they'd come back for him.'

'What?'

'He doesn't believe they're going to let him go. He doesn't trust anybody, Harry. In the department. Except you. He knows you're his friend.'

Bosch was silent. He wasn't sure what to say.

'Harry, find him, would you? Then call me back. I don't care what time it is.'

Bosch looked through the glass doors to the deck and from this angle saw something on the deck railing. He stepped over to the wall and flipped on the outside light. He saw five amber beer bottles lined up on the railing.

'Okay, Margie. Give me your number.'

He took the number and was about to hang up when she spoke again.

'Harry, he told me you got married and divorced already.'

'Well, I'm not divorced but … you know.'

'Yes, I know. Take care, Harry. Find Francis and then one of you call me back.'

'Okay.'

He put down the phone, opened the slider and went out onto the deck. The beer bottles were empty. He turned to his right and there, lying on the chaise longue, was the body of Francis Sheehan. Hair and blood were splattered on the cushion above his head and on the wall next to the slider.

'Jesus,' Bosch whispered out loud.

He stepped closer. Sheehan's mouth was open. Blood had pooled in it and spilled over his bottom lip. There was a saucer-sized exit wound at the crown of his head. Rain had matted the hair down, exposing the horrible wound even more. Bosch took one step back and looked around the deck planking. He saw a pistol lying just in front of the chaise's front left leg.

Bosch stepped forward again and looked down at his friend's body. He blew his breath out with a loud animal-like sound.

'Frankie,' he whispered.

A question went through his mind but he didn't say it out loud.

Did I do this?

Bosch watched one of the coroner's people close the body bag over Frankie Sheehan's face while the other two held umbrellas. They then put the umbrellas aside and lifted the body onto a gurney, covered it with a green blanket and began wheeling it into the house and toward the front door. Bosch had to be asked to step out of the way. As he watched them head to the front door the crushing weight of the guilt he was feeling took hold again. He looked up into the sky and saw there were no helicopters, thankfully. The notifications and call outs had all been made by landline. No radio reports meant the media had yet to pick up on the suicide of Frankie Sheehan. Bosch knew that the ultimate insult to his former partner would have been for a news chopper to hover over the house and film the body lying on the deck.

'Detective Bosch?'

Bosch turned. Deputy Chief Irving beckoned from the open slider. Bosch went inside and followed Irving to the dining room table. Agent Roy Lindell was already standing there.

'Let us talk about this,' Irving said. 'Patrol is outside with a woman who says she is your neighbor. Adrienne Tegreeny?'

'Yes.'

'Yes what?'

'She lives next door.'

'She said she heard three or four shots from the house earlier tonight. She thought it was you. She did not call the police.'

Bosch just nodded.

'Have you fired weapons in the house or off the deck before?'

Bosch hesitated before answering.

'Chief, this isn't about me. So let's just say that there could be reason for her to have thought it was me.'

'Fine. The point I'm making is that it appears Detective Sheehan was drinking – drinking heavily – and firing his weapon. What is your interpretation of what happened?'

'Interpretation?' Bosch said, staring blankly at the table.

'Accidental or intentional.'

'Oh.'

Bosch almost laughed but held back.

'I don't think there's much of a doubt about it,' he said. 'He killed himself. Suicide.'

'But there is no note.'

'No note, just a lot of beers and wasted shots into the sky. That was his note. That said all he had to say. Cops go out that way all the time.'

'The man had been cut loose. Why do this?'

'Well … I think it's pretty clear …'

'Then make it clear for *us*, would you please?'

'He called his wife tonight. I talked to her after. She said he might have been cut loose but he thought that it wouldn't last.'

'The ballistics?' Irving asked.

'No, I don't think that's what he meant. I think he knew that there was a need to hook somebody up for this. A cop.'

'And so then he kills himself? That does not sound plausible, Detective.'

'He didn't kill Elias. Or that woman.'

'Right now that is only your opinion. The only fact we have is that it appears this man killed himself the night before the day we would get the ballistics. And you, Detective, talked me into cutting him loose so that he could do it.'

Bosch looked away from Irving and tried to contain the anger that was building inside.

'The weapon,' Irving said. 'An old Beretta twenty-five. Serial number acid-burned. Untraceable, illegal. A throw-down gun. Was it your weapon, Detective Bosch?'

Bosch shook his head.

'Are you sure, Detective? I would like to handle this now, without the need for an internal investigation.'

Bosch looked back at him.

'What are you saying? I gave him the gun so he could kill himself? He was my friend – the only friend he had today. It's not my gun, okay? We stopped by his house so he could get some things. He must've gotten it then.

I might have helped him do it but that didn't include giving him the gun.'

Bosch and Irving held each other's stares.

'You're forgetting something, Bosch,' Lindell said, interrupting the moment. 'We searched Sheehan's place today. There was no weapon found there.'

Bosch broke away from Irving and looked at Lindell.

'Then your people missed it,' he said. 'He came here with that gun in his bag because it wasn't mine.'

Bosch moved away from them before he let his anger and frustration get the better of him and he said something that might bring departmental charges. He slid down into one of the stuffed chairs in the living room. He was wet but didn't care about the furniture. He stared blankly out the glass doors.

Irving stepped over but didn't sit down.

'What did you mean when you said you helped him?'

Bosch looked up at him.

'Last night I had a drink with him. He told me things. Told me about how he got carried away with Harris, how the things Harris claimed in his lawsuit – the things he said the cops did to him – were true. All of it was true. You see, he was sure Harris had killed the girl, there was no doubt in him about that. But it bothered him what he had done. He told me that in those moments in the room with Harris that he had lost it. He said he became the very thing he had hunted all these years. A monster. It bothered him a lot. I could see it had been eating at him. Then I come along tonight and drive him home ...'

Bosch felt the guilt rising up like a tide in his throat. He had not been thinking. He had not seen the obvious. He had been too consumed with the case, with Eleanor and his empty house, with things other than Frankie Sheehan.

'And?' Irving prompted.

'And I knocked down the one thing he believed in all these months, the one thing that kept him safe. I told

him we had cleared Michael Harris. I told him he was
wrong about Harris and that we could prove it. I didn't
think about what it would do to him. I was only
thinking about my case.'

'And you think that put him over,' Irving said.

'Something happened to him in that room with
Harris. Something bad. He lost his family after that, he
lost the case … I think the one thread he held on to was
his belief that he'd had the right guy. When he found
out he was wrong – when I stumbled into his world and
told him it was bullshit – the thread snapped.'

'Look, this is bullshit, Bosch,' Lindell said. 'I mean, I
respect you and your friendship with this guy, but you
aren't seeing what is right here in front of us. The
obvious. This guy did himself because he's the guy and
he knew we'd come back to him. This suicide is a
confession.'

Irving stared at Bosch, waiting for him to come back
at Lindell. But Bosch said nothing. He was tired of
fighting it.

'I find myself agreeing with Agent Lindell on this,'
the deputy chief finally said.

Bosch nodded. He expected as much. They didn't
know Sheehan the way Bosch did. He and his former
partner had not been close in recent years but they had
been close enough at one time for Bosch to know that
Lindell and Irving were wrong. It would have been
easier for him to agree. It would lift a lot of the guilt off
him. But he couldn't agree.

'Give me the morning,' he said instead.

'What?' Irving asked.

'Keep this wrapped up and away from the press for
half a day. We proceed with the warrants and the plan
for tomorrow morning. Give me time to see what
comes up and what Mrs Kincaid says.'

'If she talks.'

'She'll talk. She's dying to talk. Let me have the
morning with her. See how things go. If I don't come

up with a connection between Kincaid and Elias, then you do what you have to do with Frankie Sheehan. You tell the world what you think you know.'

Irving thought about this for a long moment and then nodded.

'I think that would be the most cautious route,' he said. 'We should have a ballistics report by then as well.'

Bosch nodded his thanks. He looked out through the open doors to the deck again. It was starting to rain harder. He looked at his watch and saw how late it was getting. And he knew what he still needed to do before he could sleep.

30

Bosch felt the obligation to go to Margaret Sheehan in person and tell her what Frankie had done to himself. It didn't matter that the couple had been separated. She and Frankie had been together a long time before that happened. She and their two girls deserved the courtesy of a visit from a friend instead of a stranger's dreadful phone call in the middle of the night. Irving had suggested that the Bakersfield Police Department be prevailed upon to send an officer to the house, but Bosch knew that would be just as clumsy and callous as a phone call. He volunteered to make the drive.

Bosch did prevail upon the Bakersfield cop shop, but only to run down an address for Margaret Sheehan. He could have called her to ask for directions. But that would have been telling her without telling her, an old cop's trick for making the job easier. It would have been cowardly.

The northbound Golden State Freeway was almost deserted, the rain and the hour of night having cleared out all but those motorists with no choice but to be on the road. Most of these were truckers hauling their loads north toward San Francisco and even further or returning empty to the vegetable fields of the midstate to pick up more. The Grapevine – the steep and winding stretch of the freeway up and over the mountains lying north of Los Angeles – was littered with semis that had slid off the roadway or whose drivers had chosen to pull over rather than risk the already treacherous run in the pounding rain. Bosch found that once he cleared this obstacle course and came down out of the mountains that he was finally able to pick up some speed and lost time. As he drove he watched branches of lightning spread across the purple horizon to the east. And he thought about his old partner. He tried to think about old cases and the old Irish jokes that Sheehan used to tell. Anything to keep from thinking about what he had done and Bosch's own guilt and culpability.

He had brought a homemade tape with him and played it on the car stereo. It contained recordings of saxophone pieces Bosch particularly liked. He fast-forwarded until he found the one he wanted. It was Frank Morgan's 'Lullaby.' It was like a sweet and soulful funeral dirge to Bosch, a good-bye and apology to Frankie Sheehan. A good-bye and apology to Eleanor. It went well with the rain. Bosch played it over and over as he drove.

He got to the house where Margaret Sheehan and her two daughters were living before two. There was an outside light still on and light could be seen through the curtains of the front windows. Bosch got the idea that Margie was in there waiting for his call, or maybe for him to show up. He hesitated at the door, wondering about how many times he had made this kind of call, then finally knocked.

When Margie answered the door Bosch was reminded of how there was never any planning for these things. She stared at him for a moment and he thought she didn't recognize him. It had been a lot of years.

'Margie, it's—'

'Harry? Harry Bosch? We just—'

She stopped and put it together. Usually they did.

'Oh, Harry, no. Oh no. Not Francis!'

She brought both hands up to her face. Her mouth was open and she looked like that famous painting of someone on a bridge screaming.

'I'm sorry, Margie. I really am. I think maybe I should come in.'

She was stoic about the whole thing. Bosch gave her the details and then Margie Sheehan made coffee for him so he wouldn't fall asleep on the ride back. That was a cop's wife thinking. In the kitchen Bosch leaned against a counter as she brewed the coffee.

'He called you tonight,' he said.

'Yes, I told you.'

'Tell me how he seemed.'

'Bad. He told me what they did to him. He seemed so … betrayed? Is that the right word? I mean, his own people, fellow cops, had taken him in. He was very sad, Harry.'

Bosch nodded.

'He gave his life to that department … and this is what they did to him.'

Bosch nodded again.

'Did he say anything about … '

He didn't finish.

'About killing himself? No, he didn't say that … I read up on police suicide once. Long time ago. In fact, back when Elias sued him the first time over that guy he killed. Frankie got real depressed then and I got scared. I read up on it. And what I read said that when people tell you about it or say they're going to do it, what they are really doing is asking you to stop them.'

Bosch nodded.

'I guess Frankie didn't want to be stopped,' she continued. 'He didn't say anything about it to me.'

She pulled the glass coffeepot out of the brewer and poured some into a mug. She then opened a cabinet and took down a silver Thermos. She started filling it.

'This is for the road home. I don't want you falling asleep on the clothesline.'

'What?'

'I mean the Grapevine. I'm not thinking straight here.'

Bosch stepped over and put his hand on her shoulder. She put the coffee pot down and turned to him to be hugged.

'This last year,' she said. 'Things … things just went haywire.'

'I know. He told me.'

She broke away from him and went back to filling the Thermos.

'Margie, I have to ask you something before I head back,' Bosch said. 'They took his gun from him today to run ballistics. He used another. Do you know anything about that one?'

'No. He only had the one he wore on the job. We didn't have other guns. Not with two little girls. When Frankie would come home he'd lock his job gun up in a little safe on the floor of the closet. And only he had the key. I just didn't want any more guns than were required in the house.'

Bosch understood that if it was her edict that there be no more weapons than the one Sheehan was required to carry, then that left a hole. He could have taken a weapon in and hidden it from her – in a spot so obscure even the FBI didn't find it when they searched his house. Maybe it was wrapped in plastic and buried in the yard. Sheehan also could have gotten the weapon after she and the girls moved out and up to Bakersfield. She would never have known about it.

'Okay,' he said, deciding not to pursue it.

'Why, Harry, are they saying it was your gun? Are you in trouble?'

Bosch thought a moment before answering.

'No, Margie, I'm fine. Don't worry about me.'

31

The rain continued through Monday morning and slowed Bosch's drive into Brentwood to a frustrating crawl. It wasn't heavy rain, but in Los Angeles any rain at all can paralyze the city. It was one of the mysteries Bosch could never fathom. A city largely defined by the automobile yet full of drivers unable to cope with even a mild inclemency. He listened to KFWB as he drove. There were far more reports of traffic tie-ups than incidents of violence or unrest during the night. Unfortunately, the skies were expected to clear by midday.

He arrived twenty minutes late for his appointment with Kate Kincaid. The house from which Stacey Kincaid had allegedly been kidnapped was a sprawling white ranch house with black shutters and a slate-gray roof. It had a broad green lawn stretching back from the street and a driveway that cut across the front of the house, and then back around to the garage in the side yard. When Bosch pulled in there was a silver Mercedes Benz parked near the covered entryway. The front door of the house was open.

When he got to the threshold Bosch called out a hello and he heard Kate Kincaid's voice telling him to enter. He found her in the living room, sitting on a couch that was covered in a white sheet. All the furniture was covered in this way. The room looked like a meeting of big, heavy ghosts. She noticed Bosch's eyes taking in the room.

'When we moved we didn't take a single piece of

furniture,' she said. 'We decided just to start over. No reminders.'

Bosch nodded and then studied her. She was dressed completely in white, with a silk blouse tucked into tailored linen pants. She looked like a ghost herself. Her large black leather purse, which was on the couch next to her, seemed to clash with her outfit and the sheets covering the furniture.

'How are you, Mrs Kincaid?'

'Please call me Kate.'

'Kate then.'

'I am very fine, thank you. Better than I have been in a long, long time. How are you?'

'I'm just so-so today, Kate. I had a bad night. And I don't like it when it rains.'

'I'm sorry to hear that. It does look like you haven't slept.'

'Do you mind if I look around a little bit before we start talking?'

He had a signed search warrant for the house in his briefcase but he didn't want to bring it up yet.

'Please do,' she said. 'Stacey's room is down the hall to your left. First door on the left.'

Bosch left his briefcase on the tiled entryway floor and headed the way she had directed. The furniture in the girl's room was not covered. The white sheets that had covered everything were in piles on the floor. It looked like someone – probably the dead girl's mother – had visited here on occasion. The bed was unmade. The pink bedspread and matching sheets were twisted into a knot – not as if by someone sleeping, but maybe by someone who had lain on the bed and gathered the bedclothes to her chest. It made Bosch feel bad seeing it that way.

Bosch stepped to the middle of the room, keeping his hands in the pockets of his raincoat. He studied the girl's things. There were stuffed animals and dolls, a shelf of picture books. No movie posters, no photos of young television stars or pop singers. It was almost as if the room belonged to a girl much younger than Stacey Kincaid had been at the end. Bosch wondered if the design was her parents' or her own, as if maybe she had thought by holding on to the things of her past she could somehow avoid the horror of the present. The thought made him feel worse than when he had studied the bedclothes.

He noticed a hairbrush on the bureau and saw strands of blond hair caught in it. It made him feel a little easier. He knew that the hair from the brush could be used, if it ever came to the point of connecting evidence – possibly from the trunk of a car – to the dead girl.

He stepped over and looked at the window. It was a slider and he saw the black smudges of fingerprint powder still on the frame. He unlocked the window and pulled it open. There were splinter marks where the latch had supposedly been jimmied with a screwdriver or similar tool.

Bosch looked out through the rain at the backyard. There was a lima bean-shaped pool that was covered with a plastic tarp. Rainwater was collecting on the tarp. Again Bosch thought of the girl. He wondered if she ever dove into the pool to escape and to swim to the bottom to scream.

Past the pool he noticed the hedge that surrounded the back yard. It was ten feet high and insured backyard privacy. Bosch recognized the hedge from the computer images he had seen on the Charlotte's Web Site.

Bosch closed the window. Rain always made him sad. And this day he didn't need it to feel that way. He already had the ghost of Frankie Sheehan in his head, he had a crumbled marriage he didn't have time to think about, and he had haunting thoughts about the little girl with the lost-in-the-woods face.

He took his hand from his pocket to open the closet door. The girl's clothes were still there. Colorful dresses on white plastic hangers. He looked through them until he found the white dress with the little semaphore flags. He remembered that from the web site, too.

He went back out into the hallway and checked the other rooms out. There was what looked like a guest bedroom, which Bosch recognized as the room from the photos on the web page. This was where Stacey Kincaid had been assaulted and filmed. Bosch didn't stay long. Further down the hall were a bathroom, the master suite and another bedroom that had been converted into a library and office.

He went back out to the living room. It did not look as though Kate Kincaid had moved. He picked up his briefcase and walked into the room to join her.

'I'm a little damp, Mrs Kincaid. All right if I sit down?'

'Of course. And it's Kate.'

'I was thinking that I'd rather keep things on a formal basis for the moment, if you don't mind.'

'Suit yourself, Detective.'

He was angry at her, angry at what had happened in this house and how the secret had been locked away. He had seen enough during his tour of the place to confirm in his own mind what Kizmin Rider had fervently believed the night before.

He sat down on one of the covered chairs across from the couch and put his briefcase on his knees. He opened it and started going through some of the contents, which from her angle Kate Kincaid could not see.

'Did you find something of interest in Stacey's bedroom?'

Bosch stopped what he was doing and looked over the top of the briefcase at her for a moment.

'Not really,' he said. 'I was just getting a feel for the place. I assume it was thoroughly searched before and there isn't anything in there that I could find. Did Stacey like the pool?'

He went back to his work inside the briefcase while

she told him what a fine swimmer her daughter had been. Bosch really wasn't doing anything. He was just following an act he had rehearsed in his head all morning.

'She could go up and back without having to come up for air,' Kate Kincaid said.

Bosch closed the case and looked at her. She was smiling at the memory of her daughter. Bosch smiled but without any warmth.

'Mrs Kincaid, how do you spell *innocence?*'

'Excuse me?'

'The word. *Innocence.* How do you spell it?'

'Is this about Stacey? I don't understand. Why are you—'

'Indulge me for a moment. Please. Spell the word.'

'I'm not a good speller. With Stacey I always kept a dictionary in my purse in case she asked about a word. You know, one of those little ones that—'

'Go ahead. Try it.'

She paused to think. The confusion was evident on her face.

'I-double n, I know there's two. I-double n-o-c-e-n-s-e.'

She looked at him and raised her eyebrows in a question. Bosch shook his head and reopened the briefcase.

'Almost,' he said. 'But there's two c's, no s.'

'Darn. I told you.'

She smiled at him. He took something out of the briefcase, closed it and put it down on the floor. He got up and walked across to the couch. He handed her a plastic document envelope. Inside it was one of the anonymous letters that had been sent to Howard Elias.

'Take a look,' he said. 'You spelled it wrong there, too.'

She stared at the letter for a long time and then took a deep breath. She spoke without looking up at Bosch.

'I guess I should have used my little dictionary. But I was in a hurry when I wrote this.'

Bosch felt a lifting inside. He knew then that there would be no fight, no difficulty. This woman had been waiting for this moment. Maybe she knew it was coming. Maybe that was why she had said she felt better than she had in a long, long time.

'I understand,' Bosch said. 'Would you like to talk to me about this, Mrs Kincaid? About everything?'

'Yes,' she said, 'I would.'

Bosch put a fresh battery into the tape recorder, then turned it on and put it down on the coffee table, the microphone pointed up so that it would capture his voice as well as Kate Kincaid's.

'Are you ready?' he asked.

'Yes,' she said.

He then identified himself and said who she was, noted the date, time and location of the interview. He read off a constitutional rights advisement from a printed form he had taken from his briefcase.

'Do you understand these rights as I have just read them?'

'Yes, I do.'

'Do you wish to talk with me, Mrs Kincaid, or do you wish to contact an attorney?'

'No.'

'No what?'

'No attorney. An attorney can't help me. I want to talk.'

This gave Bosch pause. He was thinking about how best to keep hair off the cake.

'Well, I can't give you legal advice. But when you say, "An attorney can't help me," I'm not sure that that is going to constitute a waiver. You see what I mean? Because it is always possible that an attorney could—'

'Detective Bosch, I don't want an attorney. I fully understand my rights and I don't want an attorney.'

'Okay, then I need you to sign this paper at the bottom and then sign again where it says that you do not request an attorney.'

He put the rights form down on the coffee table and watched her sign it. He then took it back and made sure she had signed her own name. He then signed it himself as the witness and put it in one of the slots of the accordion file in the briefcase. He sat back down in the chair and looked at her. He thought for a moment about talking to her about a spousal waiver but decided that could wait. He'd let the district attorney's office handle that – when and if the time came.

'Then I guess this is it,' he said. 'You want to start, Mrs Kincaid, or do you want me to ask you questions?'

He was using her name frequently on purpose – in case the tape was ever played before a jury there would be no misunderstanding of whom the voices belonged to.

'My husband killed my daughter. I guess that's what you want to know first. That's why you are here.'

Bosch froze for a moment and then slowly nodded.

'How do you know this?'

'For a long time it was a suspicion ... then it became my belief based on things I had heard. Eventually, he actually told me. I finally confronted him and he admitted it.'

'What exactly did he tell you?'

'He said that it was an accident – but you don't strangle people by accident. He said she threatened him, said that she was going to tell her friends what he ... what he and his friends did to her. He said he was trying to stop her, to talk her out of doing it. He said things got out of hand.'

'This occurred where?'

'Right here. In the house.'

'When?'

She gave the date of her daughter's reported abduction. She seemed to understand that Bosch had to ask some questions that had obvious answers. He was building a record.

'Your husband had sexually abused Stacey?'

'Yes.'

'He admitted this to you?'

'Yes.'

She started to cry then and opened her purse for a tissue. Bosch let her alone for a minute. He wondered if she was crying because of grief or guilt or out of relief that the story was finally being told. He thought it was probably a combination of all three.

'Over how long a period was she abused?' he finally asked.

Kate Kincaid dropped the tissue to her lap.

'I don't know. We were married five years before … before she died. I don't know when it started.'

'When did you become aware of it?'

'I would rather not answer that question, if you don't mind.'

Bosch studied her. Her eyes were downcast. The question was at the foundation of her guilt.

'It's important, Mrs Kincaid.'

'She came to me once.' She got a fresh tissue from her purse for a fresh torrent of tears. 'About a year before … She said that he was doing things she didn't think were right … At first, I didn't believe her. But I asked him about it anyway. He denied it, of course. And I believed him. I thought it was an adjustment problem. You know, to a stepfather. I thought maybe this was her way of acting out or something.'

'And later?'

She didn't say anything. She looked down at her hands. She pulled her purse onto her lap and held it tightly.

'Mrs Kincaid?'

'And later there were things. Little things. She never wanted me to go out and leave her with him – but she'd never tell me why. Looking back, it is obvious why. It wasn't so obvious then. One time he was taking a long time in her room saying good night. I went to see what was wrong and the door was locked.'

'Did you knock on the door?'

She sat frozen for a long moment before shaking her head no.

'Is that a no?'

Bosch had to ask it for the tape.

'Yes, no. I did not knock.'

Bosch decided to press on. He knew that mothers of incest and molestation victims often didn't see the obvious or take the obvious steps to save their daughters from jeopardy. Now Kate Kincaid lived in a personal hell in which her decision to give up her husband – and herself – to public ridicule and criminal prosecution would always seem like too little too late. She had been right. A lawyer couldn't help her now. No one could.

'Mrs Kincaid, when did you become suspicious of your husband's involvement in your daughter's death?'

'During Michael Harris's trial. You see I believed he did it – Harris. I mean, I just didn't believe that the police would plant fingerprints. Even the prosecutor assured me that it was unlikely that it could be done. So I believed in the case. I wanted to believe. But then during the trial one of the detectives, I think it was Frank Sheehan, was testifying and he said they arrested Michael Harris at the place where he worked.'

'The car wash.'

'Right. He gave the address and the name of the place. And it hit me then. I remembered going to that same car wash with Stacey. I remembered her books were in the car. I told my husband and said we should tell Jim Camp. He was the prosecutor. But Sam talked me out of it. He said the police were sure and he was sure that Michael Harris was the killer. He said if I raised the question the defense would find out and use the information to twist the case. Like with the O.J. case, the truth meant nothing. We'd lose the case. He reminded me that Stacey was found right near Harris's apartment … He said he probably saw her with me at the car wash that day and started to stalk us – stalk her. He convinced me … and I let it go. I still wasn't sure it wasn't Harris. I did what my husband told me.'

'And Harris got off.'

'Yes.'

Bosch paused for a moment, believing the break was needed before the next question.

'What changed, Mrs Kincaid?' he finally asked. 'What made you send those notes to Howard Elias?'

'My suspicions were never far away. Then one day, a few months ago, I overheard part of a conversation my husband was having with his … his friend.'

She said the last word as if it was the worst thing you could ever say about anybody.

'Richter?'

'Yes. They thought I wasn't home and I wasn't supposed to be. I was supposed to be at lunch with my girlfriends at the club. Mountaingate. Only I stopped going to lunches with my girlfriends after Stacey … well, you know, lunches and that sort of thing didn't interest me anymore. So I would tell my husband I was going to lunch but instead I'd go visit Stacey. At the cemetery …'

'Okay. I understand.'

'No, I don't think you could understand, Detective Bosch.'

Bosch nodded.

'I'm sorry. You're probably right. Go on, Mrs Kincaid.'

'It was raining on that particular day. Just like today, hard and sad. So I only visited with her for a few minutes. I got back to the house early. I guess they didn't hear me come in because of the rain. But I heard them. They were in his office talking … I'd had my suspicions so I went to the door. I didn't make a sound. I stood outside the door and listened.'

Bosch leaned forward. This was the payoff. He'd know in a moment how legitimate she was. He doubted two men involved in the killing of a twelve-year-old girl would sit around reminiscing about it. If Kate Kincaid said that was the case, then Bosch would have to think she was lying.

'What did they say?'

'They weren't talking in sentences. Do you understand? They were just making short comments. I could tell they were talking about girls. Different girls – it was disgusting what they said. I had no idea how organized this all was. I had deluded myself into thinking that if something had happened with Stacey it was a weakness on his part, something he struggled with. I was wrong. These men were organized predators.'

'So you were at the door listening ... ,' Bosch said by way of getting her back on track.

'They weren't talking to each other. It was like they were commenting. I could tell by how they spoke that they were looking at something. And I could hear the computer – the keyboard and other sounds. Later I would be able to use the computer and find what it was they were looking at. It was young girls, ten, eleven ...'

'Okay, we'll get back to the computer in a couple of minutes. But let's go back to what you heard. How did this ... these comments lead you to conclude or know something about Stacey?'

'Because they mentioned her. I heard Richter say, "There she is." And then my husband said her name. The way he said it ... almost with a longing – it wasn't the way a father or a stepfather would have said it. And then they were quiet. I could tell, they were looking at her. I knew.'

Bosch thought about what he had seen on Rider's computer screen the night before. It was hard for him to imagine Kincaid and Richter sitting in an office together watching the same scenes – and with decidedly different responses to them.

'And then Richter asked my husband if he'd heard from Detective Sheehan. My husband said, "About what?" and Richter said for the payoff for putting Harris's prints on Stacey's book. My husband laughed. He said there was no payoff. He then told Richter what I had told him during the trial, about my having been to that car wash. When he was done telling it, they both laughed and my husband said, and I remember this so clearly, he said, "I've been lucky like that all my life ..." And that's when I knew. He did it. That they did it.'

'And you decided to help Howard Elias.'

'Yes.'

'Why him? Why didn't you go to the police?'

'Because I knew they'd never charge him. The Kincaids are a powerful family. They believe they are above the law and they are. My husband's father put money into the pockets of every politician in this town. Democrat, Republican, it didn't matter. They all owed him. And besides, that didn't matter. I called Jim Camp and asked him what would happen if they ever found somebody else besides Harris that they thought took Stacey. He told me they'd never be able to try him because of the first case. All the defense would have to do was point to the first trial and say that last year they thought it was somebody else. That was enough for reasonable doubt right there. So they'd never go ahead with a case.'

Bosch nodded. He knew she was right. Going to trial against Harris put hair on the cake forever after.

'This might be a good point to take a break for a couple minutes,' he said. 'I need to make a phone call.'

Bosch turned the tape recorder off. He got his cell phone out of his briefcase and told Kate Kincaid that he was going to check out the other side of the house while he made his call.

As he walked through the formal dining room and then into the kitchen Bosch called Lindell's cell phone. The FBI agent answered immediately. Bosch spoke quietly, hoping his voice wouldn't carry into the living room.

'This is Bosch. It's a go. We've got a cooperating witness.'

'On tape?'

'On tape. She says her husband killed her daughter.'

'What about Elias?'

'Haven't gotten there yet. I just wanted to get you people going.'

'I'll put out the word.'

'Anybody been seen yet?'

'Not yet. It looks like the husband is still at home.'

'What about Richter? He's involved. She's giving me stuff on him.'

'We're not sure where he is. If he's at his home, he hasn't come out yet. But we'll find him.'

'Happy hunting.'

After disconnecting he stood in the kitchen doorway and looked at Kate Kincaid. Her back was to him and she seemed to be staring at the spot where he had been sitting across from her. She didn't move.

'Okay,' Bosch said, as he came back into the room. 'Can I get you something? A glass of water?'

'No, thank you. I'm fine.'

He turned the tape recorder on and once again identified himself and the subject of the interview. He gave the exact time and date as well.

'You have been advised of your rights, correct, Mrs Kincaid?'

'Yes, I have.'

'Would you like to continue the interview?'

'Yes.'

'You mentioned earlier that you decided to help Howard Elias. Why is that?'

'He was suing on behalf of Michael Harris. I wanted Michael Harris completely exonerated. And I wanted my husband and his friends exposed. I knew the authorities probably wouldn't do it. But I knew Howard

Elias was not part of that establishment. He wouldn't be controlled by money and power. Only the truth.'

'Did you ever speak with Mr Elias directly?'

'No. I thought my husband might be watching me. After that day when I heard them, when I knew it was him, it was impossible for me not to be completely repulsed by him. I think he realized I had come to a conclusion. I think he had Richter watch me. Richter or people working for him.'

Bosch realized that Richter could be nearby, having followed her to the house. Lindell had said the security man's whereabouts were currently unknown. He looked at the front door and realized he had left it unlocked.

'So you sent Elias notes.'

'Yes, anonymous. I guess I wanted him to expose these people but leave me out of it … I know it was selfish. I was a horrible mother. I guess I had this fantasy that the bad men would be shown to the world without it happening to the bad woman.'

Bosch saw a lot of pain in her eyes as she said it. He waited for the tears to start again but it didn't happen.

'I just have a few more questions at this point,' he said. 'How did you know the web page address and about how to get to the secret site?'

'You mean Charlotte's Web? My husband is not a smart man, Detective Bosch. He is rich, and that always gives the appearance of intellect. He wrote the directions down so he wouldn't have to memorize them and he hid them in his desk. I found them. I know how to use a computer. I went to that awful place … I saw Stacey there.'

Again no tears. Bosch was puzzled. Kate Kincaid had dropped her voice into a monotone. She was reciting the story, it seemed, out of duty. But whatever impact it personally had on her was done with and compartmentalized, put away from the surface.

'Do you believe that to be your husband on the images with Stacey?'

'No. I don't know who that was.'

'How can you be sure?'

'My husband has a birthmark. A discoloration on his back. I said he wasn't smart, but he was at least smart enough not to appear on that web site.'

Bosch thought about this. Though he did not doubt Kate Kincaid's story, he also knew that hard evidence backing it up would be needed to prosecute Kincaid. For the same reason she felt she could not bring her story to the authorities, Bosch needed to be able to go into the district attorney's office with Sam Kincaid solidly locked down by the evidence. Right now all he had was a wife saying evil things about her husband. The fact that Kincaid apparently was not the man in the web site images with his stepdaughter was a major loss of corroborative evidence. He thought about the searches. Teams were descending on Kincaid's home and office at that moment. It was Bosch's hope that they would find evidence that would prove his wife's story.

'Your last note to Howard Elias,' he said. 'You warned him. You said your husband knew. Did you mean your husband knew that Elias had found the secret web site?'

'At the time, yes.'

'Why?'

'Because of the way he was acting – on edge, suspicious of me. He asked me if I had been on his computer. It made me think that they must have known someone was poking around. I sent the message, but now I'm not so sure.'

'Why is that? Howard Elias is dead.'

'I'm not sure he did that. He would have told me.'

'What?'

Bosch was thoroughly confused by her logic.

'He would have told me. He told me about Stacey, why wouldn't he tell me about Elias as well? And the fact that you know about the web site. If they thought

Elias knew, wouldn't they have closed it down or hidden it somewhere else?'

'Not if they were just going to kill the intruder instead.'

She shook her head. She didn't see it the way Bosch obviously did.

'I still think he would've told me.'

Still confused, Bosch said, 'Wait a minute. Are you talking about the confrontation you mentioned at the start of this interview?'

Bosch's pager went off and he reached down and silenced it without taking his eyes off Kate Kincaid.

'Yes.'

'Well, when was this confrontation?'

'Last night.'

'Last night?'

Bosch was shocked. He had jumped to the conclusion that the confrontation she had mentioned had been weeks or even months earlier.

'Yes. After you left. I knew by the questions you asked that you had probably found my notes to Howard Elias. I knew you would find Charlotte's Web. It was a matter of time.'

Bosch looked down at his pager. The number belonged to Lindell's cell phone. The emergency code 911 was printed on the little screen after it. He looked back up at Kate Kincaid.

'So I finally summoned the courage I didn't have for all those months and years. I confronted him. And he told me. And he laughed at me. He asked me why I cared now since I didn't care while Stacey was alive.'

Now Bosch's cell phone began to ring inside his briefcase. Kate Kincaid slowly stood up.

'I'll let you take that in private.'

As he reached to his briefcase, he watched her pick her purse up and walk across the room in the direction of the hallway to her dead daughter's bedroom. Bosch fumbled with the briefcase's release but eventually got it open and got to the phone. It was Lindell.

'I'm at the house,' the FBI agent said, his voice tight with adrenaline and excitement. 'Kincaid and Richter are here. It's not very pretty.'

'Tell me.'

'They're dead. And it doesn't look like it was an easy ride for them. They were knee-capped, both of them shot in the balls … You still with the wife?'

Bosch looked in the direction of the hallway.

'Yes.'

Just as he said it he heard a single popping sound from down the hallway. He knew what it was.

'Better bring her over here,' Lindell said.

'Right.'

Bosch closed the phone and placed it back in the briefcase, his eyes still on the hallway.

'Mrs Kincaid?'

There was no answer. All he heard was the rain.

32

By the time Bosch cleared the scene in Brentwood and got up the hill to The Summit it was almost two o'clock. Driving through the rain on the way he could think only of Kate Kincaid's face. He had gotten to Stacey's room less than ten seconds after hearing the shot, but she was already gone. She had used a twenty-two and placed the muzzle in her mouth, firing the bullet up into her brain. Death was instant. The kick of the gun had knocked it out of her mouth and onto the floor. There was no exit wound, often the case with a twenty-two. She simply appeared as though she was sleeping. She had wrapped herself in the pink blanket that had been used by her daughter. Kate Kincaid looked as though she was serene in death. No mortician would be able to improve on that.

There were several cars and vans parked in front of the Kincaid residence. Bosch had to park so far away that his raincoat was soaked through by the time he got to the door. Lindell was there waiting for him.

'Well, this certainly's turned all to shit,' the FBI agent said by way of greeting.

'Yeah.'

'Should we have seen it coming?'

'I don't know. You never can tell what people are going to do.'

'How'd you leave it over there?'

'The coroner and SID are still there. A couple RHD bulls – they're handling it.'

Lindell nodded.

'I saw what I needed to see. Show me what you have here.'

They went into the house and Lindell led the way to the huge living room where Bosch had sat with the Kincaids the afternoon before. He saw the bodies. Sam Kincaid was in the same spot on the couch where Bosch had last seen him. D.C. Richter was on the floor below the window that looked out across the Valley. There was no jetliner view now. It was just gray. Richter's body was in a pool of blood. Kincaid's blood had seeped into the material covering the couch. There were several technicians working in the room and lights were set up. Bosch saw that numbered plastic markers had been put in place where .22-caliber shells had been located on the floor and other furniture.

'You have the twenty-two over in Brentwood, right?'

'Yeah, that's what she used.'

'You didn't think about searching her before you started talking, huh?'

Bosch looked at the FBI agent and slightly shook his head in annoyance.

'Are you kidding me? It was a voluntary Q&A, man. Maybe you've never done one over there at the bureau, but rule number one is you don't make the subject feel like a *suspect* before you even start. I didn't search and it would have been a mistake if—'

'I know, I know. Sorry I asked. It's just that …'

He didn't finish but Bosch knew what he was getting at. He decided to change the subject.

'The old man show up?'

'Jack Kincaid? No, we sent people to him. I hear he is not taking it well. He's calling every politician he ever gave money to. I guess he thinks maybe the city council or the mayor will be able to bring his son back.'

'He knew what his son was. Probably knew all the time. That's why he's making the calls. He doesn't want that to come out.'

'Yeah, well, we'll see about that. We've already found

digital video cameras and editing equipment. We'll tie him to Charlotte's Web. I feel confident of that.'

'It won't matter. Where's Chief Irving?'

'On the way.'

Bosch nodded. He stepped close to the couch and bent over, his hands on his knees, to look closely at the dead car czar. His eyes were open and his jaw was set in a final grimace. Lindell had been right when he'd said it had not been an easy ride down. He thought of Kincaid's expression in comparison to his wife's death look. There was no comparison.

'How do you think it went down?' he asked. 'How'd she get the two of them?'

He continued to stare at the body while Lindell spoke.

'Well, you shoot a man in the balls and he's going to be pretty docile. From the blood on them, I'd say that was where they got it first. Once she got past that point, I think she had pretty good control of the situation.'

Bosch nodded.

'Richter wasn't armed?'

'Nope.'

'Anybody find a nine-millimeter around here yet?'

'No, not yet.'

Lindell gave Bosch another *we fucked up* look.

'We need that nine,' Bosch said. 'Mrs Kincaid got them to admit what they did with the girl but they didn't say anything about Elias. We need to find that nine to tie them in and end this thing.'

'Well, we're looking. If anybody finds the nine, we'll be the first to know.'

'You have people on Richter's home, office and car? I'm still putting my money on him being the shooter.'

'Yeah, we're on it but don't count on anything there.'

Bosch tried to read the FBI agent but couldn't. He knew that something was not being said.

'What?'

'Edgar pulled his file from the police academy this morning.'

'Right. He was a washout way back. How come?'

'Turned out the guy was blind in one eye. The left eye. He was trying to make it through with nobody noticing. He did all right until the weapons course. He couldn't shoot for shit on the range. That's how they found out. Then they washed him out.'

Bosch nodded. He thought of the expert shooting that had taken place on Angels Flight and he knew this new information on Richter changed things. He knew it was unlikely Richter could have been the shooter.

His thoughts were disrupted by the muted roar of a helicopter. He looked up at the windows and saw a helicopter from Channel 4 drifting down and hovering outside the house, about fifty yards away. Through the rain Bosch could barely make out the cameraman in the open sliding door.

'Fucking vultures,' Lindell said. 'You'd think the rain would keep them inside.'

He stepped back to the doorway where there was a panel of light switches and other electronic controls. He pushed a round button and kept his finger on it. Bosch heard the whine of an electric motor and watched an automatic window shade drop down over the windows.

'They can't get near this place on the ground,' Bosch said. 'Because of the gates. So the air's their only shot.'

'I don't care. Let's see what they get now.'

Bosch didn't care either. He looked back down at the bodies. Judging by the coloring and the slight odor already apparent in the room, he guessed that the two men had been dead for several hours. He wondered if this meant that Kate Kincaid had been in the house all that time with the bodies or had gone to Brentwood and spent the night in her daughter's bed. He guessed the latter.

'Anybody come up with a TOD?' he asked.

'Yeah. Coroner puts time of death at sometime last night, anywhere from nine to midnight. He said the blood flow indicates they could have been alive as long as a couple hours from first to last bullet. It looks like she wanted some information from them but they didn't want to give it up – at first.'

'Her husband talked. I don't know about Richter – she probably didn't care about him. But her husband told her everything about Stacey. Then, I guess, she finished him. Finished them both. It wasn't her husband with the girl on the web site images. You should get the coroner to take torso photos of Richter and do a comparison. It might have been him.'

Lindell gestured toward the bodies.

'Will do. So what do you think? She did this last night and then what, went up to bed?'

'Probably not. I think she spent the night in the Brentwood house. It looked to me like the girl's bed had been slept in. She had to see me and tell the story before she could finish her plan.'

'The finish being her suicide.'

'Right.'

'That's hard-core, man.'

'Living with her daughter's ghost, what she let happen to her, that was even more hard-core. Suicide was the easy way out.'

'Not if you ask me. Like I keep thinking about Sheehan, man, and wondering. I mean, how dark out could it have been for him to do that?'

'Just hope you never know. Where are my people?'

'Down the hall in the office. They're handling that.'

'I'll be in there.'

Bosch left Lindell then and went down the hall to the office. Edgar and Rider were silently conducting a search. The items they wished to seize were being piled on top of the desk. Bosch nodded his hello and they did the same. A quiet pallor hung over the investigation now. There would be no prosecution, no trial. It would be left to them to explain what had happened. And they all knew the media would be skeptical and the public might not believe them.

Bosch approached the desk. There was a lot of computer equipment with connecting wires. There were boxes of thick disks used for data storage. There was a small video camera and an editing station.

'We've got a lot, Harry,' Rider said. 'We would have had Kincaid cold on the pedo net. He's got a Zip drive with all the images from the secret web site on it. He's got this camera – we think it's what was used to take the videos of Stacey.'

Rider, who was wearing gloves, lifted the camera up to show him.

'It's digital. You take your movie, plug the camera into this dock here and download what you want. Then you upload it on your computer and put it out on the net. All from the privacy of your home. It's literally as easy as—'

She didn't finish. Bosch turned to see what the distraction was and saw Deputy Chief Irving standing in the doorway of the room. Behind him stood Lindell and Irving's adjutant, Lieutenant Tulin. Irving moved into the office and handed his wet raincoat to Tulin. He told him to take it and to wait in another room of the house.

'Which room, Chief?'

'Any room.'

Irving closed the door after Tulin left. That left him, Lindell and Bosch's team in the office. Bosch had an idea what was coming. The fixer was here now. The investigation was about to go through the spin cycle where decisions and public pronouncements would be made based on what best served the department, not the truth. Bosch folded his arms and waited.

'I want to finish this up now,' Irving said. 'Take what you have found and clear out.'

'Chief,' Rider said, 'we still have a lot of the house to cover.'

'I do not care. I want the bodies removed and then I want the police removed.'

'Sir,' she persisted, 'we still haven't found the weapon. We need that weapon to—'

'And you are not going to find it.'

Irving stepped further into the room. He looked around and when his eyes finally came to Bosch's face they stopped.

'I made a mistake listening to you. I hope the city does not have to pay for it.'

Bosch paused a moment before responding. Irving never took his eyes off him.

'Chief, I know that you are thinking in … political terms about this. But we have to continue our searches of this house and other locations related to the Kincaids. We need to find the weapon in order to prove that—'

'I just told you, you are not going to find the weapon. Not here or anywhere else related to the Kincaids. All this was, Detective, was a diversion. A diversion that caused three deaths.'

Bosch didn't know what was going on but he felt defensive. He gestured toward the equipment on the desk.

'I wouldn't call this a diversion. Kincaid was involved in a major pedophile ring and we—'

'Your assignment was Angels Flight. I obviously gave you people too much latitude and now here we are.'

'This *is* Angels Flight. That's why we need the weapon. It will tie it all—'

'Damn it, man, we have the weapon! We have had it for twenty-four hours! We *had* the killer as well. *HAD!* We let him go and now we will never get him back.'

Bosch could only stare at him. Irving's face had turned the deep red of anger.

'The ballistics analysis was completed less than an

hour ago,' Irving said. 'The three slugs taken from the body of Howard Elias were matched unequivocally to bullets test-fired in the firearms lab from Detective Francis Sheehan's nine-millimeter Smith and Wesson pistol. Detective Sheehan killed those people on that train. End of story. There are those of us who believed in that possibility but were talked out of it. The possibility is now fact but Detective Sheehan is long gone.'

Bosch was speechless and had to work hard to keep his jaw from dropping open.

'You,' he managed to say. 'You're doing this for the old man. For Kincaid. You are –'

Rider grabbed Bosch by the arm to try to stop him from committing career suicide. He shrugged off her grip and pointed in the direction of the living room where the bodies were.

'– selling out one of your own to protect that. How can you do that? How can you make that kind of a deal with them? And with yourself?'

'You are *WRONG!*' Irving yelled back at him. Then, quietly, he said, 'You are wrong and I could crush you for saying what you just said.'

Bosch said nothing. He continued to hold the deputy chief's stare.

'This city expects justice for Howard Elias,' Irving said. 'And for the woman killed with him. You took that away, Detective Bosch. You allowed Sheehan a coward's way out. You took justice away from the people and they are not going to be happy about that. Heaven help us all for that.'

33

The plan was to hold the press conference quickly, while the rain was still falling and could be used as a tool to keep people – angry people – off the streets. The entire investigative team was assembled and lined along the wall at the rear of the stage. The chief of police and the FBI's Gilbert Spencer were to lead the briefing and answer all questions. This was standard operating procedure in highly sensitive situations. The chief and Spencer knew little more than what was on the press release. Therefore, questions about the details of the investigation could be easily and honestly deflected with the *I am not aware of that* or *Not to my knowledge* sort of answer.

O'Rourke, from press relations, did the warm-up, telling the mob of reporters to act responsibly and that the briefing would be short with further information furnished in the days to come. He then introduced the chief of police who took a spot behind the microphones and read from a carefully prepared statement.

'During my short tenure as chief of police I have had the responsibility of presiding over the funeral of police officers who have fallen in the line of duty. I have held the hands of mothers who have lost their children to the senseless violence of this city. But my heart has never been heavier than right now. I have to announce to the people of this great city that we know who killed Howard Elias and Catalina Perez. And it is with deep, deep regret that I report that it was a member of this department. Earlier today ballistics tests and analysis matched the bullets that killed Howard Elias and Catalina Perez to the service weapon used by Detective Francis Sheehan of the Robbery-Homicide Division.'

Bosch looked out across the sea of reporters' faces and saw shock on many of them. The news gave even them pause, for they knew the consequences. The news was the match, they the gasoline. The rain probably wouldn't be enough to put out this fire.

A couple of reporters, probably wire service men, pushed through the standing-room-only crowd and went out the door to be the first to spread the word. The police chief pressed on.

'As many of you know, Sheehan was one of several officers being sued by Howard Elias on behalf of Michael Harris. The investigators on this case believe Sheehan became overwrought with emotions relating to this case and the dissolution of his marriage in recent months. He may have become unbalanced. We may never know because Detective Sheehan took his own life last night, as he understood that it was only a matter of time before he was revealed as the killer. As a police chief, you hope never to have to make a statement such as this. But this department hides nothing from its citizens. The bad must be aired so that we can fully celebrate the good. I know the eight thousand good people of this department join me in apologizing to the families of these two victims as well as to every citizen in this city. And we ask that the good citizens in return react responsibly and calmly to this truly horrible turn of events. Now, I have other announcements but if there are questions relating specifically to this investigation I can take a few at this time.'

Immediately there was a chorus of unintelligible shouts and the chief simply pointed to one of the reporters in the front center. Bosch didn't recognize him.

'How and where did Sheehan kill himself?'

'He was at a friend's home last night. He shot

himself. His service weapon had been confiscated for the ballistics exam. He used another weapon, the source of which is still under investigation. It was the investigators' belief that he did not have a weapon at his disposal. They obviously were wrong.'

The cacophony began again but it was coming in behind the booming voice of Harvey Button. His question was clear and it had to be answered.

'Why was this man free? He was a suspect yesterday. Why was he released?'

The chief looked at Button for a long moment before answering.

'You just answered that yourself. He was a suspect. He was not under arrest. We were awaiting the results of the ballistics examination and there was no reason to hold him at that time. At that time there was no evidence with which to charge him. We got that evidence with the ballistics report. Of course, we got it too late.'

'Chief, we all know that the police can hold suspects up to forty-eight hours before charging them. Why wasn't Detective Sheehan held in custody?'

'Frankly, because we were pursuing other avenues of investigation. He was not a full-fledged suspect. He was one of several people we were looking at. We felt there was no reason to hold him. He had satisfactorily answered our questions, he was a member of this department and we did not believe he was going anywhere. We also didn't believe he was suicidal.'

'A follow-up,' Button yelled above the ensuing din. 'Are you saying that his status as a police officer got him the privilege of being released so that he could go home and kill himself?'

'No, Mr Button, that is not what I am saying. I am saying we didn't know for sure it was him until it was too late. We knew today. He was released and he killed himself last night.'

'If he had been a regular citizen – say, a black man

like Michael Harris – would he have been allowed to go home last night?'

'I'm not going to dignify that with a response.'

The chief held his hands up to fend off the shouts of other reporters.

'I have other announcements here.'

The reporters continued to shout out questions and O'Rourke stepped forward and shouted louder, threatening to end the news conference and clear the room if there was not quiet. It did the trick. The chief took it from there.

'This announcement is indirectly related to the events I just mentioned. I have the grim duty of also announcing the deaths of Sam Kincaid, Kate Kincaid and Donald Charles Richter, a security specialist who worked for the Kincaids.'

He went on to read from another sheet of paper that described the double murder and suicide, couching the events as the actions of a distraught Kate Kincaid who had let mounting grief over the loss of her daughter get the better of her. No mention was made of her husband's defilement of that daughter or his ongoing pedophilia or involvement in a secret web site dedicated to that perversion. There was also no mention of the ongoing investigation of that site by the bureau and the department's computer fraud team.

Bosch knew it was the old man at work. The original car czar at work, pulling strings to save his family name. Bosch guessed that chits were being called in all over the city. Jackson Kincaid would not allow his son's reputation to be destroyed – along with his own. It might cost him too much business.

When the chief had finished reading from the page there was a smattering of questions.

'If she was distraught, why did she kill her husband?' asked Keisha Russell of the *Times*.

'We'll never know that.'

'And what about the security man, Richter? Why would she kill him if it was about her daughter?'

'Again we're not sure. We are looking into the possibility that he happened to be in the house or happened by when Mrs Kincaid took out the gun and announced the intention of killing herself. There is a strong possibility that both of the men were killed while trying to prevent Mrs Kincaid from doing that. She then left the house and went to their previous home, where the couple had lived with their daughter. She killed herself in the bed where her daughter had slept. It is a very sad situation and our hearts go out to the family and friends of the Kincaids.'

Bosch was disgusted. He almost shook his head but knew that since he was standing against the wall behind the chief such a gesture would be picked up by the cameras and reporters.

'Now, if there is nothing further, I would ask that—'

'Chief,' Button cut in. 'Inspector General Carla Entrenkin has scheduled a press conference at Howard Elias's office in an hour. Do you know what she is going to say and do you have any comment on it?'

'No. Inspector Entrenkin operates independently of this department. She does not answer to me and therefore I have no idea what she'll be saying.'

But by the tone of the chief's voice it was clear that he did not expect whatever Entrenkin was going to say to be positive for the department.

'I want to end this now,' the chief said. 'But before I do, I want to thank the FBI and particularly Special Agent Spencer for the help that was provided. If there is any solace to be found in all of this, it is that the citizens of this community can rest assured that this department is dedicated to weeding out the bad apples, no matter where they might be. This department is also willing to place and accept responsibility for its members' actions without cover-up, no matter what the cost to our pride and reputation. I hope the good citizens of Los Angeles

353

will remember that and accept my sincerest apology. I hope the good citizens of Los Angeles will act calmly and responsibly in reaction to these announcements.'

His last words were drowned out by the scraping of chairs and equipment as the reporters began to get up en masse and move toward the exit doors. There was a story to get out and another press conference to go to.

'Detective Bosch.'

Bosch turned. Irving had come up close to him.

'Any problems with what was announced? Any problems for you or your team?'

Bosch studied the deputy chief's face. The implication was clear. Make any waves and *your* boat will be the one that gets swamped and sinks – and you'd be taking others down with you. *Go along to get along*. The company motto. That's what it should say on the side of the cop cars. Forget about *To protect and serve*.

Bosch slowly shook his head when what he wanted to do was put his hands around Irving's throat.

'No, no problem at all,' he said through a tight jaw.

Irving nodded and instinctively knew it was time to step away.

Bosch saw the exit doors were now clear and headed that way, his head down. He felt that he didn't know anything. His wife, his old friend, his city. Everybody and everything was strange to him. And in that feeling of aloneness he thought he began to understand what it was that Kate Kincaid and Frankie Sheehan were thinking about at the end of the line.

34

Bosch had gone home to watch it all on television. He had his portable typewriter on the coffee table and was leaning over it, typing out the final reports on the investigation with two fingers. He knew he could have given it to Rider to do on her laptop and it would be done in a tenth of the time, but Bosch wanted to write this case summary himself. He had decided to write it exactly the way it had happened – everything, not protecting anyone, the Kincaid family or even himself. He would turn the final package over to Irving and if the deputy chief wanted to rewrite it, edit it or even shred it, then it was up to him. Bosch felt that as long as he told it like it was and put it down on paper there was still a small degree of integrity in that.

He stopped typing and looked at the television when the broadcast broke away from the street reports of sporadic unrest and violence to recap the day's events. There were several outtakes from the press conference – Bosch saw himself standing against the wall behind the police chief, his face giving the lie to everything that was being said. And then the report cut to Carla Entrenkin's press conference in the lobby of the Bradbury. She announced her immediate resignation as inspector general. She said that after she had conferred with the widow of Howard Elias it was decided and agreed upon that she would take over the law practice of the slain attorney.

'I believe that it is in this new role that I can have the most positive effect on reforming this city's police department and rooting out the bad seeds within,' she said. 'Carrying on Howard Elias's work will be an honor as well as a challenge.'

When questioned by the reporters about the Black Warrior case, Entrenkin said that she planned to continue the case with minimal delay. She would ask the presiding judge in the morning to reschedule the start of the trial for the following Monday. By then she would be up to speed on the intricacies of the case and the strategy Howard Elias had been planning to follow. When a reporter suggested that the city would likely go out of its way to settle the case, in light of the day's developments, Entrenkin demurred.

'Like Howard, I don't want to settle this,' she said, looking right at the camera. 'This case deserves a full airing before the public. We will go to trial.'

Great, Bosch thought, as the report ended. It won't rain forever. If a full-blown riot is avoided now, Carla I'mthinkin' would be sure to deliver it the following week.

The broadcast switched to a report on reaction from community leaders to the day's events and the announcements by the chief of police. When Bosch saw the Reverend Preston Tuggins appear on the screen he picked up the remote and switched channels. He caught reports on peaceful candlelight vigils on two other channels and Councilman Royal Sparks on a third before finally finding a broadcast that showed a helicopter shot from above the intersection of Florence and Normandie. The same spot where the 1992 riots flared was packed with a large crowd of protestors. The demonstration – if it could be called that – was peaceful but Bosch knew it was only a matter of time. The rain and the dimming light of the day were not going to hold back the anger. He thought about what Carla Entrenkin had said to him on Saturday night, about anger and violence filling the void left when hope is taken away. He thought about the void that was inside himself now and wondered what he would fill it with.

He turned the sound down and went back to his report. When he was done, he rolled it out of the typewriter and put it in a file folder. He would drop it off the next morning when he got the chance. With the end of the investigation, he and his partners had been assigned to twelve-and-twelve status like everybody else in the department. They were to report in uniform at six o'clock the next morning at the South Bureau command center. They'd be spending the next few days, at a minimum, on the streets, riding the war zone in two-car, eight-cop patrols.

Bosch decided to go to the closet to check out the condition of his uniform. He hadn't worn it in five years – since the earthquake and the last use of the department's emergency response plan. While he was taking it out of its plastic wrap the phone rang and Bosch hurried to answer it, hoping that it might be Eleanor checking in from some place to say she was safe and okay. He grabbed the phone off the night table and sat down on the bed. But it wasn't Eleanor. It was Carla Entrenkin.

'You have my files,' she said.

'What?'

'The files. The Black Warrior case. I'm taking the case. I need the files back.'

'Oh, right. Yeah, I just saw that on the TV.'

There was a silence then that made Bosch uncomfortable. There was something about the woman that Bosch liked, though he seemed to care so little for her cause.

'I guess that was a good move,' he finally said. 'You taking his cases. You worked that out with the widow, huh?'

'I did. And no, I didn't tell her about Howard and me. I didn't see the need to spoil the memories she will have. She's had it rough enough.'

'That was noble of you.'

'Detective …'

'What?'

'Nothing. I just don't understand you sometimes.'

'Join the club.'

More silence.

'I have the files here. The whole box. I was just typing out my final report. I'll pack it all up and try to drop it off tomorrow. But I can't be held to it – I'm on patrol until things calm down on the Southside.'

'That will be fine.'

'Are you taking over his office, too? Is that where I should bring everything?'

'Yes. That's the plan. That would be fine.'

Bosch nodded but he knew she couldn't see this.

'Well,' he said. 'Thanks for your help. I don't know if Irving has said anything but the lead to Sheehan came out of the files. One of the old cases. I guess you heard about that.'

'Actually … no. But you're welcome, Detective Bosch. I'm curious, though. About Sheehan. He was your former partner …'

'Yes. He was.'

'Does all of this seem plausible? That he would first kill Howard and then himself? That woman on the train, too?'

'If you asked me that yesterday I would have said never in a million years. But today I feel like I couldn't read myself let alone anybody else. We have a saying when we can't explain things. The evidence is what it is … And we leave it at that.'

Bosch leaned back on the bed and stared up at the ceiling. He held the phone to his ear. After a long moment she spoke.

'But is it possible that there is another interpretation of the evidence?'

She said it slowly, concisely. She was a lawyer. She chose her words well.

'What are you saying, Inspector?'

'It's just Carla now.'

'What are you saying, Carla? What are you asking me?'

'You have to understand, my role is different now. I am now bound by attorney-client ethics. Michael Harris is now my client in a lawsuit against your employer and several of your colleagues. I have to be care—'

'Is there something that clears him? Sheehan? Something you held back before?'

Bosch sat up and now leaned forward. He was staring wide-eyed at nothing. He was all internal, trying to remember something he could have missed. He knew Entrenkin had held back the trial strategy file. There must have been something in there.

'I can't answer your—'

'The strategy file,' Bosch cut in excitedly. 'It was something in there that puts the lie to this. It ...'

He stopped. What she was suggesting – or the suggestion he was reading in her words – did not make sense. Sheehan's service weapon had been linked to the Angels Flight shootings. There was a ballistics match. Three bullets from the body of Howard Elias, three matches. End of argument, end of case. The evidence is what it is.

That was the hard fact he was up against, yet his gut instinct still told him Sheehan was all wrong for this, that he wouldn't have done it. Yes, he would have gladly danced on Elias's grave but he wouldn't have put the lawyer in that grave. There was a big difference. And Bosch's instincts – though abandoned in light of the facts – were that Frankie Sheehan, no matter what he had done to Michael Harris, was still too good a man at his core to have done the latter. He had killed before, but he was not a killer. Not like that.

'Look,' he said. 'I don't know what you know or think you know, but you've got to help me. I can't—'

'It's there,' she said. 'If you have the files, it's there. I held something back that I was bound to hold back. But part of it was in the public files. If you look, you'll find it. I'm not saying your partner is clear. I'm just saying there was something else here that probably should have been looked at. It wasn't.'

'And that's all you are going to tell me?'

'That's all I can tell you – and even that I shouldn't have.'

Bosch was silent for a moment. He didn't know whether to be angry with her for not telling him specifically what she knew, or just happy that she had given him the clue and the direction.

'All right,' he finally said. 'If it's here I'll find it.'

35

It took Bosch nearly two hours to make his way through
the Black Warrior case files. Many of the folders he had
opened previously, but some had been viewed by Edgar
and Rider or left to others on the squad Irving had put
together at Angels Flight less than seventy-two hours
earlier. He looked at each file as if he had never seen it
before, looking for the thing that had been missed – the
telling detail, the boomerang that would change his
interpretation of everything and send it in a new
direction.

That was the problem with gang-banging a case –
putting multiple investigative teams on it. No single
pair of eyes saw all of the evidence, all of the leads or
even all of the paperwork. Everything was split up.
Though one detective was nominally in charge, it was
rare that everything crossed his radar screen. Now
Bosch had to make sure it did.

He found what he believed he was looking for – and
what Carla Entrenkin had hinted at – in the subpoena
file, the folder where receipts from the process server
were stored. These receipts were received by Howard
Elias's office after the subject of the subpoena had been
served with the summons to appear for a deposition or
as a witness in court. The file was thick with the thin
white forms. The stack was in chronological order of
service. The first half of the stack consisted of subpoenas for depositions and these dated back several
months. The second half of the stack consisted of
witness subpoenas for the court case that had been

scheduled to start that day. These were summonses to the cops being sued as well as other witnesses.

Bosch remembered that Edgar had looked through this file earlier – he had come across the subpoena for the car wash records. But that discovery must have distracted him from other things in the file. As Bosch looked through the subpoenas another filing caught his eyes as being worthy of a second look. It was a subpoena for Detective John Chastain of the Internal Affairs Division. This was surprising because Chastain had never mentioned any involvement in the lawsuit. Chastain had headed the internal investigation of Michael Harris's allegations that had cleared the RHD detectives of any wrongdoing, so the fact that he had been called wasn't unusual. It would stand to reason that he would be called as a witness in defense of the detectives accused of wrongdoing by Michael Harris. But the fact that Chastain had not told anyone he was a subpoenaed witness for the *plaintiffs* in the lawsuit was. If that had been known he might have been disqualified from the team investigating the murders for the same reason that the RHD bulls had been removed. There was a clear conflict. The subpoena needed explanation. And Bosch's interest in it increased further when he saw that the date of service was Thursday, the day before Elias's murder. But curiosity turned to suspicion when Bosch saw the note handwritten by the process server at the bottom of the subpoena.

Det. Chastain refused acceptance at vehicle. Server placed under wiper.

The note made it very clear that Chastain didn't want any part of the case. And it turned Bosch's attention into a sharp focus. The city could have been burning from Dodger Stadium to the beach and he probably wouldn't have noticed the television now.

He realized as he stared at the subpoena that the subject – Chastain – had been given a specific date and time to appear in court to give testimony. He shuffled through the court subpoenas and realized that they were placed in the file in order of service, not in the order that those summoned would appear in trial. He knew then that by placing them in order according to the appearance dates and times, he would have the chronological order of Elias's case and a better understanding of how he planned the trial.

It took him two minutes to put the subpoenas in the proper order. When he was done, he looked at the documents one by one, envisioning the process of the trial. First Michael Harris would testify. He would tell his story. Next would come Captain John Garwood, head of RHD. Garwood would testify about the investigation, giving the sanitized version. The next subpoena was for Chastain. He would follow Garwood. *Reluctantly* – he had tried to refuse service – he would follow the RHD captain.

Why?

Bosch put the question aside for the moment and began going through the other subpoenas. It became clear that Elias was following an age-old strategy of alternating positive and negative witnesses. He was planning to alternate the testimony of the RHD men, the defendants, with witnesses who would obviously benefit Michael Harris. There was Harris, the doctor who treated his ear, Jenkins Pelfry, his boss at the car wash, the two homeless men who had found Stacey Kincaid's body, and finally Kate Kincaid and Sam Kincaid. It was clear to Bosch that Elias was going to attack the RHD case, expose the torture of Michael Harris and establish his defense of having done nothing wrong. He would then blow the RHD completely out of the water by bringing in Kate Kincaid to detail the car wash connection and the explanation for the fingerprints. Then most likely it would be Sam Kincaid's turn. Elias would use him to expose the Charlotte's Web Site and the horror of Stacey Kincaid's young life. It was clear that the case Elias was going to present to the jury followed the same line of investigation Bosch and his team had followed – that Harris was innocent, that there was an explanation for his fingerprints, and that Sam Kincaid or someone connected to him and the pedo net killed his stepdaughter.

Bosch knew it was a good strategy. He believed Elias would have won the case. He flipped back to the front of the court subpoenas. Chastain was third in line, putting him on the positive side of the alternating strategy – coming after Garwood and before one of the RHD defendants. He was going to be a positive witness for Elias and Harris but he had attempted to refuse being served the subpoena.

Bosch read the name of the service company off the form and called information. It was late but process serving was an odd-hours job. People weren't always served nine to five. A man answered the phone and Bosch, reading from the Chastain subpoena, asked for Steve Vascik.

'He's not here tonight. He's home.'

Bosch identified himself and explained that he was conducting a homicide investigation and needed to talk to Vascik immediately. The man on the other end of the line was reluctant to give out Vascik's phone number but agreed to take Bosch's number and contact Vascik with the message.

After disconnecting the call Bosch got up and paced around his house. He wasn't sure what he had. But he had the fluttering feeling in his stomach that often came when he was on the edge of a breakthrough to something hidden. He was flying on instinct and his instinct told him he was close to something he would soon be able to wrap his hands around.

The phone rang and he grabbed it off the couch and pushed the connect button.

'Mr Vascik?'

'Harry, it's me.'

'Eleanor. Hey, how are you? Are you all right?'

'I'm fine. But I'm not the one in a city about to burn. I've been watching the news.'

'Yeah. It looks bad.'

'I'm sorry it turned out that way, Harry. You told me about Sheehan once. I know you guys were close.'

Bosch realized that she didn't know that the friend's home where Sheehan had killed himself was theirs. He decided not to say anything. He also wished he had call waiting service on his line.

'Eleanor, where are you?'

'I'm back in Vegas.' She gave an unhumorous laugh. 'The car barely made it.'

'At the Flamingo?'

'No … I'm somewhere else.'

She didn't want to tell him where and that hurt.

'Is there a number I can call you at?'

'I'm not sure how long I'm going to be here. I just wanted to call and make sure you were okay.'

'Me? Don't worry about me. Are you okay, Eleanor?'

'I'm fine.'

Bosch didn't care about Vascik anymore.

'Do you need anything? What about your car?'

'No. I'm fine. Now that I'm here I'm not worried about the car.'

There was a long moment of silence. Bosch heard one of the electronic sounds that he had once heard somebody call digital bubbles.

'Well,' he finally said, 'can we talk about this?'

'I don't think this is a good time. Let's think about things for a couple of days and then we'll talk. I'll call you, Harry. Be careful.'

'Do you promise? To call?'

'I promise.'

'Okay, Eleanor. I'll wait.'

'Good-bye, Harry.'

She hung up before he could say good-bye. Bosch

stood there next to the couch for a long time, thinking about her and what had happened to them.

The phone rang while still in his hand.

'Yes?'

'Detective Bosch? I got a message to call you.'

'Mr Vascik?'

'Yes. From Triple A Process. My boss Shelly said you—'

'Yes, I called.'

Bosch sat down on the couch and pulled a notebook onto his thigh. He took a pen out of his pocket and wrote Vascik's name on the top of a page. Vascik sounded young and white to him. He had some Midwest in his voice.

'How old are you, Steve?'

'I'm twenty-five.'

'You been with Triple A very long?'

'A few months.'

'Okay, last week, on Thursday, you served paper on an LAPD detective named John Chastain, do you remember that?'

'Sure. He didn't want to be served. Most cops I've done don't really care. They're used to it.'

'Right. That's what I wanted to ask you about. When you say he didn't want to be served, what do you mean exactly?'

'Well, the first time I tried to serve him he refused to take the subpoena and walked away. Then when—'

'Wait a minute, go back. When was the first time?'

'It was Thursday morning. I went to the lobby at Parker Center and had the cop at the desk call him and tell him to come down. I didn't say what it was for. It said on the paper he was IAD so I just said I was a citizen with something for him that he needed. He came down and when I said who I was he just backed off and went back to the elevator.'

'What you're saying is that it was like he knew you had a subpoena and even what case it was?'

'Right. Exactly.'

Bosch thought about what he had read in Elias's last notebook. His feuding with a source named 'Parker.'

'Okay, then what?'

'Well, then I went and did some other jobs and I came back about three-thirty and watched the employee lot at Parker. I saw him come out to go home, I guess, and I cut between some cars and ducked down and sort of came up just as he was opening his door. I had my spiel all worked out and told him he was served and said the case number and all of that. He still wouldn't take the paper but that didn't matter because under California law all you—'

'Right, I know. You can't refuse a subpoena once you have been advised that it is a legal, court-ordered subpoena. So what did he do?'

'Well, first he scared the shit out of me. He put his arm under his coat like he was going for his gun or something.'

'Then what?'

'Then he sort of stopped. I guess he thought about what he was doing. He relaxed a little bit but he still wouldn't take the paper. He told me to tell Elias to fuck off. He got in his car and started pulling out. I knew he was served so I just put the paper under his windshield wiper. He drove off with it like that. I don't know what happened to it after that. Could've blown off but it doesn't matter. He was legally served.'

Bosch thought for a moment while Vascik went on about the intricacies of process serving. He finally cut him off.

'Did you know Elias got killed Friday night?'

'Yes, sir. Sure. He was our client. We did all his cases.'

'Well, did you ever think to call the department after he was killed and tell someone about this thing with Chastain?'

'I did,' Vascik answered defensively. 'I called.'

'You called? Who'd you call?'

'I called Parker Center and said I had information. I was transferred to an office and told the guy who answered who I was and that I had some information. He took my name and number and said someone would call me back.'

'Nobody ever did?'

'No, somebody called in like five minutes. Maybe less. Right away. I told him.'

'When was this?'

'Sunday morning. I was out climbing all day Saturday. Up at Vasquez Rocks. I didn't hear about Mr Elias until I read the *Times* on Sunday morning.'

'Do you remember the name of the cop you told this to?'

'I think his name was Edgar but I don't know if that was his first or last name.'

'What about the person who took your call in the first place? Did he give a name?'

'I think he said his name but I forget it. But he did say he was an agent. So maybe it was an FBI guy.'

'Steve, think for a minute. What time did you make this call and when did Edgar call you back? Do you remember?'

Vascik was quiet while he thought about it.

'Well, I didn't get up till about ten 'cause my legs were killing me from the climb. I then kind of lazed around and read the paper. It was all over the front page, so I probably read it right after the sports. And then I called. So maybe about eleven. Thereabouts. And then that Edgar guy called back pretty quick.'

'Thanks, Steve.'

Bosch clicked the phone off. He knew there was no way Edgar had taken a call at Parker Center on Sunday morning at eleven. Edgar had been with Bosch all Sunday morning and most of the rest of the day. And they were on the road, not working out of Parker.

Someone had used his partner's name. A cop. Someone inside the investigation had used Edgar's name.

He looked up Lindell's cell phone number and called. Lindell still had it turned on and he answered.

'It's Bosch. You remember Sunday morning, after you and your people came into the case, you spent most of the morning in the conference room with the files, right?'

'Yeah, right.'

'Who was answering the phones?'

'Me mostly. A couple of the others.'

'Did you take a call from a guy said he was a process server?'

'Sounds familiar. But we were getting lots of calls that morning. Reporters and people thinking they knew something. People threatening the cops.'

'A process server named Vascik. Steve Vascik. He said he had some information that might be important.'

'Like I said, it's familiar. What about it, Bosch? I thought this case was over.'

'It is. I'm just checking some loose ends. Who'd you give the call to?'

'I gave those kind of calls – you know, info off the street – to the IAD guys. To keep them busy.'

'Which one did you give the process server to?'

'I don't know, probably Chastain. He was in charge of that group. He might've taken it or told one of the others to call the guy back. See, Irving set up some shitty phones in there. We couldn't transfer one to the other and I wanted the main line free. So we took numbers and passed them on.'

'Okay, thanks, man. Have a nice night.'

'Hey, what is—'

Bosch disconnected before he had to answer any questions. He thought about the information from Lindell. He believed there was a high probability that the call from Vascik had been routed to Chastain himself, who then called back – probably taking the message to his own office for privacy – and posed as Edgar.

Bosch had one more call to make. He opened his phone book and found a number that he had not used in many years. He called Captain John Garwood, head of Robbery-Homicide Division, at home. He knew it was late but he doubted very many people were sleeping in Los Angeles tonight. He thought about what Kiz Rider had said about Garwood reminding her of Boris Karloff and only coming out at night.

Garwood answered after two rings.

'It's Harry Bosch. We need to talk. Tonight.'

'About?'

'John Chastain and the Black Warrior case.'

'I don't want to talk on the phone.'

'Fine. Name the place.'

'Frank Sinatra?'

'How soon?'

'Give me half an hour.'

'I'll be there.'

36

In the long run, Frank Sinatra got ripped off. Decades ago, when the Hollywood Chamber of Commerce put his star down on the sidewalk, they put it on Vine Street rather than on Hollywood Boulevard. The thinking probably was that the Sinatra star would be a draw, people would come down from the boulevard to see it, to take a picture. But if that was the plan, it didn't work. Frank was alone in a spot that probably saw more hypes than tourists. His star was at a crosswalk between two parking lots and next to a residence hotel where you had to convince the security guard to unlock the lobby door if you wanted to go in.

When Bosch had been in RHD years before, the Sinatra star had often been a meeting spot between detectives in the field or between detectives and their snitches. It hadn't surprised Bosch that Garwood had suggested it for their meeting. It was a way of meeting on neutral ground.

By the time Bosch got to the star Garwood was already there. Bosch saw his unmarked Ford LTD in the parking lot. Garwood flashed his lights. Bosch pulled to the curb in front of the hotel and got out. He crossed Vine to the parking lot and got in the front passenger seat. Garwood was wearing a suit, even though called from home. Bosch realized that he had never seen Garwood in anything other than a suit, the tie always pulled tight, the top button of his shirt never undone. Again Bosch thought of Rider's Boris Karloff comment.

'Those fucking cars,' Garwood said, looking across the street at Bosch's slickback. 'I heard about you getting potshotted.'

'Yeah. That wasn't fun.'

'So what brings you out tonight, Harry? How come you're still investigating a case that the chief of police and everybody else has already closed?'

'Because I have a bad feeling about it, Cap. There are loose ends. Things can unravel when you have loose ends.'

'You never could leave things alone. I remember that from when you worked for me. You and your fucking loose ends.'

'So tell me about Chastain.'

Garwood said nothing, just stared ahead through the windshield, and Bosch realized that his former captain was unsure about things.

'We're off the record here, Captain. Like you said, the case is closed. But something about Chastain and Frankie Sheehan bothers me. You should know, a couple nights ago Frankie told me everything. About how he and some of the guys lost it, did things to Michael Harris. He told me all the Black Warrior stuff was true. And then I made a mistake. I told him that I had cleared Harris. That I could prove he didn't take that girl. And that put the hex on Frankie and later on he did what he did. So when they came up with the ballistics today and said that Frankie did it all, including Angels Flight, I went along to get along. Now I'm not so sure. Now I want all the loose ends tied up and Chastain is one of them. He was subpoenaed for the trial. Nothing unusual about that – he handled the internal investigation of Harris's complaint. But he was subpoenaed by Elias and he didn't tell us. He also tried to duck the service. And that makes it all the more unusual. That tells me he didn't want to be in that courtroom. He didn't want to be on the stand and have Elias asking him questions. I want to know why.

There's nothing in Elias's files – at least the files I have access to – that says why. I can't ask Elias and I don't want to ask Chastain yet. So I'm asking you.'

Garwood reached into his pocket and took out a pack of cigarettes. He got one out and lit it, then offered the pack to Bosch.

'No thanks, I'm still off.'

'I decided that I'm a smoker and that's that. Somebody a long time ago told me that it was like destiny or fate. You were a smoker or you weren't, there was nothing you could do about it. You know who that was?'

'Yeah, me.'

Garwood snorted a little and smiled. He took a couple of deep drags and the car filled with smoke. It kicked off the familiar craving in Bosch. He remembered giving Garwood the smoking sermon years before when someone in the squad complained about the cloud of smoke that always hung over the bullpen. He lowered his window a couple of inches.

'Sorry,' Garwood said. 'I know how you feel. Everybody smoking and you can't.'

'It's no problem. You want to talk about Chastain or not?'

One more drag.

'Chastain investigated the complaint. You know that. Before Harris could sue us he had to file a complaint. That went to Chastain. And from what I understood at the time, he made the guy's case. He confirmed it. Fucking Rooker had a pencil in his desk – the tip was broken off and there was blood on it. Kept it like a souvenir or something. Chastain got it with a search warrant and was going to match the blood to Harris.'

Bosch shook his head, at both the stupidity and the arrogance of Rooker. Of the whole department.

'Yeah,' Garwood said, seeming to know what he was thinking. 'So the last thing I heard was that Chastain was going to file departmentals against Sheehan,

Rooker, couple of the others, then go to the DA for criminal charges. He was going all the way with this one because that pencil and the blood were hard evidence. He had Rooker at least in the bag.'

'Okay, so what happened.'

'What happened was that the next thing is we get the word that everybody's clear. Chastain filed the case as unfounded.'

Bosch nodded.

'Somebody reached down.'

'You got it.'

'Who?'

'Irving's my guess. But maybe higher. The case was too volatile. If the charges were sustained and there were suspensions, firings, DA charges, whatever, then we start a whole new round of "kick the LAPD" in the press and in the south end with Tuggins and Sparks and everywhere else. Remember, this was a year ago. The new chief had just come on board. It wouldn't be a good way to start out. So somebody reached down. Irving's always been the department fixer. It was probably him. But for something like this, he might have enlisted the chief's okay. That's how Irving survives. He hooks the chief in, then he can't be touched because he has the secrets. Like J. Edgar Hoover and the FBI – but without the dress. I think.'

Bosch nodded.

'What do you think happened to that pencil with the blood on it?' he asked.

'Who knows? Irving's probably using it to write personnel evaluations. Though I'm sure he's washed the blood off it.'

They were silent for a moment as they watched a group of a dozen young men walking north on Vine toward the Boulevard. They were mostly white. In the street light Bosch could see the tattoos covering their arms. Head-bangers, probably going up to the stores on the boulevard to replay 1992. A quick memory of

Frederick's of Hollywood being looted flashed through his mind.

The group slowed as they passed Bosch's car. They considered whether to do something to the car and then decided against it and moved on.

'Lucky we didn't meet in your car,' Garwood said.

Bosch didn't say anything.

'This place is going to come apart tonight,' Garwood continued. 'I can feel it. Pity the rain stopped.'

'Chastain,' Bosch said, getting back on track. 'Somebody put a cork in him. Complaint unfounded. Then Elias files his suit and eventually subpoenas Chastain. Chastain doesn't want to testify, why?'

'Maybe he takes the oath seriously. He didn't want to lie.'

'There's got to be more than that.'

'Ask him.'

'Elias had a source inside Parker. A leak. I think it was Chastain. I don't mean just on this case. I mean a longtime leak – a direct conduit inside to records, everything. I think it was Chastain.'

'It's funny. A cop who hates cops.'

'Yeah.'

'But if he was Elias's big important conduit, why would Elias put him on the stand and expose him like that?'

That was the question and Bosch had no answer. He was silent for a while, thinking about this. He finally put together the thin beginnings of a theory and said it out loud.

'Elias wouldn't have known Chastain had been corked unless Chastain had told him, right?'

'Right.'

'So just by putting Chastain on the stand and asking him about it would be revealing Chastain as his source.'

Garwood nodded.

'I can see that,' he said. 'Yeah.'

'Even if Chastain sat up there and denied every

question, Elias could ask the questions in a way that they would still get the point – and in this case, the truth – across to the jury.'

'It would also make the point at Parker Center,' Garwood said. 'Chastain would be exposed. Question is, why would Elias expose his source? Somebody who had been helping him a hell of a lot over the years. Why would he give that up?'

'Because this was Elias's home run case. The big one that would put him on the national map. It would put him on *Court TV*, *Sixty Minutes*, *Larry King* and everything else. It would make him. He would be willing to burn his source for that. Any lawyer would.'

'I see that, too. Yeah.'

The next part was left unsaid. That being the question of what Chastain would do to prevent being publicly burned on the stand. To Bosch the answer was obvious. If he were exposed not only as Elias's source but as the investigator who compromised the internal investigation of Michael Harris's complaint, he would be vilified both inside and outside the department. There would be nowhere for him to go and that would be untenable for a man like Chastain, for any man. Bosch believed Chastain would be willing to kill to prevent that from happening.

'Thanks, Captain,' he said. 'I've got to go.'

'It doesn't matter, you know.'

Bosch looked over at him.

'What?'

'Doesn't matter. The press releases have been made, the press conferences given, the story's out and the city is ready to go like kindling. You think the people in the south end care *which* cop killed Elias? They don't give a shit. They already have what they want. Chastain, Sheehan, doesn't matter. What matters is that a badge did it. And if you go making noise you'll just be adding more fuel to the fire. You bring up Chastain and you bring up the cover-up. A lot of people might get hurt, lose their jobs, all because they wanted to head this off in the first place. You better think about that, Harry. Nobody cares.'

Bosch nodded. He understood the message. Go along to get along.

'I care,' he said.

'Is that enough of a reason?'

'What about Chastain then?'

Garwood had a thin smile on his face. Bosch could see it behind the glowing point of his cigarette.

'I think Chastain deserves whatever he gets. And someday he'll get it.'

Now there was a new message in that. And Bosch thought he understood that as well.

'And what about Frankie Sheehan? What about his reputation?'

'There's that,' Garwood said, nodding. 'Frankie Sheehan was one of my guys ... but he's dead and his family doesn't live here anymore.'

Bosch said nothing but that answer wasn't acceptable. Sheehan was his friend and partner. Tainting him tainted Bosch himself.

'You know what bothers me?' Garwood asked. 'And maybe you might be able to help me, being that you and Sheehan were partners at one time.'

'What? What bothers you?'

'That gun Sheehan used. That wasn't yours now, was it? I know they asked you that.'

'No, not mine. We had gone by his house on the way to mine. To get clothes and things. He must've picked it up then. The FBI must've missed it when they searched his place.'

Garwood nodded.

'I heard you made notification to his wife. Did you ask her about that? You know, about the gun.'

'I asked. She said she didn't know about any gun but that doesn't—'

'No serial number,' Garwood said, cutting in. 'A

throw-down gun, everybody knows that's what that was.'

'Yeah.'

'And that's what bothers me. I knew Sheehan a lot of years. He worked for me a long time and you get to know your guys. I never knew him to be the kind of guy who would have a throw-down … I asked some of the other guys – especially the ones that partnered with him since you went to Hollywood. They never knew about a throw-down. What about you, Harry? You worked with him the longest. Did he ever carry an extra piece?'

It hit Bosch then, like a punch in the chest. The kind where you have to keep perfectly still and silent and wait it out until you slowly get your breath back. He had never known Frank Sheehan to carry a throw-down on the job. He was too good for that. And if you were too good to carry one on the job, why have one hidden at home? That question and its obvious answer had been there right in front of him all along. But he had missed it.

Bosch remembered sitting in his car outside Sheehan's house. He remembered the set of headlights he saw in the mirror and the car pulling to the curb down the block. Chastain. He had followed them. To Chastain, Sheehan alive was the only loose end that could cause things to unravel.

He thought of his neighbor's reports of three to four shots being fired at his house. In his mind a drunken cop's suicide was now a calculated murder.

'Motherfucker,' Bosch whispered.

Garwood nodded. He had successfully led Bosch down the road to where he apparently already was.

'Now, do you see how it could have been done?' he asked.

Bosch tried to slow his thoughts and let it come to him. Finally, he nodded.

'Yes, I see now.'

'Good. I'll make a call. I'll have whoever is on duty in

the basement let you have a look at the sign-out log. No questions asked. That way you'll be sure.'

Bosch nodded. He reached over and opened the door. He got out without another word and started back toward his car. He was running before he got there. He didn't know why. There was no hurry. It was no longer raining. He just knew he had to keep moving to keep from screaming.

37

Outside of Parker Center there was a candlelight vigil and a funeral procession. Two cardboard caskets – one marked JUSTICE, the other marked HOPE – were being carried aloft by the crowd as they marched back and forth across the front plaza. Others carried signs that said JUSTICE FOR PEOPLE OF ALL COLORS and JUSTICE FOR SOME IS JUSTICE FOR NONE. Above news helicopters circled and on the ground there were at least six news crews that Bosch could see. It was getting close to eleven and all of them were getting ready to put out live reports from the protest front.

At the front door a phalanx of cops in uniforms and riot helmets stood ready to defend the police headquarters if the crowd turned from peaceful demonstration to violence. In 1992 a peaceful demonstration had turned violent and the mob roamed downtown destroying everything in its path. Bosch hurried toward the lobby doors, skirting behind the procession of protesters and through a crack in the human defense line, after holding his badge up high over his head.

Inside, he passed the front counter, which had four cops behind it, also wearing helmets, and went through the elevator lobby and took the stairwell. He went down to the basement level and then followed the hallway to the evidence storage center. He realized as he went through the door into evidence that he hadn't passed a soul since the front counter. The place seemed empty. Under the emergency response plan, all available hands of the A shift were out on the street.

Bosch looked through the wire-mesh window but didn't recognize the man on duty. He was an old vet with a white mustache on a face flushed with gin blossoms. They moved a lot of the old broken-down ones to the basement. This one got off his stool and came to the window.

'So what's the weather like outside? I don't have no windows in here.'

'The weather? It's partly cloudy with a chance of riots.'

'I figured. Tuggins still got his crowd out front?'

'They're there.'

'Yeah, the mutts. Wonder how'd they'd like it if there were no coppers around. See how they'd like life in the jungle then.'

'That's not their point. They want police. They just don't want cops that are killers. Can you blame 'em for that?'

'Yeah, well some people need killing.'

Bosch had nothing to say to that. He didn't even know why he was parrying with this old dog. He looked down at his nameplate. It said HOWDY. Bosch almost laughed. Something about seeing the unexpected name cracked through the tension and anger that had been twisting him all night.

'Fuck you. It's my name.'

'Sorry. I'm not laughing at – it's something else.'

'Sure.'

Howdy pointed over Bosch's shoulder at a little counter with forms on it and pencils tied to strings.

'You want something you gotta fill out the form with the case number.'

'I don't know the case number.'

'Well, we must have a couple million in here. Why don't you take a wild guess?'

'I want to see the log.'

The man nodded.

'Right. You the one Garwood sent over?'

'That's right.'

'Why didn't you say so?'

Bosch didn't answer. Howdy reached below the window to someplace Bosch couldn't see. Then he came up with a clipboard and put it into the pass-through slot beneath the wire mesh.

'How far back you want to look?' he asked.

'I'm not sure,' Bosch said. 'I think just a couple days will do it.'

'There's a week on there. That's all the sign outs. You want sign *outs* not sign *ins*, right?'

'Right.'

Bosch took the clipboard over to the forms counter so he could look at it without Howdy watching what he was doing. He found what he was looking for on the top page. Chastain had checked out an evidence box at seven that morning. Bosch grabbed one of the sign-out forms and a pencil and started filling it out. He noticed as he wrote that the pencil was a Black Warrior No. 2, the first choice of the LAPD.

He took the clipboard and form back to the window and slid them through the slot.

'That box might still be on the go-back cart,' he said. 'It was just checked out this morning.'

'No, it will be back in place. We run a tight ship' – he looked down at the form and the name Bosch had filled out – 'Detective Friendly.'

Bosch nodded and smiled.

'I know you do.'

Howdy walked over and got on a golf cart and then drove away into the bowels of the huge storage room. He was gone less than three minutes before the cart came back into view and he parked it. He carried a pink box with tape on it over to the window, unlocked the mesh window gate and passed the box over to Bosch.

'Detective Friendly, huh? They send you around to

the schools to talk to the kids, tell 'em to say no to drugs, stay out of the gang, shit like that?'

'Something like that.'

Howdy winked at Bosch and closed the window gate. Bosch took the box over to one of the partitioned cubicles so he could look through its contents privately.

The box contained evidence from a closed case, the investigation of the shooting of Wilbert Dobbs five years earlier by Detective Francis Sheehan. It had fresh tape sealing it, having just been signed out that morning. Bosch used a little knife he kept on his key chain to cut the tape and open the box. The process of unsealing the box actually took longer than it did for him to find what he was looking for inside it.

Bosch walked through the crowd of protesters as if they weren't even there. He didn't see them or hear their chants of *No justice, no peace*. Some of them yelled insults directly at Bosch but he didn't listen to those either. He knew that you didn't win justice by carrying a sign or a cardboard coffin. You earned it by being on the side of the righteous, by being unswayed from that path. And he knew that true justice was blind to all colors except one: the color of blood.

Bosch opened his briefcase after getting to his car and looked through all the paperwork until he found the call-out sheet he'd had put together on Saturday morning. He called Chastain's pager and punched in the number of his cell phone. He then sat in the car for five minutes, waiting for the callback and watching the protest march. As he watched several of the television crews broke away from their positions and hurried with their equipment toward their vans and he realized that the helicopters were already gone. He sat up straight in his seat. His watch said ten minutes to eleven. He knew that if the media were leaving all at once, and before making their broadcasts, then something must have happened – something big. He flipped on the radio, which was already tuned to KFWB, and caught the middle of a report being delivered in an urgent, quavering voice.

'– out of the truck, then the beating began. Several bystanders attempted to stop the attack but initially the angry mob of youths held them back. The firefighters were pulled into separate knots of attackers and were being assaulted until a platoon of LAPD units stormed the intersection and rescued the victims, who were pulled into the patrol cars and then driven away – to receive medical attention, we assume, at nearby Daniel Freeman Hospital. The fire engine, left behind, had been set ablaze after the mob unsuccessfully tried to turn it over. The police quickly established a perimeter in the area and calmed things. While some of the attackers were arrested, several escaped into the residential neighborhoods bordering Normandie Boul—'

Bosch's phone began ringing. He cut off the radio and flipped the phone open.

'Bosch.'

'It's Chastain, what do you want?'

Bosch could hear lots of voices and radio squawking in the background. Chastain wasn't at home.

'Where are you? We have to talk.'

'Not tonight. I'm on duty. Twelve and twelves, remember?'

'Where are you?'

'In wonderful South L.A.'

'You're A shift? I thought all detectives were B shift.'

'All except IAD. We got the shaft – night shift. Listen, Bosch, I'd love to talk about the schedule but—'

'Where are you? I'll come to you.'

Bosch turned the car's ignition and started backing out of his spot.

'I'm at the Seventy-seventh.'

'I'm on my way. Meet me out front in fifteen minutes.'

'Forget it, Bosch. I'll be swamped. I'm on arrest

processing and I hear they're bringing in a dozen mooks who just attacked a fire truck, for chrissakes. These guys were trying to put out a fire in *their* neighborhood and these animals go after them. I tell you, it's un-fucking believable.'

'It never is believable. Be out front in fifteen minutes, Chastain.'

'You're not *listening* to me, Bosch. Things are going to hell out there and Big Blue is about to put down the boots on it. I don't have time to talk. I have to get ready to put people in jail. You want me to stand out front like a target for some mook with a gun? What is this about, Bosch?'

'Frank Sheehan.'

'What about him?'

'Fifteen minutes. Be out there, Chastain, or I'll come find you. You won't want that.'

Chastain started another protest but Bosch closed the phone.

38

It took Bosch twenty-five minutes to get to the Seventy-seventh Street Division station. He was delayed because the 110 Freeway had been closed in all directions by the California Highway Patrol. The freeway was a conduit from downtown to the South Bay area, directly through South L.A. In the last riot, snipers had fired on cars passing through and concrete blocks had been dropped from pedestrian overpasses onto cars below. The CHP was not taking any chances. Motorists were advised to take the circuitous route of the Santa Monica Freeway to the San Diego Freeway and then south. It would take twice as long but it was safer than a run through the expected war zone.

Bosch took surface streets the whole way. Almost all of them were deserted and he never stopped once for a traffic light or stop sign. It was like driving through a ghost town. He knew there were hot spots of looting and arson, but he never passed through them. He thought about the picture the media was projecting compared to what he was seeing. Most of the people were inside, locked down and waiting for this to pass. They were good people waiting out the storm, staring at the television and wondering if that was really their city that was being shown on fire.

The front of the Seventy-seventh station was also strangely empty when Bosch finally pulled up. A police academy bus had been pulled across the entranceway as a guard against drive-by shots and other attacks. But there were no protesters out front and no cops. As

Bosch pulled to the no-parking curb in front, Chastain stepped out from the rear of the bus and approached. He was in uniform, his weapon holstered on his hip. He came to Bosch's window and Bosch lowered it.

'Where you been, Bosch, you said fif—'

'I know what I said. Get in.'

'No, Bosch. I'm not going anywhere with you until you tell me what the hell you're doing here. I'm on duty here, remember?'

'I want to talk about Sheehan and the ballistics. About the Wilbert Dobbs case.'

He noticed Chastain take a slight step back from the car. Mentioning Dobbs had landed a punch. Bosch noticed the sharpshooter ribbon on Chastain's uniform below the badge.

'I don't know what you're talking about but the case on Sheehan is closed. He's dead, Elias is dead. Everybody's dead. That's it. Now we have this – the whole city coming apart again.'

'And whose fault is that?'

Chastain stared at him, trying to read him.

'You're not making sense, Bosch. You need to get some sleep. We all do.'

Bosch opened the door and stepped out. Chastain moved back another step and drew his right hand up a little until he hooked his thumb on his belt near his gun. There were unwritten rules of engagement. That was one of them. Bosch was now on deadly ground. He understood this. He was ready.

Bosch turned and swung his car door closed. While Chastain's eyes involuntarily followed that movement, Bosch swiftly reached inside his coat and pulled his pistol out of his holster. He had it pointing at Chastain before the IAD detective could make a move.

'All right, we do it your way. Put your hands on the roof of the car.'

'What the hell are you—'

'PUT YOUR HANDS ON THE CAR!'

Chastain's hands went up.

'Okay, okay ... easy, Bosch, be easy.'

He moved to the car and put his hands flat on the roof. Bosch came up behind him and took his gun from its holster. He stepped back and put it into his own holster.

'I guess I don't have to check you for a throw-down. You already used yours on Frankie Sheehan, right?'

'What? I have no idea what you are talking about.'

'That's okay.'

Keeping his right hand pressed against Chastain's back, Bosch reached around and took the handcuffs off the man's belt. He pulled one of Chastain's arms behind his back and cuffed his wrist. He then pulled the other arm back and completed the handcuffing.

Bosch walked him around and sat him in the backseat of the slickback opposite the driver's side. He then got back behind the wheel. He took Chastain's gun out of his holster, put it into his briefcase and reholstered his own weapon. Bosch adjusted the rearview mirror so he could quickly see Chastain at a glance and flicked the lock switch which rendered the rear doors inoperable from the inside.

'You stay right there where I can see you. At all times.'

'Fuck you! What the hell do you think you're doing? Where are you taking me?'

Bosch put the car in drive and headed away from the police station. He headed west until he could turn north on Normandie. Almost five minutes went by before he answered Chastain's question.

'We're going to Parker Center,' he said. 'When we get there you're going to tell me about killing Howard Elias, Catalina Perez ... and Frankie Sheehan.'

Bosch felt anger and bile back up in his throat. He thought about one of the unsaid messages he had received from Garwood. He wanted street justice, and at that moment so did Bosch.

'Fine, we'll go back,' Chastain said. 'But you don't know what you're talking about. You are full of shit! The case is CLOSED, Bosch. Live with it.'

Bosch started reciting the list of Constitutional rights against self-incrimination and then asked Chastain if he understood them.

'Fuck you.'

Bosch pressed on, glancing up at the mirror every few seconds.

'That's okay, you're a cop. No judge in the world would say you didn't understand your rights.'

He waited a moment and checked his prisoner in the mirror one last time before going on.

'You were Elias's source. All these years, you were the guy giving him whatever he needed on whatever case he had. You –'

'Wrong.'

'– sold out the department. You are the lowest of the low, Chastain. Isn't that what you called it before? The lowest of the low? That was you, man, a bottom feeder, a scumbag … a motherfucker.'

Bosch saw police barricades across the street ahead. Two hundred yards beyond them he saw flashing blue lights and fire. He realized they were heading toward the hot spot where the firefighters had been attacked and their truck set ablaze.

At the blockade he turned right and started looking north at each intersection he passed through. He was out of his element here. He had never worked an assignment at any of the department's South Central divisions and didn't know the geographic territory well. He knew he could become lost if he strayed too far from Normandie. He gave no indication of this when he checked Chastain in the mirror again.

'You want to talk to me, Chastain? Or play it out?'

'There is nothing to talk about. You are enjoying your last precious moments with a badge. What you're doing here is pure suicide. Like your buddy, Sheehan. You're killing yourself, Bosch.'

Bosch slammed on the brakes and the car swerved to a stop. He drew his weapon and leaned over the seat, pointing it at Chastain's face.

'What did you say?'

Chastain looked genuinely scared. He clearly believed that Bosch was on the edge of losing it.

'Nothing, Bosch, nothing. Just drive. Let's go to Parker and we'll get this all straightened out.'

Bosch slowly dropped back into the driver's seat and started the car moving again. After four blocks he turned north again, hoping to run parallel to the disturbance spot and cut back onto Normandie after they were clear.

'I just came from the basement at Parker,' he said.

He glanced in the mirror to see if that had changed anything in Chastain's face. It hadn't.

'I pulled the package on Wilbert Dobbs. And I looked at the sign-out log. You pulled the package this morning and you took the bullets. You took the bullets from Sheehan's service nine, the bullets he shot Dobbs with five years ago, and you turned three of them into ballistics saying they were the bullets from the Howard Elias autopsy. You set him up to take the fall. But it's your fall, Chastain.'

He checked the mirror. Chastain's face had changed. The news Bosch just delivered had hit like the flat side of a shovel in the face. Bosch moved in for the finish.

'You killed Elias,' he said quietly, finding it hard to pull his eyes away from the mirror and back onto the road. 'He was going to put you on that stand and expose you. He was going to ask you about the true findings of your investigation because you had told him the true findings. Only the case was too big. He knew how high he could go with it and you became expendable. He was going to burn you in order to win the case ... You lost it, I guess. Or maybe you've always been cold in the blood. But on Friday night you followed him home and when he was getting on Angels Flight, you made your move. You put him down. And then you looked up and there was the woman sitting there. Shit, that must've shocked the hell out of you. I mean, after all, the train car had been sitting there. It was supposed to be empty. But there was Catalina Perez on that bench and you had to put one in her, too. How am I doing, Chastain? I have the story right?'

Chastain didn't answer. Bosch came to an intersection, slowed and looked left. He could see down to the lighted area that was Normandie. He saw no barricades and no blue lights. He turned left and headed that way.

'You lucked out,' he continued. 'The Dobbs case. It fit perfectly. You came across Sheehan's threat in the files and took it from there. You had your patsy. A little research on the case and a little maneuvering here and there and you got to handle the autopsy. That gave you the bullets and all you had to do was switch them. Of course, the coroner's ID markings on the bullets would be different but that discrepancy would only come up if there was a trial, if they took Sheehan to trial.'

'Bosch, shut up! I don't want to hear anymore. I don't—'

'I don't care what you want to hear! You're going to hear this, douche bag. This is Frankie Sheehan talking to you from the grave. You understand that? You had to put it on Sheehan but it wouldn't work if Sheehan ever went to a trial. Because the coroner would testify and he'd say, "Wait a sec, folks, these aren't my marks on these bullets. There's been a switch." So you had no choice. You had to put Sheehan down, too. You followed us last night. I saw your lights. You followed us and then you did Frankie Sheehan. Made it look like a drunken suicide, lots of beers, lots of shots. But I know what you did. You put one in him, then you fired a couple more with his hand wrapped around the gun.

You made it all fit, Chastain. But it's all coming apart now.'

Bosch felt his anger overtaking him. He reached up and slapped the mirror so he wouldn't have to look at Chastain's face. He was coming up to Normandie now. The intersection was clear.

'I know the story,' Bosch said. 'I know it. I just have one question. Why did you snitch to Elias all those years? Was he paying you? Or did you just hate cops so much that you'd do whatever you could to nail them any way you could?'

Again there was no answer from the back seat. At the stop sign Bosch looked to his left and could see the blue lights and the flames again. They had circumnavigated the police perimeter. The barricades started a block down and he paused with his foot on the brakes and took in the scene. He could see a line of police cruisers behind the barricades. There was a small liquor store on the corner with the windows shattered and jagged pieces of glass still hanging in the frames. Outside its doors the ground was littered with broken bottles and other debris left by the looters.

'You see that down there, Chastain? All of that? You –'

'Bosch –'

'– did that. That's –'

'– you didn't go far enough!'

'– all on you.'

Picking up on the fear in Chastain's voice, Bosch began turning to his right. In that instant the windshield shattered as a chunk of concrete crashed through it and hit the seat. Through the falling glass Bosch saw the crowd moving toward the car. Young men with dark angry faces, their individualities lost inside the mob. He saw a bottle in midair coming at the car. He saw it all so clearly and with seemingly so much time that he could even read the label. Southern Comfort.

His mind began registering some kind of humor or irony in that.

The bottle came through the opening and exploded on the steering wheel, sending a blast of glass and liquid into Bosch's face and eyes. His hands involuntarily came up off the wheel to cover himself too late. His eyes began burning from the alcohol. He heard Chastain begin screaming from the back seat.

'GO! GO! GO!'

And then there were two more explosions of glass as other windows in the car were shattered by missiles of some sort. There was a pounding on the window next to him and the car began to rock violently right to left. He heard someone yanking on the door handle and more glass being shattered all around him. He heard shouts from outside the car, the angry, unintelligible sounds of the mob. And he heard shouts from the back seat, from Chastain. Hands grabbed at him through the broken windows, pulling at his hair and clothes. Bosch slammed his foot down on the gas pedal and yanked the wheel to the left as the car jerked forward. Fighting against the involuntary instincts of his eyes to stay closed, he managed to open them enough to allow a small slice of blurred and painful vision. The car jumped into the deserted lanes of Normandie and he headed toward the barricades. He knew there was safety at the barricades. He kept his hand on the horn all the way and when he got to the barricades he crashed through and only then did he hit the brakes. The car slid into a tailspin and stopped.

Bosch closed his eyes and didn't move. He heard footsteps and shouts but he knew they were cops coming for him this time. He was safe. He reached forward and put the car into park. He opened his door and quickly there were hands there to help him out and the comforting voices of the blue race.

'Are you okay, man? You need paramedics?'

'My eyes.'

'Okay, hold still. We'll get somebody here. Just lean here against the car.'

Bosch listened as one of the officers barked orders into a rover, announcing he had an injured officer needing medical attention. He demanded that attention right now. Bosch had never felt safer than at that moment. He wanted to thank every one of his rescuers. He felt both serene and yet giddy for some reason; like the times he had emerged unscathed from the tunnels in Vietnam. He brought his hands up to his face again and was trying to open one of his eyes. He could feel blood running down the bridge of his nose. He knew he was alive.

'Better leave that alone, man, it doesn't look too good,' one voice said.

'What were you doing out there alone?' demanded another.

Bosch got his left eye open and saw a young black patrolman standing in front of him. A white officer was standing to the right.

'I wasn't.'

He ducked and looked into the back seat of the car. It was empty. He checked the front and it was empty, too. Chastain was gone. Bosch's briefcase was gone. He straightened up and looked back down the street at the mob. He reached up and cleared the blood and booze from his eyes so that he could see better. There were fifteen or twenty men down there, all gathered in a tight group, all looking inward at what was at the center of their undulating mass. Bosch could see sharp, violent movements, legs kicking, fists raised high and then brought down out of sight and into the center.

'Jesus Christ!' the patrolman next to him yelled. 'Is that one of us? They got one of us?'

He didn't wait for Bosch's reply. He brought the rover back up and quickly called for all available units for an officer-needs-assistance call. His voice was frantic, infected with the horror of what he was seeing a block away. The two officers then ran to their patrol cars and the vehicles stormed down the street toward the crowd.

Bosch just watched. And soon the mob changed its form. The object of its attention was no longer on the ground but was rising, being brought up. Soon Bosch could see Chastain's body raised above their heads and held aloft like a trophy being passed by the hands of the victors. His shirt was now badgeless and torn open, his arms were still bound by the handcuffs. One shoe and the accompanying sock were gone and the ivory-white foot stood out like the white bone of a compound fracture through the skin. It was hard to tell from where he stood but Bosch thought Chastain's eyes were open. He could see that his mouth was wide open. Bosch heard the start of a sharp shrieking sound that at first he thought might be the siren of one of the patrol cars racing to the rescue. Then he realized it was Chastain screaming, just before he dropped back into the center of the mob and out of sight.

39

Bosch watched from the barricades as a platoon of patrol officers flooded the intersection and attempted to chase down members of the mob. The body of John Chastain remained sprawled in the street like a sack of laundry that had fallen off a truck. They had checked him and left the body alone once it was determined that the rescue was too late. Soon the media helicopters were overhead and paramedics came and tended to Bosch. He had lacerations on the bridge of his nose and left eyebrow that needed cleaning and stitches but he refused to go to the hospital. They removed the glass and closed the wounds with butterfly bandages. Then they left him alone.

Bosch spent the next period of time – he wasn't sure how long – wandering behind the barricades until a patrol lieutenant finally came to him and said he would have to return to Seventy-seventh Street Division to be interviewed later by the detectives coming in to handle the investigation. The lieutenant said he would have two officers drive him. Bosch numbly nodded and the lieutenant started issuing orders for a car into his rover. Bosch noticed the looted store across the street and behind the lieutenant. The green neon sign said FORTUNE LIQUORS. Bosch said he would be ready in a minute. He stepped away from the lieutenant and walked across the street and into the store.

The store was long and narrow and prior to that night had had three aisles of merchandise. But the shelves had been cleared and overturned by the looters who had stormed through. The debris on the floor was a foot high in most places and the smell of spilled beer and wine was heavy in the place. Bosch carefully stepped to the counter, which had nothing on it but the plastic rings of a liberated six-pack. He leaned over to look behind the counter and almost let out a scream when he saw the small Asian man sitting on the floor, his knees folded up to his chest and his arms folded across them.

They looked at each other for a long moment. The entire side of the man's face was swelling up and coloring. Bosch guessed it had been a bottle that had hit him. He nodded at the man but there was no response.

'You okay?'

The man nodded but didn't look at Bosch.

'You want the paramedics?'

The man shook his head no.

'They take all the cigarettes?'

The man did not respond. Bosch leaned further over and looked under the counter. He saw the cash register – the drawer open – lying on its side on the floor. There were brown bags and matchbooks scattered all over the place. Empty cigarette cartons, too. Placing his body on the counter he was able to reach down and weed through the debris on the floor. But his hunt for a smoke was fruitless.

'Here.'

Bosch raised his eyes to the man sitting on the floor. He was pulling a softpack of Camels out of his pocket. He shook the pack and held it out, the last soldier in it protruding.

'Nah, man, it's your last one. That's okay.'

'No, you have.'

Bosch hesitated.

'You sure?'

'Please.'

Bosch took the cigarette and nodded. He reached down to the floor and picked up a pack of matches.

'Thank you.'

He nodded again to the man and left the store.

Outside, Bosch put the cigarette in his mouth and sucked air through it, tasting it. Savoring it. He opened the matches and lit the cigarette and drew the smoke fully into his lungs and held it there.

'Fuck it,' he said.

He deeply exhaled and watched the smoke disappear. He closed the matchbook and looked at it. One side said FORTUNE LIQUORS and the other said FORTUNE MATCHES. He thumbed open the cover again and read the fortune printed on the inside above the red match heads.

HAPPY IS THE MAN WHO
FINDS REFUGE IN HIMSELF

Bosch closed the matchbook and put it in his pocket. He felt something in there and pulled it out. It was the small bag of rice from his wedding. He threw it up into the air a couple of feet and then caught it. He squeezed it tightly in his fist and then put it back into his pocket.

He looked out across the barricades to the intersection where Chastain's body was now covered with a yellow rain poncho from the trunk of one of the patrol cars. A perimeter had been set up within the larger perimeter and an investigation of the death was just beginning.

Bosch thought about Chastain and the terror he must have felt at the end, when the hands of hate reached in and grabbed him. He understood that terror but felt no sympathy. Those hands had begun reaching for him long ago.

A helicopter came down out of the dark sky and landed on Normandie. Doors opened on either side of the craft and Deputy Chief Irvin Irving and Captain John Garwood climbed out, ready to take control and direct the investigation. They walked briskly toward the clot of officers near the body. The air wash from the helicopter had blown a flap of the poncho off the body. Bosch could see Chastain's face staring up at the sky. An officer stepped over and covered him again.

Irving and Garwood were at least fifty yards away from Bosch but they seemed to know of Bosch's presence and at the same time they both looked toward him. He looked back and didn't flinch in his stare. Garwood, still in his perfect suit, gestured toward Bosch with a hand holding a cigarette. There was a knowing smile on his face. Irving finally looked away and focused his attention on the yellow poncho he was walking toward. Bosch knew the score. The fixer was on the job now. He knew how it would be handled and what the official story would be. Chastain would become a department martyr: pulled out of a patrol car by the mob, bound with his own handcuffs and beaten to death, his murder the justification for whatever else happened at the hands of the police this night. In an unspoken way, he would become the trade – Chastain for Elias. His death – broadcast from the mechanical vultures above – would be used to end the riot before it started. But no one would know outside of a few that it had been Chastain who also started it.

Bosch knew he would be co-opted. Irving could get to him. Because he held the only thing that Bosch had left, that he still cared about. His job. He knew Irving would trade that for his silence. And he knew he would take the deal.

40

Bosch's thoughts kept returning to that moment in the car when he had been blinded and he felt the hands reaching and grabbing for him. Through the terror a lucid calmness had come over him and he now found himself almost cherishing the moment. For he had been strangely at peace. In that moment he had found an essential truth. He knew somehow that he would be spared, that the righteous man was beyond the grasp of the fallen.

He thought about Chastain and his final scream, a wail so loud and horrible as to be almost inhuman. It was the sound of fallen angels in their flight to hell. Bosch knew he could never allow himself to forget it.

All Orion/Phoenix titles are available at your local bookshop or from the following address:

Littlehampton Book Services
Cash Sales Department L
14 Eldon Way, Lineside Industrial Estate
Littlehampton
West Sussex BN17 7HE

telephone 01903 721596, *facsimile* 01903 730914

Payment can either be made by credit card (Visa and Mastercard accepted) or by sending a cheque or postal order made payable to *Littlehampton Book Services*.

DO NOT SEND CASH OR CURRENCY.

Please add the following to cover postage and packing

UK and BFPO:
£1.50 for the first book, and 50P for each additional book to a maximum of £3.50

Overseas and Eire:
£2.50 for the first book plus £1.00 for the second book and 50p for each additional book ordered

---

BLOCK CAPITALS PLEASE

name of cardholder ....

address of cardholder ....

....

....

postcode ....

delivery address
(if different from cardholder)

....

....

....

postcode ....

[ ] I enclose my remittance for £................................

[ ] please debit my Mastercard/Visa (delete as appropriate)

card number ☐☐☐☐ ☐☐☐☐ ☐☐☐☐ ☐☐☐☐

expiry date ☐☐☐☐

signature ....

prices and availability are subject to change without notice